Santa Fe Solo

Santa Fe Solo

A DEATH IN THE
SHADOW OF THE SANGRE
DE CRISTO MOUNTAINS

David Hoekenga

To order additional copies of this book, contact:
Xlibris Corporation
1-888-795-4274
www.Xlibris.com
Orders@Xlibris.com
41172

To
Helen Mary Beattie Hoekenga
A lover of books

"The moment I saw the brilliant, proud morning shine high up over the deserts of Santa Fe, something stood still in my soul . . ."

D. H. Lawrence

PART 1

CHAPTER 1

Signe Sorensen walked along the rutted dirt track between the large green-gray horse barns. The ground was wet and sloping and horse droppings lay everywhere. Her black leather city shoes were already spattered with a brownish material and wet mud and manure clung to the soles of her shoes. Horses neighed and pawed on both sides of her creating a pleasant opus of sound. Trainers and owners moved easily along the track leading animals to the show pen or to grooming stations. Signe raised her gaze a bit as she entered a dry patch of ground and saw three large cottonwoods whose leaves had turned a brilliant brain rattling yellow. Above the cottonwoods, she saw a broad mountain range with dark green forested slopes. The Sangre de Cristo mountain range edged northward as a broad-shouldered part of the Rocky Mountains. On the barer tops of the peaks a white dusting of snow could easily be seen as October marched toward cooler days and longer nights.

Signe (pronounced "seena") Sorensen, on loan from the Copenhagen Metropolitan Police, was not here for the scenery even though Santa Fe was as different from downtown Copenhagen as the Grand Canyon was from its nearby city of Phoenix. She was here because of a death.

As Detective Sorensen turned into the stall which had already been cordoned off, three New Mexico state policemen abruptly terminated their banter and shifted uneasily from foot to foot. It was the fifth day of the 68th annual New Mexico State Fair and the body of a young woman had been found in the horse stalls. The officers wore black uniforms with silver grey trim and a peaked hat. When combined with black leather belts, a holster and shoulder straps the uniform bore a striking resemblance to the dreaded uniforms of the Gestapo. It was an unintentional similarity that always gave law abiding New Mexicans pause when approached by their law enforcement officials.

In the corner of the stall lay a young woman. She was moderately tall with long pale blond hair. She wore tan jodhpurs, tall tailored boots with long black perfectly clean uppers topped above her calves by a four inch band of rich brown leather. Her shirt was a soft purple western style garment with a pointed collar and mother of pearl buttons. She lay on her back in seeming repose with both hands at her sides palms up almost in supplication. A very large dirty hoof print was noticeable in the middle of the victim's chest. Detective Sorensen looked at each officer in turn and then said, "Has anyone else been in here?"

The tallest officer said, "No ma'am," in a hesitant voice.

"Did any of you touch the body?" she asked the three accusingly. In unison they shook their heads vigorously from side to side.

The first State Police officer on the scene was Vincent Jaramillo a rookie with only five months on the force. Traditionally, the State Police provided security at the State Fair even though the fairgrounds were well within the city limits of Santa Fe. Officer Jaramillo had been on duty since seven a.m. that morning and it was now 2 p.m. He made regular rounds through the livestock areas, the carnival rides, the Indian village and the Hispanic Pavilion. He had been raised in Santa Fe, so that he knew many of the people visiting the fair. He was always cordial and stopped to talk to each of them.

"How're you doing? How's your kid? Are you enjoying the fair this year?" he repeated frequently.

He looked forward to a lunch of fry bread and beans in the Indian Village. The fry bread was cooked by the Indians from Cochiti Pueblo in a large kettle of oil heated over an open fire and was one of Vincent's favorite foods. He picked up the fourteen inch circle of hot crispy brown bread still shiny with oil in his left hand and spooned beans into his mouth with his right hand.

Just as he was enjoying his second bite of fry bread a stable hand from the livestock area ran up very excited and out of breath. He was talking too fast to understand at first and waving his arms wildly.

Officer Jaramillo said to the man, whom he didn't know, "sit down, calm down and speak more slowly, please."

The stable hand was wiry and less than five feet tall. He looked to be in his late 50's with a wrinkled face, tanned skin and graying black hair. It took him two minutes to settle down a little. Only then did he begin to speak still in an excited voice with a heavy Spanish accent. "I theenk I found a bawdy," he said excitedly.

He had been cleaning the area between the last two rows of horse stalls. He was using a rake and a large shovel to transfer straw and droppings into a wheelbarrow. As he passed stall number 17 he heard a loud thumping sound. He looked over and noticed that the stall door stood open. It was swinging gently. The stall consisted of an eighteen by eighteen square foot space in the "old" horse sheds built in the 1920's. A Dutch door nine feet tall separated the stall from the wide alley between buildings. The timbers were of a large dimension no longer used and the interior was unfinished bare studs weathered a dark brown. The inside consisted of an outer area that was half the stall. It was used for tack, as well as buckets, brushes and soaps and polishes. Extra feed consisting of bags of oats and bales of alfalfa were also stored there. Sometimes the owners or keepers of the horses sat or rested here. On occasion a groom might even curl up on a broken bale of alfalfa in this area to nap. The other side of the stall was where the horse bedded down. The two sides were separated by a sturdy fence that was supported by six by six inch timbers driven well into the ground every five feet. On the side away from the horses stall sturdy boards one and a half inches thick and seven inches tall were screwed to the supports up to a height of seven and one half feet.

Toney Anaya, the stable man was surprised to find the door to stall #17 swinging open. He dropped his rake and shovel and went over to investigate. In the dim light on first looking in the stall he noticed that the latch holding the gate to the side of the stall was open and the gate itself was swung wide open. The horse was missing. Then looking back into the corner of the other part of the stall he saw bales of alfalfa, a tangle of tack and an overturned folding chair. Next to the chair was something larger than a sack of oats with a vaguely human form. He came closer and despite the dim light he saw a beautiful young woman, who wasn't moving and somehow still managed to look rich.

Toney had a criminal record and had spent time in the New Mexico penitentiary. His very first goal in life, no matter what the cost, was to not be locked up again. He ran from the area, his tan work shirt dislodged from his torn and worn jeans and flowing out behind him. He went as hastily as his worn cowboy boots would let him. He ran into Stephen Samuels first. Tony knew him to be one of the judges of the horse shows at the State Fair-English pleasure class-and one of directors of the fair that year. Without revealing what he had seen Toney asked Mr. Samuels excitedly where he might find a police officer. Stephen said that he had seen officer Jaramillo heading toward the Indian Village on the exact opposite side of the fairground.

On his way there Tony Anaya strongly considered bolting from the fair and from Santa Fe. He had only a few possessions and could easily be on the road to friends in Chama in the northern mountains of New Mexico within the hour. But he also knew that the authorities could find him. New Mexico is a very large state but not very populous so it isn't easy to "get lost" in a throng because no throng exists anywhere in the state.

Despite a rising panic and dread he headed quickly to the Indian Village, found Officer Jaramillo in his Gestapo like uniform, and after a long pause told him of his fear. Officer Jaramillo commandeered an ATV that the Indians used to haul supplies. He jumped up on the seat between the four large knobby tires and slammed the ATV into gear. He had never driven a sports vehicle like this before. How hard could it be? He sped out of the Indian Village and swerved to miss some hay bales as he entered the Hispanic Village. He over corrected and unfortunately caught a rope supporting a long string of colorful Mexican flags. The rope wrapped around the axle of the right front tire and quickly wound up like a fishing line. Twenty-five red, green, and white flags pelted the ATV as they came thumping down. Unfortunately for Officer Jaramillo, a crowd was gathering around him as the flags fell. In another bit of bad luck, the rope that held the flags was attached to two long cords holding dozens of piñatas which began crashing down upon the tables and chairs of the booths and also hitting the ground. As they hit, the *Papier-mâché* piñatas broke open and spilled hard candy in every direction. Pieces of yellow butterscotch and red and white striped peppermints pelted him on the shoulder and arm and then fell onto the floor and seat of the ATV. Vincent sprang off the ATV. Despite his brown complexion; he was bright red with embarrassment as children ran forward from the crowd to scoop candy from the dirt. He took a large knife from his belt and started cutting the ropes wound around the axle of the ATV. He pitched the ropes, the flags and a grey donkey, a pink elephant, and a brightly hued Chiquita banana piñata off the vehicle. He slammed the ATV into first and headed off to the horse barns.

In stall #17 he discovered the body of a young lady with a muddy hoof print on her chest and for a minute wasn't sure what he was supposed to do next. Later he confessed to Signe that he thought he might be sick. He was barely 20 years old, new on the force, and growing up in Santa Fe had never seen a dead body, certainly not the body of an otherwise healthy young woman just about his age.

He radioed for help once the nausea passed. Two other officers in a squad car patrolling on the north side of Santa Fe responded quickly, even though it seemed an eternity to Vincent. The officers had been instructed in crime scene management at the state policy academy. But all three were religious viewers of Crime Scene Investigation shows on television watching the Las Vegas, Miami, and New York versions avidly. Most of their ideas about forensics came from this video indulgence. Despite knowing better the senior officer disturbed the body and tramped around the area near the victim. Evidence was destroyed and displaced. However, all three officers quickly came to the same conclusion. Somehow, the horse had escaped from his stall. The size of the hoof print suggested he was a very large animal. In lumbering from the confines the horse had struck his presumed owner in the chest with one of his large hooves accidentally killing her with one heavy sudden blow. The horse must have then galloped out of the stable area. The oldest state trooper turned to his two fellow officers and said, "An open and shut case."

CHAPTER 2

Detective second rank Signe Sorensen was the officer assigned to accidental deaths, homicides, and burglaries in Santa Fe on the Thursday, October 3rd, 2002. Santa Fe, New Mexico a tourist mecca and art center with a population of 60,000 was not known as a nexus for violent crime. With a mixed population of Hispanics, Anglos, Indians and movie stars, it was the second oldest city in America after St. Augustine, Florida. It was a relatively quiet city however there was an occasional explosive family feud that resulted in a wounding or death. Despite the prejudice of the local paper this was as likely to occur in the elegant homes with four car garages on the shoulders of the Sangre de Cristo Mountains as in the narrow small abode houses in the older, poorer part, of town. Almost always mixed into these family tragedies were the synergistic combination of firearms and alcohol. Still part of the "wild west", New Mexico was home to Billy the Kid, who managed to kill 21 people by the time he reached his majority. Treated as a hero in his home state, he was hidden and protected by the simple ranchers and farmers of the southern part of the state. He was surprised one night in a house of prostitution by Sheriff Pat Garrett and shot in cold blood. His legacy is that guns are still everywhere in New Mexico in every size and shape and caliber.

Alcohol is also plentiful in the land of enchantment and figures in a higher percentage of auto accidents there than anywhere else in the country. In 2002 most liquor stores in New Mexico had drive up windows allowing patrons to purchase beer, wine and tequila without setting a foot out of their vehicles. The liquor was brought out of a badly painted, dirty steel side door of the establishment and placed in the vehicle. In other words, a person in Santa Fe County could get alcohol even if they were too drunk to walk 10 steps into the bar or package store to buy beer or tequila.

The combination of family strife, ethanol and bullets usually resulted in twenty five maimings and 6 to 8 deaths per year in the county. Of course, other homicides occurred, but rarely. In 2001 a well known young defense attorney was gunned down during mid day on a busy street near the Plaza. His life was ended by a single bullet fired from a passing car. This murder remains unsolved.

Detective Signe Sorensen sometimes wondered why *she* was in Santa Fe as it was a backwater for violent crime. After all she was a homicide detective.

Signe Sorensen was born in 1966. She was the oldest of three children in a close knit family from the little town of Odense, on the island of Fyn, in Denmark. The island of Fyn is only a short ferry ride from the capitol Copenhagen. But of course, everything in Denmark is only a concise ride away from everything else. Denmark is a small country of only 16,000 square miles. The *state* of New Mexico is over seven and half times as large as that entire charming little country.

Signe's father built small wooden sailboats in a modest old factory in Odense. The boats were 24 feet long, lapstracked with a pointed prow and stern. They were perfect for traditional sailors who wished to sail from island to island in Denmark. Signe's mother was a house wife who volunteered two days a week at the local hospital. No one in the family was interested in criminology. Signe grew up playing with her two younger brothers in the fields and small harbors near her rural home. The farthest the family went on vacation was to Copenhagen where they visited museums, castles and Tivoli, the world famous amusement park. Signe loved these trips and daydreamed about them for weeks before they departed on the ferry. She loved the exotic sites, the crowds, and the shimmering lights on the amusement park rides.

As a youngster, Signe, was dedicated and hardworking in grammar school and she excelled. She brought home several ribbons and plaques for academic excellence. When she got to the higher forms she became less studious. She bridled at the long classroom hours from eight until four, five days a week and especially the half day of school on Saturday. She would rather be out playing in the fields or by the shoreline. She tested high enough on standard exams, given to every student in Denmark, at age sixteen to get into a university. It was the very last thing she wanted to do.

When she graduated from the twelfth form at age eighteen she surprised her parents by applying to be a police officer in Odense. She commuted daily to the police academy for sixteen weeks and graduated at the top of her class because she was engaged in something she liked. She started out walking a beat in a neighborhood by the harbor in a suburb of Odense. It was a less prosperous area in a country where no one is allowed to be "poor" because of the welfare state. She liked the day shifts when she could interact with people on her beat and help with lost pets and minor domestic disputes. She hated the night shifts, especially in the winter, when the northern nights were long and cold. The gloominess, dark and lack of contact with the denizens of her suburb made the hours just drag on.

After two years she was allowed to take a test for promotion to Sergeant. She passed easily at the top of her class. However, the job meant lots of paper work in the station house and more time with the less savory Danish miscreants. After a year of underperforming in this job she applied for consideration as a detective. Again, she easily passed the test and was duly promoted.

Signe was five feet ten inches tall with a slender figure. Her face was longer than it was wide with pretty, regular features. She had very pale Danish skin and beautifully shaped grey-blue eyes. She was a natural blond with small high breasts and a strikingly svelte figure. Her lips turned down ever so slightly at the corners. She liked boys from age thirteen and had two "steadies" in upper form before she left high school. Her good looks and sunny personality attracted lots of male admirers.

While a rookie cop, she met Axel Rasmussen, a fellow cop, who often worked the night shift with her. They hit it off immediately, and were constantly together, at work but also in their off hours. Signe's parents began to talk of a possible marriage, but both were "first borns" and always wanted to have their own way. They went their own directions after eight months of each of them struggling for complete control. Signe was left with a pregnancy that resulted from a careless night of fun in Copenhagen. She wanted the pregnancy and she didn't want the pregnancy and in the end her indecision carried her toward term. One evening she wasn't feeling well and had a fluctuating pain in her back that she had never experienced before. Signe called her mother who said she would drive her daughter to the hospital, perhaps she was in labor. She delivered a 6 pound 10 ounce baby boy in the local hospital after eight hours of labor. Her mother and father were in attendance and she named her son after his father even though she wasn't anxious for Axel to be involved in her son's upbringing.

As soon as she could, Signe and her son soon moved to Copenhagen where she was employed as a detective second grade in the Homicide Division of the Copenhagen Metropolitan Police. She rented an apartment in a large old stone building near headquarters where several officers lived.

CHAPTER 3

Officer Jaramillo pulled Detective Sorensen outside so he could speak with her away from his fellow officers.

"They moved the body," he blurted out with considerable embarrassment. Officer Jaramillo stated that Sergeant Gallegos, the senior officer had felt the victim's neck for a pulse and turned her head from facing the wall to pointing toward the ceiling at the same time he was closing her eyes. He then felt for a wallet or other ID in her riding pants and moved her hands from palm up by her shoulders, as if fending something off, to palm down at her side in repose.

Detective Sorensen could feel the anger rising in her as she stormed back into the stall yelling, "You miserable excuses for policemen! You violated my crime scene! Get out of here! I'll charge you all with tampering with evidence!"

They slunk away.

It took her five minutes to slow her breathing and for her anger to abate once she was alone. When calm, she turned her full attention to her victim as the light began to fade. The body looked small and peaceful lying in the corner and it filled Signe with sadness. The department's crime scene investigator was in Farmington, New Mexico helping local police with a violent armed robbery. She took her Nikon out of her pack and shot a series of pictures from a middle distance and also up close. She found a small expensive purse hidden beneath the tack. It contained five $100 bills, three platinum credit cards, and the New Mexico driver's license of Chloe Angela Patterson. She also found two 'joints' and a small glassine packet of a white powder that tasted like cocaine in her purse. The victim was only twenty-eight years old with a home address on the exclusive Rio Grande Drive on the north side of Albuquerque. Large homes with extensive lawns lined the broad street with outsized cottonwood and elm trees along the edge of the highway and around the homes.

"How did this happen and more importantly why did this happen?" Detective Sorensen wondered. She knew so little and ached to know more quickly. At the beginning of a case, she always had this familiar feeling of looking at a large book that had no writing in it. Each page was blank and her job was to fill each page as accurately and completely as possible. Right now the task seemed enormous. As she worked her way around the stall she dusted for prints and lifted several sets of good quality. She also searched for anything no matter how small that seemed out of place. She found some hair of large caliber and uniform length obviously from horses but also some long and short hairs that appeared to be human. She found a small piece of milky white plastic, the end of a cable tie and a torn piece of red paper that she studied and then bagged. Overall not a lot of clues were present and the ones that were there were disrupted by the three inept policemen. Perhaps the victim had been killed by an errant kick from a large quadruped, Detective Sorensen wondered.

She brought years of working homicides to this stable. Many coworkers in Denmark found her work on cases slapdash, apparently disorganized and tangential. However, her successes were real, particularly in such high profile case as the case of the vanishing German banker. Often she did her best work on cases that were complex and took a long time to solve. The other detectives in Copenhagen attributed her successes to luck or a sharpened sense of intuition. She had only been in Santa Fe for five months so the other local detectives didn't have a firm opinion about Signe's ability, yet. Perhaps, this was the big case that was going to make or break her reputation in New Mexico. Now, she took a small folding chair and set it near the body, and sat down alone in the semi dark and let the scene flow over and into her. A half an hour later she knew that this was a murder.

Once she had collected her thoughts she had a lot to accomplish quickly. She called Officer Jaramillo on the radio and asked him to come back to the scene. He appeared to be the least useless of the three officers who had been there and he appeared to be honest. She watched closely as the attendants from the coroner's office bagged and removed the body for transport to the Coroner's Office in Santa Fe. Next she had dispatch patch her through to the Patterson home on the north side of Albuquerque. The phone rang several times and she found herself hoping no one would answer. On the sixth ring, Dirk Patterson, esquire, a prominent plaintiff's attorney who advertised on billboards for accident victims answered. She delivered the sad news as gently as she could. She ended with the stock phrase of American law enforcement, which she learned quickly after arrival in the US. "I'm sorry for you loss," she said with real sincerity in her voice.

Mr. Patterson sounded sad but even more than sad, he sounded angry. Signe suspected her problems with him were just beginning. She was sure she would meet Mr. Patterson soon and she wasn't looking forward to it.

When Officer Jaramillo sheepishly reappeared, Detective Sorensen questioned him. "May I call you Vincent?" She said.

"Yes, ma'am," he said emphatically.

"Open your mind and go back to the scene, Vincent. As you first entered the stall tell me about all that you saw, heard or smelled. Nothing is too small or unimportant." she said in a friendly voice.

"At first, it was very quiet; the young woman had a frightened look on her face. Her eyes were wide open and staring right at me, Detective. I knew she was dead. Then I felt a little sick." he said.

"Oh yes, just as I entered the stall I heard a low pitched thumping sound nearby," he offered hurriedly.

None of these random statements seemed to help Detective Sorensen as she scribbled hurriedly in Danish in her little notebook. She sent Vincent out to search the area around the stall with strict instructions to come and get her if he found anything that even resembled evidence. He left willingly.

Stephen Samuels, a State Fair director, came by. Signe thought he was nosy and wanted a good story to tell later at the bar in the La Fonda Hotel. Detective Sorensen was very unimpressed with her male help that afternoon. The grounds man, Toney Anaya, was not forthcoming. The three State Police had been a destructive influence on the crime scene. She stopped him at the door and declined to answer his questions. Then she had a good idea.

"Mr. Samuels would you be good enough to find Toney Anaya for me?" she said in her pleasant Danish accent.

He hurried off to find Toney. Detective Sorensen noticed the area around the entrance to the stall for the first time. The ground was quite wet from a dripping hose connected to a spigot between stall #17 and stall #18. A variety of people had been in and out since discovery of the body. Despite that, a series of clear boot prints remained on both sides of the doors. She quickly taped off the area and reluctantly planned to have Officer Jaramillo make plaster of Paris casts of the imprints.

Toney Anaya showed up following Mr. Samuels. Toney looked very ill at ease. Detective Signe Sorensen had done a background check through the Santa Fe Police Station. The National Criminal Data Bank had turned up a moderately long rap sheet on the grounds man. Along with several misdemeanors and dropped charges for shoplifting there was a felony conviction for armed robbery. Toney had served four and a half years at the State Penitentiary in Cerrillos. Since he had been released his record was notably cleaner.

Now that she knew she had the upper hand, she motioned Toney to a folding chair across from the crime scene.

"I know you touched the body, Mr. Anaya," she said sternly and without preamble.

"Pleese ma'am, I deedn't," he whined. "I came right away from theyer," he implored.

Signe waited without saying another word. Finally he went on to say that he had actually gone right up to the body.

"I've seen dead guys in the pen," Toney said. "I knew right away she wasn't alive. I saw something sparkling on her left wrist so I yanked it off and took it. I knew she wouldn't need it anymore."

"You are under arrest, Mr. Anaya for grand theft and as an accessory to murder!" she shouted.

She whipped the cuffs off the back of her black slacks and handcuffed him to a hitching post. Officer Jaramillo arrived back just then with the report that someone had seen suspicious tire tracks just behind the stables. Detective Sorensen cut him off and ordered him to read Mr. Anaya his Miranda rights, and then make casts of the foot prints outside the door to the stall.

"Officer Jaramillo, have Mr. Anaya transported to jail," Signe said with authority.

Signe began to have a sense that she was making some progress. Just then she caught site of a uniformed officer approaching from the stable parking lot. It was her old "friend" Sergeant Raymond Gallegos of the New Mexico State Police, the very person that had moved the victim's body. The officer had a cocky, self assured swagger.

"You're new detective," Sergeant Gallegos began. "Even though we are squarely inside the city limits of Santa Fe, the NMSP had jurisdiction on the fairgrounds through decades of tradition. I spoke with my captain and I will take control of the investigation now. Take your things and leave."

Signe felt the heat rise into her face. She opened her black suit jacket with alacrity, snapped open the shoulder holster on her .38 caliber Smith and Wesson and said, "*Knep*" in Danish. Then quickly reverting to English she continued, "Get the fuck away from my crime scene now you lying pervert or I will shoot you in the forehead and call it self defense."

CHAPTER 4

Dirk Wilkes Patterson, esquire, raced north toward Santa Fe on I-25 in his red Mercedes 570 convertible. A flat and busy road, I-25 runs along the western edge of the Sandia Mountains. It's a four lane highway that should have been widened to six lanes before Indian Gaming Casinos the size of super domes lined the interstate. Even before gambling I-25 was the busiest stretch of road in the state going from the biggest city to the third biggest city. Now hundreds of people from Albuquerque and surrounding towns travel the interstate daily to lose money relentlessly on the slot machines housed in an ever enlarging string of casinos. Mr. Patterson got the Mercedes up to eighty. Beyond Bernalillo the road starts to get hilly but traffic also lightens. The rolling hills are dotted with occasional piñon trees and creosote bushes. The lawyer punched the little convertible up to 115 mph. He didn't even slow for La Bajada hill the huge mesa before Santa Fe that gave the early settler so much trouble. He had little to fear from the State Police. His bright car with a vanity plate that stated, quite correctly, **IBURNU** was recognized by every peace officer in the northern part of the state. As an aggressive defender of the rights of all peoples hurt in motorcycle, truck, and car accidents Dirk depended on the authorities. Mr. Patterson's firm needed at least 3 referrals a week to pay for his full page, full color yellow pages ad, and seven billboards around Albuquerque that displayed his jowly face eleven and a half feet tall. Six months ago he added TV spots twenty times per week on seven different channels. TV advertisements alone cost him $165,000 a year. The two major sources of referrals to his law practice were EMTs that rode in all the local ambulances and police officers. Mr. Patterson's firm paid a "stipend" of $200 for the name and phone number of any person injured in an accident and $500 if there was a fatality. Usually these "stipends" were paid promptly in cash. This allowed the recipient to make his or her own decision about whether to report this income and pay tax on it. Mr. Patterson's favorite accident was a motorcyclist, preferably without a helmet, being struck by a semi truck owned by a large corporation. The weight disparity between the two objects almost always resulted in a death or severe paralysis. Often a large corporation would settle for $1,000,000 to avoid a lot of publicity. Mr. Patterson took 50% of the settlement plus his cost which were always exorbitantly and shamelessly inflated. Often on a million dollar judgment he ended up with $850,000 or more.

Because of his close relationship with law enforcement Dirk could drive 115 miles per hour with impunity. If he struck and killed three hitchhikers with aged mothers and disabled infant sons along the way the authorities would simply turn a blind eye.

The fifty-eight mile trip from Albuquerque to Santa Fe took Mr. Patterson just under thirty-two minutes, a new record for him. He screeched to a halt in front of the Santa Fe County Morgue under a sign that said, "Positively No Parking. Violators Will Be Towed." He burst from the car, slammed the door and marched purposefully up the steps. Detective Sorensen who was to meet Mr. Patterson was running late. The lawyer was directed to a wooden arm chair in the dingy old anteroom of the coroner's office. While waiting very impatiently for twelve minutes he managed to make three calls on his cell phone, one resulted in a settlement of $80,000 in a case involving a motorcyclist who had broken his leg. Detective Sorensen arrived slightly out of unfocused and disheveled. While still out of breath she spoke haltingly, "Sir, I am Detective Signe Sorensen and I will be investigating you daughter's death."

"I believe that this is a case of mistaken identity, young woman, and I will file a written complaint over being compelled to rush to Santa Fe this evening. There is also a $400,000 dollar horse that is missing." The lawyer blustered.

"Come with me, sir. I hope you are correct," Signe said in a more normal tone.

I never imagined that one animal could be worth that much money, she thought. One of her friends on Fyn got a horse for her sixteenth birthday and she remembered that this pleasant looking bay mare cost 2000 Krøner which was about $330. She thought that she might have a motive for murder.

"Tell me about this horse, sir." Signe said. "This extraordinarily valuable horse might be implicated in this crime. Do you have a picture?"

"I have pictures, I have documents, and I have a complete pedigree on this astonishing animal." Mr. Patterson snapped.

She led the way quickly through two sets of swinging doors battered by years of use and into a large room with light green institutional tile on the walls and matching worn linoleum on the floor. The room was cool and it sent a shiver down Detective Sorensen's spine. An attendant in a long white lab coat entered and briskly walked to a wall of stainless steel doors with a five digit number next to each handle. He consulted a clipboard after a whispered conversation with the detective and then quickly opened a shoulder high door and pulled out a long steel tray. A blast of cold air fell on Detective Sorensen making her shiver again. Resting on the tray was a slender form covered by a perfectly white, carefully tucked sheet. Without ceremony the attendant lifted the sheet upward and back off of the victims face. The countenance of a dead young woman that was now a grey color with some shades of blue was revealed. She had blond hair and regular features and even in death was quite beautiful.

"That is my daughter," Mr. Patterson gasped as he turned away and held the edge of a sink for support. "I want the son of a bitch that killed her and I want him now!" he shouted.

"We just found her body four hours ago, sir, and I'm not even sure this is a homicide," she offered.

"That's ridiculous," he shouted, "a young woman doesn't just fall over dead even if she's had a few problems! I want to speak to your supervisor right now, Detective, and I want every available officer working through the night on this case!"

"Sir, we need to evaluate the evidence we have and perform an autopsy before we even know if this was a murder." she said with some irritation in her voice. "I feel the autopsy should be performed at the Office of the Medical Investigator in Albuquerque, they have the most experience, and they need time to do a thorough job." she went on.

She suspected that the autopsy wouldn't be done until Monday. From past experience she thought the microscopic sections of various tissues would be first collected, then embedded and stained. This process would require two days. Toxicology and gas chromatography of fluids would take three to five days at the very least.

"I want the autopsy tonight," Mr. Patterson shouted. "I'm well known in Albuquerque and I have lot of friends in law enforcement!"

"I'll let you talk to the Chief of Homicide here in Santa Fe, but nothing is going to happen tonight," Signe said. "Don't you need to be with your wife, sir?"

At that Mr. Patterson spun on his heels and rushed out of the room without saying another word.

Detective Sorensen took a moment with the help of the attendant to examine the victims unclothed body. There were no signs of external trauma or marks from defending herself, in fact, she had perfect skin. Specifically, there was no bruise or abrasion from a hoof print to the anterior chest. She had a small dark blue tattoo of an oriental design on her lower right groin. She had three pierced ear rings in her right ear and four in her left. Her tongue was pierced with a single gold stud but surprisingly her navel wasn't pierced. She was slender with a well proportioned figure and some superficial skin depressions from tight underwear and socks.

Detective Signe Sorensen was as tired as she had ever been. She walked quickly to her black Jetta. At an altitude of 7000 feet it was dark and cold in Santa Fe at 8 p.m. Her black suit failed to protect her from the cold. Her legs and sides were instantly cold. She stopped quickly at the Coyote Café, her favorite restaurant, for take out and sped home to her apartment at Fort Marcy Park. She ate quickly with Axel, her son, who had finished his homework and then headed to bed. After pounding the pillows and twisting in the sheets for forty-five minutes, she realized she couldn't sleep. A hot shower didn't help. A glass of red wine didn't help. Signe had been here before. Her head was spinning with questions about the murder she was going to solve. Most of her cases began this way and the intense insomnia that often lasted the first week made even thinking difficult.

CHAPTER 5

She awoke at six a.m. Friday morning with sandy feeling eyes and achy muscles from tossing all night. She dressed quickly and ate a Danish breakfast of pumpernickel bread and slices of Tilsit cheese washed down with very strong coffee. She sped across town to the 1930s style Police Station. The four hundred year old town had narrow roads laid out for one way wagon traffic which didn't accommodate the modern automobile. However, this Friday the sun was streaming down from the mountains and no one much was about. Fallen leaves flew up behind the stubby rear end of the Jetta. She made it across town in a remarkable eight minutes.

As she walked into the detective's area behind the booking desk she noticed that her desk was the messiest. Piles of case reports, photos of crime scenes, analyses of crime scene reconstruction experts, and even some pieces of physical evidence balanced precariously on her desk. Even the central writing area, always the last to disappear on a messy person's desk, was buried under disordered papers. She had meant to reorganize it Tuesday when nothing much was happening in the criminal underworld of Santa Fe, but had gotten distracted by an NCDB computer search for a petty thief that had stolen cash from a rock and mineral store just off the plaza. Now she grabbed the piles and after glancing briefly at the top paper briefly stuffed them unceremoniously in an old green file cabinet.

She pulled out a yellow legal pad and wrote down what she knew about the death of Chloe Angela Patterson. It was very early in the investigation, but the list was surprisingly and disturbingly short and vague. The lack of real evidence was perhaps the most daunting. She knew that in a few minutes she would have to present the case to the chief of detectives, Gerald Hartford.

Gerald Hartford was from St. Louis but had lived in New Mexico for twenty-five years. He had started as a patrolman in Taos, New Mexico and had risen through the ranks. For a town that was quite well known, Taos was a very small village of only 6,000 people. It had a well known pueblo, a famous ski area for intermediate and advanced skiers and over 80 art galleries. However, it wasn't a hotbed of crime. During Chief Hartford's service in Taos there was one four and a half year stretch with no homicides. He became chief of detectives in Santa Fe when his predecessor was fired in a scandal over a large amount of cocaine which went missing from the evidence room. Detective Hartford was fifty-five, but looked ten years older, probably because he still smoked two packs of unfiltered Marlboros a day, down from three packs a day. He was honest, reasonably hard working, surprisingly kind to those working under him and smart. His main goal was to skate along to his retirement without a breath of scandal. However, his retirement was still eight years in the future.

He arrived at work about fifteen minutes after Detective Sorensen. He was wearing a rumpled brown suit that went out of style ten years ago with a worn white shirt, a blue tie and scuffed brown loafers that didn't enhance his overall rundown look. He carried two coffees from Starbucks one with cream and sugar for himself and one black for Signe. They were both called "grande" so that Starbucks could charge twice as much as the fanciest restaurant in downtown Copenhagen for their brew. Chief Hartford motioned Signe into his office, handed her a coffee and closed the door.

"I got two irate calls late last night from senior law enforcement in Albuquerque about this Patterson case. What can you tell me about it?" he said without any preamble.

"I would have called you last night if there was anything substantial to report, Chief." she began. "A young woman was found dead in a horse stall at the State Fair yesterday with a hoof print on her chest. It may not be a murder but her $400,000 horse is missing." she continued.

"Why all the heat, Signe?" he enquired.

"The victim's father is a wealthy, arrogant ambulance chasing lawyer from Albuquerque. You'll recognize him when you meet him. His face is on billboards all over The Duke City." the detective said with some sarcasm.

"Well it looks like we will have to expend some major effort on this case to keep the big city boys off of our backs, Signe. Mr. Patterson already brow beat the OMI into doing the autopsy this afternoon. I don't think I've ever seen them respond this quickly before. I'm taking you off all other cases. I want you present to talk with the pathologist and take your own excellent set of notes even if they are in a foreign language", he concluded.

She yelled, "Yes sir", over her shoulder as she headed out the door.

She didn't really mind the drive to Albuquerque which took a law abiding law enforcement officer about 70 minutes if it wasn't rush hour in the southern city. It gave her some alone time which she never got in Santa Fe between her demanding job and her son Axel. She reflected on the strange turn of events that had brought her to New Mexico.

She had felt stuck in Copenhagen. She had been involved in three high profile murders in the last two years and none had been solved. She knew that one third of murders go unsolved worldwide, and it may just have been a run of unlucky cases. Something like black coming up three times in a row at roulette. The chances of that happening were one in eight she remembered from statistics. The newspaper articles about the cases however made it worse. After a time the articles were critical of the police in general and her in particular. Her confidence sagged. Just then the chief of detectives, Thor Nielsen, got a flyer from The International Detective about officer exchanges as an aid to improving homicide investigations. He put her name in without even telling her. He thought a change of venue might help restore her confidence. When she was selected he broached the idea to her. She would go to a police force in the western United States and they would send an officer to Denmark. Each would learn the other force's new methods and then come back and mentor others.

She was shocked when she first learned she was coming to New Mexico. She didn't even realize it was a *part* of the United States. Trips to the main library in Copenhagen quickly made her realize that she was going to a very different part, of a very different country from Denmark. She was going not just to a totally dissimilar environment of dry land, sparse plants, and big skies but an altered view of the world. An uncle, Tage Sorensen, had visited the US four years ago. When he returned he described his pure fright at seeing the deep, wide, cavernous Grand Canyon. He found it so vast that it was overwhelming to him. It fit nothing in his experience coming from a crowded and very small country. He longed for the humid closeness of Denmark where you were never more than 40 feet from a tree and the highest spot in the country was only 370 feet above sea level. She had some anxiety about her new posting but also some excitement at a chance to spread her wings. Overall, her first five months had been a good experience but she prayed every night for more heinous crime and murder in Santa Fe.

When she arrived at the Office of the Medical Investigator on the campus of the University of New Mexico she wheeled into an "Official Parking Only" spot and shut down the engine. In truth, law enforcement officer and other people in public office have no idea how much time ordinary citizens spend trying to find a legal parking spot. She brushed through the door flashing ID and asking for Autopsy #3. When she arrived Dr. Bernadette Gilchrist was already there. Signe recognized her from previous visits to the OMI. She greeted her and got a grunt in return. Dr. Gilchrist was in her late thirties and might once have been pretty, Signe thought. She now looked worn, with little makeup, and a disorganized dirty blond ponytail. She wore faded green scrubs with a three cornered rent over her abdomen. They were ill fitting and far from fresh. She was a very bright pathologist and very thorough so Detective Sorensen considered herself lucky to have this pathologist working on the Patterson case.

Dr. Gilchrist wore a voice activated head set with a microphone the size of a grain of rice that sat at the left side of her mouth. As Detective Sorensen entered Dr. Gilchrist, continued to dictate the findings of the external examination. She noted no external trauma. Particularly no bruising to the anterior chest was apparent despite the history of a hoof print on the victim's clothing. Breast implants were noted without palpation by the doctor as the nipples of Chloe's very large breasts pointed right at the harsh halogen lights above the autopsy table. There was none of the natural sloping of the breast tissue toward the axilla that occurs with real breast tissue. When a woman without breast augmentation lies supine it creates a beautiful curve that is totally lost with silicon, Dr. Gilchrist explained. There was evidence of a remote rhinoplasty (nose job). The Asian tattoo in the depth of her right groin was noted as were the piercings. Dr. Gilchrist remarked that the tongue piercing appeared red and quite irritated. The abdomen was scaphoid (flat) with no scars. As her eyes drifted lower she noted easily visible markedly enlarged lymph nodes in both groins. The victims closely shaved and waxed pubic region made the multiple lumps at the fold of each groin very visible even to Signe.

Dr. Gilchrist ripped off her microphone and stepped away from the body quickly.

"This could be the sign of a dangerous and contagious infection," she said flatly handing Detective Sorensen a mask. Signe was motioned to a table where they both sat down. Dr. Gilchrist said, "We have some unusual, dangerous and potentially fatal infections in northern New Mexico that don't occur in Europe".

She stated that one such dangerous infection is Hantavirus Pulmonary Syndrome. It's a virus she said that is carried by the deer mouse and secreted in its droppings. A person can get the disease by unknowingly disturbing a nest. After fever and chills the victim can develop swollen lymph nodes. Or the victim may develop abrupt severe respiratory distress.

"I don't think our victim had this even though it has a very high mortality and she could have been exposed in the stables at the State Fair. It's a perfect habitat for the deer mouse. The environment is unoccupied by people fifty weeks out of the year so the mice can nest and reproduce. Then for two weeks there is intense human activity disturbing not only the mice but their nests and droppings exposing everyone especially an immune suppressed drug addict to the virus."

"The disease I'm really worried about, in this case, is the plague," she continued in a more animated voice. "Actually this disease was common in Europe centuries ago and a form of it caused the Black Death killing millions on the continent. It has been eradicated there."

Unfortunately, she stated, plague is endemic in northern New Mexico and we have few fatalities every year. The disease comes from a bacterium, which is carried on a flea that lives on a rat, and then passes to humans. If you tried to sell a fictional story based on such a preposterous chain of events and made it a killer, your story would be promptly rejected by any editor. However, just such a vector caused more death and grief to humans than any other pathogen in recorded human history. In most cases the patient develops fever and chills followed by the most characteristic sign-swollen lymph glands. These often occur in the groin region and are referred to as a 'bubo'. Hence the name-bubonic plague.

"Our victim presents in just this way, Detective Sorensen," Dr. Gilchrist continued.

She went on to say that it would be dangerous to go on with the autopsy at this time. The bacterium *Yersinia pestis* could be spread by contact or worse yet, aerosolized and inhaled into the lungs of employees and visitors throughout the building as it traveled through ventilation system causing a more dangerous form of the infection. A variety of tests including gram stain, immunofluorescent stain, and attempted culture of the bacterium would need to be done before the necropsy could proceed.

"I'm afraid we won't know much until Monday or Tuesday," Dr. Gilchrist concluded.

Signe was disappointed since there was no way to go forward with the case until she had the test results. Perhaps this unfortunate young woman was a victim of bubonic plague a dreaded historical killer with fifteen percent mortality when treated appropriately and aggressively. She had already warned Axel that, most likely, she would be working the whole weekend. Now, she felt like a young girl who had been suddenly and unexpectedly let out of school.

CHAPTER 6

After a quick call to Chief Hartford explaining the possible diagnosis of plague in the recent decedent, Signe drove back to Santa Fe. Starting in Copenhagen, Signe had read avidly about New Mexico. She consumed guide books, histories, biographies and even novels about the state. Every spare weekend, since being stationed in New Mexico five months ago, Signe and Axel had explored most of the northern part of the state. New Mexico is the fifth largest state, just behind Montana, but Santa Fe, fortuitously for the traveler, is in the upper fifth of this huge expanse. Many of the most spectacular sights are in the northern third of the state.

Signe hit Albertson's for food, drink and camping supplies and missed the Friday afternoon crush of shoppers. She sped to the apartment and chucked the camping gear in the back of the Jetta. She arrived at Santa Fe High School five minutes before the last bell and surprised Axel before he could board the yellow-orange school bus that usually took him home. He was delighted not to be spending the weekend alone and even better to be going camping with his mother. Signe had packed his hiking boots, blue jeans and t shirts.

Axel was sixteen years old and six feet four inches tall. He towered over almost every student in the Santa Fe High School. He had dark blue eyes and wavy blond hair. He had recently grown so quickly that he still moved with a gawky gait as if he weren't quite sure where his arms and legs were headed. He was bright but undisciplined.

Signe pointed the Jetta back onto I-25 for the third time that day. She headed south to the seedy little town of Bernalillo with its unruly buildings and unkempt yards. Somehow this little burg completely escaped the prosperity of Albuquerque to the south and Rio Rancho to the west. Signe turned west onto US 550 and crossed the Rio Grande River. The drive out past Zia Pueblo is through open country with sparse vegetation and distant views of the Jemez Mountains. The road takes a turn south past red cliffs and then heads north toward the small village of Cuba. This would be their last sign of 'civilization' so Signe got gas here and they ate a greasy, below average, cheeseburger at the Dairy Queen. The next forty miles was through open country with very few houses and some pine covered hills. Cabezon Peak shaped exactly like a Mexican hat was off to the left. Finally, they reached Nageezi, a small Navajo trading post with just a few desolate buildings and turned south on the dirt road to their destination, Chaco Canyon.

During the first two hours of the drive, Axel and Signe had their first long talk in three weeks. Axel was doing poorly in school. It wasn't a language problem as his English was good. He was taking history, biology, English and metal shop. His disliked all of them except shop. His girlfriend, Irma Perez, was a freshman who didn't like school either. Her family came from the Aqua Fria area on the south side of Santa Fe. This was an old area of small adobe homes with bare dirt yards. No one in her family had graduated from High School. Signe desperately hoped that Axel would tire of Irma. She knew if she volunteered her opinions which included-underachiever, bad manners, slutty dresser, and no goals-it would only drive them closer. So she bit her tongue. Axel wished that he could leave school like in Denmark at age sixteen and study a trade. He had as little interest in college as his mother had when she was his age. His academic future didn't look bright to mother or son. When they passed through Cuba they agreed to table the discussion until after the weekend was over.

The road from Nageezi to Chaco Canyon was abysmal in good weather and a washed out track if it had rained. Huge ruts ran from side to side across the road. When it was dry the dust was impenetrable. The Jetta could barely navigate it during daylight and under the best of conditions. The twenty-nine mile drive would take two hours if they were lucky. The swerving and braking started immediately and wore on both of them. By seven thirty they reached the small campground at the eastern edge of the Chaco Culture National Historic Park. Most of the summer travelers had gone back to Indiana, so they got a choice spot along the bluffs to the north and set up camp quickly before the light faded. Axel built a small campfire and they sat beside it as darkness descended. There were millions of stars as the nearest artificial light was dozens of miles away. Before it was late they retired to their small tents and read by candle lanterns until sleep overtook them.

When Signe awoke in full light Axel was already up. He had the fire started and was cooking breakfast. After eating, they planned a hike to some of the ruins. So far, in their exploration of northern New Mexico, Chaco Canyon was their favorite place. It was isolated, mysterious and had complicated and extensive ruins. From 900 to 1200 AD as many as 5,000 people lived in this area. It was the political and economic center of the Anasazi people. A wide-ranging network of roads, arrow straight, headed out from the large settlements in every direction. The ruins revealed a high level of planning with multistory buildings, religious sites and solar observatories.

On Saturday morning Axel and Signe planned a long hike east to Wijiji. The pair hiked easily along the road to this site. It was a large house constructed around 1100 AD with grinding stones and petroglyphs. The petroglyphs showed ibex with huge curved horns, sun symbols and playful people with flailing arms and wide spread legs. It was oriented as a viewing station for the winter solstice. The sun rises first on December 4th in a notch in the wall and then proceeds for seventeen days allowing preparation for the solstice. On the day of the solstice the sun reaches the southern end of the notch allowing precise timing for feasting and dancing. Signe and Axel sat against a stone wall enjoying the warm New Mexico sun. After an hour at the site the two headed back along the flat road. Signe thought of Chloe and the unsolved case every few minutes but the motive wasn't becoming any clearer. She had no revelations.

After lunch and a rest, they walked westward to Chetro Ketl a large pueblo containing over 500 rooms and twelve kivas. Signe had read that kivas are large circular underground rooms used for the religious ceremonies of a clan. In the floor is a spirit hole called a sipapu. Many kivas were thirty or forty feet in diameter and sixteen to eighteen feet deep. The roofs of the kivas were covered with cleverly engineered timbers. This was a longer hike but the October day remained cool despite the sun. They studied the precise masonry which was as carefully cut and laid as anything made with modern power tools. An elegant banded pattern with a narrow darker stripe between broader layers of stone was present in most areas. On returning to camp they cooked a large meal of potatoes, corn on the cob and steaks over the campfire. The hiking had made them ravenous. They retired early.

At 2 a.m. Signe was suddenly fully awake. It looked as though someone was shining a huge, white spotlight on the campground. She grabbed her jacket and went outside to see a full moon as big as a dinner plate rising over the mesa. It cast an eerie white light over the campground, rock formation and a few nearby trees. She felt that the Anasazi had seen a similar magical sight 1000 years ago and it made her problems seem quite small.

In the morning they broke camp and drove to Pueblo Bonito or 'pretty village'. It is the largest and most famous ruin in Chaco Canyon. It contained 800 rooms in five stories and was the first apartment building in North America. The second apartment house was one built in Brooklyn. Some of Pueblo Bonito has collapsed but the monumental back wall still rises over forty feet and is nearly 500 feet long. They leisurely explored the rooms and some of the thirty-nine kivas remarking on the perfectly square door ways and tall precise interior walls. Signe could imagine hundreds of the skilled Anasazi people making clothing, building multistory buildings and gathering crops here. On the long ride back to Santa Fe Signe began to think more about the puzzling case she would try to solve. No matter what the next week brought she was glad for her weekend retreat to a quiet and special place with Axel.

CHAPTER 7

Monday morning started even worse than Signe had suspected. Chief Hartford called at 6 a.m. He had been on duty that weekend and had received three long threatening calls from the barrister, Mr. Patterson. Signe was just as glad the calls were addressed to someone higher up and with more authority. Since there was no new information all the badgering was for naught. Chief Hartford also reported there were no answers from the OMI and he wanted their results as soon as they opened. Detective Sorensen had known that the plague tests wouldn't be ready until Monday at the soonest. Finally, the Chief reported that Mr. Patterson had hired a private investigator to 'help' with the investigation. Chief Hartford seemed most disturbed about this development. A PI, named Anthony Squitero, had come from New Jersey to New Mexico. He would stay until the case was solved to Mr. Patterson's satisfaction. Chief Hartford ran the name through the NCDB and found a series of misdemeanors that the PI committed in the eighties. Mr. Squitero, sometimes called, 'Tony the Squid' also had extensive ties with the New York La Cosa Nostra.

The chief had scheduled a meeting for himself, Mr. Squitero and Signe at the station house at 8 A.M. The Chief felt they could give the PI the cold shoulder and shut Mr. Squitero out. However, on reflection Hartford thought it might be better to at least seem to include 'Tony the Squid' so they would know what he was up to. Signe bolted out of bed and raced her naked self to the shower. She had her fourth chill since starting the case on Thursday and it wasn't from the cold.

Arriving 15 minutes early Signe found Chief Hartford and Mr. Squitero already waiting. The Chief rolled his eyes in Signe's direction as she entered his office. Then he made the introductions. Mr. Squitero was short and very heavy set with three chins, a sallow complexion, and a shiny double breasted sharkskin suit that looked *very* out of place in New Mexico. "Pleased ta meet ya," he said.

"Likewise, I'm sure," Signe said with no conviction in her voice. After grabbing some coffee she sat down between the two men. She briefly reviewed the little that they knew about the case. She intentionally overlooked some parts of the case, as she didn't see Mr. Squitero as being on their side.

"Who killed this beautiful lady?" Mr. Squitero asked.

"I'm still not sure this was a homicide, Sir," Detective Sorensen replied.

"I'll start lookin' at the fairground," 'Tony the Squid' said loftily. "Mr. Patterson is high up in this state and he will want answers quick. May I have your cell phone number and may I call you Signe?" Mr. Squitero asked.

"No and no," she said quickly. "The number of the station house is 955-5080. May I write it down for you?" she said sarcastically.

Mr. Squitero swaggered out of the police station. The chief went into his office, and Signe tried to order her thoughts in view of this new and unwanted complication. She called the OMI and was surprised to get Dr. Bernadette Gilchrist.

"Hello, Signe we had some bad moments over the weekend. We aspirated the buboes, those swellings in Chloe's groin, and Gram stained the aspirate. Christian Gram was a Danish doctor, a countryman of yours, who invented the test in 1882 to differentiate one bacterium from another. We still use it today. There are four groups of bacteria based on the shape of the individual bacterium and whether or not they are avid for a blue stain or a red stain. Basically, you can get four results. The bacteria can stain acid and red, or basic and blue. That's the Gram stain. Then the bacteria can be round or rod shaped. We found Gram negative, that is blue, cocco, that is round, bacilli in the bubo. This was an uncommon result and very consistent with the characteristics of the bacterium that causes plague. We quarantined the whole lab, not just Autopsy #3 where the victim's body was located. The police yellow taped the entire building on the outside. I mobilized our disaster response team and called all the lab techs in. Saturday evening we had forty-two people crawling all over the building in white contamination suits. We were the feature story on KOB TV for the ten o'clock news. The laboratory people did the definitive immunofluorescence test that usually takes thirty-eight hours in just seventeen hours. I'm surprised, but pleased, to tell you that it was negative," she said with relief in her voice.

"She didn't die of the plague. I'm just about to perform the autopsy and when I'm done I'll call you on your cell," Dr. Gilchrist concluded.

Signe sat at her desk and thought. Something is missing here, and it has been eluding me for four days she decided. She looked over at the detective's secretary, Andrea, a new hire just out of high school. Suddenly, Andrea's purse began to ring. She reached inside and pulled out a slender cell phone. Of course, Signe thought. How obvious. The rich young victim had a cell phone and I didn't even search for it!

Detective Sorensen raced to her car and headed for the fairgrounds. On the way she called Mr. Patterson and got Chloe's cell phone number. So much talk of cell phones today. First Mr. Squitero asked for her cell number. Then Dr. Gilchrist said she would call Signe on her cell, and still it didn't sink in. Signe walked quickly to stall #17 and climbed through the yellow tape. Unfortunately, 'Tony the Squid' was inside. "Would you like to be arrested for disturbing this crime scene, Tony?" Detective Sorensen said angrily.

"Hey, lady. I'm just taking a look see. No need to be so hostile. I was sorta just goin'," he stammered and promptly left.

When he was gone Signe took out her cell and dialed Chloe's number. She heard nothing. Of course, she would search every square inch of the stable and surroundings. The cell phone had last been charged on Thursday and the battery had to be weak or dead. If only she had thought to look for the phone on Friday. Then in the corner of the stall she heard a barely audible, intermittent, fading ring. She walked hurriedly to the corner of the stall and under a bale of alfalfa saw a sleek pink cell phone. She pulled a pair of latex gloves from her purse and quickly put them on so she could pick up the phone. She immediately shut it off so no data would be lost despite the low battery. She spent another hour in the stall combing through the horse paraphernalia there and searching, but to no avail. She found no other clues. It was disturbing to Detective Sorensen how clean this crime scene was.

On the way back to the station house she got a call from Dr. Gilchrist. The autopsy revealed no internal trauma. No cracked ribs or sternum that would have been present if a fifteen hundred pound horse had kicked Chloe in the thorax. No broken hyoid bone in the neck from subtle strangulation. Her internal organs showed fatty changes in the liver probably from alcohol abuse. Her heart was mildly dilated especially the left ventricle which is the main pumping chamber of the heart. Her lungs showed early emphysematous changes from smoking. Both antecubital areas, the inside of the elbows showed needle tracks covered with makeup. Examination of her reproductive organs showed marked scarring of her ovaries and fallopian tubes. She had a raging case of gonorrhea at the time of her death explaining her massive lymphadenopathy (the swollen nodes in her groin). In other words, this twenty-eight year old female looked twenty-one on the outside due to cosmetic surgery and makeup, but on the inside Dr. Gilchrist said she looked fifty-one.

Chemical and chromatographic analysis of tissue and serum showed ethanol, cocaine, chloroform, and cannabis in her blood stream. She was taking an antibiotic. No heavy metals or standard poisons were detected. However, she did have detectable levels of hydrazine, a rocket fuel, in her blood stream. Some specialized tests were sent to laboratories in California.

At this time, however, Dr. Bernadette Gilchrist said, "The cause of this young woman's sudden and untimely death is completely unknown."

CHAPTER 8

For no reason that she could discern, when she awoke Tuesday, Detective Sorensen felt better about this case and therefore about herself. She was, after all, a workaholic and therefore validated by the solving of cases. She had no life away from the squad except for her son, Axel. Her job was in many ways like being a basketball player for the University of New Mexico. Her occupation wasn't like that of a writer, doctor or accountant who at the end of the year could assess their accomplishments in some sort of 'soft' way. For example, the writer could declare, even though I had 'writer's block' from January to June, I wrote three short stories and one fifth of the 'great American novel'. The writer could conclude, "I had a successful year." Few would be able to dispute it. A surgeon could remember the young auto accident victim he saved, and forget the three operations that even he knew he botched with resulting unnecessary mortality. "It was a successful year!" He could crow to his colleagues.

On the other hand, the starting forward during the U.N.M. Lobos successful 2001 basketball season would know his team won eighteen games lost seven and tied two. Individually he would know that he scored 12.7 points per game, had 5.6 rebounds per game and successfully shot 75.4% of his free throws. Like the basketball player, Signe could say that in 2001 she worked forty-one robberies and solved twenty-nine of them or 71% of them and that she worked fourteen homicides in two venues and solved eleven of them or 79%. This figure was enough above the national average for solving murders, which is 66%, to get her an invitation to the detective's equivalent of the NCAA tournament's sweet sixteen basketball tournament, affectionately known in the United States as 'March Madness'.

Yes, she felt good about this case even though she didn't have a murder weapon, a suspect or a solid motive. Recovering the pink cell phone was a coup even though she only gave herself 'two points' for it. Had she thought of that Thursday, or Friday it would have been a clear 'three pointer'.

Just as she got to the mud and dust spattered Jetta in the fairgrounds parking lot she got a call. It was from Jefferson Barclay, a concierge at the La Fonda hotel. La Fonda was an old warhorse of a hotel in the abode style that hunkered on the southwest corner of the Plaza. Much of the inside was a mixture of Indian and Hispanic decors. It had a comfortable worn look that suggested no major redecorating had been done since before the war, World War I, that is. It was very dark inside but somehow comforting and homey. Signe maintained an extensive group of informers or 'snitches' in Santa Fe, more than any of the other detectives. She had learned the value of informants in Copenhagen, and perhaps it was her secret weapon.

Jefferson's large cluttered desk sat right in the middle of the tortuous and heavily beamed lobby. He could see every tourist and local in the lobby by merely turning his gaze and looking down the three separate hallways that converged where he stood. He was gay and hid it half heartedly. Late at night he could be found in a Santa Fe night club always accompanied by a young 'nephew'. More important than his sexual orientation was the fact that he was acquainted with everyone in town and knew everybody's business.

"Hello love," Jefferson said. "I heard about your nasty little murder. I called to tell you about three gentlemen that stayed at the hotel last week. They wore cowboy boots, dress western pants and long brown dusters. I'm sure you're thinking, well it was State Fair then and the town was packed to the gills with horsy types. However, these three talked with an extraordinary accent, South American, I believe. They left in a hellacious hurry on Thursday and when I heard about Chloe's death on Saturday I thought of you."

"Thank you, Jefferson. I'll come and look at the guest register later. I owe you a dinner." Signe purred into the phone.

Her first objective was to secure the cell phone and her second objective was to reestablish contact with Officer Vincent Jaramillo of the New Mexico State Police. The last four days she had found herself thinking about him as she daydreamed while waiting on hold on the telephone or driving. At night after getting into bed and while waiting for sleep she actively tried to visualize him-his large brown eyes, regular features, smooth brown skin and slender frame.

Signe had come to the US in April. In the past five months she hadn't had sex or even been held and she was quite horny. In Denmark she began having sex with her boyfriends when she was sixteen. Sex was more open and accepted in the Scandinavian countries than in the US, with its puritanical background. Once she got on the police force there were heaps of handsome fellow officers, married and unmarried, looking for a dalliance. Signe found them fun and the sex the first time with a new partner was powerful. She liked the unexpected moves each new male made even if she tired of it by the third or fourth time. The married ones were less of a problem because, of course, they didn't want a commitment. She thought their guilt made them more attentive. Looking back, Signe wondered if she would ever be in a committed, loving relationship. Perhaps something about that much intimacy scared her.

"How's the case going?" Chief Hartford said.

Signe had managed to drive back to the station house, park the car, and walk inside all the while daydreaming about Vincent and her nonexistent sex life.

"Not to bad," Signe said in a voice a bit too loud but overall making a good recovery. "I found her cell phone," she said triumphantly as she held a plastic bag over her head with a sleek pink object in it.

"Good work, Detective Sorensen!" he said heartily.

She walked back into the lab and handed the phone to the technician. After dusting for prints, Signe asked the tech to record the number of all the victim's calls for the week prior to last Thursday. As soon as she got a little privacy she called the State Police Post and asked that Officer Vincent Jaramillo give her a call. "Was this an emergency?" The dispatcher wanted to know.

"Oh, no. Definitely, not." Detective Sorensen responded nervously.

Signe jumped in her car and headed across town to meet with a rocket scientist. As she turned onto Galisteo Street, a BMW 750 sped around her crossing the double yellow line and narrowly missing a visitor. A large man was driving. She noticed an expired New Jersey license plate. She pulled the red flashing light from under her seat and turned it on. It was dusty as she never made pullovers in Santa Fe, but she thought this might be fun. She stepped out of the car after calling the tag number into dispatch. Detective Sorensen sauntered up to the side of the car and tapped on the window. 'Tony the Squid' rolled the window down and smiled.

"Good morning detective. How can I help ya?" Mr. Squitero said cheerily.

"Well, Tony, I believe I have you for speeding, reckless driving, expired tags and could I see your driver's license please?" Signe barked into the car. Tony turned out to be without a driver's license. "In New Mexico we send reckless drivers to jail, Tony."

Detective Sorensen got on the radio and had an officer come by, cuff Tony and cart him off to jail. Smiling, Signe continued on to her meeting at Tante Maria's coffee house. When she had first come to Santa Fe the second person she met was Dr. Lawrence Abramowitz from Los Alamos. They met at the local bookstore and had dinner together twice. They tried to have a romance but Signe found him too short, too curly headed and too self-centered. He had a degree in theoretical physics and worked at Los Alamos National Laboratory as a rocket scientist. He had been at the lab for the past eighteen years. Signe slid into a booth and ordered a regular coffee. "How are you Larry?" Signe sang.

"Not as good as when we were having romantic dinners, Signe. I still have the two corks from those wonderful Chilean cabernets we shared."

"We'll do it again, Larry. Those dinners were great. However, right now I need to pick your beautiful brain. What do you know about hydrazine?" She queried.

"Well it's an old time rocket fuel. The Germans used it and we did up until recently. I think the Germans may have used it in those awful V2 rockets that went from Peenemünde to London. I know that we used it in liquid fuel rockets right after the war. More recently I think we use it to fuel small multistage research rockets. Why do you ask?" Dr. Abramowitz asked inquiringly.

"I'm investigating a murder and the victim had high levels of several drugs and hydrazine in her bloodstream, Signe continued. "Could marijuana, cocaine, ecstasy or any other drug breakdown into hydrazine?"

"I don't think so, Signe, but I know people who could answer those questions easily. Hydrazine is quite simple to make and the ingredients are easy to find. Honestly, I don't have any good ideas about where that compound came from or how it got there. I'm sorry," Dr. Abramowitz concluded.

"I appreciate it your help, Larry, and we will have dinner soon. Please call me when you have some answers." Signe said as she slid out of the booth, hugged Larry and walked to her car again feeling discouraged about her mystery.

CHAPTER 9

Vincent Jaramillo called Signe back at 4 o'clock and said he still had the casts of the footprints from the fairgrounds. Signe suggested a meeting after work at Coyote Café for a drink so she could thank him properly for his help with the case. She also wanted to bring him up to date on the State Fairground murder, and pick his brains about the case. She didn't say that she also wanted to jump his bones in the worse possible way.

Signe went home early so she could get out of her navy blue suit and put on a more casual black sweater and a figure flattering skirt. She splashed some perfume on her throat as she raced out the door. Signe arrived first and took a seat at the near end of the bar with her long legs dangling invitingly toward the floor. The Coyote Café wasn't crowded at 6:30. Vincent rushed in 10 minutes late, still in his uniform looking as self-conscious as the first time they met. Signe had ordered a martini and Vincent ordered a Coors. They scooped up their drinks and headed to a quiet, dark table in the corner. The popular bar was beginning to fill up and now had the pleasant buzz of multiple conversations. Neither really seemed to want to talk about work. Signe talked about Axel and their recent trip to Chaco Canyon with its elegant architecture and mystical spirituality. Vincent talked about his family and his struggles as an officer with little experience and no mentors. Two drinks later, Signe still felt Vincent was too young but he looked even more desirable, if that was possible. Vincent suggested dinner at The Pink Adobe and Signe agreed after some hesitation. She knew that Axel was at an away football game for the evening, but she hesitated just a bit so that she didn't seem too eager before agreeing. The restaurant was only a few blocks away and the evening was mild so they decided to walk. Vincent took her arm as they walked down hill to the Santa Fe River. This was a narrow stream, completely dry in October, and a major source of water for this parched city in the desert. When she saw this 'river' she was always reminded of the abundance of water in her home land. They wound up a narrow old road toward the capitol to the Pink Adobe restaurant.

They had a delicious dinner of *chateau briand* for two that was prepared at table side with medium rare beef that melted in their mouths and an inexpensive bottle of red wine. They talked and laughed comfortably through dinner. Signe would touch Vincent's hand to emphasize a point until he took her hand under the table and held it gently. On the way back to her car they walked leisurely arm in arm. Signe didn't want the evening to end. When they got to the Jetta it was on a quiet narrow Santa Fe side street. The street was dark and empty. Vincent gently pressed her against the car and kissed her full on the mouth. She kissed him back. It felt wonderfully warm and tingly to her and she leaned comfortably into his muscular young body. She quickly unlocked the Jetta and pulled Vincent into the not very big back seat. She could lie partway back and she eased Vincent toward her so she could kiss him deeply with an open mouth while running her hands over his shoulders and back. Vincent kissed her neck and then fondled her shoulders and belly before settling his left hand on her breast. Even through the sweater and bra his hand felt wonderful there and she felt warmth in her loins. She kissed him even harder now with her sharp little tongue exploring his sweet mouth.

She wanted him right then, mostly because she liked him and found him sexy and a good kisser. Partly though, it was just that she hadn't had sex in six months, and was unbelievably horny. In Denmark she would have taken him to her empty apartment and had the sex with him that she so badly wanted. However, this was America and even though things were changing in this country the rules were different. If she went as far as she wanted to this night it might ruin her long run chances with this handsome young man. She tamped her desire down and took Vincent's hand from under her sweater where it had just strayed. She gently kissed the tips of his fingers.

"Vincent, I have to stop," she said breathlessly. "I had a perfect time and you were wonderful, but I have to get home. I want to see you again, soon."

Signe kissed Vincent goodbye and slid into the front seat wishing she wasn't alone. When she got home she was sad, discouraged about her murder case and still horny. Signe had had too much to drink, was alone in bed, and dreaded a meeting with the victim's family the next day. Not surprisingly, she slept poorly.

Wednesday morning she had a nine o'clock meeting at the station house with Mr. and Mrs. Patterson. Both Signe and Chief Hartford had received numerous calls from the Mr. Patterson on Tuesday so a meeting had finally been set. As she arrived and stopped at the coffee pot she could see that both of the Patterson's were in the conference room. Dirk Patterson was his usual jowly self in a double breasted pinstriped suit with a bright yellow tie. He looked the stereotypical part of an egotistical, pretentious barrister. Signe fought back her revulsion. Unlike her husband, Mrs. Svelty Patterson was striking. She was only 5 foot 5 inches tall but had a curvaceous figure with an hourglass waist, softly curled auburn hair and dainty features set off by brilliant green eyes. She looked twenty-five years younger than Dirk and was the *perfect* trophy wife. As she walked into the conference room, Detective Sorensen was truly at a loss for words. She strongly suspected that Svelty was not Chloe's mother as mother and daughter appeared to be very similar in age. Also the woman didn't appear to be grieving. The Detective finally found her voice and reviewed the highlights of the case for the past week. As she finished she was struck again by how little she truly knew about this transgression. It had been six days and they still had no suspects, no murder weapon and no real motive.

"I don't appreciate you jailing and mistreating my associate, Mr. Squitero," Dirk Patterson began. "He is only here to help you and the other officers solve this heinous crime."

"Sorry sir, but he was speeding, driving recklessly with expired tags and possessed no driver's license. The Mayor of Santa Fe would have been jailed for that," Detective Sorensen responded. "I want to know more about the horse that was stolen." Signe continued.

"I purchased the horse for Chloe two years ago." Mr. Patterson began. "She learned about those horses from a rich young girlfriend she met in rehab. Chloe learned everything there was to know about the breed. I've never seen her so focused and excited. Then she got on the internet to find out how to buy one. She had her heart set on this particular horse. Hercules was a two year old Lipizzaner stallion from Grenada, Spain. Chloe and I went to Grenada to the Alhambra Farms to see the horse and consider purchase. He was seventeen and a half hands high and quite dark. He is a huge animal with a high proud head. You know, Lipizzaner don't turn white until they are 5 or 6 years old. It was a beautiful farm with rolling hills covered in rich green grass and huge oaks trees. Chloe and I had a special time there. I felt closer to her than I had in years. They wanted €525,000 for the horse. I negotiated for two days with a Spanish interpreter and got the price down to $400,000. It cost me $18,000 just to ship him to Albuquerque." Dirk said with a wistful voice.

"Was this horse so valuable that someone would commit murder to obtain him?" Signe asked.

"I've been racking my brain over that question, and regretfully, I believe the answer is yes." Mr. Patterson said thoughtfully.

"Mr. Patterson, please tell me a bit about Chloe's drug problem," Signe enquired.

"Chloe has been totally drug free for two years!" Mr. Patterson bellowed.

"Perhaps sir, but she, has a record of alcohol and drug abuse prior to that," Signe yelled back.

"All right, she had 2 DUI's when she was a teen." Mr. Patterson said. "She had trouble with cocaine in her early twenties. Then she went to drug rehabilitation three times. The first program she went to was in Scottsdale and it was expensive but the staff smuggled cocaine and crystal meth in for the clients. The second program was in Austin and I really had it checked out before hand. She worked hard in the program but relapsed after three weeks. The third program was in New York it cost more than a Rolls Royce. The hospital looked like an Ivy League campus but they had electrified fences and TV cameras everywhere, even in the showers. However, for the last two years she has been clean. Totally drug free."

"Thank you, Mr. Patterson, Signe asked. "Are you Chloe's mother, Mrs. Patterson?" she continued.

"No I'm not," Svelty said. "I married Dirk five years ago. We met on an airplane. I was a stewardess or rather a flight attendant. Chloe's mother lives in St. Louis. She's remarried. She and Dirk divorced in 1979. Chloe never really accepted me. I think she saw me more as a competitive older sister than a step mom."

"Thank you, Mrs. Patterson; do you two have any questions for me?" Signe asked.

"No I don't, Miss Sorensen," Svelty said with a catch in her voice. "But please find Chloe's killer. What happened shouldn't happen to anyone. Despite her problems, Chloe didn't deserve this."

The Patterson's rose in unison and walked toward the door and Signe escorted them past the clerk's desk. On the way out, Svelty surreptitiously slipped Signe a note.

CHAPTER 10

When she first awoke on Thursday, Signe was hoping for a break of any kind. She needed to review all her evidence and clues, and then think and think and think. First she checked on the foot prints that Vincent had cast. There were three different boot tracks. They were size 10, 12 and 13. They were not distinctive except for the right imprint of the size twelve boots which showed a jagged broken heel on the instep.

Next the piece of red paper found at the scene was of foreign manufacture and may have come from South America. It might have been part of a travel voucher but most of the writing was obscured. Forensics could tell her little more. There was a broken cable tie. Finally there was a white piece of plastic found in the stable that seemed to be part of the handle of a ten cc hypodermic syringe made by Becton Dickinson.

The cell phone only showed fingerprints from Chloe. She had made or received twenty calls in the week before she died. Four were to her family. Most were to or from her girlfriends scattered all over the Southwest. Three were to a Johnny Armijo in Albuquerque and three were to Tommy Rice. One call on Thursday afternoon was to a number in area code 862 which could not be traced. Rice was a well known drug dealer according to the NCDB. He lived in the south valley of Albuquerque. The south valley was an anomaly in New Mexico. A poor barrio in an otherwise prosperous and modern city, the south valley bred drug use, child and spousal abuse and shockingly violent crime. Tommy dealt crystal meth, cocaine and heroin. He had been convicted twice of dealing drugs and had served two years in the county jail. Johnny Armijo appeared to have been Chloe's most recent boyfriend. He was the rich, spoiled only son of a family that owned a many section ranch in nearby Mountain Air. Signe planned on interviewing both of these gentlemen.

Signe suddenly remembered that she had a note from Svelty in her pocket. She pulled it out. The note, written on a small piece of paper, asked Detective Sorensen to call her and included her cell phone number. Signe dialed the number. Svelty answered.

"This is detective Sorensen, can you talk?" Signe asked.

"Yes, Dirk is at the office. I'm so glad that you called," Signe said. "I'm so sorry about Chloe's death. Dirk is very domineering and seldom lets me speak. I wanted to talk with you today when we visited the police station but he threatened me before we went in. Detective Sorensen, I don't know who's responsible for this terrible crime. However, there are some things that you should know. Mr. Patterson appears to be very prosperous and quite honestly, it was one of the things that attracted me to him. However, despite his Mercedes and $4,000 suits he is in desperate financial difficulty. He hid this from me. I used to go on shopping sprees to New York and spend $50,000 in a weekend on dresses, shoes and purses. Dirk never seemed to mind until recently."

"The rent on his new 15,000 square foot office is very expensive." Svelty continued. "Dirk spent a quarter of a million dollars on paintings and tapestries for the office. His advertising budget alone is hundreds of thousands of dollars a year. He has had a lot of little settlements but no 'rainmakers' in the last three years. Just after we married, Dirk represented 7 people in a horrendous bus accident. The bus was struck by a semi traveling at high speed and there was a fire. The truck driver was on drugs. There were horrendous injuries and burns; Dirk settled for millions. Since then things haven't ever been the same." Svelty said wistfully.

"Six months ago Dirk took out life insurance policies on Chloe and me. They were for $2,000,000 each in the event of our deaths and he was named the sole beneficiary. The only reason I know about this is that I had to have a physical and sign some forms at the time. He said that he took out a policy on himself also but I never saw such a policy. When I asked him about the insurance later he just got angry and changed the subject. I've been afraid to bring it up ever since."

"I'm not sure how any of this relates to Chloe's death or even if it does," Svelty said plaintively. "But Dirk is under tremendous financial pressure and hasn't been himself for the past year."

"Thank you for this information," Signe said. "I will keep it very confidential. If you learn anything more please call me at any time, day or night." The conversation with Svelty left Signe unsettled. Certainly, Mr. Patterson wasn't responsible for his difficult daughter's death, but he and

Mr. Squitero might have a hidden agenda. She would have to be more careful around both of them.

Detective Sorensen was late for a luncheon engagement and she raced out of the police station to her car. When she arrived at The Shed just to the east of the plaza, Jefferson Barclay was already sipping a margarita on the porch. He wanted to enlighten Signe about the South American strangers. As a trusted long time employee of La Fonda he had ready access to the hotel's computers, and had taken the liberty to print some confidential information for Signe. He reminded her that three men had checked into the hotel just before the beginning of the New Mexico State Fair. He didn't hear about the crime until Saturday. Jefferson was very surprised that it took him two days to get the scoop. Normally, he prided himself on knowing everything that happened in Santa Fe, quickly. He was particularly suspicious because he had seen the three South American cowboys leave in such a hurry late Thursday afternoon.

Signe ordered the blue corn enchiladas with red chile sauce. When she had first arrived in New Mexico she had never tasted anything as hot as the local food. It seared her northern European palate. In Denmark spices were a rarity. However, underneath the heat she found a complex mix of appealing tastes. Since the spring, she had graduated to hotter and hotter dishes. Initially she needed two large glasses of water and an iced tea to get through a meal. Now she was a veteran and hardly ever gasped, although she still perspired particularly while eating very hot red chile.

"Here is the registration form for the three gents that I told you about," Jefferson purred. Signe saw the three Spanish looking names written in one man's flowery hand. The three all had the same last name, Fortuna. Their addresses were all the same-a number with no street name (perhaps a post office box?) followed by Santa Rosa, Argentina 8042.

"It may not mean anything, but I thought they looked 'shifty'," Jefferson continued after a big sip of margarita. "They dressed like working cowboys with worn boots and hats and they wore long brown dusters that no one in New Mexico wears. They sped through the lobby about 6 p.m. on Thursday without even checking out. They were sweating and dusty. One of them had a lariat over his shoulder and their black cowboy hats were pulled down over their faces."

"Well it's not much to go on, but I appreciate the tip," Signe stated. "Could you identify them from a photo?"

"I believe I could," Jefferson said. "The tallest one had a scar on his left cheek that would be hard to hide."

"Let me buy lunch, Jefferson," Signe concluded.

They said their goodbyes and then Signe raced back to the station and her computer. On the way she had the vague feeling that she was being followed. A small blue sedan seemed to take all the twisting turns that she did as she crossed town on the old narrow streets. The car stayed about a block and a half behind her. She would watch for it later.

The police computer was old, had been misused, and it was slow. Sometimes Signe did math puzzles in her head will she waited for the next prompt. Part of the 'c' key was broken off and its jagged shape startled Signe finger every time she struck it. She read some general information about Argentina, a large country with people of Indian, Spanish, and Italian descent. It is the second largest country in South America and occupied most of the southern part of the continent. The country's name comes from the Latin name for silver *Argentum*. Despite being poor in all the precious metals; it is a rich country. They produced cattle, sheep, wheat, corn and flax in abundance. The little ranching town of Santa Rosa is on the eastern edge of the Pampas, the sea of grass that occupied a large part of the center of the country. This fertile area with rich soil and endless grass extends for over 500 miles, Signe read. It is home to millions of cattle and horses and not many people.

She contacted Immigration and Naturalization with the three names of the men that stayed at the La Fonda Hotel, but it would be days before she heard back from them.

CHAPTER 11

Signe Sorensen had been thinking about Vincent Jaramillo everyday and especially every night since they had dinner. Of course, she was busy with the case which now had a series of tentacles and clues but overall it was still quite murky. As the older, more experienced, member of the pair Signe decided to plan an assignation. Since they were both unattached it wasn't as complicated as her meetings with married men on the police force in Copenhagen, however, both were known in the little village of Santa Fe. Some discretion was appropriate. First she found a school night when Alex would be away all night for a basketball game in Belen, south of Albuquerque. Then she hired a car and driver so that they could relax and have some wine and not worry about driving. Signe's mind went into high gear as she planned this tryst. Vincent had been calling her daily but on this particular day she said she had a surprise for him that would take fourteen hours. Vincent said he was game without any hesitation. She gave him a short list of the things he would need for their tryst.

She went home early took a leisurely bath before fixing her hair and putting on makeup. She had a new sapphire blue dress that set off her slender figure. The car, a white Lincoln, picked her up at six thirty. She had the driver take her to Vincent's apartment. The limo driver went up to Vincent's door while Signe relaxed on the spacious back seat crossing her legs in an unladylike fashion. Vincent appeared promptly in a well tailored black suit with a grey shirt and silver tie. He carried a single white rose that he presented to Signe as he climbed through the open door and kissed her both tenderly and deeply.

They started at the Coyote Café, where they had met the week before, for a drink, soft words, and hand holding. Signe thought Vincent was as relaxed as she had seen him and she adored looking into his large soft brown eyes.

After a leisurely drink the car headed north out of the city past the veteran's cemetery with the sad quiet rows of headstones lined up the hillside, and then past the massive soaring wings of the Santa Fe Opera, dark since August. The driver turned smoothly to the right onto a side road. Soon they were in the town of Tesuque buried in a valley where the two could find the anonymity that that they sought. The driver glided to a halt by El Nido an old adobe style restaurant that hulked only 10 feet from the roadway. They had a private table that Signe requested. She had their special house smoked salmon and *Coquilles Saint-Jacques.* Vincent had ceviche and a rib eye steak. The food was spectacular. They lingered over each bite of their appetizers talking and laughing. Signe had the main course delayed so they would have more time to converse. After they finished eating, a small band set up in the corner by the bar. A piano player, trumpet player and bassist created plenty of sound in the confines of the room. They danced slow and close and fast and apart. Signe liked the slow tunes when Vincent pulled her in close and she could feel his warm lanky body along hers. The crowd thinned about eleven thirty and they felt comfortable dancing even closer sharing long and deep kisses right on the dance floor. After a particularly long slow dance Signe handed Vincent a card with the name of the Kokopelli Bed and Breakfast in Pojoaque. The limo driver headed north as soon as he received the card. Tesuque is nestled in the piñon covered hills above Santa Fe. Pojoaque is a few miles further north just before the road turns west toward Los Alamos and the cottonwood trees replace the piñons. On the way Vincent caressed Signe's shoulders under her coat and ran his hand up the inside of her thigh. He discovered she was wearing silk stockings with a European style garter belt. Signe hoped the ride would be over very soon.

The owners were still up and walked the couple to their suite nestled in the pine trees. The B&B was furnished with antiques. The sitting room had a curving brocaded sofa and a chair with a large fireplace. A piñon fire had been laid with its perfumed smell and crackles from little bits of exploding pitch. The bedroom had a large four poster bed with an antique quilt. Once they were alone, the couple lost no time settling on the capacious sofa kissing with soft open mouths and fondling each other with light almost tickling touches. Soon their clothes lay in a tangled pile on the rug. Vincent could admire Signe's slender white body, pert breasts and the curly tuft of blond brown hair between her legs. She saw his slender brown body for the first time and a darker brown erection sprouting from a curly mat of black hair. She had been very patient but now she was in a frenzy of boiling desire inside. She gently removed his mouth from her nipple, pulled him up and walked with him hand in hand toward the bed. As she walked she realized how wet and warm she was between her legs.

As they reached the bed the quilt was unceremoniously pushed to the floor. Signe lay down on her back, legs demurely but at the same time invitingly apart. Vincent lowered himself slowly onto her and entered her without any fanfare. As he gently moved deeper Signe remembered how much she had missed this feeling. As she began to focus on the wonderful filling sensation Vincent gave a soft moan and came. Signe pulled him close and kissed him tenderly, however she was immensely aroused now and far short of her own fulfillment. This is what I get, she thought for picking an inexperienced partner half my age!

After a very short pause, she used her soft hand to caress him back to a pleasing stiffness. She pushed him firmly down on his back and toyed with his erection briefly using her mouth and tongue. Next she moved her body over him and guided him in to her now double wetness. She took charge with the long slow strokes that she liked and at the deepest spot pressed her clitoris against his pubic bone. After a few minutes she exploded in wave after wave of pleasure that started where they were attached but radiated into her belly, her ass and even down the fronts of her legs. Vincent joined in at the end. After holding each other for a few minutes they move around the bedroom and sitting room making love in a variety of different positions. At three a.m. they took a hot soapy bath together and collapsed into bed. Both of them had work the next day so they got up at six a.m. on Friday and after a 'quickie', they dressed and walked outside just as the sun lit the Sangre de Cristo Mountains. Still in a daze, Vincent half expected to see the white Lincoln parked there with the driver sitting attentively behind the wheel in his neatly pressed uniform. Instead Signe had had two of her friends bring the Jetta to the bed and breakfast the day before for a quick get away. Signe flipped the keys to Vincent.

One the way back to Santa Fe Signe's cell phone rang. "Hello. Yes this is she," she said warily. After listening for several minutes she said, "This is extremely bad news and I can't believe that what you are saying is true." She hung up abruptly. She closed the phone and threw it angrily on the floor barely missing Vincent's feet.

PART 2

CHAPTER 12

When her cell phone rang she was hoping it was a break on the mystifying murder she was intent on solving. Instead it was a call from a Mister Manuel Perez. He identified himself as the father of Miss Irma Perez and asserted that her son, Axel, had been dating his daughter for five months. He had gotten her cell phone number from Axel. He was calling to say that Irma was three months pregnant and he thought that the families should meet.

She was too shocked to respond intelligently and after mumbling, "This is extremely bad news." Signa had hung up the phone and threw it across the car.

Vincent was surprised. He asked some questions she was in no mood to answer. She had Vincent 'hot footed' it into town to Vincent's apartment and after a brief but very pleasant kiss they said their goodbyes.

She pulled out her flashing red light and activated it so she could traverse Santa Fe, in her rage, at a completely reckless speed. She screeched to a halt on the south side of town in front of Santa Fe High School. She parked illegally by the flagpole and left the red light on her dashboard oscillating as she ran into the school. As she bounded up the steps she realized how sore she was from last nights activities with Vincent. She uncharacteristically flashed her badge as she pulled the high school office door open.

"Where can I find Axel Sorensen?" She demanded in a loud voice.

The flustered student clerk, with mousy brown hair, took some time after rustling through several large stacks of paper to report that he was in metal shop. The clerk yelled directions out the door as Signe turned on her heels and left.

She ripped open the door of the metal shop to the noise and heat of the machines. Axel was working under a hood heating a piece of metal in a bright blue flame. He was unaware of her presence until she grabbed his ear.

Startled he dropped the heavy piece of metal with a loud clank and turned to see his furious *Moder* glaring at him. While his mother was tall, at 6'5" Axel towered over her. When he saw the look in her eyes he was truly afraid. She held his arm tightly as she steered him out of class.

"He's going with me," she yelled in the direction of the startled teacher. No words were spoken by either as she hustled him out of the school.

When they hit the front steps she began to yell. "*Fandens!*" Which is Danish for "damn it!" "What is going on here? Are you responsible for Irma's pregnancy? How did *this* happen to that little *luder?* How long have you known?"

In addition to being afraid, Axel was confused by the barrage of questions and didn't know which one to answer first. Despite his size he felt tears welling up in his eyes. He started with what he thought his mother would find most damning.

"I've known for six days, but I was afraid to tell you. I could never find the right words. Yes, I think I'm responsible. We've been having sex for four months. I think I love her, mother." he continued warily.

"Son, you know nothing about love," Signe began. "Don't confuse love with lust and the fact that you like having sex. You've known about sex since you were nine, and I taught you about birth control when you were twelve. I even offered to buy condoms for you. What went wrong?" she continued now more exasperated than angry.

"Well we started using condoms and I was very careful. Then Irma said she didn't like the 'feel' of them and if we were careful she wouldn't get pregnant. Sometimes though, we both got in such a hurry that we weren't careful." He said wistfully. "Sometimes we screwed in our apartment and I was afraid you might come home and find us doing it," he said.

"We have to come up with a plan, Axel." Signe said with some anxiety in her voice. "We need to help the Perez family consider all of the options: abortion or adoption rather than trying to force you into a long term relationship. You are too young to marry. Both you and Irma will grow into different people in the next ten years."

"Mom, Irma is Catholic. She won't look at this pregnancy the way you do. She already said that she thinks an abortion is a sin and if she were forced to have one she would surely go to hell." Axel said plaintively.

"We need to work together on a plan, son." Signe reiterated. "But right now I need to go to the station house and you need to do some serious thinking about your future. I'll set up a meeting for both of us with Irma's parents."

Signe dropped Axel off at their apartment and raced off to the police station. When she arrived Detective Hartford was in his office. She knocked and was waved in. She felt very out of touch after a wonderful night with Vincent and a horrible morning with Axel. "What's up chief?" she began.

"That's the very question I was going to ask you, Signe." he replied.

"There are no major breakthroughs, I'm afraid." she began. "I still don't know *how* the victim was murdered. Dr. Gilchrist provided less guidance than usual from her autopsy report. The motive may well have been that very expensive horse. However, Mrs. Patterson reports that Mr. Patterson held a two million dollar life insurance policy on Chloe and that he is sole beneficiary. She says he's in financial difficulty and she seems afraid of him. Three suspicious men from Argentina may have actually taken the horse even if they didn't commit the murder. That information, however, is very circumstantial right now. In summary, unfortunately, I'd say we still have a long ways to go." she concluded.

"Albuquerque PD called yesterday and said they were holding Tommy Rice on a crystal meth distribution charge. That's the guy that Chloe called three times during her last week of life. Also, my sources in Albuquerque say that Johnny Armijo is around town. He spends his afternoons at an off track betting parlor and parties every night in the VIP room of a strip club on Central called The Wild Pony Gentlemen's Club. You have the full resources of the department behind you Detective Sorensen in trying to solve this case. Don't hesitate to ask." Chief Hartford concluded.

"I'll go to Albuquerque Monday, chief, and interview both of those 'gentlemen'. Thanks for the tip," Signe said as she rose to leave.

When she got to her desk she found a stack of messages. None of them were important, although one was from Mr. Perez and contained his work number. She called him at the Atalaya Elementary School, where he was a custodian, and arranged a meeting with the Perez family at their home at 6 p.m. that evening. She spent the rest of the day clearing the files off her desk. She did manage to squeeze in a quick handholding lunch with Vincent at her old favorite The Coyote Café. Signe relaxed some in the presence of two things she enjoyed—hot New Mexican food and Vincent, in that order.

Signe and Axel arrived ten minutes early for the meeting at the Perez's residence. Axel wore his usual rumpled chinos with an untucked shirt. Signe wore her trim dark blue suit from work. The family lived in Agua Fria, an old neighborhood, south and west of the Capital. The land is lower with a few large cottonwood trees and narrow, tortuous, dirt streets. On some corners the adobe houses come within two feet of the roadway. The Perez's home was a modest old adobe with a large garage and workshop behind it. Signe parked in the dirt side yard. She brought some cut flowers for Mrs.

Perez which she made Axel carry. It was a cool October evening and the cozy house felt warm.

Manuel Perez introduced his wife, Maria and his other three daughters. One carried an eighteen month old baby on her hip. No other men were present which Signe regarded as a bad sign. Signe and Axel towered over the Perez family. Mr. Perez was the tallest member at five foot three inches. Mr. Perez did the talking. He reviewed the facts—Irma was twelve weeks pregnant, Axel was the father and the family wished to secure the new baby's future with a marriage. The bride's family would pay for the marriage at St. Genevieve's church nearby or even at the downtown cathedral. Since it was the fall and not many marriages were planned, several Saturdays were open in the next six weeks.

Before Signe could begin to object Mrs. Perez invited the guests into the cramped kitchen to eat. Everyone, eight in number, crowded around the small table with a green oilcloth table covering. Small wooden chairs with loose joints were placed along the sides and corners of the table. Mrs. Perez and the oldest daughter served flautas, chile rellenos, and the hottest and best tasting green chile enchiladas that Signe had ever eaten. She ate pinto beans and homemade flour tortillas along with the enchiladas to reduce the burning in her mouth.

After a barely decent interval Signe began to speak. "Thank you, Mr. and Mrs. Perez for your hospitality, but I will not allow Axel to marry your daughter. They are both children and their chance of success as a couple is vanishingly small. Their only relationship is based on some furtive sex. Besides, children should not raise children. I will bear the full cost of an abortion and accompany Irma to the clinic. Surely, you both must realize that this is the right thing to do." Signe concluded as she pushed her chair back from the table.

There were nods of disagreement from all of the women at the table but only Mr. Perez spoke.

"You must realize ma'am that for Catholics abortion is an unpardonable sin. You son took advantage of my youngest daughter, she is pregnant and he must marry her!" Mr. Perez shouted as he stood up from the table. Signe rose nodded toward the door at Axel and moved in that direction.

"This marriage will *not* take place as long as I have breath, Mr. Perez. Good night." Signe shouted back as she and Axel went out the door into the cold, crisp New Mexican night. Signa sensed Axel's confusion and ambivalence. She knew that sex was a powerful drug for a young man.

"I'm sorry that ended that way, son," Signe said with real sympathy in her voice.

"It's all going so fast, Mom. It's just hard to keep up," Axel replied forlornly.

One the way home Signe and Axel reviewed their limited options. Axel bravely said that he would marry Irma, but Signe realized that this would be tragedy for three people—Irma, Axel and the new baby. Signe considered some type of lump sum payment to Irma in return for no further contact by mother or child. However, such an agreement would be too easy to break after the Perez's had gotten their money. Signe was stumped, and could think of no other options. She also had a headache and her stomach was upset by her anxiety combined with the chile she had eaten. She fell into bed for what she knew would be another sleepless night.

She spent a frustrating weekend with Axel worrying about Irma's pregnancy. Axel was alternating between being discouraged and seeing a future with Irma. Signa tried to be the voice of reason for the son that she loved so much. On Sunday they drove to the nearby Jemez Mountains for a fast six mile hike over a dusty, rocky trail that helped them both forget their worries temporarily.

CHAPTER 13

Signe dragged herself out of bed at 6 a.m. having slept fitfully. Her case was going nowhere and her personal life was a wreck except for one small very bright spot-Vincent. She dressed and headed to the department. There were no new developments overnight. She got in the Jetta and pointed out Old Pecos Trail and then south toward Albuquerque on I-25. I-25 goes south out of Santa Fe in both directions, Signe noticed. On the map the road is shaped like a little hill as it goes past the Capitol with Santa Fe at its highest point. In one direction the road goes southwest to Albuquerque. In the other direction the road goes southeast toward Pecos and Las Vegas, New Mexico. The interstates avoidance of the Capitol is reminiscent of the famous railroad that serves northern New Mexico. Before the mergers of all of the railroads it was called the Atchison, Topeka and the Santa Fe. Despite this sobriquet, which was one of the best corporate names in America, the railroad never went to Santa Fe. The train stopped at the little town of Lamy which is fourteen and a half miles south of Santa Fe. In the old days, a dusty stagecoach ride up a tall mesa followed a long train before the weary passenger actually arrived in the Capital.

As she headed past the State Penitentiary in Cerrillos she accelerated with traffic and headed southwest. When she arrived in Albuquerque, she went directly to the local barbed wire encased detention center. After checking her gun, badge and handcuffs she was ushered into a small dingy green detention room and Tommy Rice was brought in. He was a slight young man with bad teeth, a collapsed nose and a noticeable limp. He had watery pale blue eyes and was balding. His skin was so pale Signe though he hadn't been out in the sunlight once in the past ten years. He wore a Bernalillo County detention center orange uniform and his legs and hands were manacled. He walked with the strange crablike gait of a person who could not swing his arms and legs normally. Tommy Rice had been dealing drugs in the most deadly and violent place in New Mexico since he was thirteen, Albuquerque's south valley. He had a rap sheet as long as the neck of one of the famous giraffes at the Albuquerque Zoo. Most of the charges had been dropped or reduced in punishment, but fortunately for Detective Sorensen, Tommy had been convicted twice and had done time. Now at the age of thirty-four, Tommy faced New Mexico's three times loser law. If he was convicted this time he would spend the rest of his life in jail, without the possibility of parole.

"Tommy I'm Detective Sorensen of the Santa Fe Police and I want to ask you about on of your customers, an attractive blond woman, in her late twenties named Chloe Patterson." Signe began.

"I don't know who you're talking about," Tommy said with some attitude.

"Let me remind you about the seriousness of the charge against you. This is a potential third conviction for you Tommy. If you are convicted no one will be able to keep you from spending the rest of your life in jail without the possibility of parole. Not even the judge." Signe fired back.

"I don't have anything to say," Tommy shot back.

"You can't be that dumb," Signe retorted. "I'm asking questions about someone who is dead, and if you don't come clean you spend the rest of your miserable life in jail. You don't have the resources or the network to feed your habit for the next forty years."

"Okay, okay. This little rich *puta* started buying from me several years ago. First she bought marijuana in big quantities. She must have been peddlin' to her friends. Later she bought mongo amounts of cocaine. Then I wouldn't hear anything for months. I heard she was doin' the rehab thing. Then one day she'd be back always flashing a big roll of bills and buying several big bags of dope. I loved it when she came by. She had big pillowy tits. She was great to look at and she always flirted. She laid so much green on me when she came by high I didn' have to hustle for a week. But I heard from some of her doper friends that she went straight. I haven't seen her in, unnh, two, two and a half years." Tommy concluded.

"She called your cell phone twice in the last two weeks, Tommy. You are really starting to piss me off. I'm glad I get to make a report to your arresting officer about our visit and the level to which you are *not* cooperating." Signe spat out as she leaned toward him.

"Okay. Jesus. She called, I don' know ten, eleven days ago and said she needed some 'ice', you know some 'crank', some crystal meth and some heroin. I'd never sold her that shit before. We set up a meeting at my place a week ago Wednesday. She bought the 'ice' and the 'h'. That's the last I time I saw her, honest." Tommy concluded.

"She was found dead the day after she got the drugs from you. Is there anything else you want to tell me, Tommy?" Signe asked.

"No, it wasn't from my shit." he replied.

"Now, how would you know that, Tommy? She couldn't have OD'ed on your drugs, particularly if she had never used heroin before? Give me a break, Tommy." Signe said with an exasperated voice as she motioned for the guard to take Tommy away.

She collected her things and left. She met with Albuquerque PD to check information on any of her other suspects including the three vaqueros from Argentine, but she learned nothing new. She spent the rest of the afternoon at the Bernalillo County Sheriff's Office working on some other cases.

As night fell she headed east on Central Avenue through the rebuilt downtown where the KiMo Theater stands, past the University and then through the Yuppie area around Scalo's Restaurant. After a slight dip in the road the character of the street changes dramatically. The buildings were older, some were boarded up. There was more trash and hookers could be seen loitering along the roadside in six inch skirts. Suddenly a sixty foot tall neon sign announces The Wild Pony, A Gentleman's Club. She parked and walked inside. The bar was nearly full at this early hour and girls hung from every pole. She flashed her badge and asked for the VIP lounge. A waitress took her there. She hesitated briefly on the threshold, and wondered if she should have brought back up, and then plunged in. The main part of The Wild Pony was dark but the VIP lounge was several times darker. The only light was weak indirect red light bouncing off of the ceiling. Several people were moving around in the room but Signe could make out nothing clearly. She pulled out her badge in desperation and called out Johnny Armijo's name. She heard a grunt ahead of her, and to the left as her eyes were just starting to adjust. She started to stumble over a narrow armless chair, but a strong hand grasped her left upper arm, turned her 180 degrees and pulled her down into a velvet chair.

"What can I do for ya?" Johnny Armijo said.

She found herself sitting next to a handsome heavy featured man in a tailored suit and silk shirt open at the neck with heavy gold chains around his neck and wrist. A tall brunette wearing high heels and a thong was straddling him and rubbing her large, augmented breasts against his neck and upper chest.

"Beat it," he said. She unfolded, stood up and walked away on her seven inch spike heels shaking her ass as she went.

"Mr. Armijo, I'm Detective Sorensen and I'm investigating the death of Miss Chloe Patterson. I understand that you were 'close' with the deceased." Signe began.

"We had known each other for about two years. We met in drug rehab and we'd been seeing more of each other this past six months. A real loss, her death I mean. She was beautiful, smart, rich and fun. We really had a thing for each other." Johnny said with some real sadness in his voice.

This is the first person I've talked with that seems truly sorry about her death Signe noted.

"We partied a lot," Johnny continued as he shifted to look Signe directly in the eye. He was powerfully built and very handsome she noted. "The best was when we drank and smoked some marijuana. She did okay on cocaine. It made her happy. When she switched to crystal meth three months ago everything changed. Oh, it made her very horny, but she stopped eating and she had to be moving all the time. After she'd been using 'crank' for three or four days, she would get very suspicious. Then later she'd get anxious, then depressed, and sometimes violent. I got hit in the shoulder by a broken bottle she threw and had to have stitches. We weren't as close the last month. She was using more 'speed' and couldn't get any sleep without shooting heroin. God, I miss her," he nearly sobbed.

"I'm sorry that you lost her. If she had lived maybe she could have beaten her drug habit." Signe said. "Who would have wanted to kill her, Johnny?"

"I heard the horse got stolen, and it was almost valuable enough to be grounds for a murder." Johnny wondered. "Perhaps it was a drug deal gone bad, or a drug dealer robbed her. She was always flashing big wads of cash around especially when she was high. She was very careless with money. You know, she didn't get along with her dad. He was tired of footing the bill for rehab and then watching her relapse. She said that he felt that she needed to stop being such a financial drain on him now that she was almost thirty. I guess, detective, I don't know who did it or why, but I sure hope you catch him or her." Johnny said wistfully as his voice trailed off.

"Thank you for your time Mr. Armijo. If you think of anything more call me on my cell," Signe said scribbling the number on a paper napkin. As she rose and walked away she saw the brunette prance back toward Johnny with her flat stomach pointed at Signe and her breasts bouncing. As she drove back toward Santa Fe Signe called Chief Hartford and Vincent and told both of them what she had found out. She called mostly because she was very tired, and it was a very dark night with little traffic, and the talking would keep her from falling asleep at the wheel. As she traveled along the dark road between the two cities her eyelids were heavy but her mind wandered over the mystery of Chloe's murder.

CHAPTER 14

As Signe got close to Santa Fe the sleepiness returned and she had real trouble keeping her eyes open. After the long climb of La Bajada hill there are no services on either side along the road into Santa Fe except for a rest area on the right side of the road just after the crest of the hill as the lights of the city come into view. She passed the first exit, Cerrillos Road where most of the already light traffic got off. Cerrillos Road was the main artery into town but first it made a long curve to the west before turning north into the city. In this proud old city, this street was lined by every fast food joint, retail outlet and gas station with an irregular pile of discarded tires beside it that American capitalism had to offer. It was a glaring neon jumble. At St. Francis Drive, the next exit, the remaining traffic got off.

Next, is a long dark slow curve to the right with no lights, and no buildings before the Old Pecos Trail exit to the old part of Santa Fe. Halfway along the curve with Signe dangerously close to sleep a large jacked up pickup with iron bars across the radiator approached from behind at high speed. She heard the roar of its unmuffled engine before she saw the vehicle. The trucks headlights were higher than the top of the Jetta. A row of piercing lights along the top of the roll bar was also illuminated. She was suddenly wide awake expecting the truck to pull into the passing lane and shoot by. However, the truck didn't deviate or slow, and it smashed hard into the stubby rear end of the Jetta. Signe gripped the steering wheel hard with both hands as she felt fright spreading from the pit of her stomach. As the trunk crumpled, the right rear tire of the car locked causing the car to swerve to the right.

First, she felt the bumps of the warning strip along the shoulder and then gravel as the car veered to the right. The front end just missed a metal guard rail, and the car plunged down a gentle embankment. The Jetta was still going fast from its own highway speed plus the kinetic energy it received from the thump of the truck. Fortunately for Signe the ground was smooth and a little soft which slowed the vehicle some. The car ran over several creosote bushes and some small piñon trees. The small branches and trunks and her brakes combined to slow the vehicle until the front bumper suddenly hit a large rock. The Jetta stopped abruptly, and the air bag deployed. Signe may have lost consciousness for a minute or so.

When she awoke her left arm hurt badly and her chest and face felt bruised and abraded. She was alive, though, and not badly hurt. Signe felt confined in her seat and claustrophobic for the first time in her life. She batted the airbag out of the way, and unfastened her seatbelt. She felt around in the dark on the floor of the car with her good arm for her cell phone. She called the station and reported what happened. She asked for an ambulance, a wrecker, and the canine unit in case the vehicle was hard to find as she knew none of the lights in the vehicle worked. She also asked for the detective on call to be dispatched as she knew the 'accident' was deliberate without knowing why yet. She called Axel and explained as gently as she could what had happened. Then she dialed Vincent on his cell. He was worried about her and he said he would meet her at St. Vincent's Hospital. As she sat in the dark for the next twenty-five minutes, she got colder and colder and shivered for the fifth time since the murder occurred. Instead of thinking about the murder she focused on her problem with Axel. No clear way out of her son's thorny problem had yet revealed itself to her.

Help arrived all at once. Some large spotlights from the road flashed off the back window of the car and then she heard the barks and breathing of the department's two canines-Jethro and Jasmine. They were a pair of large German shepherds that worked in the department for drug detection, and also walked beats with patrolmen in downtown Santa Fe during the night. Signe always petted them, and slipped them a treat on her way into the department. Both jumped up on the driver's side door, barked and then slobbered on the driver side window.

Two uniformed officers arrived next, and were unable to open the door on Signe's side of the car. Two EMTs were close behind. They came around to the passenger side and were able to open the door, took a pulse, felt to make sure none of her long bones were broken, and passed two scratchy grey wool blankets to her through the passenger door to ward off the cold. In five minutes the shivering stopped. The officers returned with a crowbar and pried the Jetta's door open. She tried to get out and stand, but the whole world suddenly started spinning and got very black. When she awoke she was strapped on a stretcher being carried through the New Mexico sagebrush.

The first thing she saw as she looked up was the constellation Orion rising above the dark mass of the Sangre de Cristo Mountains and suddenly she also knew what to do to help Axel.

Perhaps she drifted off, and when she awoke she was on the third floor of St. Vincent's Hospital with a splint on her left arm and bandages on her face and shoulder. Vincent and Axel were at her bedside both looking worried. She reassured both of them that she would be okay, and planned on coming home in the morning. She asked Axel to step outside for a moment.

"This accident was deliberate, Vincent. The driver of that truck had every intention of hurting or killing me." Signe began. "I told you what I learned in Albuquerque. Maybe I am closer to solving this murder than I thought. Someone is getting scared. Please, take Axel home and make sure he is all right, and then think over everything I told you. The terrified feeling is going away, and I'll be okay here tonight. Call me in the morning. I'm counting on you and I want you to hold me." Signe said softly.

Vincent crawled awkwardly into the tall, hard hospital bed with his boots on. He wrapped his long arms around Signe trying not to squeeze her.

"You know I will, babe." Vincent answered and left.

Despite all the noise and bright lights, Signe managed to sleep until eight. The doctor came by and examined her. After saying how lucky he thought she was, he gave her some instructions and sent her home. Vincent drove her home and after a quick shower she went to bed. Every muscle in her body ached, and he head pounded in rhythm with her heart.

When she awoke in the afternoon the sun was already getting lower in the sky and a golden light shone into her room. Even though she felt she knew little about the murder, someone sensed she was getting too close. She reviewed what she had learned about Chloe from Tommy Rice and Johnny Armijo yesterday. While useful, none of it seemed earth shaking. She was missing something, but what? How did the perpetrators know she was on the interstate last night? After a strong cup of coffee the headache was better, but she had no clear answers. Everything about the case was murky. Nothing was crystal clear.

As the caffeine began to course into her veins, she started working on her plan for Axel. She called the Odense, Denmark police station and asked to speak to senior detective Rasmussen talking in her beloved Danish. Despite the late evening hour the detective was on duty and soon came on the line. They hadn't spoken in two years. They made some small talk. Detective Rasmussen had heard indirectly that she was in the States. He was between girlfriends and was doing some sailing and horseback riding. Signe explained

Axel's problem and talked about him at length as a confused young man who had good qualities but was drifting. Then she asked him to consider taking Axel for a year or two, and wondered if he could get him into a trade school in Denmark. She expected a brusque and very prompt rejection. Much to Signe's surprise Axel's father said he would consider it, and call her back in a couple of days.

Signe then went back to thinking about the 'accident'. Someone had heard about what she had learned. It was Tommy Rice, Johnny Armijo or Detective Gerald Hartford. Tommy was in jail; Johnny seemed too addled by the brunette, and Chief Detective Hartford had always seemed to be on her side. Something was missing. She couldn't easily query Tommy or Johnny again so she called Detective Hartford and set up a meeting for Wednesday morning. Despite some pain medicine everything on her hurt, mostly her ego though, and she spent a quiet evening at home with Axel.

Early the next morning a uniformed officer picked Signe up at 7:30 a.m. Every muscle ached when she was moving but her left elbow hurt the most even in the sling. The doctor thought she caught it on the steering wheel, before the airbag deployed, and it had severely sprained her elbow.

Detective Hartford was in his office with his usual two large coffees. She sat down gingerly, and reviewed what she had learned in Albuquerque before the accident from Tommy and Johnny. She was now suspicious of everyone and she watched his face for some sign of insincerity. Finding none she quizzed him about his ideas on the murder and the accident.

"I think that the ridiculously expensive horse was the motive." Chief Hartford began. "That animal was at the fair for five days before it disappeared. Neither that large well founded horse nor that flashy rich woman kept a low profile. They were all over the fair, and they were both very ostentatious. I heard that in addition to being good looking and have a great figure that Chloe was very flirtatious. You and I both know how many 'neer do wells' and hangers on the fair attracts. There are no vagrants or bums on the streets of Santa Fe during the Fair. Someone just couldn't resist that 1400 pounds of horse flesh worth about three hundred dollars a pound. Hell, I hear he was a young stallion. If they can keep him hidden for a couple of months, they could collect and freeze enough semen to generate $3 or $4 million dollars in stud fees. Then the bastards could turn the horse into dog food and no one would ever be the wiser. That arrogant lawyer is too much of a 'city boy' to even think of that."

"I think the murder was an unfortunate and unintended side effect of the theft." Detective Gerald Hartford concluded.

"I think you may be right and I'm going to redouble my efforts to find that horse." Signe started. "You're right about the size of that beast. How could anything that large just vanish from as busy a place as the State Fair? There are people around those animals twenty-four hours a day. Someone saw something and I will find them." Signe said forcefully even though everything was starting to hurt again.

"What are your thought about my accident?" she continued.

"You know, I suspect it was just a random act of aggression. Some young cowboy had been drinking and drugging all night, and was tired of his shitty dead-end job, his bitchy girlfriend, and his loser life style. I think you just got in his way at the wrong time. He could take his rage out on you with little consequence because of that ridiculous jacked up truck and the steel pipe he probably welded to the front end himself. I doubt he even dented his rig. We are seeing more random violence-hit and runs, drive by shootings, and assaults on strangers over the past five years. It's just part of the unraveling of our society made worse by drugs and alcohol. I know you think this was related to the murder and that someone feels you are getting too close. Honestly, Signe, I don't think you are that close. We still lack the big three-motive, method and perpetrator."

Signe walked out of the chief's office with more unanswered questions than ever. However, she was pretty certain that he wasn't complicit, and maybe he was right about the accident.

CHAPTER 15

She left the station after checking her tragically disorganized desk and finding nothing of importance. The department gave her a 1997 black and white Ford Crown Victoria squad car to drive until she could get the Jetta fixed or replaced. She hated the Crown Vic from the moment she saw it. Despite her long frame and legs it was too big inside. She couldn't reach across the front seat to grab something while driving. It didn't fit in any parking spaces. She didn't think it even fit on the streets of Santa Fe. She also had a European's prejudice about the poor quality of American cars. As she headed across town she got a call that a large white horse was running loose at the Santa Fe Opera. She pointed the long hood of her vehicle, which resembled the flight deck of an aircraft carrier to her, toward the Opera.

As she pulled into the parking lot she was met by security. The brown adobe mass and soaring timbers of the Opera's performance hall rose in the background with the Jemez Mountains behind it. The setting had gotten dusty and forlorn since the last opera of the summer season was performed in August six weeks ago. Then crowds of elegant easterners and Texans would gather in the parking lot for a cold supper of lobster and chardonnay before the performances began at nine p.m. They would mingle beside beds of pure white petunias and amongst ushers in colorful serapes. Now the venue was deserted. The guards drove her to the area behind the stage house where all the sets were stored. There, tied to a piñon tree, was indeed a large white horse. However, Signe's hopes fell. She knew little about horses but this spavined creature with rheumy eyes and a swayed back was no $400,000 beast even if Chloe's horse had been cruelly abused for the last eleven days. She waited a bit until animal control arrived and then pointed her capacious car back toward the city.

When she started down the long hill to the city she got a call from Mr. Manuel Perez, Irma's Dad. They had decided against the abortion and he wanted to know if Axel would marry the young mother in the sanctuary of St. Genevieve's Church. Signe was caught off guard, once again by Mr. Perez.

However, she recovered quickly and replied, "I appreciate your keeping me informed, Sir, about your daughter but Axel will not be marrying her. I think you are making a mistake for Irma's young life. Please don't call us again." She said with finality as she hung up.

She raced home and placed a call to Odense, Denmark. Detective Rasmussen answered on the second ring. She explained the latest call from Mr. Perez and again asked if Axel could come and live with him. Her fallback plan was to beg her parents to take her son when she got the expected 'no' from Axel's father. However, after some preamble Axel Rasmussen senior gave a resounding 'ya'. The only precondition was that she pay his airfare to Denmark, and get him started on his journey. She was on the phone immediately, and got a reasonable fare on Scandinavian Airways System. The summer rush was over and the 'shoulder' between the high travel season and winter resulted in a large savings. Signe was strapped for money right now because of her low salary and expenses that she was expecting from the little car accident, but she could spare $950 dollars to save her son. Suddenly the aches went away and she felt better than she had since the accident.

When Axel got home she explained the plan to him. It was okay with him. He would miss his mother; of course, they had been together since the moment of his birth. However, New Mexico still seemed a foreign and barren place to him and he would not languish without it. He would truly pine for Irma (or at least her shapely sinuous body and hot little mouth), but the thought of getting married, dropping out of school and getting a low paying job at Circle K wasn't very appealing. He didn't relish the thought of years of changing diapers and warming bottles of formula. Both Signe and Axel realized that he wasn't progressing in the American educational system. A change of direction at this time might be beneficial. Axel headed to his room to pack. Later Signe and Axel went to The Pink Adobe for a quiet dinner. She had Chicken Marengo the dish that Napoleon's chef whipped up after the great French victory in 1800. The rich combination of chicken, tomato, mushroom and wine gently simmered together filled her stomach and warmed her soul. The only sour note that evening was the PI Tony Squitero sitting in the corner of the restaurant with a very pretty young brunette. He had nodded pleasantly when they entered. Axel and his mother spent the rest of the evening reminiscing and planning for the future.

The next morning Signe was back to normal except for a sling on her left arm. She would work on how that magnificent horse was spirited out of the fairground, and who could have possibly seen it. First she called Mr. Stephen Samuels, the English pleasure class judge, from the State Fair. Signe knew he was around near the time of the disappearance of the horse. In real life he was a CPA in town. She set up an appointment in an hour. She also wanted to talk to Toney Anaya, the grounds man, and the difficult State Police Officer-Raymond Gallegos.

Stephen Samuels had an office in a thirty year old building south of the plaza. Signe took a seat in his waiting room and was offered some lukewarm coffee by his secretary. Mr. Samuels was in his fifties and portly. Like most accountants his office contained three faded and uninteresting prints that had been unchanged in the last fifteen years. The magazines *Modern Accountant* and *Accounting Today* were even more tragic. She was ushered in to sit in a very uncomfortable chair across from Mr. Samuels.

"I want to go back to the afternoon of the murder at the fairgrounds, Mr. Samuels." Signe began. "Someone took that valuable horse out of the stall either before or after the murder. You were in the vicinity. You must have noticed something, Sir. What did you see or hear?"

"I'm afraid I don't have much information detective," Mr. Samuels began tentatively. "I was in the horse barns around that time. I'm afraid I didn't see anything. However, just after I arrived I heard a truck leave the area. It was behind the last row of stalls. It accelerated slowly, like it had a load, but it was clearly a diesel pickup truck. You know the sound that diesels make? It's very distinctive. It has a low clicking sound, as it accelerates, that isn't anything like a gasoline truck. Is it the tappets? I wouldn't confuse it with anything else. It sounded to me like a Dodge Ram but I can't tell you why." he continued.

"You didn't see anything?" Signe asked.

"No. I was completely blocked by the last row of stalls." Mr. Samuels concluded.

"Thanks for your time, sir. If you think of anything please call." Signe said as she scribbled in her notebook in Danish and left.

Next she met with Sergeant Raymond Gallegos of the New Mexico State Police. She purposely set the meeting at the State Police post. She already knew that he was a liar, and could be at least verbally abusive. She had witnessed those things the day of the murder at the State Fair when he moved the body. She didn't want to take any chances with him. He ushered her into a small conference room and offered her coffee. The coffee was terrible with the bitter taste the beverage gets if it has been on the heat for four or five hours. She told him very little about the progress of the case but some things just to elicit his cooperation.

"Do you have any ideas how that horse was removed from the fairgrounds?" she asked.

"I thought you would have this case solved by now Detective Sorensen with your amazing powers." Sergeant Gallegos began sarcastically. "You must be pretty desperate if you want my help. Officer Jaramillo called me and my partner for backup you'll recall. When we arrived, a dirty, white, rusty old horse trailer was being pulled out from behind the horse barns. I didn't see the vehicle that was pulling it, the barns blocked my view. I didn't think much of it at the time. I think I wrote down at least a partial license plate number on a scrap of paper out of habit. But the scrap hasn't turned up again. Other than that I don't recall any other activity, Detective."

"Thank you, that's helpful, Sergeant. If you do find that partial tag number, please call me," Signe said pouring the wretched coffee down the sink and walking out.

Next Detective Sorensen drove south of town to the New Mexico State Penitentiary. She had arranged a visit with Toney Anaya, the grounds man that had stolen Chloe's diamond bracelet after the murder. After signing in and checking her weapon she was brought to a small interrogation cell where Toney was waiting. No shackles were apparent under his orange uniform. He obviously wasn't regarded as dangerous by the guards.

"I need to ask you some questions Toney." Signe began in the stern voice that seemed to work best with him. "Did you see any unusual activity around the horse barns on the day of the murder? Were there any horse trailers coming or going on that day? Did you see any suspicious looking men?"

"I deed see a beeg peekup that afternoon it was *marron* colored." Toney began. "I deed see tree men earlier around stall number 17. That's all I remember." Signe asked several more questions but got mumbled answers and no additional information from the thief. Overall, the three interviews had been very productive. Each man, in his own way, had provided a useful and different glimpse of the crime scene on that October afternoon when the murder occurred and the horse disappeared. She knew of several state data bases that could help her refine and narrow her search. After she left the 'pen' she pointed the Crown Vic back toward the station. Once inside she noticed that her disordered desk was again growing precariously tall stacks of paper. Once Axel left she would have more time and she made a solemn resolution to fix this problem then. She worked for some hours on the old computer. She wasn't surprised to learn that there were over 11,000 maroon pickup trucks in the state. She saw pickups everywhere. In the west even petite, stylish young women seemed to prefer a large truck to ride around in. She was surprised that there were 34,000 horse trailers registered in the state. Also numerous other horse trailers were nearby in the neighboring states of Arizona, Utah, Colorado, Oklahoma and Texas. The thieves could easily have come from out of state and gone back to another state with the horse. The two lane highways in northern New Mexico were sparsely populated and seldom traveled. Rural Colorado was particularly close to Santa Fe. She couldn't think of a way to use the data base to match owners of maroon diesel pickups with owners of white horse trailers. She needed the license tag numbers that Sergeant Gallegos had recorded. However, she didn't think she was going to get any real help from the likes of him. She had run into another dead-end. Rather than get depressed she decided on a quick lunch with Vincent. It felt good to eat some really hot green chile at The Shed and hold hands under the table. Vincent offered to accompany her to Albuquerque the next day to see Axel off. Signe readily agreed. She was already dreading her son's departure. Signe and Axel had been with each other from the evening he drew his first breathe. She loved him fiercely even if her Scandinavian reserve kept her from expressing it often in word or touch. Vincent was becoming more of a force in her life with each passing day. Perhaps Vincent would fill some of the void when Axel departed.

CHAPTER 16

The ride to Albuquerque in the Crown Vic on Friday morning was uneventful. For once its capacious size paid off. It accommodated three large people and all of Axel's belongings easily. The trunk looked bigger to Signe than her first apartment in Copenhagen. Signe wondered out loud how this motoring behemoth would have done on the dirt road to Chaco Canyon. Both of the males thought the car would do well on that, rutted, washed out, dirt track because of its weight. Axel seemed jaunty and excited. Only Signe was pensive on the ride down to the Albuquerque Sunport. Axel's plane was on time so they took him to security where after many hugs and kisses Signe said a tearful goodbye. It was only thirteen months since the 9/11 tragedy and security was tight. Everyone in the airport seemed edgy. Airline personnel, security people, and especially other passengers seemed overwrought and anxious.

Signe and Vincent strolled out of the Sunport hand in hand stopping every thirty or forty feet for a warm wet kiss. Vincent drove them to Signe's favorite restaurant, Scalo's for some northern Italian cuisine. It was barely evening and the restaurant was deserted. They settled into a banquette in the back corner. She ordered her favorite salad, *Panzanella al Pane di Segale e Balsamico*. She loved the combination of ripe tomato, yellow onion and small cubes of rye bread with balsamic vinegar dressing. Vincent was picking a bottle of Tuscan red but one hand was exploring Signe's thighs and lower back. Abruptly, she was more horny than hungry, and she was quite hungry. She leaned over and kissed Vincent fervently with an open mouth. Slowly she explored his lips, tongue and palate with her languorously probing tongue while softly touching the inside of his right forearm with the soft finger tips of her right hand. She wanted him. She thought their night together would slake her desire after six months of abstinence but if anything she was more desirous now. She slid toward the edge of the banquette. As she moved she turned her eyes toward Vincent and said in a husky voice, "Meet me in the ladies' lounge in 30 seconds." She thought about proposing a longer time interval so she could primp but knew that if she did she would lose her nerve. She loved the look of utter surprise on Vincent's face.

She walked slowly across the back of the dark, deserted restaurant to the lounge on her high heels. As she pushed open the heavy wooden door to the ladies' lounge she ran her right hand up under her skirt, hooked her thumb around her panties and pulled them down with a quick motion. She hopped up on the black granite vanity, in front of the large makeup mirror and started to work her panties over her high heeled shoes and then decided to just kick the elegant black leather heels off. She stuffed her panties into her small purse just as Vincent entered. He looked sheepish, but one glance at Signe perched on the vanity with her bare thighs exposed changed the look in his brown eyes from astonishment to longing.

In one motion Signe pulled him toward her, kissed him and unzipped his pants. She reached in very gently and freed his erection. She lifted her body slightly so Vincent could push her skirt up to her waist. She felt the cold of the granite on her ass and thighs as he pushed into her. He moved quickly with shallow strokes and she knew she would be lucky to come before he did even though the real chance of getting caught in the act increased her ardor. She was close, but he started to come, and at that very moment her cell phone rang in the small black purse beside her. Her desire evaporated as she realized how vulnerable and exposed they both were. She pushed him backward and reached for her purse. Years of being a detective gave a mental quickness that allowed her to answer the phone on the third ring. "Hello?" she said in a husky, wavering voice.

"Detective, this is Johnny Armijo. I know who killed Chloe and why they did it. I need to meet you right away." He said in a nervous voice.

"Just tell me on the phone, Johnny, please." she begged.

"It's too dangerous. I have to tell you in person. Can you be here in an hour? I'm at The Wild Pony and I'll wait." he said nervously.

"I'm just down the street, Johnny. I'll be there in ten minutes. Don't leave." she said in a loud voice as she started for the door. Signe grabbed her shoes in one hand and took Vincent's hand in the other. As she pulled him toward the door, walking quickly on bare feet, she told Vincent what Johnny had said. Vincent threw some money on the table as they exited. The Crown Vic was parked in front pointing the right way on Central Avenue. The old cruiser had real flashing red and blue lights and a siren. Vincent switched both on as he squealed away from the curb. They were at the club in five minute after running five red lights. An old lady nearly 'T boned' them at the Louisiana Avenue crossing. The startled woman braked and swerved to a halt at the last second.

Vincent stopped the cruiser across the front door of the club and both ran inside. Signe led the way to the VIP room, but as they approached they heard three shots. One shot was followed by a pause and then two more in rapid succession. Vincent and Signe hunkered down and unholstered their weapons. Vincent called 911 on his phone. Signe cracked the door open from a crouch and was greeted by a bullet splintering the door just above her head. Small pieces of dark wood landed on her head and shoulders. Vincent moved up behind her.

"We need back up," he said. "Do you have vests in the car?" he said hurriedly.

"Yes, in the trunk," she whispered back.

"Here are the keys. Go get them. I'll cover the door. Keep down," he said in rapid staccato fashion.

As she came back into the club with the vests three Albuquerque blue and white patrol cars pulled up with lights flashing and sirens on. Four officers spilled out the doors of the cruisers with guns drawn. Signe flashed them her ID, told them about the shots and sent one officer around to the back of the club. After slipping on her vest Signe led the three patrolmen across the club. She had one patrolman herd the patrons, strippers and bartenders from the large main part of the club out the front door. The girls complained loudly about being led out into the cool fall air with next to nothing on. The patrons seemed embarrassed to be discovered there and were very cooperative. Vincent was still at the door of the VIP room and had heard nothing since Signe left. Cautiously, he cracked the door and stuck his weapon into the room first. He could hear some soft sobbing off to the right side. He opened the door and moved into the room in a crouch with Signe right behind him. Two Albuquerque policemen followed with weapons drawn.

The large body of a young male lay in the center of the floor. He wasn't moving. Signe felt for a carotid pulse; there wasn't one. It was Johnny Armijo, dead. Vincent checked the rest of the room. A scantily clad brunette stripper was hiding behind a chair and crying loudly. A red head dressed the same way came timidly out of another corner. The bouncer got up off the floor sheepishly. Near him, hiding behind a chair, was a portly grey haired man in a suit not as well tailored as Johnny's suit. He was wearing a wedding ring and seemed unable to speak. APD took him into the other room to get his ID and question him. Signe examined Johnny Armijo. He had been shot once in the left thigh and then twice in the center of the chest.

All four witnesses told the same story. Two heavy set nondescript men came into the VIP lounge. There faces were obscured by the very dim lights. They ordered drinks and then started arguing with Johnny. As the disagreement got more heated, the two masked men waved the three bystanders and the bouncer away with the barrels of their drawn pistols. None of the four survivors heard what the men were arguing about. Then the taller masked man shot Johnny in the left leg and before Johnny could even turn to run; the other man shot Johnny twice in the chest. When the door to the room creaked open a few seconds later the taller man spun and fired his pistol at the door. That was the shot that just missed Detective Sorensen's head. Then both men ran out the back door. One of the girls caught a glimpse of a dark sedan lit by a streetlight through the open door. She knew little about automobiles. She was still very frightened and couldn't provide a further description. No one knew if there was a driver waiting in the vehicle. However, there almost certainly was as the car squealed away very quickly.

Signe went over to exam Johnny. She had liked him and he was the only person she had found so far that really cared for and maybe even loved Chloe. His eyes were open and no one else was in the dim room so she closed them. His wallet contained the usual ID with a few hundred dollars in cash and horse racing tickets in it. She did find a scrap of yellow paper in his trouser pocket that had numbers written on it—8142501-153336. Too long for a phone number or license plate, perhaps it was a bank account or safety deposit box number. She folded the paper and put it in her pocket. She worked quickly because she didn't want to get caught disturbing the crime scene. What she was doing wasn't that different from what the state police had done to her crime scene. But, damn it, she thought Johnny had called me and said he had information for me. The number is mine, she decided. As the minutes passed, her heart had stopped racing and the adrenalin jangle was wearing off. She realized she was working the crime scene in a very short, tight skirt and that she was wearing no panties. As she stood up, a small rivulet of warm liquid inched slowly down the inside of her left thigh. She reflected on how peculiar and dangerous her life had become.

CHAPTER 17

On the ride back to Santa Fe, Signe and Vincent were both lost in thought about their close call and spoke little. She dropped him off at his apartment and after a brief kiss, pointed the Crown Vic toward the Coyote Café. She knew she wouldn't sleep for hours. The evening had been too startling and she was really missing Axel. The bar was deserted. She sat at a table by the fireplace and sipped some Kahlua and cream. She opened her purse, pushed her panties aside and pulled out a yellow scrap of paper. On the paper was a string of thirteen numbers written in pencil. She had found this paper in the pocket of Johnny Armijo, the man who said he knew who had killed Chloe Patterson, just before he had himself been killed. Signe puzzled over the numbers, cataloguing them, tabulating then and re-arranging them. Nothing meaningful came to mind.

She had always been a 'counter'. In school she would count the tiles in the classroom endlessly. When driving with her dad she counted the white center stripes on the highways in Odense. She sorted all of her clothes by color both in the drawers and on the hangers. Even when very tired if a blue blouse had gotten mixed in with the white ones she was compelled to move it before she left the room. At one point she was evaluated by the counselor in her grade school because her parents were concerned. First the counselor thought she might be a polymath, accomplished in math, history, and music. However, her IQ test wasn't quite high enough for that. Next he considered obsessive compulsive disorder. She had concerns about symmetry and order but lacked a fear of germs, dirt, fires and disasters. She had some daily rituals like making her bed in a certain way but they never became endlessly repetitive or more complex. He finally diagnosed her as having mild OCD largely manifest as 'counting'.

In Denmark her most famous case was the case of the disappearing German Banker. It made her reputation in the department and new detectives were told about it in hushed voices. The case involved Otto Müller who was a Vice President of Deutsche Bank in Bonn. In 1997 he came to Copenhagen with 4,000,000 Krøner in bearer bonds in an old leather suitcase. After two days at the Tivoli Hotel he vanished with the bonds. He was a solid family man with a wife and three daughters in Bonn. He had no vices. He didn't drink, gamble or chase women (or men). He was a stolidly placid, overweight financier who listened to Schubert lieder in his spare time if he needed excitement. The local police spent months searching for him. With only 6,000,000 inhabitants and little migration in or out the police can canvas Denmark very thoroughly. Forensics swept his room three times for clues. When the chief of detectives sent them back the third time, to the same hotel room, there was a lot of grumbling amongst the technical staff. The third time they found a seven digit number written in the dust behind the radiator cover as the light was fading, and wrote it down for Detective Sorensen. It was too short for a Danish phone number. She checked over forty banks in the city for such an account number or safe deposit box number. She checked license numbers for cars in all of Denmark and in northern Germany. She showed the number to other detectives, bankers, financial advisors and snitches. No luck. After months of research and leg work she had drawn a blank. The case was put aside; however, Signe kept the number on her bathroom mirror.

Every morning when she was putting on her make up she played with the number-6612574. One spring morning she thought Otto has three daughters and he is a banker, a numbers man; I'll just add three to each number giving me-9945807. She worked with that for a while with no success. However, she realized that she hadn't applied the rule exactly. Seven plus three was actually 10 not zero. That made the number-99\458107 and that looked like a phone number. She called and pretended to be from the Copenhagen gas company. The address was in a north suburb of Copenhagen. The owner of this large suburban house, in the department's reverse telephone book, was Inge Johannsen, a well known soprano with the Danish State Opera. Signe staked out the house. She felt as if she were on her one hundredth wild goose chase. She parked in plain sight across the street. Low and behold on the second morning, just as Signe was getting sleepy despite a large cup of strong Danish coffee, Otto Müller walked out of the front door! What a high! After fourteen months of work and hundreds of dead ends, there he was looking even more portly in a banker's suit. She suspected Inge stripped, and sang him Schubert naked before bed each night. She followed him and arrested him at a Danish Bakery. The story made the front page of the Copenhagen newspaper, *Ballerup Bladet,* with Otto's picture and also a picture of Signe and Inge. Nearly all of the 4,000,000 Krøner were recovered. Her reputation at central headquarters improved temporarily but immensely. Now she had a new number to work with, from Johnny Armijo's pocket, even if she wasn't a polymath.

She got a call from Dr. Bernadette Gilchrist early Saturday afternoon about the autopsy on Johnny Armijo. The cause of death was two 9mm gunshot wounds to the chest. He had cocaine, marijuana and benzodiazepines on board but not in large quantities. The microscopic studies weren't back yet, but she didn't expect any surprises. Dr. Gilchrist was coming up to Santa Fe the next night for the Santa Fe Chamber Music concert. She had an extra ticket and wanted to know if Signe could go. Signe missed the abundant cultural events in Copenhagen, and readily said yes. Signe spent the rest of the afternoon in a futile attempt to clear her desk and to bring chief Hartford up to speed on the latest developments. The murder seemed to be getting more Byzantine and complex as the days went by.

She spent the next day drawing a time line for the case and placing all of the few known facts on it. She also started working with her thirteen digit number trying to see the pattern. Just before she left work in the afternoon she got a surprise call from Sergeant Gallegos of the New Mexico State Police. He was shockingly cordial and chatty on the phone. He had found the piece of paper in the pocket of a dirty uniform. The horse trailer license plate had a bright yellow background with red numbers; so it was a New Mexico plate and not a neighboring state. He had written down F 53or8 but probably a 3. Trailer licenses in the state usually consisted of a letter followed by four numbers so if it was F 53_ _ then her search was narrowed down to one hundred trailers. Signe thanked him with real sincerity in her voice. She had some time before her dinner date, and immediately got on the Department of Motor Vehicles data base. There was only one white horse trailer with those letters and numbers. It was F 5356 and it was licensed to a Richard Lederback in Wagon Mound, New Mexico. Signe wrote the information down and raced home.

She dressed quickly for the concert and sped along narrow Canyon Road to Geronimo's. The valet made a face when the Crown Vic pulled up which changed to a smile as she slid her long bare shapely legs out of the driver's door topped by a tight dark blue knit dress. The very act of turning from the driver's seat and placing her high heels on the ground caused her skirt to rise even higher. Dr. Bernadette Gilchrist was sipping a martini in the bar. Signe had a cosmopolitan. Then the hostess showed them to a table in an elegant white high-ceilinged room with an adobe fireplace in the corner. Bernadette Gilchrist looked enticingly different than when she was working at the OMI. Signe noticed her hair was softly curled and much blonder than she remembered. She was wearing makeup which set off her blue eyes. She wore an attractive, low cut black dress. They talked over a beef tartare appetizer and pumpkin soup. They shared a large salad of farm greens. Both had the Chilean sea bass entrée. Signe noticed that Bernadette often touched the back of her hand softly for emphasis when she talked. It felt pleasant. They roared off to the concert in Dr. Gilchrist's white BMW 530i. Signe loved being wrapped in European leather again as she slid into her seat.

The concert began with a Brahms's clarinet trio that Signe had always enjoyed. It was followed by a Mozart quintet. After the break, they played a dense Beethoven string quartet #59, the "Razumovsky". Growing up in Europe Signe had several years of exposure to classical music, and there were concerts all the time even in a small town like Odense. When the family went to Tivoli they heard bands playing Strauss and Neilsen, not the fare you would here at an American amusement park. After the concert Signe and Bernadette headed to the Coyote Café for some coffee. Bernadette slid over next to Signe and held her hand tenderly. They talked like long lost sisters. After the bar was empty they strolled out to Bernadette's BMW and drove back to Geronimo's where Signe's car was parked. It was cold at first in the BMW but it warmed up quickly inside. When they got to the Crown Vic before Signe could open the door of the BMW Bernadette leaned over and kissed Signe on the mouth. Her lips were small but very soft. It was a gentle, tender kiss and Signe was caught utterly by surprise. Compared to Vincent's kisses it was more expressive and also much warmer and softer. Signe had never had a thought about being attracted to a woman sexually. When she was thirteen, she had had her friends over for slumber parties. Sometimes they explored each others developing bodies with hands and rarely lips, but she remembered it didn't even feel erotic. She was confused as their lips remained on each other. Signe decided she needed to know more about this, so she kissed Bernadette back. Bernadette took the signal and pulled Signe close with both of her arms. Their bodies fit together nicely. Signe tried to relax and focus on the feelings. They were warm, tender and comfortable but without that tingling sensation that spread down into her loins as she kissed Vincent. They had managed to fog up the windows of the 530i. After a few minutes there was a loud tap on the driver's window.

Both women were startled and pulled away from each other in astonishment. Both had lipstick and makeup smeared over most of their faces. Bernadette put the power window down to be greeted by a patrolman shining a bright flashlight into the car.

"Are you all right ladies?" Officer Art Johnson said. "You need to move it along."

"Everything is okay, Art," Signe said.

"Oh is that you, Detective Sorensen? Sorry. Good night."

Great, Signe thought, now everyone in the department will think I am gay and it probably isn't even true. How do I combat that rumor?

Signe turned to Bernadette. "I had a wonderful time. Let's do it again soon." Signe said as she opened the door, and slid off the aromatic warm leather seat of the BMW.

The Ford had cold seats, a cold steering wheel and the power steering groaned when she made a sharp turn. When she got home she flopped into bed, and pushed her knit dress off over her head rolling it into a ball, and throwing it onto the floor, before falling into a deep dreamless sleep.

CHAPTER 18

Signe got up early on Monday and ate her Danish breakfast of pumpernickel, cheese and coffee. She missed Axel all of the time but even more acutely in the morning when they always had time to talk. She threw on a blue work suit, and headed out to the Crown Vic. Today she was going to find out about the horse trailer that had been seen at the State Fair on the afternoon of Chloe's death. She headed out Old Pecos Trail and got on I-25 going toward Las Vegas. When she first got to Santa Fe, with her poor grasp of US geography, she was startled to learn that Las Vegas was only fifty-seven miles from the state capitol. She imagined being amongst all those bright lights and shows and gambling within an hour. She wasn't really into big city glitz but the idea of it being in the neighborhood was appealing. Of course, this was Las Vegas, New Mexico not the infamous Las Vegas, Nevada. Another thirty-nine miles beyond Las Vegas is the tiny village of Wagon Mound, New Mexico. With a population of 359, it was home to Richard Lederback.

The two hour drive to this village, through low mountains covered with piñon and ponderosa pine was pleasant. It gave her a chance to think about all the confusing and troubling events of the past two days. She didn't come to any solid conclusions, however. If it weren't for the big green sign on the highway, she was so lost in thought, that she would have missed Wagon Mound. It had seen better days. It was named for a nearby butte that looked like a covered wagon, to some. It was on the old Santa Fe Trail that went from Missouri to New Mexico in the 1900s. She headed east out of town into the morning sun. There was rolling grass in every direction which had already turned a golden brown and no trees in sight, even on the far away horizon. The road quickly turned to gravel and Signe flew along, except for cattle guards, to the Lederback spread 19 miles east of town. The house was small, squat, square and once white but it needed paint. A small barn and a large corral stood out back. Four horses were loose in the corral, none were white.

Signe rapped on the screen door. A worn woman in her fifties came to the door, wiping flour from her hands onto an apron. She invited Signe in and the detective showed Mrs. Lederback her ID. Signe explained that she was investigating the 'disappearance' of some horse trailers and wondered if they had any. "Why, yes," Mrs. Lederback said. "They are out back."

"Mind if I take a look?" Signe asked.

"Not at all, but come back in for a piece of apple pie when you are done." Mrs. Lederback sang back. Signe headed out behind the house and gave the light blue horse trailer with flat tires a cursory look. Then she focused her attention on a white trailer with a current registration and tag number F5356. She collected some samples from the treads of the tires. There was some green gray paint in a scrap on the curved front of the horse trailer. Inside on the wooden floor she found some manure but also small clumps of horse hair that she placed in plastic bags. She went back in the house and was enjoying the warm apple pie, unlike anything that they make in Denmark, when a truck screeched to a halt outside.

A man, presumably Mr. Lederback, burst through the screen door and in a loud voice demanded an explanation for Detective Sorensen's visit. He was powerfully built, well over six feet tall with tattered overalls, and large arms and chest. Mrs. Lederback tried to explain, but Mr. Lederback broke in.

"Get the hell off my property, now!" He yelled, moving menacingly toward her. Without a word Signe got up, and while mustering as much courage as she could, walked out of the house slowly.

As she went to her car she noticed that Richard Leterback's maroon pick up truck was jacked up two feet and he had black steel bars welded across the radiator. Was this the testosterone powered truck that had forced her off the road that dark night? She brushed her sleeve against the pipes as she went by hoping she would pick up a paint sample. She tried not to be too obvious. Then she swung into her patrol car and drove off particularly slowly. As soon as she was off the property she slowed by the side of the road. She removed her jacket carefully and placed it left sleeve up on the seat beside her. Now she had some hair samples to compare to the ones she had found at the horse stall where Chloe had been murdered. In fact, she had a variety of samples from the Lederback ranch for the lab to analyze as soon as she got back to Santa Fe. On the drive back a light dusting of snow began to fall. The white flakes reminded her of happy days when she got to stay home from school in Denmark.

She pulled into the station house early on Tuesday. Were people staring at her now that they knew she was a lesbian, or was it just her imagination? She took her suit jacket that she had carefully bagged to the lab first. She wanted to know if there were paint flecks on the steel bumper of Richard Lederback's truck that matched the paint on her wrecked Jetta. Unfortunately, both the bumper and her car were black so she had been unable to tell by simply looking if this was the truck that caused her accident. However, she was also in quandary. If she submitted the sample as evidence and listed when and where she got it she might have a problem. If there was a match, she wasn't sure she could use the evidence in court as it was obtained without a search warrant. She didn't have probable cause. If the judge threw out the evidence the case would go out the window also. She hated the America legal system where the cops always had to play fair, and give every defendant every possible opportunity to avoid conviction. In Europe, she thought, if you found evidence of a murder you didn't know about, while investigating a robbery, you simply escalated the charge and sent the miscreant to prison. In America that person would go free.

She decided to submit the sample without a name and date and ask the tech to do a comparison as a favor to her and to report the results verbally. She had wondered before if this tech, Valerie, was gay. Was Valerie making more eye contact with her now because of what she thought she knew? Had Officer Art Johnson told everyone in the station house about Signe necking with the blond lady? Signe was tempted to spend a night with the most indiscrete male detective in the department to crush this lesbian subplot. At least then it would move her over the 'switch hitting' bisexual category rather than the gay label.

When she got back to her desk from the lab she had a phone message from a Sven Torvaldson of the American National Assurance Company requesting an urgent meeting. When Signe reached him he said that his company had insured Chloe Patterson's life for $2,000,000. However, if her death was accidental then the pay out was $4,000,000. Mr. Torvaldson had heard that the unfortunate young woman had a hoof print in the middle of her chest when she was found. He had been receiving daily phone calls and e-mail from Mr. Patterson about payment. Recently the barrister had threatened to sue the insurance company for breach of contract if he didn't receive his money in a week. Signe had wondered why she had heard so little from Mr. Patterson recently and why Mr. Anthony Squitero had faded into the background. Perhaps the lawyer, while making a big show of wanting the murder solved at the beginning, really just wanted the insurance money. Signe set up a meeting with the insurance man for that afternoon.

She went out alone for a quick lunch at The Shed. The blue corn enchiladas with red chile burned her mouth first and then seared the doubt from her mind. She was making progress on the case as more and more players became involved. She would turn them against each other and discover what had, in actual fact, happened. She missed Axel terribly. Despite the difficulties of his teen years they had been so very close. She had just received a short letter from him. It was upbeat. He had enrolled in a woodworking apprenticeship and looked forward to starting that soon. Maybe, he would follow in his grandfather's foot steps. Happily, here was no mention of a Danish girlfriend.

When she returned to the station house the insurance man was waiting. Sven Torvaldson was 6'4" tall with wavy blond hair and deep blue eyes. He looked to be about 3thirty-five. He had come to America from Sweden ten years ago and lived in Albuquerque. He still had a Swedish accent. At the bottom of the Kattegat, the countries of Denmark and Sweden are only separated by a scant two miles of the North Sea. Their languages however are quite different. A Dane can understand most of what a Swede says, but not speak their language and vice versa. Signe and Sven were sitting at her desk in the center of the large unpartitioned detective's bullpen. Lots of officers and clerks were working at their desks this early fall afternoon. Signe decided immediately to flirt with this man for her own selfish reasons. She moved from her chair to a perch on the edge of the desk so that her legs flowed languorously to the floor. She thought her long, shapely legs were her best feature. She stared into his eyes more than Valerie, the technician, had recently stared into hers. In the midst of all the flirting, she did accurately describe what was known about the case, up to this point. She also said it was her belief that this was a murder. Sven seemed puzzled, but not displeased by all the personal attention. He was elated that this was looking like a murder, and not an accidental death. He committed all the resources of his company to aid in solving this crime. His company had a cadre of investigators and computer experts in Chicago who investigated insurance fraud. American National Assurance Company would be willing to commit between 30 and 50,000 dollars to catch the murderer. He said even more money might be available if it looked like they were making some progress. Signe quickly realized that if Mr. Patterson was implicated in anyway in his daughter's death that Mr. Torvaldson's company would be in the clear.

Signe pulled out a yellow legal pad from the rubble of her desk and quickly made a list of what she wanted. It consisted of five items:

1. Investigate and follow Richard Lederback, 2. Get background on the three gauchos in Santa Rosa, Argentina, 3. Complete her initial investigation into Anthony Squitero, 4. Find the history and ownership of The Wild Pony where Johnny Armijo had been shot, and 5. Search the United States for any thefts of Lipizzaner horses, particularly stallions, in the past three years.

Sven took the list and said that he would start on all five of her enquires that day. He suggested that they meet for dinner in two days to discuss the progress he had made. She wasn't surprised at his offer, given the signals she had been sending him. She assented to a dinner meeting at 7 p.m. three nights hence at The Palace, one of the busiest and most public restaurants in Santa Fe.

Right now she was sick of her job, sick of the murder, and sick of all the games she had to play. So she did two things. She asked her boss for a new desk, after she told him about the insurance company's generous offer. He readily agreed and she left the teetering pile of paper on her old desk to gather dust in the center of the detective's bullpen. Her new desk was a smaller unused one in the corner of the large room with nothing on its barren top. She placed a few of the Patterson files on the desk just to claim ownership. Next she drove the Crown Vic to Santa Fe BMW on Camino Entrada to buy a new car. Her large Ford automobile resulted in some stares from the showroom. She picked out a female salesperson so she wouldn't have to deal with the hormone driven jousting and ogling from a male car salesman. She had been called by her insurance company that morning. The poor Jetta had been totaled and they were giving her $24,000 toward a new car! Signe thought that was quite generous. She would have liked a white 5 series BMW like Bernadette had with a leather interior. However, at $56,000 that was way out of her price range. As she went for a test ride with Sharon, the sales person, the BMW seemed small inside compared to the Crown Vic. She liked the smell of the partial leather interior. The handling was great. She loved the responsiveness of the rack and pinion steering. The 325 they were driving lacked quick acceleration so Signe and Sharon walked around to the back of the lot and found a dark blue sedan and picked the BMW 330i. The 325i was less money but only had 184 horsepower. The 330i had a 3.0 liter 224 horsepower engine with much better 'punch'. She had no ideas what all those "i's" were about, but she got the car for $34,000 plus title, tax and license. Being a European Signe didn't know she should have 'haggled' on the price as Sharon would have come down $3,000 and change to make the sale. Sharon was happy. Signe was happy. Signe drove out in her new dark blue BMW with tan leather seats. She felt like a snake that had just freed itself from its old skin and a shiny new exterior was now revealed for all to see. One of the patrolmen was kind enough to drive over and get the Crown Vic.

CHAPTER 19

Signe worked on paper work the next morning. Reports were due on all of her cases but especially the murder. She typed them dutifully on the broken down department computer, avoiding words with the letter 'c' in them whenever possible because of the broken key. She talked Vincent into playing hooky for the afternoon. She picked up picnic food at the Wild Oats Community Market, grabbed some wine and beer and headed for Vincent's apartment. Driving across town she mused on the fact that everything she did with Vincent was thought up and organized by her. They took Vincent's 1996 Ford F-150 as the road would be rough. Fall in the high desert of New Mexico is perfect. The sunny cloudless skies at 7,000 feet are a deep azure blue; there is no wind and temperatures are in the low eighties during the day cooling to fifty at night. They drove south from Santa Fe on I-25. After going down the 900 feet of La Bajada hill they turned to the west on state route 22 and drove through Cochiti Pueblo. The comfortable old adobe structures crowded the road. The chocolate brown finish coat on the buildings blended well with the brown red color of the earth. Nondescript spotted dogs lay next to the houses soaking up the warm sun. Long strings of dried red chiles, called ristras, hung from every doorway. Then the pair turned left on to the wash boarded forest service route 266. They bounced through low hills creating a huge plume of dust behind them. This road was the reason Signe didn't want to bring her new BMW. They pulled into the parking lot for *Kasha-Katuwe* a state park. The name means 'white cliffs' in the Keresan language of the pueblos of Northern New Mexico. However, Vincent knew that local Hispanics and Anglos called it 'Tent Rocks'.

Seven million years ago volcanic eruptions left a 1,000 foot thick layer of soft pumice, ash and tuff in the area. Later volcanic explosions spewed harder rock fragments often only two or three feet in diameter, called 'pyroclasts', randomly onto the thick layer of pumice. When the rain and wind came over eons of time, the small hard rock caps protected the soft ash just under them from disintegrating. All the rest of the soft tuff washed down the canyon. The result was dozens of tall uniformly shaped columns of rock, some up to 90 feet tall standing in groups or rows. The spaces between them on the canyon floor were sometimes so narrow, that a slender person like Signe had to turn sideways to pass through the opening.

They were alone at the park that day and after going up the canyon headed off the trail into the columns or 'hoodoos' in violation of all the posted regulations. They found a flat area in the dirt and spread out the foam pads that each carried in their back packs. They spread a blanket over the foam; kicked off their hiking boots and enjoyed their picnic of pasta salad, kiwi and raspberry mix, sandwiches, beer and wine. After eating they stretched out in the warm New Mexican sun. The sun at this altitude warmed them quickly and gradually they began to shed their clothing. Soon they were lying naked beside each other on their backs enjoying the heat. They touched hands, then kissed and started making love. Signe had learned to start by taking Vincent in her mouth so he came quickly. He was young enough that he recovered with alacrity. Then she could lie back and let him take her. She relaxed into the earth with her legs invitingly but still demurely apart, feeling the warm sun on her breast, her belly, her curly bush and her thighs before he covered her moving slowly and deliberately. Just before she came she opened her eyes and saw three 80 foot tall columnar rocks with rounded caps that looked exactly like giant phalli in a perfect row over Vincent's right shoulder. That sight triggered her orgasm. She enjoyed the waves of pleasure that began slowly and softly and built to a shuddering climax. When they were both finished she lay there laughing with contentment and satisfaction.

After a few minutes of holding each other tenderly, she got up abruptly and pulled her hiking boots on but nothing else. She walked proudly and otherwise completely naked behind a nearby rock to pee. When she returned looking satisfied and regal in her nakedness she said, "When are you going to learn some Da-anish?"

"As sooon as you learn some Spa-anish," he replied without a pause.

"I can already swear in Spanish," she said. Then she fell upon his naked body and tickled him and held him down as best she could with his arms over his head; as her firm taut breasts jiggled invitingly over him. He reached his mouth up to taste and caress her right nipple. However, they heard other people coming up the trail. They were well hidden and knew they would be overlooked by humans. However, these people had dogs (they could hear them barking and snuffling) and the dogs would seek them out and sniff their emissions and secretions from far away; so they quickly pulled on their jeans and tops with no underwear. Just then Jasmine and Jethro bounded up to them with noses on the ground and then quickly on Signe's and Vincent's crotches. Patrolman, Art Johnson had the German Shepherds out for a run. He was the young officer that had interrupted Signe and Bernadette in Geronimo's parking lot, the other night. Signe hoped he was thoroughly confused to now find her in a compromising situation with a red-blooded male. They gathered their things up quickly and headed for Vincent's truck. On the ride back Vincent wanted to talk about their future together. Signe had had a great afternoon and her pale Nordic skin burned from the sun, but she did not want to talk about the future. She deflected his questions as soon as he asked them.

Signe loved driving to work in her blue BMW. She arrived at work early on Thursday morning. First, she checked with Valerie in the lab. The horse hairs found in the white trailer at the Lederback's ranch matched the hairs found at the crime scene. Presumably both came from the big white Lipizzaner. More ominously, the paint flecks from Signe's jacket sleeve that she obtained from brushing against Richard Lederback's grill exactly matched samples from the smashed trunk of her Jetta. She was pleased to have this connection but she also knew that she had a problem. She went to Chief Hartford's office right way. After grabbing a cup of coffee she sat down in the chief's office. She explained to him the evidence she collected with Mrs. Lederback's permission from the white horse trailer and that the horsehairs matched those found at the crime scene. Then she went on to her 'accident'. She described how Mr. Lederback came home while she was in the house and ordered her off the property. She told the chief she thought she recognized Richard's truck as the one that forced her off I-25 and into the 'drink' even though the night of the accident had been very dark. She brushed her sleeve against the bumper on the way by and paint flecks matched the paint on her Jetta. She felt the evidence would be inadmissible in a trial and Chief Hartford agreed. He suggested they get a search warrant as quickly as possible and only mention the horse hair.

Signe filled out the paperwork and headed off to the courthouse. Half the police force was there waiting for various cases to be heard on a trailing docket. Signe chatted amicably with the other patrolmen and detectives. Citizens in the courthouse on other business would wonder, correctly, who was out on the street protecting them? The system was incredibly wasteful. Officers often spent a half a day in the courthouse waiting to give one minute of testimony on a traffic case. After waiting over an hour she caught Judge Terecita Armijo in her office. Judge Armijo had been helpful and sympathetic in the past. The judge motioned Signe into her office while she pulled her long black robe off, throwing it in on chair. After Signe explained her situation the Judge readily scrawled her name on the warrant. Signe collected three other officers and headed out to Wagon Mound in the department's crime scene investigation van. One the way there they all talked about their current cases, the Lobo football team and new restaurants in Santa Fe.

When they got to the ranch the jacked up truck was gone. Mrs. Lederback was cooking and savory smells came from the kitchen. Detective Sorensen showed Mrs. Lederback the search warrant and asked after her husband. Mrs. Lederback said that Richard left one hour after the detective's last visit towing the white horse trailer and that she hadn't heard from him for the past four days. The four officers searched the house. They found several firearms that they confiscated, an old IBM computer that they took and boxes of financial records. In a cursory look nothing seemed to link Mr. Lederback to the horse theft or the murder. They stopped at the Santa Clara Café in Wagon Mound for lunch. It's an authentic place with branding irons and deer heads on the wall. Each of the four officers had chicken fried steak, the house specialty for lunch. They picked among ten kinds of homemade pie for dessert.

CHAPTER 20

Heading back to Santa Fe all four officers were sleepy from such a big lunch. Signe was sitting in the right front seat of the big CSI suburban. As they started down the on ramp in Wagon Mound onto I-25 a high caliber bullet tore through the windshield three inches from Signe's head and struck patrolman Art Johnson exploding his cranium. The sound of the shot inside the vehicle was deafeningly loud. The driver turned around and saw his friend who had been sitting behind him with most of his head blown away. Pieces of brain and bone and blood were splattered all over the back of the vehicle. As the driver looked back he jerked the steering wheel to the right sending the suburban into the grassy ditch at thirty-five miles per hour. The heavy vehicle rolled over on its right side and skidded to a halt in the grassy ditch. The other three officers were banged up but each felt there might be more shots coming. They crawled out the driver's door one at a time, using the door for protection. Each of officers was carrying their service revolver and the truck was equipped with a sawed off shotgun. They had nothing to match a sharp shooter with a high powered rifle and scope, and each of them knew it individually without any need for discussion.

They radioed for help but the nearest police force was thirty-nine miles away to the south in Las Vegas, New Mexico. Raton was the nearest city to the north but it was smaller and almost seventy miles away. The three officers needed to survive for the better part an hour before help would come. They hunkered down along the underside of the vehicle which was toward the interstate since the shot appeared to have come from the right side of the road. As the first car slowed to offer assistance one patrolman crawled out to it, and explained the danger of the situation. The officer got in the car with the civilian and headed back to Wagon Mound where he used the vehicle to block traffic on the south bound interstate. He told the first two drivers that stopped about a possible sniper, and ask them to pass the word along to the cars that would soon be waiting behind them. The remaining patrolman kneeling in the grass with Signe snuck up to the front of the vehicle and peeked around. On reflection Signe was sure that the fatal round had been intended for her. The patrolman was peering around the front of the suburban trying to figure out where the sniper was hiding. Across a narrow pasture he saw a thin stand of Ponderosa pines and with bushes underneath them. The underbrush would provide excellent cover for a man with a high powered rifle. He searched the area with binoculars but saw no sign of movement or reflection. He slid back along the underside of the massive vehicle for protection and waited with Detective Sorensen.

Three squad cars from Las Vegas arrived at high speed forty minutes later with lights flashing and sirens blaring at the same time that the police helicopter from Albuquerque arrived. The helicopter landed on the freeway. A four man SWAT team deployed from the chopper with automatic weapons at the ready and rushed to the suburban. A medic wearing a bullet proof vest followed. Two SWAT team members set up at the front of vehicle, and two at the back with automatic weapons pointing across the pasture. Signe and the patrolman boosted the medic into the suburban, but there was nothing to do for patrolman Art Johnson who had died instantly from a massive head wound. The SWAT team members moved across the pasture with the Las Vegas policemen behind them. Once they reached the trees they all began searching for evidence. They gave the signal to allow traffic to flow on I-25. After an hour of searching one partial boot print and a .357 magnum rifle shell casing were found and bagged.

Art Johnson's body was sent to Albuquerque in the chopper. Detective Sorensen and the two remaining patrolmen were placed in a cruiser and driven by the Las Vegas policemen to police station in Santa Fe where Chief Detective Hartford personally debriefed each of them and set up psychiatric evaluations for the next day. Signe cancelled her dinner meeting with the insurance man. She went home and showered and changed. She called Axel in Denmark. It was midnight there and she woke him, but she needed to hear his voice. She didn't tell him the events of the day but ask about his apprenticeship and told him how very much she loved him. She called Vincent. He had heard the bad news but unfortunately was on duty that night. She spent the evening eating alone at the Coyote Café and drinking more than she should have. She knew sleep was unlikely so later she met Jefferson Barclay at a small jazz club north of the Plaza.

Worn out from tossing and turning all night she got to her psych eval the next morning ten minutes late. Dr. Vivian Goldiamond conducted Signe's evaluation. She was understanding about the detective's late arrival, given the events of the previous day and let her speak uninterrupted for thirty minutes. Signe told Dr. Goldiamond about her injury from the car accident caused by the jacked up pickup. Signe also affirmed that she felt the bullet that killed patrolman Johnson was meant for her. Often, she felt she was being followed when she drove around town. Someone had shot at her the night Johnny Armijo was killed. All of this mayhem had been directed at her since she took on the Chloe Patterson murder investigation. She wasn't even close to solving it, but someone seemed increasingly threatened and was lashing out at her with more and more lethal means. Signe said she was increasingly anxious and not sleeping well.

"Do you want to be taken off this case?" Dr. Goldiamond asked. "This case must have taken a toll on you psychologically."

After a minutes thought Signe said, "No. I can handle the anxiety and I wouldn't mind some sleeping pills. But I will reorder my life and get the protection and extra resources I need to get these criminals incarcerated. If they aren't caught I will never be safe, and I think I can catch them."

"I will clear you to go back to work," Dr. Goldiamond said sympathetically. "But I want to re-evaluate in one month. In the meantime here is my home phone number and my cell. Call anytime." She concluded.

Signe left the conference room and grabbed a whole pot of coffee, and two cups before striding into the chief's office and closing the door behind her. As soon as he was off the phone she reviewed the Patterson murder including the horrible shooting just yesterday. She forced him to admit that her 'accident' was an attempt on her life. Signe avowed her belief that she was the intended victim in Wagon Mound, and that Richard Lederback was the 'perp' for both attempts on her life.

That morning over breakfast she had drawn up a list things she wanted to continue working on this case and solve it. She would move to a gated apartment in a complex with a guard in the gate house at all times. The department would pay for it. She would go back to driving the Crown Vic with a patrolman escort at all times. She wanted two searchlights installed on the car. She also wanted two sawed off shotguns and a .223 sniper rifle with a scope in the car. She wanted one of the departments new high powered global positioning systems put in the car. She and the patrolman would wear Kevlar vests whenever they were working the case. In addition to her

Smith and Wesson she would carry a snub-nosed .32 caliber on her ankle. No more skirts.

Chief Gerald Hartford had no choice but to agree. He suggested a task force of at least two other detectives. Signe considered it; however, at this time she didn't know how she would employ them. She drove the Crown Vic to the police garage herself so they could start modifying it. Then she drove to Santa Fe Gunsmithing to purchase some firearms.

PART 3

CHAPTER 21

As Signe walked out of Santa Fe Gunsmithing with the stock boy carrying four new guns and a large box of ammo, she felt back in charge. However, as she drove up Galisteo Street she again had the feeling she was being followed. A Chevy Neon was about one and a half blocks back. She turned right on Palace fighting the urge to signal first. When she got to the Plaza she went along the west side, then turned left along the south side and stopped at the light. She proceeded past the La Fonda Hotel and headed toward the cathedral past a row of bakeries, camera shops and dry goods stores. The cathedral was a massive brown-red structure in the French Romanesque style on the east side of town. It was finished in 1869 by Jean Lamy the first archbishop of Santa Fe. The steeples on each tower had never been built. Two large flat-topped structures rose above each side of the sanctuary. Signe thought this gave the building an unfinished look. Signe glanced in her rearview mirror. The Neon followed at a leisurely distance. She called a squad car on the radio, as she did a series of four right turns that brought her back to the imposing cathedral. The squad car picked up the Neon and radioed the license number to Signe before the officer pulled the car over. The car was registered to a Wanda De Berneres who lived in Santa Fe but was recently from Newark, New Jersey. When Signe pulled up her registration on the Department of Motor Vehicle site she recognized her as the young brunette she had seen eating with Tony Squitero at The Pink Adobe. So "Tony the Squid" was still in play. She had seen little of him in the past two weeks.

That afternoon Signe, attired in her dress uniform, attended Officer Art Johnson's funeral at the Immaculate Heart of Mary Catholic Church. He was unmarried, but his parents sitting in the front row were clearly, and very publicly devastated. Burial was in the beautiful Santa Fe National Cemetery

(Art had been in the Army before he joined the force) that was situated on a long slow rise on the north side of town. Nearly every one of the three hundred police officers from Santa Fe attended in dress uniforms and spotless white gloves. Long sad, silent rows of uniform white tombstones stretched up the hillside surrounded by grass that remained green despite the late season. The Sangre de Cristo Mountains provided a massive green-black backdrop. At the conclusion of the service the sun was setting and for a few minutes the mountains did turn a deep red color and resemble their Spanish name-blood of Christ. Signe was overwhelmingly sad as she walked down the hill peeling off the gloves in her uncomfortable black dress shoes.

It was after five but she headed back to the office. She pulled out the large white bulletin board that she had started ten days ago and added recent events connected with the murder to her time line. She sat back and stared at the facts and events of the case. Three attributes of Chloe's murder jumped out at Signe. First the crime was not the work of a single killer but of a group whose size was unknown. Secondly, the perpetrators were ruthless and would stop at nothing to protect themselves. Thirdly, they had an enviable information management and communication system. They knew where she was at all times, as demonstrated by the two attempts on her life and they were precisely aware of who had information that might help Signe in her investigation: witness what happened to Johnny Armijo. Detective Sorensen promised herself that she would focus her new resources on each of these three problems. Before she left work Signe called Sven Torvaldson and changed their dinner meeting to a conference in the station house early the next morning. She didn't want to be distracted.

Mr. Torvaldson appeared blond, handsome and well dressed at the appointed hour the next day. Signe offered him coffee and then got down to business. He stated he had, at least, some information on each of the five topics she asked him to investigate. She had asked about Richard Lederback. Sven stated that he had a long record of criminal infractions including, but not limited to, robbery, horse theft and assault. He had done some time years ago. He had never used a gun in any of his previous crimes although he had assaulted one victim with a knife. According to an interview with Mrs. Lederback he often disappeared for weeks at a time and then would suddenly reappear. She had no inkling where he went, and he became furious if questioned.

Mr. Torvaldson's contacts had investigated the three Argentinean men who attended the state fair. The information was sketchy, but they were upscale ranchers who focused on finely bred horses. They had several thousand head of cattle and almost eight hundred horses. One of the three had a criminal record but no details were available. He had no way of knowing if they had one new Lipizzaner stallion on their vast ranch near Santa Rosa, Argentina which covered 1900 hundred square miles.

Detective Sorensen's third enquiry had been about Anthony Squitero, sometimes know as 'Tony the Squid'. Signe knew his early history as a petty thief and his association with the New York mob. Sven reported that he had become increasingly marginal and violent in the past seven years. His name came up after the kidnapping and ransom of a prominent New Jersey banker and later the disappearance of the scion of a pharmaceutical heir. A large ransom was paid in both cases but neither man was ever found. Tony had an office in Santa Fe now that bristled with antennas and at least one 'employee' or girlfriend Wanda De Berneres from Secaucus, New Jersey. She had arrests for shoplifting and solicitation. Signe wondered if Sven could put a 'tail' on Tony. Mr. Torvaldson said that he would be happy to.

The fourth item on Signe's list was the background on The Wild Pony gentleman's club. Sven had learned that the club was a closely held corporation owned by ten Albuquerque attorneys. One owner was none other than Dirk Patterson. The club was often in trouble with the law over drug dealing and unregistered firearms. The authorities had once shut it down for six months. It had shown a big loss on its tax return for the past five years. Signe was glad to know this but wasn't sure how it helped.

The fifth item was Signe's inquiry about the Lipizzaner horses. The horse that had been stolen the afternoon of Chloe's death had been of that breed. Sven had made inquiries of the American Lipizzaner Horsemen's Association. They had active chapters in forty-seven states. The breed had become increasingly popular over the past decade and a half. With the increase in popularity the value of Lipizzans with good pedigree had quintupled. The space required by such animal's means that they are often left in areas that are unattended. Sven found that some national organizations think 40,000 horses are stolen in the US every year. The most valuable equine, purebred Arabians and Lipizzaners were most likely to be stolen. She thanked Mr. Torvaldson for all his help. He suggested a dinner meeting for an update in a week.

"Let's meet here, at the station house," she suggested in Danish. She didn't want to deal with this handsome large man on ambiguous territory just yet.

CHAPTER 22

The next morning she was picked up by patrolman Jack Gallegos at her new gated and guarded apartment. Jack was a four year veteran of the force known to be smart, easy going, and a good shot. He was driving the newly refurbished and now heavily armed Crown Vic. To start Jack out easy she made the rounds of her Santa Fe contacts. She went to State Police headquarters to talk with Sergeant Raymond Gallegos. He also happened to be a distance cousin of Jack's. Signe thanked him for the tip on the horse trailer license plate, and filled him in on what had happened. She also wanted to know if he had any further recollections from the state fair that day. He thought for a bit and then said that he didn't. He said he would talk to Stony Jones the other officer on the scene.

"I hope you solve this case detective," Raymond said to Signe and then to Jack. "Say 'hi' to your mother for me Jack."

Signe directed Jack to the La Fonda next. They both visited with Jefferson Barclay. Signe showed him a poor quality mug shot of Richard Lederback. Jefferson thought he might have seen Mr. Lederback in the hotel the week of the state fair, maybe for lunch. He remembered him because of his worn clothing and was sure he was alone. He was sure he hadn't seen him with the three men from Argentina. Signe thanked him for the information. She asked for a call if he remembered anything further.

Signe was meeting Dr. Lawrence Abramowitz at La Fonda for lunch. Jack and Signe took a table in the La Plazuela restaurant in the center of the first floor of the hotel. It featured large glass panels with brightly colored tiles and frames painted blue, green and red that reminded Signe of Mexico or Spain. Dr. Abramowitz arrived promptly and Signe made the introductions. They ordered South American food. Larry Abramowitz had called Signe two days ago and requested a meeting. He had been puzzling about the hydrazine found in the dead girl's body since their last visit.

Dr. Abramowitz found several old books and journal articles about the chemical in the library at the Los Alamos National Laboratory. Many were from the Second World War and in German and Polish so it took him some time to puzzle them out. Hydrazine had been used by the Nazis to fuel the V2 rockets that terrorized London during the Blitz. The Germans also used hydrazine as a rocket fuel during the war in a plane, the Messerschmitt Me 163, he said. At that time Allied bombers flew at 260 miles per hour and fighters at 380 miles per hour. This very advanced German rocket plane went 623 miles per hour in 1941 and production of this plane was given highest priority. It was shaped like a plane but only 18 feet long with a 30 foot wing span.

"That plane was three feet shorter than your Crown Victoria, Signe." Larry said. Signe remembered now that Larry went on like this about science and history. She just wished he would get to the point. Dr. Abramowitz went on to say that hydrazine and methanol were used to fuel the rocket plane. Hydrazine is an oily clear liquid that smells like musty ammonia. Several mechanics lost their lives fueling the plane before they realized how toxic the hydrazine was.

"The LD 50 is the scientific way," Larry said, "Of reporting the amount of a chemical or toxin that will be lethal to 50% of the animals exposed to it. For hydrazine it is only 25 milligrams per kilogram. If your victim weighed 120 pounds, Signe, converting to English units, only 3 grams of hydrazine would have been rapidly fatal to Ms. Patterson. That is about one quarter of a teaspoon."

There is another angle on the hydrazine beside the rocket fuel Dr. Abramowitz went on. "There is a wonderful tasting mushroom called a morel. It grows under big trees deep in the woods, and when cooked in butter tastes delicious. Mushroom hunters go out in the spring before leaves come out and collect them. However, in a case of mimicry, there is also a false morel that looks a lot like the real mushroom but is poisonous. The false morel contains a compound called gyromitrin which metabolizes into monomethyl hydrazine in the body. So the toxic effects of the mushroom are identical to hydrazine poisoning."

"Now I don't think Chloe was a victim of mushroom poisoning but you did say she used drugs and maybe she was experimenting. However, there was a science teacher here in Santa Fe that taught high school students an elective on rockets. He helped them build small liquid fueled missiles that used hydrazine and methanol just like the Germans. The teacher got the hydrazine from Los Alamos. That's the best I could do," Dr Abramowitz concluded.

"I'm amazed, Larry. You did your usual thorough job. I owe you dinner." Signe said enthusiastically.

"One more thing," Dr. Abramowitz continued. "I may have found the hydrazine that the science teacher used in storage up in Los Alamos. There is an access number and it should be brought to my office this afternoon. If you want to drive up tomorrow I can give you a sample. It will have some unique impurities in it that would match up with the sample taken from that unfortunate young woman if they came from the same source."

Jack, Signe and Larry finished their lunches and continued talked about the case over coffee. Jack drove Signe to her new apartment so she could finish unpacking. They agreed to meet at 7 a.m. for the drive up to Los Alamos.

It was chilly but sunny the next morning when Jack maneuvered the Crown Vic into the apartment parking lot, like the Queen Mary 2 docking at a wharf that was too small. They headed north out of town past Camel Rock, past Tesuque and at Pojoaque took the overpass and headed west. The land rose quickly and the desert gradually got hilly and was covered with more vegetation. They crossed the Rio Grande and the road grew even steeper. They passed a startling mesa top airstrip with a cliff just off the end of the tarmac. Soon they were in the village of Los Alamos and then in the National Lab, itself. They found Dr. Abramowitz office with no difficulty and collected the sample from a secretary. Dr. Abramowitz was up the canyon, at one of the nuclear reactors, doing an experiment and wasn't expected in the office at all that day.

Jack stopped at a gas station to fill the Crown Vic, a very thirsty car and then headed back down 'the hill' as Los Alamos locals say. He drove out of town and down the long decline by the airport and then wound through rolling hills toward the Rio Grande River at a place called Otowi crossing. The bridge was an old two lane steel structure with most of the supports overhead. As he approached he observed a long row of orange construction cones diverting traffic into the right hand lane on the bridge. Next he noticed a sign that said, 'Slow to 5 mph'. He knew that these road work signs weren't here on the way up. He cut his speed and started over the bridge. Half way across, he hit a tire deflation device that he hadn't seen in time to avoid. The open metal diamonds snaked across the road and every two inches a sharp three inch metal spike pointed skyward. The Crown Vic's two front tires were flat in seconds, and a gun shot to the right rear tire stopped the vehicle in an exposed position on the middle of the bridge. When the shot hit the right tire Jack and Signe instinctively ducked and move toward the driver's door. Before they tumbled out Signe made an automated 911 call while Jack scooped up the three long guns and ammunition from the back seat.

A bullet tore through the front door on the passenger side. Signe reached in the back seat for the Kevlar vests and threw one at Jack. She motioned him to the front of the car and indicated with her hand that she would go around the back of the vehicle. Her position wouldn't have been safe if she hadn't known that the gas tank was on the left side of the vehicle and the shots were coming from the right side of the bridge. As she inched along the back of the car a bullet tore through the back windows scattering glass in every direction. She peaked out cautiously and focused on the large sandstone boulders across the river and up about fifty feet which would have given the shooter a commanding view of the bridge without increasing the length of his shot too much. A bullet dug into the surface of the bridge just six inches from her shoulder spraying bits of gravel onto Signe and the car. Signe realized that their adversary was an excellent marksman. Before she flinched involuntarily she saw a glint of metal beside one of the rocks as the shot was fired.

"Jack, the shooter is about eighty yards away behind that rock with the broken trunk of a Ponderosa beside it." Signe called out. "I don't think the shotguns will reach that far. Try the .223." She pulled out her Smith and Wesson and waited for more movement. When she saw some motion she squeezed off two rounds just before the man in the rocks got off another round at them.

"I'm hit," Jack cried. Signe moved quickly back behind the car and along the left side until she got to Jack's body. It looked like a shoulder wound. She tried to pull him back out of the line of fire but he was too heavy.

She lay on top of him so that she could reach the .223 sniper rifle and eased it back slowly into her grasp. She pointed the weapon at the rock with the tree beside it. The view through the scope magnified everything and gave her a clear view. She waited patiently for eight or ten minutes and then the shooter began to move out from the behind the rock. She waited until his right side came into view with the rifle on his shoulder. She knew she was exposed and taking a chance but she wanted a clean shot. She didn't think the shooter would expect the police in a routine looking patrol car to have a high powered rifle with them. When half of his body was exposed she fired and saw him lurch forward. He remained partially exposed so she took another shot. Then she checked on Jack who was only semi conscious but had a strong pulse. A small puddle of blood was growing on the tarmac beside his body. She crawled back into the car and put in an emergency call for an ambulance. Then she came back to Jack took off her jacket and pressed the folded fabric over the wound where his left shoulder met his chest just an inch from his Kevlar vest.

Five minutes later two black and whites police cars came screaming down the hill. No shots had been fired from the rim rocks for the past fifteen minutes. Perhaps the shooter was wounded or had slunk away. Either way, Signe got help from the Los Alamos police officers. First they pulled Jack behind the safe bulk of the Crown Vic. He was beginning to respond. Signe stayed with Jack while the four officers ran crouching across the bridge and dispersed on the hillside. The ambulance arrived next and the EMTs evaluated Jack's wound and decided it wasn't life threatening. Signe helped the attendants load Jack in the ambulance, which they did in a crouching rush, and then joined the officers on the bouldery hillside. The four officers were eight to ten yards apart and working slowly up the hillside crouching behind boulders, weapons drawn.

Suddenly one of the officers shouted, "I found him. He's wounded." Signe and the other three officers scrambled to the spot.

The shooter was lying on his back with an entrance wound in his right upper chest. He was barely conscious. His breathing was rapid and shallow. Signe realized immediately that it was Richard Lederback.

"Did you kill Chloe Patterson? Did you kill Officer Johnson? Did you kill Johnny Armijo? Who are you working for?" Signe demanded in a loud voice while shaking him. Mr. Lederback did not say anything even though his eyes were open. He gave her a look of pure hate and expired.

CHAPTER 23

The Los Alamos police worked the crime scene at Otowi crossing while one of the remaining officers drove Signe into Santa Fe. She wanted to spend some time going through the material they had confiscated at Richard Lederback's ranch, but first she wanted to report to Chief Hartford. He had heard most of what happened on the radio but he wanted Signe to fill him in the details. She told him everything that had happened that morning. Signe replayed every memory of the morning searching for hidden clues.

She dwelt upon the drive up, particularly the ride across the old bridge at Otowi crossing. It had been a clear cool morning and the water in the Rio Grande sparkled as it dashed over the rocks. The Jemez Mountains rose above the mesas to the west. Even as she replayed it in her mind's eye nothing seemed amiss. She thought she should have spotted the set up before it unfolded and been able to get her partner and herself out of harms way. Certainly, Richard Lederback had been in place as the officers approached Los Alamos. Probably he was sitting against a tree enjoying a smoke. As the Crown Vic approached he would have stubbed the cigarette out slowly and scanned their vehicle with binoculars or through the scope of his rifle. He would have noted Signe's position in the vehicle and gazed at Jack for the first time. She had been assured that Jack would be okay.

"I haven't seen a case like this since I came to Santa Fe, Detective Sorensen," The Chief began. "The people involved in this crime are both desperate and ruthless. That is a treacherous combination. There may be layers to this case that we haven't even uncovered. I'm glad you beefed up your car and insisted on a driver. Without that sniper rifle you would have been sitting ducks. The modifications to the car were expensive, but it paid off a lot faster than I thought it would. I want to reassign you to another case, Signe. I can't afford to lose you."

"Thanks, Chief," Signe began. "Dr. Goldiamond already asked me about a transfer when Art Johnson was murdered. I told her the only way I will really feel safe is if I solve this crime. Otherwise the perps will be out there and they could strike at anytime and that is not a good feeling. So far I've been able to adjust to their outbursts. Right now I want to sift through the stuff we got from the search warrant for the Lederback ranch and see if there are any clues. I got to Richard Lederback before he died, Chief. The bastard wouldn't tell me who killed Art Johnson or Johnny Armijo let alone Chloe Patterson. I know he could hear me. He just gave me this look of unadulterated hate and then he died."

"You and Jack were very lucky, Signe," Chief Hartford concluded.

Signe pulled out the four cardboard boxes that they had collected at Mr. Lederback's house. She spread the papers out on her desk and let her OCD take over. She spent two hours looking through Richard Lederback's papers and sorting then by date and making lists. The balance in his account had fluctuated wildly over the years. In 1995 his balance had been down to $37.06 however a month later it has risen to $42,000. She found herself wondering if Richard had been a bank robber or a cat burglar. There was nothing in any of the records that connected Lederback to any of the other suspects. The techs had analyzed Richard's computer in detail. There were few files on the machine and most were badly done pornography.

A Sergeant from the Los Alamos Police Department called just before five. He stated that they had found four shell casings from a .357 magnum bullet at the shooter's location. They collected a .357 magnum rifle from next to the body that had prints on it, but all matched the dead man. The assailant bled to death from a gunshot wound to the right upper chest that must have torn a major artery. He also had a flesh wound about waist high on the right side. A pair of binoculars and a small backpack were also found at the site. A wider search of the surrounding area led to the discovery of Mr. Lederback's truck hidden in an arroyo along the shoulder of the road toward Santa Fe with brush piled behind it to hide its location. Signe thanked the Sergeant for the information. She carefully put the records from the Lederback search warrant back into their four boxes.

Signe slipped into her blue BMW and drove north toward Los Alamos. She stopped at the Los Alamos Medical Center to visit Jack. She found her new partner sore but in good spirits. The bullet had struck his right clavicle at its distal end reducing the harm from the bullet and making it easier to extract. He would be discharged in the morning. Signe had brought him some green chile enchiladas from the Coyote Café since they both had a passion for hot Mexican food.

On the way back down 'the hill' Signe called Vincent and invited him over to her apartment that evening. They spent two hours reading and listening and then made love. Signe sent him home afterwards. She liked sleeping next to his warm body but in the morning he would ask her questions about their future. She found the questions increasingly irritating for reasons she couldn't fathom. Sunday she took a leisurely drive back to Los Alamos to visit Jack and then drive him home.

Monday morning she had another meeting with Dr. Goldiamond to review the latest shooting.

"How are you feeling, Signe?" Dr. Goldiamond began. "You were involved in another potentially fatal shooting occurring so soon after that last tragedy. How is your anxiety level?"

"Actually, I feel better," Signe began. "The man that I shot was responsible for my accident, Vivian. I'm sure of it. I found paint from my wrecked car on the front of his truck. I also believe that Lederback killed Officer Johnson. You know, that shooting was within thirty miles of Lederback's home in Wagon Mound. The rifle that was confiscated at the scene yesterday was the same caliber as the rifle that was used in the murder of Officer Art Johnson. I feel that the man responsible for all three incidents is dead. It's like having a large weight lifted off of my shoulders."

"But the last time we talked you said that this crime involved others, and those miscreants are still out there." Dr. Goldiamond reminded her.

"Perhaps," Signe said thoughtfully. "But Lederback committed three violent crimes. Maybe he was also the person who murdered the star-crossed Chloe Patterson. In any case I'd like you to clear me to keep working on this crime."

"Psychologically I find you fit for duty, Signe." Dr. Goldiamond pronounced. "However, these three violent episodes occurring within such a short time span are bound to take a toll. Superficially you feel well but deep currents may be building under the surface. You must really A DEATH IN THE SHADOW OF THE SANGRE DE CRISTO MOUNTAINStune in' to yourself and call me if you become troubled."

"Thanks, and I promise I will." Signe said with relief in her voice. Signe walked to her desk and studied the time line she had drawn on the white bulletin board. The remaining list of possible suspects was very short; Al Squitero, Dirk Patterson and the three gauchos from Argentina. Suddenly, Signe knew what her next move would be.

CHAPTER 24

The next morning, Signe strode back toward the Chief's office with two large cups of coffee in her hand. She nudged the door open with her foot and walked in.

"I need to go to Argentina chief," Signe said in a voice that was just a little too loud.

"Sit down, Signe, and slow down a bit." Gerald Hartford began. "Has all this violence, directed at you, tipped you over the edge? Why, in God's name, would you want to go to Argentina? Are you leaving the department? Are you running away? I thought you told me you were Danish. Why Argentina?"

"No, no Chief, you don't understand." Signe said excitedly. "*Fandens!* It's the Chloe Patterson case, Sir. I'm drawing a blank here. Dick Lederback died, inconveniently, before I could make him talk. 'Tony the Squid' and Chloe's father are suspects but I have *no* good leads on either one of them. They are well financed and quite clever. You remember the three men that Jefferson Barclay told me about—the three gauchos from Argentina? I think that they absconded with Chloe's horse. They are my only other good lead, Chief. I need to question those men and search for that horse in Santa Rosa, Argentina. If I try to have the local authorities investigate, Chief, it will just spook the three men. Argentina is a very large country and they could hide that horse anywhere. I would never find it if they knew I was coming. I'll take some of my leave for the trip. I have two weeks of holiday coming but can the department pay for the trip?"

"I just reviewed my budget last Tuesday, Signe, and there are not enough discretionary funds to pay for such a journey." Chief Hartford said. "Besides, Detective, this *could* be a wild goose chase. All of your information is circumstantial. I know how you feel about your informants, and it is true that that Concierge has an amazing number of contacts in the county. However, you might go to Argentina, and spend a lot of money, and find nothing."

"You might be right chief, but I feel blocked in every other direction." Signe began. "I have explored ways to get at the other suspects and as you know all have come up blank. Let me see if I can get funding for the trip from other sources. If I get the funding, would you be supportive of the trip, Chief?"

"Yes, Signe." Chief Hartford said. "I'm as anxious as you are to settle this damn case."

After leaving the Chief's office Signe put in a quick call to Sven Torvaldson about money for the trip. After he called the American National Assurance Co. he informed Signe that she had up to $15,000 in financial support for the trip. After all, his company still stood to lose up to $2,000,000 on their policy. Signe got on the phone immediately and set up the air travel and hotels.

After lunch Signe drove the BMW to Albuquerque with the sample of hydrazine that Dr, Abramowitz had found. She had called Dr. Gilchrist to make sure she was working and invited her to dinner. Signe met Bernadette in her office and handed over the sample. Dr. Gilchrist also gave Signe the final report on Johnny Armijo's death. The thigh wound was from one 9mm pistol. The bullet had passed through skin and muscle of Johnny's thigh and imbedded itself in the paneling of the lap dancing lounge. The two shots that killed him came from a second 9mm hand gun and both bullets were recovered from his thorax. One bullet tore through his right ventricle and embedded in the spine. The second slug pierced the right pulmonary artery. Either would have been almost instantly fatal. The report also showed that Johnny's body contained marijuana, benzodiazepines, heroin and truly heroic amounts of cocaine. Hydrazine was notably absent. Poor Johnny, Signe found herself thinking.

Signe and Bernadette went to Garduno's for drinks along with chips and salsa. The watering hole was packed with stockbrokers, lawyers and financial planners that had left work early. Bernadette had her usual martini and Signe a cosmopolitan. Then they went to Sadie's for fiery hot Mexican food. Sadie's was a north Fourth Street fixture that had started in the back of a bowling alley. It was now in a huge building with three large noisy dining areas that seated seventy dinners each. Both had chile rellenos—hot green chiles five inches long, slit open, stuffed with cheese and then dredged in a light egg batter and fried in oil. If prepared right and served fresh the rellenos should be a combination of crispy, then spicy hot and fiery hot, at the same time, followed by a soft mild tasting center. Even when eaten with beans and rice, if done right, the diner should break out in a sweat.

After dinner they drove downtown to the old restored KiMo Theatre on Central Avenue. The theatre was constructed on old Route 66 in the center of downtown Albuquerque in 1927. It was built in the short lived Pueblo Deco style that fused Indian motifs with the flamboyance of Art Deco. Its name came from the Tewa Indian language and means 'king of its kind'. The governor of another pueblo, Isleta, won a contest to name the theater in 1927. He received $50 as a prize for his suggestion. Bernadette and Signe went to a concert by a local jazz singer that only vaguely interested them. As soon as the rococo, gold-leaf decorated, theater got dark, Signe and Bernadette started shamelessly touching and kissing each other. Bernadette was the more adventurous kissing Signe on the neck, mouth and ear. Her hands roamed over Signe's legs, belly and breasts. Signe followed Bernadette's lead and touched and kissed her back. She enjoyed holding and stroking Bernadette's breasts which were much larger than her own.

When the concert was barely over and before the encores the two walked up the aisle holding hands. They drove to Bernadette's home in the north valley. Signe was greeted inside the door by two friendly overweight Golden Labradors. Bernadette opened an eight year old bottle of Cabernet Sauvignon and poured the wine into two large wine glasses. Each glass was large enough to hold the whole bottle of wine so they easily held the bouquet of the wine when it was swirled. Bernadette put a Brahms string quartet on and smoothly led Signe to a large sofa. They kissed gently and held each other. Bernadette began to undress Signe. First she unbuttoned her blouse and slid it off while gently touching her shoulders and upper chest. Next Bernadette unzipped Signe's skirt and touched her legs particularly the inside of her thighs. Signe enjoyed the touching and started to get wet, but still felt confused about what was about to happen. Bernadette perhaps sensing this ambivalence, removed Signe's bra and panties quickly and then slipped out of her own clothing. Bernadette pulled Signe close to her naked body and gently caressed Signe's breasts and ass while kissing her deeply. Bernadette worked her left hand slowly between Signe's legs and touched and played with her folds and crevices. Signe forced herself to relax and focused on Bernadette's full breasts and pink nipples. Bernadette moved her hand faster and deeper until Signe had a mild but long orgasm that caused her to moan softly. Bernadette removed her hand, pulled Signe close and kissed her lingeringly with an open mouth and gently exploring tongue.

"That was delicious," Signe said in a husky voice. "May I return the favor?"

"There is no need," Bernadette replied softly. "This is all new to you. Let's go slow."

Bernadette took Signe's hand and walked her to her king-sized bed. Together they threw the huge pile of pillows onto the floor and crawled between the sheets. They slept contentedly in each others arms naked and warmed by the heat of each others bodies.

CHAPTER 25

Signe awoke at six a.m., quickly kissed and thanked Bernadette. She was leaving for South America that evening. She raced home and finished her packing. She went to the office and checked the messages on her desk and turned some cases over to other detectives. Vincent drove Signe to Albuquerque. They ate a quick plate of pasta at Scalo's with no visit to the ladies lounge this time. Vincent walked Signe to security and kissed her good by. Signe found herself comparing Vincent's tender kiss to Bernadette's recent probing kisses. They were both nice but there was a deeper sense of arousal with Vincent.

First, Signe had a four hour flight on American Airlines with one stop to Miami. Most of her carryon space was taken up by a large heavy book called *The Big Book of Lipizzaner Horses*. As she settled in for the first flight she pulled down this heavy volume and started reading. She knew next to nothing about horses, so she started with Chapter one. When she was a child her family had taken her and her brothers to see the Austrian Lipizzaner Stallions from the Spanish School when they appeared in Copenhagen. She remembered them as very large pure white horses that were precisely trained and amazingly agile. They could even walk on their hind feet and cross their front legs and bow. Everything about these horses was amazing to an eight year old girl.

The book stated that the Lipizzans could be traced back 2,000 years to Carthage. This Carthaginian stock was bred to the Vilano, a sturdy horse from the Pyrenees. The combination became the famous Andalusian horse of ancient Spain. The Andalusians were highly prized war horses. For 700 years the Moors dominated Spain and the breed remained the same. Occasional crossing with Arab and Oriental blood in Cordoba and Grenada improved fleetness and agility. When Spain threw off Moorish rule, the horses were exported. The most notable stud farms were in Trieste, Italy and Fredericksborg, Denmark. Signe had never heard of this link between Lipizzaner stallions and her home country but she wasn't surprised. The Danes produced excellent stock. Archduke Maximilian, Emperor of Austria, began breeding Spanish horses in Austria in 1562. Eighteen years later the royal stud farm was moved to Lipizza near Trieste. Spanish stock was added to the breed during the seventeenth and eighteenth century. With the fall of the Habsburg Empire in 1918 the Danish horses were divided between Austria and Italy.

The Lipizzaner horses are trained in precision presentations both alone and in groups. The emphasis is on coordinated motion and control and includes the art of dressage. Dressage which is French for 'training' involves six levels of training for precision horse maneuvers. They progress through various gaits and motions advances the abilities of the horse and its willingness to be trained. At the culmination there are six maneuvers where the horse actually leaps above the ground. Lipizzaners have been trained in dressage for centuries and after eight to ten years of training can perform dressage at the highest level. The horses are known for majesty, elegance, beauty and intelligence.

All of the Lipizzaner can be traced to eight stallion dynasties. Chloe's horse came from the Pluto dynasty. Pluto was born in the Danish Royal Stud Farm in 1765. The stable where Pluto was born was built by the Danish King Christian the IV in Fredericksborg, Denmark. The crenellated castle was surrounded by an extensive French park with perfectly straight paths that led directly to the stables. Pluto arrived in Lipizza in 1772. Pluto's dynasty was the most successful of all the stallion lines.

As Signe's plane made its final approach into Miami shortly after midnight she realized that she was searching for a horse that had a better pedigree and more extensive written history than her own family.

After buying a Spanish-English dictionary, Signe boarded an American Airlines flight for Buenos Aires, Argentina. During the seven and one half hour flight Signe watched the movie and slept. When she arrived in Argentina it was 10:00 a.m. Despite the fatigue she managed to get through baggage claim and customs. The firearms and ammunition in her luggage took some extra time. When she finally stepped out of the airport a fresh light rain was falling. A muscular man in his thirties held up a sign with "Detective Sorensen" written on it. He introduced himself as Juan Vivendi an inspector in the Argentinean National Police. He was a handsome man with wavy brown hair, three inches shorter in stature than Signe. He wore a well tailored European suit. He took Signe's rifle case and suitcase and threw them easily over his shoulder. His Mercedes was parked in front of the Ezeiza Airport. Inspector Vivendi drove Signe to a nearby hotel and helped her check in. They agreed to meet for dinner to discuss the case and plan their travels. Signe hurried up to her room, closed the curtain, nearly tore her clothes off, and slipped between the crisp fresh sheets. For a few seconds she realized how wonderful it felt to lie down after being up for twenty-eight hours and then she was asleep.

She awoke at 6 p.m. Buenos Aires time. She met Inspector Vivendi in the hotel restaurant. The restaurant had an Alto Plano décor and served large skewers of meat roasted over an open fire and carved table side. She was offered skewers of lamb, pork, chicken and especially beef. She was startlingly hungry and ate ravenously, sometimes forgetting good manners. Signe described the case and the central role of the horse to Juan Vivendi as he took copious notes. Then Inspector Vivendi went over their travel plans to Santa Rosa and the Terra Grande Ranch which was many miles beyond the last town. Signe had not realized that they would be traveling by train and then on horseback for three days. At the end of the meal Juan handed Signe a large package containing leather pants, a vest, and a jacket all in a rich brown suede. He also gave her a pair of cowboy boots. He apologized for not telling her about the clothes that she would need for their trip into the Pampas, but he wanted to meet her first so he would know what sizes to get for her. It had taken him the three hours she was asleep for him to find suitable garments for her as she was seven inches taller than the average Argentinean woman. Before he departed he said he would pick her up at 5 a.m. for an early train.

She left the hotel in the morning before first light. Juan Vivendi drove across the sleepy neighborhoods of Buenos Aires quickly. They boarded a worn brown passenger train and settled into velour seats with wooden arm rests. They headed out of town through suburbs and then into the country side as the sky lightened. They headed in a south westerly direction toward Bahia Blanca and then turned more westward. While they ate breakfast in the dining car they headed into the Pampa Humedo. October was spring in the Southern Hemisphere and the first 150 miles was through clover and thistle fields. The thistles were in bloom and often stood ten or eleven feet high with large spectacular purple blossoms at their tops. Signe alternately napped and read a novel as they moved steadily westward. By evening they had traveled 240 miles to the last stop on the tracks—Santa Rosa. After a modest dinner on Main Street, notable only for an excellent Chilean red wine, they retired to a small two story clapboard hotel in need of paint and with creaky wooden floors.

In the morning Signe found Juan already outside with two sturdy horses and a donkey. Juan's horse was a tall roan with black mane and tail. Signe's horse was a slightly taller palomino. Juan helped pack Signe's belongings into two big saddle bags and put her .223 rifle and shotgun in leather slings on each side of her saddle. Signe approached the right side of the horse intending to clamor up. As Juan directed her to the left side of the horse and helped her mount he realized that she had probably never ridden before. With dew still heavy on the grass and a chill in the air they headed off on a well marked trail. They went west out of the small town of Santa Rosa. In many places the grass was four or five feet tall but the trail was easy. It smelled of hay mixed with a fresh smell of vegetation that was like a subtle spice. As they rode through the endless sea of grass it got warmer and brighter. They stopped at midday for a cold lunch and let the horses graze for an hour. They spent the afternoon wending their way to the west. Signe adjusted well to her palomino but knew she would be sore in the morning from the unaccustomed activity. They rode into the evening and then camped by a stream in a grove of scrub oak trees. Juan set up two tents and started a campfire from the wood Signe had gathered. She cooked beef and corn and warmed tortillas over the fire. As it darkened, the sky lit with billions of stars, large and small, twinkling and steady, some yellow white, some rose white and some Signe's favorite, blue white. She saw the Southern Cross for the first time. Signe and Juan lay by the fire for warmth with their heads on their saddles and swapped stories about the cases they had worked on.

They had ridden almost twenty-two miles that day but had another forty-three to go. There destination was the Terra Grande Ranch owned by three prosperous brothers—Hector, Jose and Miguel Fortuna. Signe could have written or telegraphed them from the US, but if they were harboring Chloe's horse she sensed how easily this large distinctive animal could be hidden in this vast grassland. When the fire burned down to embers they retired to their tents. Signe found the ground hard and her butt, shoulders and back were already sore from riding. She didn't sleep well. In the morning Signe cooked breakfast and helped break camp while Juan saddled and fed the animals. As they departed from camp Signe reflected on the beauty and peacefulness of this majestic seemingly endless grassland.

The second day of riding was much like the first. They saw more cattle and some gauchos. They had lunch by a stream and took turns bathing. Signe went first. She folded and piled her clothes neatly by the stream side and stepped gingerly into the clear cold water. The water came from the Andes but had been warmed some by its flow through the warmer pampas. In spite of that, it was still a shock as she stepped in. She stood in thigh deep water and soaped the rest of her body before splashing water on her breasts and belly. She used a cup to dribble water over each shoulder getting the soap off of her back. She decided her dusty hair would last a couple more days before washing. She knew the frigid water on her head would give her a fierce headache. Juan went to bathe next. Just as he got soaped up the donkey, with a jerk of its head, broke the branch that held its reins. While it had been walking very slowly, despite cajoling all morning, it now gamboled across the stream and headed back along the trail. Signe saw the animal bolt first with all of their supplies and food on its back. She went running after the creature. Juan heard his hoof beats and saw the animal jump the stream as the donkey boiled out of camp. Juan jumped out of the stream and ran after their supply animal. Rocks and thorns on the ground slowed him down as he was barefooted. As he ran haltingly, his penis flopped around in every direction. He attempted to cover his privates from Signe's gaze with one hand while running and stumbling on the rough trail. Signe burst out laughing as she ran after the equine. The *burro* would stop and munch the grass until Signe got close and then run forty more feet, and start eating again. She finally snuck up on the donkey, grabbed his reins, and walked back toward camp. An embarrassed Juan was just pulling on his boots and his hair was still wet as she tied the donkey securely to a tree.

They camped in the open that night along a stream. In the middle of the night an animal screeched repeatedly in long high pitched cries nearby. Signe scooped up her sleeping bag and slipped into the other side of Juan's tent. He didn't even wake as she could hear his gentle uninterrupted snoring. Juan was surprised to see her curled up in the corner of his tent when he awoke. He asked after her, and she explained what had happened. As they rode out that day they could see the ranch house in the hazy distance as the yellow sunlight played on the dew covered grass.

CHAPTER 26

Signe and Juan arrived at the Fortuna Ranch in the mid afternoon of the third day. They had watched the ranch grow in size and detail as they got closer. The buildings sat on a gentle rise surrounded by oak trees. The buildings were all white and nestled among the vegetation. The house was one and a half stories tall with large wings that went out to each side. The corrals were extensive, and off to the left of the buildings. On the right were several barns. Two of the horse barns were larger than any Signe had ever seen. As they approached they rode through a *pato* field, the Argentinean equivalent of polo played on horseback with a six handled ball. A rider on a fast Argentinean pony holds the ball by one of the handles and throws it ahead to a teammate. The teammate grabs the ball by a handle and throws it toward a small, sock shaped net nine feet off the ground at both ends of the field. A successful throw results in a goal. As they rode up the small gradual hill to the main house the servants came out on the veranda and stared as they approached. It is the custom on the Pampas to welcome all guests as ranch houses are fifty to sixty miles apart. Juan and Signe were invited in and given a chance to bathe and change out of their riding clothes before afternoon tea.

After a bath and a delicious afternoon snack of coffee, cheeses and homemade bread they were asked about their business by the ranch manager. Both Inspector Vivendi and Detective Sorensen presented their papers and badges. They said they were at the ranch to enquire about a missing Lipizzaner stallion from America. Juan Vivendi had described the men of the Pampas on their long ride to the ranch as bold men but often lawless. The Fortuna brothers had had disputes with ranchers to the north and to the west toward Limay Mahuida over land and cattle. Jose Fortuna had spent two years in a regional prison for a brawl with a neighboring rancher that had resulted in a nearly fatal knife wound. Once the ranch manager understood their business he remained closed mouth, and guarded, but courteous. He said that all three brothers were on the far western edge of the ranch, seventeen miles away, for a large annual spring branding and castrating roundup. The manager offered to ride with them to the branding operation in the morning. After tea Juan and Signe explored the buildings and grounds of the ranch. There were dozens of elegant Arabian, Clydesdale and quarter horses. Juan knew their breeds and Signe only knew that they looked well formed, well cared for and proud. However, they saw no Andalusians and no Lipizzaners. They ate a hearty dinner that featured meats, of course, but also fresh vegetables and salad which delighted Signe. Both went to bed early. After only two nights of camping a real bed felt heavenly to Signe's aching muscles and joints.

In the morning after breakfast their horses, minus the donkey, were saddled and tied to a post out front. They headed west with the ranch manager in the lead. It rained lightly the first two hours and then gradually cleared and warmed. They rode quickly with a brief stop for a cold lunch and then continued west. The sea of grass stretched to the horizon in every direction, gently waving in light breezes. About 3 p.m. Signe began to notice a large cloud of brown dust ahead of them. It grew as they advanced. About an hour later, they entered the dusty camp. It was a maelstrom of noise and activity. Extensive wooden corrals made up the center of the camp. Off to the right were four large tents with two dozen people working at various tasks. A group of young women was tending fires and preparing food. A dozen or more *gauchos* were herding cattle into the chutes and corrals and another dozen appeared to be doing the actual castrating, inoculating of the yearlings and the branding. The dust from moving animals; cattle, horses and men was stifling and everyone except the young women wore a bandanna across their faces.

The ranch manager introduced the police to Hector Fortuna who was nearby supervising the chutes. Hector set a meeting with all three brothers for 8 p.m. The ranch manager escorted Signe and Juan to the tent farthest from the corrals and found them chairs. Two of the young women brought them wine and platters of snacks. The young servers were attractive with good figures and beautiful faces. Signe noticed each wore a tight but colorful cotton dress that dipped low across the bodice revealing more than a third of their firm breasts. As a woman, Signe found herself wondering about the real purpose of the multitudes of young women in the camp. The snacks and wine tasted delicious, but Signe enjoyed sitting in a chair and not on a horse the most. In her mind she still felt the gentle sway of animal as if she were still astride the horse.

When evening arrived Signe and Juan had a large dinner served by several of the voluptuous young women. The wine was an excellent Argentinean Malbec and the food the day's harvest of testicles from the young steers which had been battered and fried. They were crisp and delicious. Signe had heard them called rocky mountain oysters in the US. The main course was served with piles of fruit and salad. After dinner Juan and Signe met with the three Fortuna brothers. Signe began by showing a picture of Hercules, Chloe's horse, and asking the three if they had ever seen him. Hector did the talking for the brothers and was very evasive. Instead of answering the question, he asked a series of questions back. Rather than answer those questions, Signe changed tack.

"Have any of you ever seen this man?" Signe asked showing them a picture of Anthony Squitero. They each shook their heads no.

"How about this man?" Signe said showing a picture of Dirk Patterson.

"We have never seen him, senorita," Hector said answering for all of them.

"Finally, have any of you ever seen this man?" Signe said showing them a picture of Richard Lederback taken on the morgue table.

After some hesitation, Hector said "No ma'am." Signe didn't think he was telling the truth about Lederback.

The brothers asked for some time to talk in private. They seemed very wary of the police, especially Inspector Juan Vivendi. While the three were outside conferring Signe told Juan that she thought Hector was lying about having seen the shooter. Juan said that he had been involved with the three brothers during the knifing case and they always stuck together and were loose with the truth.

When Hector, Jose, and Miguel came back in looking ill at ease, Hector burst out, "We have the horse!" At last, thought Signe, some real progress on this awful case. So all this expense and travel and a sore posterior are not for naught! The scar across Hector's face looked more menacing in the fire light

"We purchased that horse legally," Hector began. "We want to establish a line of Lipizza horses here in Argentina like the lines in Spain, Italy and Austria. Hercules is from the Pluto line; the finest stallion line of all the Lipizzaners. We purchased him in America for 1,600,000 Argentine Pesos. It's many times more than we have ever paid for an animal before. We had to take a mortgage out on our land to the north to pay for him. Do you need to see him?"

"Yes, we do, and we need to see the paper work on the purchase," Juan said.

"Hercules is at our new ranch eight kilometers north of the main ranch," Hector said. "The paper work is in the office at the main ranch house. I will have you taken there tomorrow."

"I appreciate your cooperation, senor," Signe said.

"Join us for the celebration this evening. We have completed our work on 1500 cattle." Hector said as escorted Signe and Juan to an area in the center of the tents. A five piece band was already playing Latin music. Soon gauchos wandered in with the young women who had prepared and served dinner. They danced sambas, tangos, cha-chas, and lambdas for hours with only the briefest of rests. As it got later Signe noticed gauchos and senorita slipping away into the Pampas. She and Juan were shown to well appointed rooms in one of the tents. Signe was happy to be on a cot and slept deeply but had a series of vivid and disturbing dreams. In one long dream Signe was racing across the pampas with Juan on two sleek horses. They were surrounded by other horses, of every shade of brown and tan, also running at break neck speed. The manes and tails of all the horses were several feet long and streamed out behind the galloping animals. Next, was a dream about an isolated resort near the sea with black sand beaches. She was with Axel but there was a mix-up about their reservation. They didn't have a room and spent the night endlessly and sleepily roaming from beach to pool to lobby. Outside the lobby was a twenty by ten foot bed of hot coals at ground level with no fence around it. It looked like a large bed of grey dirt but a steak thrown on the coals would immediately begin to sizzle. In the final dream, Signe and Bernadette were floating and sinuously twisting in the clouds. Their skin was a rich pink and without a blemish as they gently floated around each other like a Matisse painting. As she awoke she didn't remember where she was at first and then recalled her long horse ride to the camp. She was surprised at how much she remembered of her dreams.

CHAPTER 27

Early the next morning Signe and Juan headed out on horseback with Miguel Fortuna, the youngest brother, to take a short cut to the new north ranch where Hercules was stabled. The morning was cool and clear with clouds gathering off to the west. As they rode Signe did some geometry in her head. She loved numbers. Hector said the new ranch was five miles north of the main buildings and they had traveled seventeen miles west to the branding camp. Signe knew if they went east back to the main ranch, and then north to the new stables it would be a twenty-two mile ride along two sides of the triangle she could see in her mind's eye. If they went to the new stables along the hypotenuse of the triangle it would be shorter. Squaring the two known sides and adding in her head she got an estimate of 315 and then finding the square root of that number by trial and error gave her a distance of only eighteen miles as the 'crow flew'. She was heartened by her calculation as she was still very sore from sitting in the saddle. As soon as they started though she realized how narrow and rough this little used trail would be. They headed out single file with grass and bushes brushing their legs on both sides. It got hot quickly and soon they had to ford a small river. Signe stayed mounted and the two men walked their horses across the shoulder deep water. The water felt icy on her legs as she rode across. After a rough hot ride of three hours they rounded a sharp turn and the new stables came into view close ahead. The buildings were much smaller than the main ranch but in the same style, again set among trees. The walls were stuccoed white with red tile roofs in a pleasing long low style. Pieces of cut timber and tiles lay around on the ground suggesting that the project had just recently been completed.

The three dismounted and watered and fed their horses. After a brief rest Miguel led them into the stables. The building had a tall ceiling with a central isle. Doors to the individual stalls lined each side. Bright light came through high windows at each end of the barn. The building smelled of hay and newly cut wood. Signe spotted Hercules straight away. He was spectacularly large and sturdy. Miguel said he was seventeen and a half hands tall at his back. He was pure white, with large muscular haunches, a massive neck and his head tipped in. He had large intelligent eyes that followed any movement. He held his long white tail up proudly. So this is what a $400,000 horse looks like she thought. Wow! She approached his stall but Hercules backed away, reared up on his hind legs and neighed. Miguel said he was so spirited that it took three grooms to handle him.

"That sure looks like Hercules," Signe began. "I was told by his previous owner that he had a small tattoo of six letters above the back of his right front hoof. I need to check that myself Mr. Fortuna."

"Give us some time, senorita, and we can do that." Miguel said.

In the interim, Signe sat down on a bale of hay to admire Hercules from a distance. It took twenty minutes for the three grooms with Miguel and Juan's help to rope and harness the horse. Signe moved slowly up his right side, patting him gently as she went and looked just above the horny part of his right fore hoof. In small black Spanish style letters she read DPRTVX. Mr. Patterson had told her about the letters and she had shared them with no one, nor had she written them down anywhere. So this was Hercules, not that she had had a doubt since she laid eyes on his magnificent frame. She sat and looked at the horse for another twenty minutes while the men readied the horses. The three mounted up and rode down the broad trail to the main ranch complex. Most of the way they rode three a breast enjoying the sunny afternoon and the lush grasses with an occasional clump of oak trees.

They arrived in time for the tasty small sandwiches and coffee that had been served at their first afternoon tea. The day was warm enough that they sat on the veranda with fine linen table cloths, silverware and porcelain dishes. When they were done eating Hector, who had just ridden in, took them into the office and closed the door. He handed Signe a small dark green file with Hercules's name on it. Detective Sorensen was immediately suspicious because of its slimness. Inside, were a typed description of the horse and a long genealogy of the Pluto line going back hundreds of years to Denmark. A professionally done glossy photograph showed Hercules in his entire splendor.

"Where are the financial papers?" Signe demanded. "Where are the letters from the people who sold you the horse, Mr. Fortuna?"

"We paid cash for him, detective. That was a demand of the seller." Hector said ashamedly as he hung his head.

"That is currency fraud. There may be charges brought because of that, Senor Fortuna. I will have to discuss that with the Chief Inspector when I return to Buenos Aires," Juan interrupted.

"The seller never sent us any letters or documents. We only communicated by phone and they always called us," Hector Fortuna continued.

"You mean to tell me you took 1,600,000 pesos to the US and gave it to someone you had never met?" Signe asked with disbelief in her voice.

"We didn't think we needed to know the seller. We were sure about the horse. He was real and valuable. All three of us went to New Mexico because we were carrying so much money and because Jose is a veterinarian. We needed to know we were getting a healthy and robust animal." Hector said earnestly.

"How did the transfer of the animal take place?" Juan asked. Signe hoped the answer would give her clues she needed to find the killer.

"We were told that Hercules would be at the State Fair in Santa Fe in stall 17," Hector began. "We were invited to examine and test the animal there in any way we wanted. We arrived in Albuquerque on a Sunday and drove to Santa Fe. We spent time with the horse Monday, Tuesday, and Wednesday. No one was in the stables during these visits. Urine, blood and analysis of sperm were all normal. I was called Wednesday night, and I said we wanted to make the purchase. I was told to keep the money and have one of my brothers go to the stall at noon on Thursday and put on a riding helmet with ear flaps and opaque goggles. Then he should sit down and wait. Miguel went and did exactly as he had been instructed. About 2 p.m. people came into the stall and took the horse but as they were leaving someone unexpected must have come in. Miguel could hear the first group arguing with a woman but he could make out no words. Miguel was ushered into the horse trailer, along with Hercules. First there was a loud thump and the front of the trailer dropped several inches. Apparently in their excitement, the men hadn't hooked the trailer to the truck improperly. The front of the trailer was lifted slowly before they drove off. (Signe remembered Vincent telling her there had been a thump when he first went into the empty stall). It was scary in the horse trailer because the trailer swayed and Hercules was skittish moving around with his huge hooves around. Miguel was blindfolded and afraid he would get stepped on. They drove for thirty minutes then stopped. Miguel was handed a small tape recorder and a cell phone. When he held the tape recorder up to his ear and played it a loop recording said, 'take off the helmet and call your associate.' He told me what had happened so far and said he was inside a white horse trailer. Then the recorder instructed him to put the cell phone in his pocket and put the helmet back on. They drove for another two hours. Then they unloaded Hercules. They led Miguel out of the trailer and helped him climb a short flight of stairs into an airplane. After the plane took off the tape recorder instructed Miguel to take off the helmet and call again. He told me what had happened and that he and Hercules were in the plane and from the play of sunlight in the windows Miguel knew the plane was heading south. That was my signal to give them the money."

"So, let me get this straight," Signe began. "Miguel neither saw nor heard the people that abducted the horse. However, there was an argument in the stall between the men who took the horse and a woman who may have arrived unexpectedly."

"Yes. That is correct," Hector said.

"How did you give them the money?" Juan asked. Signe already knew that this part of the story wouldn't be any more helpful as to the identity of the assailants. The transfer of the horse had been meticulously planned and carefully executed.

"I was instructed to put the money in a small red suitcase and give it to the concierge at the La Fonda Hotel." Hector said. *Fandens!* Damn, Signe reverted to English. Jefferson Barclay, my snitch, held out on me. "That was the last I saw of it." Hector concluded.

CHAPTER 28

So I have found Hercules but I'm still not close to the perpetrators, Signe thought. They are as smart and clever as they are vicious, well informed and well financed. Signe felt a wave of depression. When she heard about finding the horse last night she was elated because she knew it would open many doors. Now she wasn't sure she was any farther ahead. The many pathways that she expected to open before her were still blocked. She did realize that she had to think over everything that Hector had said during their meeting. Something might be hidden there.

A pleasant dinner followed with the usual abundance of meat and excellent Argentinean wine. Hector and Miguel joined the two detectives and the conversation was lively. After dinner they sat before a fireplace and heard stories of the brother's early days at the ranch. For many years the brothers were cut off from the outside world and had to rely on their own resources to provide themselves with food, tools and timber for building.

Juan and Signe lasted until 10:30 felled, by a combination of a long ride, rich food and more Argentinean red wine—the distinguished Malbec. The grape came from the Bordeaux region of France and was grown beside cabernet sauvignon and the mysterious cabernet franc. Malbec was prone to mildew, frost and rot and never made a good French wine. However, two decades ago winemakers in Argentina discovered that Malbec made magic. It's a rich red with dark fruit leather and spice flavors. The Fortunas got their wine from Mendoza, a sunny dry region in the foothills of the Andes. Signe crawled into her high bed and waited for one half hour. Then she quietly snuck out of her room and down the hall to Juan's room. She opened the door noiselessly and tiptoed inside. At the edge of his bed she unbuttoned her pajama top and let it fall to the floor. She pushed her pajama bottoms down, lifted the edge of the covers and slid into Juan's bed. Riding all day with undulating pressure against her pelvis had made her very horny. She slid over to him, and ran her arms around his stout firm body. He awoke and tried to speak. She covered his lips gently with an index finger to silence him and then replaced it with her warm, open, mouth and probing sharp tongue. She pushed his pajamas off and in so doing found that he was ready to please her. She let him take charge. She didn't feel the need to manage their coupling as she did with the younger, less experienced Vincent. She wasn't disappointed. He pleased her with his hands which explored every inch of her body and she came. Then he treated her to an odyssey with his mouth and tongue focusing finally on her secret hidden folds until she came multiple times with deep waves of pleasure. Finally he entered her by degrees with his short but thick erection and moved slowly, teasing her and feeling her pleasure rise. Then he would stop and kiss her deeply and caress her breasts before resuming his long steady strokes. They came together in a crashing simultaneous climax with Signe muffling her moans in a pillow. After they were both satisfied they held each other. Signe did not want to be caught in Juan's room. She grabbed her pajamas and stepped out into the hall. Hector was at the other end. She smiled at him and then turned her naked back side toward him as she walked down the hall as confidently as she could.

In the morning their horses were saddled early, and they headed east toward Buenos Aires. On the way back they would ride hard in the morning and then stop for the day in the early afternoon. Juan would spread a sleeping bag under a tree and they would make love for two hours, break for supper and then resume their coupling through the evening and into the night until they were both sated. It took them three days to make the return trip. While riding, Signe told Juan the story of her family in Denmark. He had never been to Europe and he was surprised to hear of such a little country with over 5,000,000 inhabitants. She spoke of her son Axel and her father the sailboat builder. Juan responded with the Vivendi family's migration to Argentina from Italy in 1881. He said that between 1860 and 1930 millions of Italians migrated to Argentina for a better life. The peasants of Italy were held down and starved by an ancient feudal system. Almost half of all immigrants in Argentina came from Italy. This made Italians the second largest group in the country after the *Mestizos*. His great grandfather married an Indian woman, and they moved to the capitol where the family has flourished ever since. Juan's father is still an inspector with the police in Buenos Aires. Juan had never married much to his mother's disappointment. He loved the freedom of the Pampas and would often ride and hunt with other inspectors in the tall grass on the weekends. When he had more time he would fly to the Cordillera of the Andes in nearby Chile and rock climb. He liked his job and thought his life was close to perfect. He had no intention of hobbling himself with a wife who would make demands.

Back in Buenos Aires and very saddle sore, Signe went to the metropolitan central police station. She put in a call to Chief Hartford. She forgot it was two hours earlier in Santa Fe, and she caught him just coming in the door.

"Good morning, Chief. This is Signe. I found the horse," Signe chortled. "How's my partner Jack?"

"Congratulation, Signe. I thought you were on a wild goose chase. I'm glad I was wrong," Chief Hartford said in a voice Signe could barely hear. "Jack's fine. He's back at work and awaiting your return. Unfortunately, there aren't any new developments on the Patterson murder case here. Hopefully you'll be able to close it with your new information."

"I hope you're right, Chief," Signe said with no confidence in her voice. "See you soon."

Signe spent a last afternoon with Juan at her hotel, and then he took her to the Ezeiza Airport and kissed her good-by. He promised to write, but she knew he wouldn't. She slept and read *Loving Pedro Infante* on the eight hour American Airlines flight back to Miami. After a short layover she got a direct flight from Miami to Albuquerque. Vincent met her in baggage with a big kiss, a long hug and a dozen long-stemmed red roses. It felt good to be 'home' Signe thought to herself. Vincent brought two letters from Axel. Signe tore them open and perused them for bad news. There was none. She stuffed them in her back pack for later. Vincent had also been keeping a surreptitious eye on Irma. She was now over four months pregnant and still not showing despite her small frame. She wasn't married. She had been to the doctor and mother and baby were doing well. Signe leaned into Vincent's shoulder and felt safe. On the way home both kept the conversation light. They talked about their cases, which for law enforcement officers, is the equivalent of other people talking about the weather. Signe told Vincent all about the Argentina trip and finding Hercules. She omitted some of the parts about Juan.

CHAPTER 29

Once she got back to Santa Fe, Signe needed a total reassessment of her progress or lack thereof on the case. She had spent $6,000 dollars of the insurance company's money on her trip to Argentina and she had found the horse. However, the murderers had been brainy, and the Fortuna brothers knew nothing about the people that had allowed them to purchase Hercules. She couldn't assign any criminal intent to the Fortunas. Signe had gone over and over what Hector had told her about the purchase of the horse. She was dealing with clever criminals that had experience and were very crafty. Little was left to chance. However, Signe had come up with two questions that might push the case forward: where had the money gone? And was there any record of the plane that had transported Hercules and Miguel? She worked on the second question first.

She placed a call to the Terra Rosa Ranch in Argentina and got Hector but asked that Miguel call her back. Miguel said that based on the noise the engines made and the vibrations on takeoff, the plane was probably a two engine propeller driven cargo plane. It had no seats inside. It flew due south for three and half hours before landing at a deserted dirt landing strip. On the trip Miguel felt the warm sun coming in the windows on the right side of the plane so he knew the plane was going south. The bumpy landing told him it was a dirt runway. First, Signe looked for a flight plan for that day with the FAA but wasn't surprised that she didn't find one. She talked with a pilot at the Santa Fe Airport who thought the plane was either a Convair CV-580 or a Beech 90 King Air. It would be hard to differentiate one from the other if the passenger was blindfolded, but fortunately both flew at 180 miles per hour. If Miguel's estimate of the time and direction were correct then Signe could calculate where the plane might have landed. She got out a map of North America and calipers. In three and a half hours the plane should have gone 630 miles. When she drew an arc on the map it landed her in the western part of Mexico where the Sierra Madre Mountains were and there were few towns. Moving east, only Hidalgo del Parrel and Jiménez were the correct distance from Santa Fe. She called the Mexican Federal Police and requested records for October 3rd and 4th for landings at both airports. She was told it would take several days to obtain such records.

Next she worked on the disappearing $500,000. She would meet Jefferson Barclay later but she wouldn't be buying him lunch this time. Thanks to the war on drugs no one could move a sum of money near that large around the country with impunity. The U.S. government was interested in any amount over $10,000. The three likeliest places for a felony to stash this much cash were: the Cayman Islands, Barbados or Switzerland. It wasn't possible to wire that much money any more without attracting the attention of the Drug Enforcement Administration. Most likely the person holding the cash or a mule would deliver the funds in person. Signe calculated that one hundred $100 bills would be approximately two inches tall. That would be $10,000. Therefore $500,000 would be fifty inches tall or four stacks twelve inches tall. The money would fit in an oversized brief case. The problem with having a mule do the delivery was that when the mule looked in the briefcase he would realize what he was carrying. Often times, the mule would be tempted to get 'lost' in Thailand or Venezuela where there was no extradition law. He could live luxuriously for at least ten years, more if he invested the funds even if it wasn't invested very wisely. Signe sent an enquiry to the airlines for travel by Dirk Patterson, Anthony Squitero and Wanda De Berneres for the two weeks from October 3rd to October 17th.

Signe called Sven Torvaldson and gave him a full report on her trip to Argentina. She also told him that she would like to have intensive surveillance on Mr. Patterson, Squitero and De Berneres. Sven agreed readily as most of the $50,000 he had allocated to the project was still available, and he was still looking at a payout of $2,000,000. He said that Mr. Patterson had filed suit against his insurance company last week. Sven suggested they meet in a week for dinner to go over the findings from his PIs. Signe agreed.

She was already late for her meeting with Jefferson Barclay, but she noticed a note on her desk from Bernadette. She ripped it open. There were two pieces of paper in the envelope. One was a page of flowery writing which Signe stuffed in her pocket. The second was a type written page from a lab in California that compared the hydrazine found in Chloe's body with that found in the sample from Los Alamos. The two samples had low levels of choline and aspartane in them. It appeared that the two samples came from the same source. Signe had no idea what that meant, but realized that it might be very important. She stuffed that paper in another pocket.

She jumped in her BMW and sped over to the La Fonda Hotel and parked in the tow away zone. I'm getting more like Dirk Patterson every day she thought with a shudder. She marched inside and beckoned Jefferson Barclay to come over. She didn't wait for him to finish helping the little lady who looked to be from New York with her chamber music tickets. Jefferson approached her sheepishly with eyes averted.

"Damn you, Jefferson!" Signe yelled. "You are supposed to help me! I have to go to *Knepping* Argentina to find out what my fucking friend, and so called informant already knows."

"I'm so sorry Signe," Jefferson said softly. "I knew I should tell you, but they paid me $750 to help them and I needed the money. My partner Keith had to have surgery and the money was for the urologist's fee. It wasn't for me. I knew I couldn't tell you part of the story and not tell you the rest, and I was embarrassed."

"Tell me every detail this instant, Jefferson." Signe shouted.

"All right," He began. "I got a call on Tuesday. It was a voice I didn't recognize. The chap said if I would take a red satchel from my desk to a room he would designate later, he would pay me $750. I really needed the money, Signe."

"What happened next?" Signe demanded.

"One of those South American men I told you about brought me the satchel Thursday afternoon. I had been told to put it in room 223. I took it to the room and used the pass key to get in. I laid the satchel on the bed. An envelope was also on the bed. It had $750 in it, so I took it and left. That's all, Signe. I swear it!"

Signe racked her brain. Same *modus operandi* as the horse transfer she thought and no more helpful. She just turned and strode out without saying another word to Jefferson Barclay as he slunk back to his concierge desk.

"How am I going to solve this case?" She wondered half out loud.

She went back to her apartment and grabbed the two recent letters from Axel and then drove up the road to the ski area. It was a winding pleasant uphill ride through forest and small meadows. Near the top in some tall Spruce trees where the road flattens is a Japanese bathhouse built of stone and timber called Twenty-Nine Waves. Signe got a secluded hot tub that looked out on the forest and the valley north of Santa Fe. She took a pass on the cold plunge tub. She removed her bathrobe and slid into the hot water letting it gradually inch up her lanky body. The remainder of her body that had not yet entered the water was touched by a cool breeze that made her shiver. She closed her eyes and let the hot water sooth her body and then her mind. Then she lay back and read both of Axel's letters twice.

Axel's dad was gone a lot, but when his father was off for the weekend, they sailed around the many small islands that made up Denmark. Often they would spend the night in an inn near the harbor. He enjoyed the time with his father. He'd always had his mother's rational and cerebral perspective on things, and was sure that would always be his orientation. However, the male impulsiveness and risk taking was fun and not something Axel had been exposed to. One Saturday they had been sailing on a reach, Signe thought she remembered that was when the wind came from the side of the boat, in a stiff breeze when they came across a freighter about to enter a channel. Axel's father raced the larger ship to get into the channel first and they made it!

The trade school was going well. He was good with his hands and he loved the smell and feel of the fresh wood. He was good at seeing the finished piece within the oak or beech log when it was brought into the shop. He was dating some girls but none were serious and 'yes' he was being careful about birth control. He had visited Signe's parents several times. They were well, and Signe's father had given Axel some special antique woodworking tools. Over all, he was glad he had gone back to Denmark. He missed his mother terribly and Irma hardly at all. Signe was elated at how well her son was doing even though she missed him fiercely.

For a brief moment she thought of going back to her country and leaving this vexatious murder and its three ancillary killings behind. Then she realized she couldn't quit and leave patrolman Art Johnson's vicious death unavenged. There were only three pieces left on the chess board. The horse represented by a knight had been taken out of play by her. Only a king, a rook and a pawn remained. Dirk Patterson was the king. If he was running the board he was clever and vicious as she had noted before. The rook was Anthony Squitero and he was wide ranging and powerful. The pawn was Wanda De Berneres who despite her weak moves and lack of power might know many answers. Signe decided to attack the pawn with every tool that she had. Setting the case aside, she enjoyed the rest of her soak, and then drove slowly down the twisting mountain road and had some supper at the Coyote Café.

CHAPTER 30

Friday morning Signe got to the office early. She went to her 'new' desk and sifted through all the material on the Patterson murder. She was looking for ways that Wanda could have been involved. While she wasn't the perp in any of the shootings or even the accident, she might still know about one or more of them or have overheard a conversation that was pertinent. What were her duties other than shadowing Signe? What had she done in New Jersey? Why would such an attractive young woman associate with 'Tony the Squid'? Was he holding something over her?

She wandered into Chief Hartford's office with a large cup of fresh steaming coffee in both hands. She was aghast at the coffee Americans drank. It was tasteless, insipid dishwater. She had taken to getting fresh French roasted beans every week at the Wild Oats Community Market, grinding it at home and bringing it to the station. Then she brewed it herself using lots of grounds. Starbuck's coffee was good and there was a drive through right near headquarters. However, one large cup for her and the Chief was $7.66. In one short year, the detective with polymath tendencies knew from the calculation she did in her head that that one simple habit would cost $1915. She was pleased to find that the multiplication came out to an even dollar amount. She also realized that she could buy three original Pueblo Indian pots for that amount.

She plopped down across from the Chief and handed him the steaming brew. First she wanted to pick Gerald's brain about this vexing case.

"Who did this crime, Chief?" Signe said and then looked quizzically at Gerald Hartford.

"I think that ass Dirk Patterson started this as a simple robbery, with no one getting hurt, and everyone getting paid off." Chief Hartford began. "Then as sometimes happens, the whole thing spiraled out of anyone's control. Each move they made had an unintended consequence, creating more problems and sucking more people in. It's a little like a dust devil that rustles leaves in Africa and then wanders out over the Atlantic Ocean where it grows and grows until it's a class four hurricane devastating Florida. I don't have a shred of proof and I don't know who else is involved aside from Mr. Squitero and Wanda."

"I concur with your ideas, Chief." Signe began. "I will pressure all three suspects. However, I would really like to turn the heat up on Wanda."

"That sounds like a good approach to me, Signe." Chief Hartford began. "I have a friend who is the assistant chief of police in Secaucus, New Jersey. I'll see if he can stir anything up on Wanda De Berneres."

"Thanks. How is the java?" Signe asked, as she stood to leave.

"Great," the Chief said reaching for the phone.

Signe went to her messy desk and called Sven Torvaldson. She asked about the tail and background research on Wanda. Sven had a preliminary report. Wanda lived with Anthony in a three bedroom apartment on St. Michael's Drive. They shared a small office south of the plaza. The electronic antennae on the roof were for monitoring the police band and tracking several 'bugs' they had placed on vehicles. Signe's Crown Vic had a tracking device on it as did her BMW and even the Chief's car. Wanda was usually out of the office all day. She spent her time tailing people, and lately Signe was often the objective. Signe got a funny visual of herself driving around Santa Fe with Wanda tailing behind her by one and one half blocks and Sven's tail on Wanda one and one half blocks behind that. If Signe could only hook up with Sven's tail they would complete a perfect circle. Wanda also monitored several sites around town-the La Fonda Hotel, the Coyote Café, Tanta Maria's and The Pink Adobe. She had a boyfriend, Roger, closer to her own age, that Tony Squitero didn't know about. Roger worked as a waiter at The Compound another restaurant on Canyon Road. They usually met at Roger's apartment on Calle Le Paz in the middle of the day. They had noisy sex that the person tailing her could hear from the parking lot.

The background check on Wanda De Berneres revealed that she was born to an Italian American family in Newark, New Jersey. Her folks still lived there. She grew up poor and started turning tricks at age fourteen for extra money. While engaged in these extracurricular activities she met Michelangelo Bachechi, a New York crime boss under don. She left home at age fifteen to be with him. She liked the expensive clothes and fancy hotels. He was good to her for a while but he had a history of abuse and soon began hitting Wanda. Michelangelo was very jealous and didn't care for the way other men looked at the voluptuous young Wanda. When they got to their apartment after a night of ogling, Michelangelo would lock the front door and then corner Wanda in a room. He beat her with his open hand and also with his fists. Once he stripped her, tied her up and burned her with a hot cigarette on her flank and below her breast. Wanda would be too sore and bruised after the beatings to go out for two or three days. Michelangelo was always contrite and attentive and sweet for weeks afterward but Wanda felt trapped and just wanted to disappear.

She didn't have a lot of options. Her folks made it very clear that she could not come back home. Wanda started getting cash back on every purchase and hiding it in one of her boots. After four months she had $4,000 but she realized that it might take her over two years to get enough money to leave. She started looking around for someone who would want her, and was also powerful enough to protect her from Michelangelo. She settled on Anthony Squitero. He was a hit man for Michelangelo's organized crime boss and even though physically unattractive was known to be totally ruthless. He always stared at Wanda. He was crazy for her brown eyes, black hair and angel face. His gawking had been responsible for two of her beatings. Now every time the family had a meeting, Wanda flirted with Anthony. She would meet him in closets, spare bedrooms and on roofs. She would let him fondle her breasts and run his hand up her skirt. Finally one afternoon when Michelangelo was out of town he came to her apartment and helped her pack her things.

Anthony doted on Wanda and fulfilled her every wish. Unfortunately, Wanda may have been caught up in the two fatal kidnappings of scions of New Jersey families. Anthony was certainly a player if not the mastermind in both cases. Wanda was with Anthony during the time the two unfortunate millionaires disappeared, and Wanda and Anthony seemed to work together. The New Jersey authorities were still actively investigating these two high profile cases. If Wanda or Anthony got convicted of either crime they could be looking at long jail sentences.

Signe thanked Sven for the report, and asked that he forward it to her in writing. She felt she wanted to apply some pressure on Wanda by searching her home and office. The excuse for the search warrant was the tracking device placed on the Chief's car. She told Chief Hartford about her suspicion and asked for the keys to his vehicle. She drove it over to the police garage herself, and asked the mechanics to search it thoroughly for a tracking device. They found a small device in the left rear wheel well with its antenna up and a flashing red light indicating that it was working.

Armed with the device, Signe returned to the Chief's office, and the Chief readily signed a search warrant for Wanda and Anthony's office and apartment. Signe raced off to the courthouse to find a judge. Judge Manny Ramirez, newly appointed was in his office and signed for Signe once she explained the case. Signe collected Jack and two other officers and headed toward Mr. Anthony Squitero's office. They took three squad cars to make a show and pulled up to the door with lights flashing and sirens whooping. Signe led the way with her search warrant covered in official blue paper held high in her right hand. For the very first time Signe thought 'Tony the Squid' looked surprised. Wanda was shaking. While the other officers crated up computers and files with Anthony objecting, Signe surreptitiously pulled Wanda aside.

"I need to talk to you, urgently," Signe said. "You are about to get yourself into a lot of difficulty, and the outcome will be a very long prison sentence. I may be able to help you avoid that, but we need to talk soon."

Wanda put her index finger over her lips in a 'shush' sign. She hurriedly wrote on paper, 'meet me Plaza Taos 6 tomorrow eve.' Then she walked away. Detective Sorensen realized that Wanda must be very afraid. Signe joined the other officers cataloguing and carrying Mr. Squitero's belongings out to the squad cars. Finally, with all of his bravado gone, Tony sat in one of his desk chairs looking dejectedly at his nearly empty office.

PART 4

CHAPTER 31

There was a part of Signe that really enjoyed executing a search warrant. She thought of herself as always fair and even handed when dealing with culpable criminals. However, roaring up to Anthony Squitero's office with several squad cars and busting into his little den with several other officers pleased her deeply. She had been irritated and bridling since she first met Squitero in the Chief's office. She found 'Tony the Squid' to be arrogant, clever, unkempt, anarchistic and by history vicious. She liked pawing through his papers and files and ordering his private things taken out to a squad car. Signe hoped that somewhere in this voluminous material she would find the links to the murder that so far had eluded her.

She needed an update from Sven Torvaldson on the tails he had placed on the principal players. He had already told her a great deal of useful information about Wanda but she wanted to know more. She had finally agreed to dinner with Sven, and she was looking actually forward to it. She relished the idea of being able to spend an evening of speaking Danish while puzzling out his Swedish. They had agreed to meet at The Palace. Signe was early but Sven had gotten there first. He stood, greeted her with a hug and gave her a single yellow rose. Detective Sorensen was charmed. So, he still remembers me flirting with him the first time we met, she thought. Over cocktails he told Signe what his people had discovered. First, he said there was no new information on Wanda De Berneres. Beyond the extensive info he had given her a week ago. They talked about the raid on Anthony's office and the note Wanda slipped her. Anxious to move on Signe promised to call Sven after her meeting with Wanda in Taos the next evening.

Sven's sleuths had delved into the seedy backgrounds of Anthony Squitero and Dirk Patterson. A lot was available on the barrister. However, not nearly as much information was available on Anthony Squitero. Sven attributed this fact to his Mafia ties. The Cosa Nostra had spent decades destroying records and bribing officials so that their members appeared opaque. In spite of this, the insurance company found that by increased 'application of funds' nonexistent information suddenly became available. Using this tactic they had discovered that Anthony Squitero was born in New Jersey and by age eleven was running numbers for the mob in Paterson, New Jersey. He graduated, after dropping out of school at age fourteen, to working fulltime for the mob mainly destroying property and committing robberies. Often the victims were businesses that had failed to pay protection money to the mob.

Later, Anthony moved into the 'family's' prostitution houses to provide security and bring back wayward hookers. In his mid twenties the family expanded some operations into lower Manhattan from New Jersey. As part of this expansion the Gambino family that was already operating in this area had to either be neutralized or eliminated. Tony befriended some of the young Gambino crime family members. Once these young dons trusted him, Anthony murdered more than one, usually with a garrote. His moniker was 'Tony the Squid'.

For the next fifteen years Tony worked for the family. Most of his activity during those years was lost. However, records show he wasn't rising in the ranks of the Benevento crime family at a time when the family's strength and power were growing. He wasn't promoted to section head, or under don with preparation for becoming a don. In truth the Mafia is like a University. In the latter institution faculty start out as instructors and then are promoted to assistant, associate and finally full professors. In the Cosa Nostra (literally 'our affair') the testing, winnowing, and promoting ended with a don, the equivalent of a full tenured university professor. For some reason Anthony Squitero's development in this system was thwarted. Most likely at some point he started to free lance. Whenever he could, he did work for groups outside the Benevento family. Sometimes semi-legitimate businesses or small Mafia families needed crimes committed. Most likely a person similar to Tony would be contacted and on completion paid in cash. There are no 401k's or other retirement plans in the mob (too many records); so Tony was just looking out for his future.

In his late 40's Tony almost certainly shifted into another line of work. In the early 1990's three prominent New Jersey socialites and industrialists were kidnapped. Each family worked closely with the FBI. Wiretaps were set up, ransom money was packed with exploding purple dye packs and small tracking devices were secreted in valises packed with unmarked bills. While the ransoms never got paid, none of the three victims were ever recovered. The bodies of one banker and one heiress were never found. The third victim, Madame Sarah Thompson, heiress to a Geigy drug fortune, supporter of the arts, humanitarian, and grandmother to fourteen grandchildren was found in a shallow grave near Secaucus. The publicity filled the front pages of the New Jersey papers for over a year.

The lesson prominent families took from these three cases, especially the Thompson case, was: don't cooperate with the authorities, instead pay the ransom and hopefully retrieve your loved one. Later that year, when the young scion of a Newark family, owners of a multinational software company, disappeared the large wealthy family showed remarkable cohesiveness and restraint and adhered to this lesson.

The authorities were not notified. When the ransom call was made, the family quietly assembled the $2,000,000 in cash in small unmarked bills from twenty-three banks so as not to alert the authorities. They delivered the money as instructed without tracers, radio transmitters or investigators watching through binoculars. Then they waited. The young executive did not reappear. A year later a young investigative reporter in Newark broke the story from an anonymous tip. Public opinion was on the side of the family even though the FBI struggled to say that the way the family conducted themselves seldom had a good outcome.

The next kidnapping was a carbon copy of the 'Software Steven' case, the press's name for the unfortunate Newark victim. The authorities weren't notified, the ransom was paid and the victim never reappeared. As both prominent families moved out of New Jersey and relocated their industrial and banking appendages to Arizona, the authorities continued to investigate. Their conclusion was that both crimes were committed by the same gang and that at least four people were involved. After months of pushing on 'snitches', tracking down hundreds of anonymous tips and combing abandoned buildings one possible hiding place from the 'Software Steven' case was found. The site was clean except for a fiber that may have been from the victim's shirt and a partial finger print that had only four match points on it, not enough for a positive identification. When run through all their criminal data bases they discovered there were nineteen possible matches and one was 'Tony the Squid'.

While Sven was talking and showing documents, he and Signe had shared a piquant ceviche appetizer with shrimp and fish in a cold tomato-cilantro broth. They each also had a large helping of Caesar salad made at table side.

The FBI in New Jersey was fairly certain that Mr. Squitero was involved in both brutal kidnappings and that he might have been the ringleader. Yet despite years of trying they could pin nothing on him. He had committed two perfect crimes along with several murders and would get away with it.

Sven averred that unlike Tony researching Dirk Patterson's background was much easier. He had cut a wide and public swath through his life with no destruction of documents. He was born in Beaumont, Texas in 1946. His father was an oil refinery worker who left permanently when his youngest son, Dirk, was six months old. Dirk's mom worked as a maid at the local Beaumont Hilton. With three children to raise on her own and a low paying job; they lived poor. They rented a clapboard shotgun house that abutted one of the refineries. It was noisy in the house and never dark because the huge yellow flames from the flaring natural gas at the refinery lit the sky even on the darkest night. Dirk grew up dirty and poorly dresses with few friends. He did poorly in school and dreamed of moving away and of being wealthy.

At sixteen, dropped out of high school to take a job at the Amoco refinery in town where he made four dollars an hour; twice what his mother made. After a year and a half he realized if he was very lucky and after working ten years the most he could make at that job would be nine dollars an hour. He wanted to own an oil company; *not* work in one of their refineries. So he went back and finished high school in a year and started at the local junior college while working part-time at the refinery. It took him six years to get a bachelors degree in education. The last thing he wanted to be was a teacher but the courses in that curriculum were plentiful and easy and it got him the degree he needed. More than anything, Dirk wanted to make a lot of money fast. He looked at a list of the 100 richest people in America. Almost everyone on the list from Rockefeller on down had inherited their millions. He looked in the local newspaper, the *Beaumont Enterprise*, for the names and occupations of socialites and prominent citizens. Dirk found they fell into four categories: wealthy inheritants, businessmen, doctors and lawyers. Medicine was a sure thing but it took too many years of school before the money came in. A career in business took no school, but the chances of succeeding without a brilliant idea or even with one were small. That left the law, since he hadn't inherited as much as a savings bond. Only three years of school were required to become a lawyer and there were lots of shady areas in the legal field that looked appealing to Dirk.

Dirk applied to five law schools and got rejected by each. The next year he applied to fifteen law schools, wrote an essay about his poor upbringing and invented some community service with black children in nearby Port

Arthur. Working with disadvantaged blacks in the south in 1972 was a ticket to higher education. Fourteen law schools rejected him but one school accepted him. The South Texas College of Law took the bait and without a lot of investigation into his background admitted Dirk Patterson in 1973. Located in a nondescript skyscraper in Houston, the ST College of Law was a freestanding law school diploma mill. The school was only seventy-seven miles from Dirk's home in east Beaumont so he commuted for three years. He graduated in 1976 with below average grades. Sven modified the old joke for Signe. "What do you call the dope that graduates at the absolute bottom of his law school class, at the most academically deficient law school in the country, Signe?"

"I don't know." Signe giggled back. She was 'just off the boat', so to speak, from Denmark after all.

"Councilor," Sven shot back.

CHAPTER 32

Sven and Signe's identical rare rib eye steaks arrived from The Palace's kitchen at the part of the story where Dirk was starting to drag himself up by his boot straps. After law school, he spent the next three years trying to pass the Texas bar exam and found he just couldn't. He was working as a clerk in a large Beaumont law firm that did defense and plaintiff's work, making the nine dollars per hour that he could have aspired to in the refinery. He had already decided that plaintiff's work was more financially rewarding and he wanted to practice in that area, but first he had to pass a bar exam. He checked the surrounding states and found that the State of New Mexico, immediately to the west of Texas, had an easier exam. However, Dirk didn't relish spending three more years trying to pass the New Mexico exam. He felt he had already given up $400,000 in lifetime income by failing the Texas bar repeatedly. So he hired a surrogate to take the exam for him.

Sleuthing had shown Dirk that only a New Mexico driver's license was necessary to gain admittance to the bar exam in that state. He found a brilliant young lawyer in Albuquerque, named Paul Berger, who would take the exam for Dirk. Paul Berger, esquire, was arrogant enough to offer a money back guarantee, at least verbally. Although brilliant, Paul had few clients after six years in practice in the Duke City because of his truculent marginal personality, Sven reported. Clients and other lawyers alike despised him. Paul needed the money. After some negotiation Paul agreed to take the exam for Dirk for $60,000 in cash and a fake driver's license. Dirk went to the south valley and returned with a respectable fake New Mexico license that afternoon. The cash was more of a problem, but Paul introduced the future barrister to a pawn broker who loaned him the money on the spot at an interest rate of 50% annually. The pawn broker actually opened an old brown floor safe in his office and pulled out a huge stack of worn $100 dollar bills held together by rubber bands. Dirk reluctantly and despairingly agreed to the terms; after counting the money twice he handed the bundle to Paul.

Paul, as Dirk, registered for the New Mexico state bar exam one month later, took the exam three months later, and had passed with a very high score in nine months when the New Mexico board got around to reporting the results. Dirk had already applied to several large firms in Albuquerque with the sole idea of paying off his debt to the pawn broker quickly. The day Paul called with the good news; Dirk took a job with a thirty-five lawyer firm in Albuquerque at $35,000 a year. The firm was called the Trunk law firm and named after their founder, Tyler Trunk. They had a reputation for suing anybody anytime and then working toward a quick settlement. Dirk used his contract with the firm to negotiate a loan from a bank, which was also a client, to borrow the money he needed to pay off the pawn broker. Dirk stayed at the firm for three years. The day he became debt free he resigned with no notice. Dirk realized that it had taken him two years to get into law school, three years to go to law school, four years to pass the bar and three years to pay off his debt from having someone take his bar exam. In those twelve years he could have easily gone to medical school, interned and done a residency in ophthalmology the most lucrative medical subspecialty.

After leaving the Trunk firm, Dirk opened an office on Central Avenue in a store front with one underpaid secretary. He called his former clients from the Trunk law firm and other lawyers he knew to solicit business. He did defense work for petty criminals, handled divorces and wrote contracts for small businesses. Unfortunately for Dirk in 1983 lawyers didn't advertise, so he went to social events, conferences and joined business clubs. By 2002 the advertising picture had changed and ninety-seven pages in the Albuquerque yellow pages were devoted to color, often full page ads, for attorneys. Barrister's faces appeared in color ads on the back and even front page of the book. Gradually Dirk's appointment book began to fill up mostly from contacts at Rotary and the country club.

In the spring of 1984 Dirk met a New Jersey transplant, Michelangelo Bachechi. Sven reminded Signe that he had been part of Wanda's tale. He had to leave New Jersey because of a credible death threat from a rival gang. There was little organized crime in New Mexico at the time and Michelangelo saw this as a business opportunity. He used Santa Fe Downs as his first target. There were always gamblers, shady characters and sharp dressing idlers at a track. He added prostitution, a small numbers racket and started collecting protection money from strip joints and bars. Michelangelo and Dirk hit it off and Michelangelo put Dirk on retainer for his firm-San Mateo

Enterprises. From that moment on Dirk was 'dirty'. He did anything he was asked to do to advance San Mateo Enterprises.

Sven caught Signe yawning behind her napkin so he put away the documents and they shared Bananas Foster and strong coffee. But nothing was reviving Signe. Sven walked her to her BMW and kissed her. Signe liked it. She ran her hand through his wavy blond hair, said good night, and left.

The next morning, Signe's head was still spinning with all the information Sven had given her the night before. She spent the early part of the day cataloguing and reviewing the material from Anthony's office. Many of the files related to expenses and the numbers were large. There were extensive documents from weeks of tailing multiple people in Santa Fe including Signe, Chief Hartford, two other detectives, Judge Terecita Armijo and Judge Manny Ramirez. Someone had caught Judge Ramirez in a deserted park with his hand far up the skirt of a girl who looked to be only fifteen or sixteen. There were embarrassing pictures of Signe with Vincent from the night the two were necking in her car and also from *Kasha Katuwe* where they had done more than kiss. Seeing the pictures made Signe furious. Scattered through the files were several small folders marked in the upper right hand corner with an upside down backward capital 'F'. She laid them out on the table and studied each. There seemed to be no common thread. One was about eating expenses, two about car repairs, four concerned purchases of electronic eavesdropping gear. She set those nine folders aside. She took one to the crime lab for analysis of the paper, ink and infrared scanning and heating to look for a hidden message.

After lunch she got a teletype from the Mexican aviation authorities about the plane that may have transported the Hercules out of the country. No planes had landed at Jiménez on the 3rd and 4th of October. Three planes had landed in Hildago del Parra on the 3rd and one on the 4th. Of special interest to Signe was a 9:45 p.m. landing of a Convair CV-580; the very type of plane that could have been carrying the horse. The plane was registered to a syndicate in Mexico City, and the plane flew there next. However, Signe noted an old DC 3 of Argentinean register had arrived at the airport on the afternoon of October 3rd and left after the Convair. This seemed more than a coincidence. Detective Sorensen wondered if the horse had been transferred to the DC 3. She sent more inquires to the Mexican authorities.

She also checked with all the airlines that flew to the Cayman Islands, Barbados, and Switzerland. There was no record of Wanda, Dirk or Anthony flying to those locations in October. So the money trail was still cold. Perhaps they flew to another location or traveled under an alias, Signe thought. She would check Anthony's files for aliases and check flights to Venezuela, Cambodia and Thailand.

It was time to leave for her meeting in Taos. She knew she would be tailed yet still considered going alone in her own beautiful new BMW. However, she remembered that while driving in New Mexico she had been pushed off the road and fired on twice. She revised her plan. She would go to the meeting with Jack in the Crown Vic. If that spooked Wanda and she didn't show; so be it. Jack checked all the survival supplies in the car and added extra ammo before picking Signe up at 2 PM. They both wanted to be in Taos early to investigate the Plaza area before the meeting.

Signe and Jack headed north on US 285 past the Opera, past Pojoaque and through the maze of roads into the not very prosperous and sprawling town of Espanola. On the north side of town they took route 68, following the Rio Grande River toward Taos. The road narrows and twists as the cliffs on each side rise higher and higher. The second longest river in America, the Rio Grande, has a narrow deep course here. It runs through dark almost black granular volcanic rock. In mid November the river is a slender ribbon of silver and blue splashing against the rocks. The road turns toward the east, rising, away from the river, and popping out on a flat plain before the city itself.

Taos Pueblo, a multistory adobe structure, was constructed about 1350 by the Athabascan people. Indians have occupied the pueblo ever since. The village just to the south was founded by Don Juan Onate's colonists in 1598. Religious strife between the Indian's animism and the Catholicism of the Spanish smoldered for nearly 100 years. Finally, in 1680 the pueblo dwellers revolted and massacred 70 settlers and priests in Taos. Over the next three hundred years Taos had remained a peaceful village.

CHAPTER 33

Today Taos is a small historic town of only six thousand. It is a picturesque but impractical village as evidenced by the fact that it has over eighty art galleries. The plaza is a sleepy, dusty little space much smaller than the plaza in Santa Fe or Albuquerque. Signe and Jack parked the Crown Vic out of sight, but close at hand behind the variety store on the north side of the plaza. They walked the plaza three times looking for sight lines for guns or binoculars and noticing places where a person or camera could be hidden.

After casing the plaza Jack picked a spot on the southwest corner where he could be hidden behind a kiosk with two pistols and the .223 sniper rifle. As six o'clock approached Signe stayed in the variety store with a good view of the whole plaza. By six ten Signe had not spotted Wanda. Perhaps she wasn't going to show. Signe refocused her attention on an Indian woman sitting on the west side under a portico. The woman was wrapped in a shawl with a blanket spread in front of her. On the blanket were pieces of Indian jewelry and pots. However, only three or four items of each were displayed. In Santa Fe the Pueblo Indians had the right to sell wares on the portico of the Inn of the Governors on the north side of the plaza. Signe had seen hundreds of such colorful jewelry displays in Santa Fe. There they would display bundles of turquoise necklaces and bracelets and dozens of pots on one blanket.

Signe decided to walk over and investigate. The plaza was nearly empty on this late fall evening. When she got there she picked up a necklace and handled the stones.

"This is plastic!" Signe yelled.

"You're late Detective," Wanda answered from her Indian disguise. "I saw you and your partner casing the square."

"I've been shot at twice and run off the road once, Wanda," Signe said. "I'm just trying to stay alive long enough to solve this case. Do you blame me?"

"No. I guess I don't," Wanda said pushing her shawl back some. "You know I wasn't involved in any of those crimes, don't you?"

"I was pretty sure that you weren't, Wanda." Signe replied. "But a whole lot of other stuff is starting to come out about this murder and you could easily get sucked down with it."

"I think you're right and that's why I agreed to talk with you." Wanda replied.

"You shot Dick Lederback, Detective," Wanda said. "He worked for Anthony at least some of the time. I know Anthony planned your 'accident' on the freeway. But someone else gave the order for the shootings at Otowi Crossing and in Wagon Mound. I know Anthony wasn't involved because we heard the news together after it happened both times. Anthony met with Dick several times but Lederback wasn't a big talker. I never heard him say he was working for someone else."

"After the murder did you or Anthony make any trips, Wanda?" Signe enquired.

"Yeah. Anthony sent me to the Barbados in a private plane. I traveled under an alias. How does Rosie Bachechi sound? I had a red satchel that he told me to keep with me always. He told me to never take my eyes off of it even when I was peeing or putting on makeup. I took it to a bank in Bridgetown."

"Did you look in the satchel, Wanda?" Signe asked.

"No. It wasn't locked, but Anthony told me exploding purple dye packs were in the satchel," Wanda replied. "You know, like they put with the cash in a bank robbery? I was afraid to open it. I didn't even let the satchel jiggle. That dye is permanent."

"So you don't know what was in the satchel, but you think it was money because you took it to a bank," Signe enquired.

"I know what was in it," Wanda said quickly. "The bank manager opened the satchel in front of me. Anthony was lying about the dye. It was full of bundles of $100 bills, just stuffed full."

So, Signe thought, I have solved the money trail. I know where the payoff is. Unfortunately finding out who has access to the account will be very difficult. Getting account information in the Caymans is easy with a small bribe. The Barbadians are as tight as the Swiss with account information. Maybe Sven can help.

"Tell me about Tony's relationship with Dirk Patterson." Signe said.

Wanda looked around the plaza from under her shawl and didn't seem to find anything alarming.

"I know that Dirk was supposed to pay Anthony's expenses and salary in Santa Fe." Wanda began. "They met every week for a long lunch. I was never invited. I hated to be around Mr. Patterson he would always pat my ass and rub my tits. I tried to stay away whenever I could."

"Wanda, do you think Dirk murdered his daughter Chloe?" Signe asked.

"By meeting with you Detective I'm risking my life," Wanda said in a wavering tone. "I'm done talking. We'll meet in a wee to talk more. You can tell me how you plan to protect me then." Wanda pulled her shawl up and tipped her head down further.

"Thank you, Wanda. I appreciate your openness." Signe concluded and walked to the southwest corner of the Plaza. As Signe and Jack pointed the Crown Vic south through the gorge, the black sky and black volcanic rock seemed particularly ominous to Signe. During the drive back to Santa Fe Signe told Jack what she had learned. She had gotten some answers but now had even more questions.

Just as Jack and Signe were driving by Pojoaque on the way back into Santa Fe, Signe got a call on her cell phone. It was Svelty Patterson and she was in a panic. She had been nosing around in Dirk's records and she was afraid he had become suspicious. Svelty said she had found evidence of financial irregularities at the firm and wanted to give Signe some documents. Signe offered to come to Albuquerque right then. Svelty said she couldn't get out of the house. She would meet Signe in the spa of the Hyatt's Tamaya Resort on the Santa Ana reservation near Bernalillo at 10 a.m. tomorrow and then hurriedly hung up.

Signe pulled up to the elegant adobe styled chocolate brown resort at 9:30 the next morning. The resort sat in broad field beside the bosque with a million dollar view of cottonwoods along the Rio Grande and the Sandia Mountains rising above the trees. Signe found the spa on the second floor and as she entered the smell of herbs hit her nostrils. Several well kept middle-aged women padded around in white robes with the Hyatt coat of arms emblazoned over their left breast. As a European, Signe found American women vastly pampered and yet unappreciative of all they were given. She pushed that thought down and took a seat in the ante room amongst huge colored tubes of herbal concoctions. She picked up a copy of *Cosmopolitan* and started to read.

Svelty padded up in her slippers with a white robe on and her hair wrapped in white towel done up like a turban. She had a light green sticky looking material all over her face. She looked like a gecko in a boxer's costume. Svelty motioned Signe to one of the massage rooms and Svelty lay down on the massage table. An attendant put slices of cucumber over her eyes and scurried out.

"Thanks for coming on such short notice, Detective," Svelty said. "I've been worried since we talked. Dirk has been awful. He's gone a lot but when he is around he's short and abusive. I've been more and more afraid."

"Tell me how I can help," Signe said. "Do you think he is involved in this crime?"

"I don't know at this point," Svelty said. "He's been gone so much that it's been easy to snoop. I rifled his desk first. I found the key to his files and I went through each of them. Most of them were old and related to real estate deals and stock purchases. But some are about Anthony Squitero. Dirk had been getting a lot of bills from him over the past month. I didn't see any e-mails or reports back to my husband from Mr. Squitero. Perhaps he keeps those reports elsewhere. In any case, I'm afraid. When he is home he's verbally abusive and once he got so angry he struck me. He's never behaved like that. I know that creditors are hounding him. I see the bills coming in everyday. I may just disappear."

"I don't think that's a good idea, Svelty." Signe said. She could see tears running out from under the cucumber slices and causing the green goop on Svelty's face to run. "He can find you anywhere in the world. You need to get more information, and give it to me so I can charge him with his crimes. Does he have a safe?"

"Yes. But I can't find the combination," Svelty sighed.

"The safe comes with a combination that can not be changed, Svelty." Signe began. "Since the numbers are randomly assigned at the factory they are not easy to remember." Signe, the polymath continued. "He has to have written them down perhaps in code somewhere that he can easily access. Most people aren't devious enough to hide the numbers in a page of figures like a German cryptogram. Usually what you're looking for is a chain of four or five two digit numbers. You must find the combination, Svelty. Your safety depends on it. I also want you to go back through the files and look for upside down and backward capital 'F's'."

"You should go Detective before the staff becomes suspicious. I will call you." Svelty concluded in a small sad voice that was barely audible. Driving back to Santa Fe, Signe realized that she had succeeded in flipping both Wanda and Svelty. However, she knew she needed to move quickly. Anthony and Dirk were both very closed and very clever and may have kept the information that Signe needed from the women in their lives. Both women were in grave danger.

CHAPTER 34

The crime had occurred exactly six weeks ago. Signe felt frustrated. She wanted it solved. Her former Chief in Copenhagen, would at this point, have sat her down with a good cup of strong Danish coffee and said, "Don't be so impatient, Signe." Then he would have reminded her that she had found the horse with little help from anyone. She had found the money trail. She had flipped the women that slept with two potential perps and taken the criminal's shooter out with a clean shot. Besides, he would say, that complicated murder cases, which this one certainly was, on average took six to eighteen months to solve. He wouldn't remind her that only sixty some percent of such cases are ever solved. She missed Chief Nielsen, her former boss. She had no one in New Mexico to mentor her quite like he did. Perhaps she would call him for ideas on the case.

Signe had lunch with Vincent and caught him up on the visits she had had with the two *hetaerae*. It was a Greek word she had learned in school and it meant courtesan or mistress in an ancient society where such a role was valued. Signe had started thinking of Wanda and Svelty as *hetaerae* because both were with men they didn't love yet they acquiesced to the relationships for financial reasons. What did that make her? Signe wondered. She slept with men and women for sexual release and without commitment. Did she need a 'sugar mommy or daddy'? After discussing the case, Signe asked her boyfiend how he was doing. Vincent said that he was fine. He felt he was learning everyday and getting better at the State Police work. He was just sorry Signe was so busy that they got to spend little time together, and that it was always on short notice.

After lunch Signe had her follow-up visit with the department shrink, Dr. Vivian Goldiamond. Signe reported that she was sleeping better and had such a good appetite that she had gained seven pounds. She felt less anxious and was enjoying sex, even if it was infrequent. Dr. Goldiamond admired smart patients with good memories. In two sentences Signe had given Vivian an update on all the important somatic symptoms of depression. The implication was that Signe was doing well. They talked about the case including the successful trip to Argentina and the new leads.

Signe spoke at length about her meetings with Wanda and Svelty comparing and contrasting the two *hetaerae*. Svelty broke down at one point and told Signe about a very bad period she had between the age of seven and nine. She was still wetting the bed. She beat three family cats with sticks. One died. She set fire to a shed, and also to the neighbor's garage which burned to the ground. Svelty described herself as being perfectly normal since then. After listening carefully, Vivian commented that both women appeared similar with Svelty pretending to be an iota classier but that she suspected that they were actually quite dissimilar. Dr. Goldiamond thought that Wanda was dependent and a rescuer. She was probably very manipulative with a high level borderline personality. Vivian told Signe to be wary around Wanda who saw things as black or white, and Wanda's behavior could easily flip right before Signe's eyes. Dr. Goldiamond saw Svelty as complicity in illegal activity which she had known about for years. She stayed with her husband not out of fear, but because she liked gaming the system and other people. Vivian thought Svelty might be that rare entity, a female sociopath. Of the two, Vivian thought Svelty was the more dangerous. She went on to say that almost certainly both women had suffered physical and sexual abuse as children and that if Signe delved into that area with them both, they should be more cooperative with her investigation.

Ten minutes was left in the hour and Signe was out of topics so she casually mentioned her sex life. Dr. Goldiamond perked up immediately and asked some probing questions before the hour was up. Vivian said, now, she wanted Signe back in a week and gave her some issues to think about in the mean time. Signe fervently wished she had been mute for the last ten minutes.

After a quick late lunch, she came back to the station house for a meeting with Sven. She had remembered earlier that she never heard the end of Dirk's story the other evening as fatigue had set in after their large meal. Mr. Torvaldson had agreed to drive up from Albuquerque. He breezed in with two large strong coffees from Starbucks. First he reminded Signe of Dirk's early history up until 1997 when he went to work for Mr. Bachechi, Wanda's abuser at San Mateo Enterprises.

Sven described Dirk's rise from there as meteoric. San Mateo was involved in garbage removal, construction and the laundry business as well as more traditional mob activities such as gambling, prostitution and drug dealing. Each branch of SME had legal issues which Patterson handled. Also, suddenly, Dirk Patterson was the plaintiff's lawyer in almost every major auto or industrial accident in Bernalillo County. His offices kept getting bigger and he was doing more and more advertising. It seemed that nothing could stop him. Then suddenly in November of 2001 the juggernaut stalled and later collapsed. Cases fell to 40% of what filings had been, and Dirk had never recovered. Sven had no plausible explanation at this time for the change. There was no seminal case that affected his reputation. There were no changes in the law or influx of new attorneys. Analysts at the Assurance's central office were looking at other possible parameters.

Mr. Patterson tried doubling his advertising budget to no effect. He hired consultants that showed him graphs of his dramatic decline in business, but offered no explanation for the change. He even went to a fortune teller, Mrs. Croucher in the south valley. About this time he took up with a brunette from The Wild Pony and even gave her a job as a 'secretary' in his office. None of the other secretaries and clerks liked her. Svelty took one look at Honey and knew exactly what she was about. Dirk joined the Albuquerque Shootist's League and became an expert with a pistol, rifle and shotgun. He had never owned guns before. He won several competitions at the League for accuracy.

As the cases dried up, so did the cash flow. He dipped into savings and then retirement in the first few months. Then he sold his real estate holdings in New Mexico and Texas. He was in such a hurry he often took a low ball offer. He took out a mortgage on his office and sold part of his equipment and furniture for pennies on the dollar. As quickly as he sold assets it never seemed to be fast enough and Dirk sank further and further into debt. He had always been a bit of a drinker but it got much worse. There is evidence he started to use drugs for the first time in his life.

"Right now his expenses still exceed his income by about $25,000 a month," Sven continued. "He is on the razor edge of bankruptcy just moving money every week from one bank to another, and taking out more and more credit cards. His house of cards will collapse in two or three months without a huge infusion of cash. I think, Signe that is where settling with my company comes in. He's putting as lot of pressure on American National at the corporate level."

"I hope you don't have to pay him, Sven." Signe said. "The financial pressure may help flush him out, forcing him to make a mistake so that I can see his true role in this awful murder."

"Believe me, Signe, we do not want to pay this death benefit, however, we are running out of options. I suspect we will be forced to give Mr. Patterson the money within a month." Sven said despairingly. Mr. Torvaldson was just getting up to leave when his cell phone rang. The call was brief and he hung up dejectedly. "Wanda has disappeared." He said. "That was one of her tails. They hadn't seen her since yesterday afternoon. No one thought much of it. She often holed up in the apartment for twenty-four or thirty-six hours. This morning they got suspicious and faked a visit from the phone company. She had decamped with most of her things."

Signe instantly jumped onto the department's antiquated computer. She entered the FBI's national travel net and punched in 'Wanda De Berneres'. No travel by air, bus or train showed up in the last week. Wanda had told Signe her alias, and she had written it down after their interview. At first Signe couldn't find her notebook. Her 'new' desk was now almost as cluttered as her old desk. She flipped papers and files out of the way quickly, and at last found her notebook. She checked her Danish scribbles from the interview and there, on the bottom of the second page, it was 'Rosie Bachechi'. She punched that into the computerized travel net. Rosie Bachechi had flown from Albuquerque to Houston on Continental flight 644 the previous morning and then switched to Continental Flight 779 to La Guardia arriving at 6:18 p.m. Great, Signe thought, Wanda De Berneres is in the wind.

CHAPTER 35

Signe thanked Sven for all the information. She left the station and quickly drove to Anthony Squitero's office. Fortunately he was still working. Signe knocked and then walked in.

"I should have most of your files back in two days, Mr. Squitero," Signe began.

"It's pretty fucking hard to run an office with no files and no secretary, Detective," Anthony snarled.

"Yes. I noticed that Wanda wasn't here. I actually came to ask her a question. Where is she?" Signe replied.

"How should I know, Detective? She moved out of the apartment the night before last. She didn't say a word. We've been together for seven years," Anthony said dejectedly.

"I need to find her, Tony," Signe continued. "Do you know where she would go? Does she have friends or relatives? Does she have an assumed name?

"Her family still hates her, but I love her and I want her back," Anthony said thoughtfully. "She has a friend in New Jersey, Michelle Sorrento. They're close and talk every week. Come to think of it, she does have an alias. She hasn't used it for forever, but it's Sandra Vitari. I can get you Michelle's phone number if that will help."

"Just call it to the station, Tony. I'll get right on it." Signe said as she left. As soon as she was alone she called Sven Torvaldson with the information about Wanda's friend. He said he would work on it right away. Time was running short for his company.

As Signe drove home she tried to decide why Wanda had left. Had Anthony found out about her meeting with Signe? Had he threatened her? Was she fleeing for her life? Was she just getting out of an untenable situation with a man she had never loved? Signe knew that Wanda, or Sandra, or Rosie or whatever name she was going by was her best lead right now at least until Svelty cracked Dirk's safe. Signe had to find her. She would start moving toward La Guardia before the trail got cold and hopefully by then Sven's excellent sleuths would have some more leads on Wanda's whereabouts. When she got home she booked a seat on the American Airline's early flight to O'Hare continuing on to New York's La Guardia. She packed her things and drove to Albuquerque so she wouldn't have to get up at 2 a.m.

On the drive down she noticed a blue Taurus openly tailing her. She had time, so she took the tail on a long wild goose chase through the north valley and along Central Avenue with long stops at each block for red lights. As she approached the airport the tail disappeared. She parked the BMW in long term parking and rode the shuttle to the Airport Hilton where she asked for a 5:30 a.m. wake up call. The next morning, Detective Sorensen went through security in the line for pilots and flight attendants. She got through easily with both of her guns after showing her badge, and boarded the plane first. The flight to New York was uneventful. She scanned all the other coach passengers as they got on thinking she might recognize her tail, but she didn't. Signe resumed reading *Loving Pedro Infante* the book that she had started on her trip to Argentina. She marveled at the fact that she could cross nearly the entire United States in one not very long day. It was equivalent to going from her home in northern Europe to Constantinople in Asia.

As soon as she landed, Signe put in a call to Sven so that she could get an update on Wanda's possible whereabouts. His people had staked out Michelle Sorrento's apartment in Secaucus and Wanda wasn't there. However, they thought she could have passed through on her way to another location. Signe rented a Jetta for old time's sake. She took the freeway to the Bronx Whitestone Bridge, cut across the Bronx on I 95 and then across the Hudson River on the George Washington Bridge into New Jersey. It was a short drive south to Secaucus.

It was 8 p.m. when Signe arrived outside Michelle Sorrento's apartment. A young woman answered the door and Signe introduced herself. It was Michelle and she invited Signe in. Michelle resembled Wanda a great deal: five feet tall, dark hair, large brown eyes, and full figured. Signe wondered if all young women in New Jersey looked like that. Signe explained why she was worried about Wanda's safety and that she urgently needed to talk with her. Michelle said that Wanda had stopped by yesterday but Michelle didn't know where Wanda was at present. She did know that Wanda said she wasn't going back to Anthony or New Mexico. Wanda promised to call

Michelle back in a week or so. Then Michelle remembered that Wanda had given her her cell phone number. Signe thanked Michelle as she wrote it down and then Signe wrote her number on the same pad.

"Please call me if you hear from Wanda." Signe said as she walked out the front door.

Signe headed back to Manhattan to the Roosevelt Hotel where she was staying. On the way she called Sven and told him of her progress so far. It seemed clear to both of them that Wanda was fleeing from Anthony Squitero. Sven reviewed his notes and reports on Ms. Bachechi but he found nothing that revealed where she might hide. Signe took a cab to Little Italy for some lobster fettuccini and then had the cabby drive her past all the New York sights on the way back to her hotel. She got out of the cab at the World Trade Center site, and stood against the chain link fence and stared at the ruble there for several minutes.

She awoke at 6 a.m., the next morning, with an idea about how to find Wanda. She called Sven's number and a groggy female answered. She apparently passed the phone to Sven whose voice was raspy with sleep. Signe had forgotten about the time difference. It was 4 a.m. in Albuquerque.

"Sorry to wake you, but I had an idea about how to find Wanda among the millions of people out here," Signe said.

"Ya," Sven said back with a Swedish accent.

"We had an in-service on communications last month at the station house and the state tech said over half of the cell phones now have GPS on them and the subscriber doesn't usually know it's there," Signe said slowly giving him time to comprehend. "Can your technical people trace her cell phone if I give you the number?"

"That is a very clever idea, Detective." Sven said with real enthusiasm. "I'll go to the office now and call you in two hours." Signe got up and got dressed and went across the street to Grand Central Station. She went into the grill and had a nice breakfast, while watching the bustle of commuters scurrying to their trains. The J.P. Morgan Library was nearby with its Guttenberg Bible but it was too early for it to be open. She settled for a walk to the Chrysler Building and admired its Art Deco extravagances. The ground floor murals highlight inventions of the twentieth century including airplanes in extravagant detail. Her timing was perfect and when she got back to the hotel Sven called. His technicians had pulsed Wanda's phone and then scanned for the signal. Wanda De Berneres was in Franconia Notch, New Hampshire. Signe got on the hotel computer and printed herself a map. The trip would take 7 hours.

She pulled the Jetta out into rush hour traffic and immediately realized her estimate of the driving time was wrong. She struggled, block by congested block, to get out of Manhattan. An hour later she was in the Queens-Midtown Tunnel under the east river. She cut across Connecticut then Massachusetts as the countryside got prettier even without leaves on the trees, and then drove straight up the middle of the only state shaped like a spear point. She had stopped in Lowell, Massachusetts for a late lunch before crossing into New Hampshire. The drive north was increasingly pleasant stopped with fewer buildings and denser forests. The mountains began to rise on both sides of the road. As she entered Franconia Notch she pulled off for a stretch and to admire the Old Man of the Mountain, a rock cliff beside the road in the shape of a very angular man's face. Two miles further north she turned on a dirt road to the west. She at a small log cabin nestled in pine trees by a stream. On the third knock Wanda answered the door and invited Signe in. Wanda looked relaxed in a flannel shirt and jeans.

"Nice to see you, Detective," Wanda said. "I was going to give you a call once I got settled. Anthony had gotten violent and I was afraid." Signe noticed a large bruise on the left side of Wanda's face only partially obscured by heavy make up.

"I could have hidden you in New Mexico, Wanda," Signe retorted.

"You don't know how connected Anthony Squitero is," Wanda fired back. "He would have found me in a heart beat in New Mexico. Eventually he will find me here. You did."

"You are the only one that can help me, right now, Wanda," Signe said.

"Here is what I know, Detective," Wanda began. "Since October the fifth Anthony has had a continuous tail on you. Therefore he is very interested in your investigation of Chloe Patterson's death. He has also tailed other members of your department. He is employed by Dirk Patterson for these services. They have left no paper trail. That is what I know. What I suspect is that Anthony or Dirk, alone or in together, committed the theft of the horse and the murder. I am afraid of both of them and I will do whatever you want me to do to put them behind bars. I will help you go through Anthony's records. I will wear a wire. I will come back to New Mexico but not for two weeks. I want the trail to get cold. I want 'Tony the Squid' off my case and out of my life."

CHAPTER 36

"I appreciate your help, Wanda," Signe said. "It wasn't accidental that I found you, was it?"

"I left a lot of clues just for you; the alias I used was the one I told you Detective. Anthony has never heard it. A girl has to have her secrets." Wanda said. "But you sure got here quick."

"Let me buy you supper before I drive back." Signe said. They drove down to a steak house on the main road with a view of The Old Man of the Mountain. They had a pleasant meal, talking about men, their families and New Mexico. Wanda was surprised how much she liked the southwest. It was so different from New Jersey. She liked the friendly approachable people, the sunny climate and the local Santa Fe traditions like Zozobra. She thought that once this was all over she would invite her friend Michelle Sorrento to come out and live in Albuquerque.

Signe drove Wanda back to her cabin and headed back to New York. She had an early flight from LaGuardia so after her drive, which took six hours despite light traffic, she stayed near the airport. She flew back to Chicago and spent the day there at the headquarters of the American National Assurance Company in suburban Arlington Heights. She presented every aspect of her murder case to Sven's experts, and took pages of notes in Danish about avenues that might be used to solve the Patterson murder. Two of the experts took her to Le Titi de Paris in Arlington Heights for an evening of great French food. In the morning Signe took another early flight from O'Hare to Albuquerque.

She slept most of the way, but as they came in over the Manzano Mountains it was bumpy as it usually is and she awoke with a start. Her first thought was: Wanda doesn't strike me as a student of southwestern history. How would she know about Zozobra? Was she in New Mexico for the fiesta? Would she have been in Santa Fe without Anthony Squitero? It seemed unlikely. After she landed and got her luggage and her car she called Wanda.

"Thank you for being so open with me, Wanda." Signe began. "I feel that together we can solve this murder. Flying home I remembered you mentioning Zozobra. How did you know about that strange pagan custom?"

"Anthony took me the first night we were in Santa Fe," Wanda said. "I had never seen anything like it in New Jersey. Burning that fifty foot old man gloom replica was spectacular. The way his arms move, and he moans, as he's caught up in the flames as they spread higher and higher. There was some wind the night we saw him. The flames must have shot up seventy-five feet!"

"I know. My son and I lived on Fort Marcy Park road and we saw it out our window," Signe said. "It was amazing!" Signe knew that the burning of Zozobra was the climax of 'fiestas' in Santa Fe, and always occurred in the second week of September. This comment from Wanda meant that Anthony had been in Santa Fe a full three weeks before the crime! "I'll check with you at the end of week, Wanda." Signe concluded.

The trip to Santa Fe went quickly in the BMW. She arrived in the early afternoon but was weary from her whirlwind travels. Her thoughts were on her son, Axel. Soon she was thinking of the Indian clay ware the two of them had acquired. She went to her apartment rather than the police station, and spent some time examining their growing collection of Indian pots. She and Axel had started collecting them as soon as they arrived in New Mexico. Most were purchased from Indian trading posts around the northern part of the state. The pots had been pawned by Navajo, Hopi, and Pueblo Indian families and then never reclaimed. Signe and Axel found they could spend hours examining the Indian pawn. Often there was writing on the bottom of the pot but it tended to be cryptic and incomplete. Rarely did it give a name, date, and location. Axel decided that Indians lacked the European urge beginning with Carl Linnaeus to describe, catalogue and number everything.

After examining the available pots and taking notes in Danish, Signe and Axel would retire to their campground. By firelight they would compare their finds to the dog eared books on Indian earthenware that they kept in a small wooden box in the trunk of the Jetta. Based on this research, the next day they would go back and bargain for their purchases. They had a northern European aversion to haggling over price, but the pottery was expensive and if they paid the first price asked their collection would be very small. Their first strategy was simply to offer half the asking price. However, often this tender was taken. They agreed to try proffering only a quarter of the stated price even though it embarrassed them every time they did it. Then the real haggling could begin with the Danes usually paying only 40% of the asking price. Signe had a small collection of eleven pots to show for their efforts. Signe enjoyed handling the fine vessels of clay and inspecting the painted designs.

After a couple of relaxing hours with the pots she listened to her phone messages. Two were from Vincent, and one was from Axel but there were five from Jefferson Barclay. Signe called him from home because she was worried that something might be amiss. He answered on the second ring.

"Jefferson, this is Signe. Are you all right?" She said.

"Signe dear, I have never been better," He said. "I'm glad you're back and I'm anxious to talk with you. But I'd rather not do it on the phone, love."

"Can we meet tomorrow, Jefferson?" Signe replied. She was puzzled, but it sounded as though it could wait until the next day. She relaxed with a book and went to sleep early.

When Signe arrived at the station house at 8 a.m., Jefferson was already there. This was most unusual. Signe knew he wasn't a morning person. She offered him a large cup of black coffee. She motioned him to the small conference room and closed the door behind them. Jefferson was bursting by then. He started by saying how sorry he was about lying to her about the red satchel. He realized that they had a professional relationship but he also thought of her as a friend. After she yelled at him in the lobby of the La Fonda hotel, he couldn't put his failing her out of his mind. So he decided to do something about it.

He was well connected in Santa Fe, particularly in the large gay community. He also had ties even though they weren't as strong to the lesbian tribe. He spent hours talking and meeting with members of both groups. Some people in both groups of gays were horse people, so he focused on them particularly. Over the past week he had learned a lot about the 'horsy' set in Santa Fe and Albuquerque. Even though Hercules's abduction had been disguised as a sale; he looked into the local stables where Lipizzaners or Lipizzaner crosses were kept. Jefferson found five stables and interviewed each owner. He gave Signe a list.

He had also found four gay men who had been closely involved with the State Fair. Jefferson talked with each of them about what they had seen particularly on October 3rd. One was working in the Mexican Village and saw nothing suspicious. He had seen a state police officer on an ATV become tangled in a row of Mexican flags and piñatas, but he only found that funny not suspicious. One young man that Jefferson described as very 'cut' worked in the little restaurant by the horse barn. He had seen a man with an accent, wearing a long duster eat in the Lasso Cafe everyday during lunch for the first four or five days of the fair. This sounded like one of the Fortuna brothers and fit with what Signe already knew.

The third man was a security guard at the fair. On Thursday he had worked the security booth at the north side of fairgrounds, near the horse barns. He remembered several horse trailers pulled by semi tractors or pickups leaving the grounds that afternoon. He was surprised by the flurry of departures. He recollected a Maroon Dodge Ram pulling a white horse trailer that left about 4 p.m. that Thursday afternoon. He didn't recognize pictures of the three Fortuna brothers, Anthony Squitero, or Dirk Patterson but he was pretty sure the truck windows were tinted. Guards wrote license plate numbers in a log but Signe already had this information.

The fourth man had a quarter horse he was showing at the Fair. His equine was in stall #8, right across the alley from Hercules. He was at the fair all afternoon on Thursday feeding, watering and grooming his horse. He remembered the man from Argentina in the duster. He saw two other men going into the stall around 2 p.m. but didn't really pay attention to them. The horseman said that that early afternoon was usually the busiest time in the animal arenas as shows and judgings were going on. Owners were grooming and caring for animals then. He was certain that Stephen Samuels, one of the State Fair directors and judges, had entered stall #17 about 2:15 p.m. shortly after the other two men had entered.

Signe had real reservations about this extemporaneous investigation that Jefferson Barclay had engaged in. He was interviewing potential witnesses who might be scared off. If he did stumble across a real suspect he might get hurt or killed. On the other hand the concierge had opened a whole new area of inquiry that Signe had missed. Most of his information had been merely collaborative except his last revelation which could break this complex case wide open.

CHAPTER 37

After accepting a fresh cup of coffee from Signe the concierge, stretched, then sat back down and resumed his tale. Signe was really worried, now, that Jefferson might have driven a solid witness into hiding or fleeing. Jefferson Barclay could not resist torturing Stephen Samuels once he got him in his sights. Mr. Samuels was an elder in the First Baptist Church, married and the father of three daughters. However, Jefferson also knew he was a homosexual who was a flamboyant and flagrant cross dresser. Stephen had even had a major crush on Jefferson three or four years ago and something had come of it, briefly. Jefferson set up an appointment at Mr. Stephen's office ostensibly to talk about taxes. Jefferson wore one of his best dark blue chalk stripe suits and an English cravat in pale yellow silk to the appointment.

Once he was in Mr. Samuel's office Jefferson revealed the true reason for his visit. He reminded the account of the Patterson murder, and asked Mr. Samuels what he knew about it. Stephen 'hemmed and hawed' and then enquired in a polite way why Jefferson wanted to know. Jefferson implied that he was trying to help a detective friend solve the case. Mr. Samuels said he had been at the fair that day but knew nothing about the crime that Jefferson was speaking of.

"I may have someone who can place you at the crime scene, Steve," Jefferson retorted.

"I believe that person is mistaken," Stephen replied quickly. At this point the concierge remembered that he wasn't versed in criminal interrogation beyond what he had seen watching Law and Order on television. He had no idea how to 'flip' this witness, yet he felt he was too far into it to stop.

"I know some things about you, Stephen, which if they were revealed could be damaging. You should talk to me," Jefferson said in his most honey-coated voice.

Mr. Samuel's face fell; then he rose abruptly and hurried out of the office without another word. Jefferson sat there in the client's chair in his nicely tailored chalk stripe suit puzzled but also embarrassed. Finally, he rose slowly and left. Feeling that he had blown his opportunity to help Signe, he went back to work at the La Fonda.

Nothing happened for the next two days and Jefferson was sure he would have to report another failure to his detective friend. Then just as he was putting his tickets and restaurant reservation forms away on the third afternoon, Mr. Stephen called. He was apologetic and asked Jefferson if they could meet that night at 10 p.m. at a notorious gay bar on the north side of Albuquerque. Jefferson quickly agreed.

Jefferson dressed in a purple silk shirt and tight black slacks with pumps. When he arrived at The Satyr, Steve was already at a table. Jefferson ordered a scotch and water. Jefferson went on the offensive immediately and reminded Steve that on their last 'date' Steve had worn stylish red pumps, a low cut black dress, false eyelashes and a bustier. Jefferson hinted that he had pictures even though he really didn't. Steve lowered his eyes. Then Jefferson pushed forward.

"I need to know what you saw at the fairgrounds, Steve," Jefferson began. "I have a reliable witness that saw you go into stall #17 shortly before the murder. If I have to, I can set up a meeting between you two, but he seems to be an unimpeachable source. This person has no reason to lie about you. I'm sure you had a good reason for being there that was unrelated to the crime, but I need to know what happened."

"Okay. I was there," Steve said reluctantly. "I wanted to inform Chloe of the time for the dressage event that Hercules was entered in and make sure she didn't need anything. It was dark in the stall but Chloe and heavy set swarthy middle aged man appeared to be having a heated conversation which I interrupted. They stopped talking the minute I entered so I don't know what the disagreement was about. I had not seen the man before or since. I said a hurried goodbye and left."

"Could you recognize him, Steve?" Jefferson asked.

"I'm not sure," Steve replied. "As I said, it was dark and I clearly was interrupting. Do you know how you act when you think you are some place you shouldn't be? I looked away and down and then hurried out. Perhaps I could recognize him."

"Well. Let's have a drink Steve, for old times sake." Jefferson said. "I want to tell you about my new boyfriend, Keith."

Jefferson headed home a couple of hours later. On the dark drive home he had a bad moment when a large pickup truck approached rapidly from behind. He remembered Signe's description of her accident on the same poorly lit road. But at the last minute the truck veered into the left lane and shot past. He was cheered by the fact that he had some real information with which to redeem himself with Signe.

Signe thanked Jefferson for all his work on the investigation. She asked him not to do any further investigation, because he could endanger himself and lacked the expertise and back up that the police could provide. Jefferson promised that he wouldn't as long as he was fully back in Signe's good graces. She assured him that he was. Signe mentioned that she had visited with Mr. Samuels twice about the case, and he had told her nothing. She planned to show Stephen Samuels a picture of both Dirk and Anthony, but first she would take him to the police sketch artist so he wasn't just focused on those two faces.

Just as Jefferson and Signe finished talking, Signe got a call from a Lieutenant Archuleta of the Albuquerque Police Department. Their computers showed that a Mrs. Svelty Patterson was a person of interest in a murder in Santa Fe. Signe confirmed that that was true. Officer Archuleta said that he had been called to the family home at 11:45 p.m. the night before. Mrs. Patterson had been found in the den by her husband when he came home from the Albuquerque Shootists meeting. She was in her nightgown and barely breathing. Officer Archuleta and his partner administered CPR and called for assistance. She had been transferred to St. Joseph's Hospital in a deep coma and not breathing on her own.

Signe asked the officer what had happened. He said the house was ransacked as if a burglar had gone through several rooms. Books were pulled down in the den and files were pulled out and dumped on the Turkish rugs. The safe stood open and empty. At first blush everything looked like a robbery. However, the master bathroom was also torn up and medicine bottles were strewn around the floor. A large empty bottle of Seconal was found on the bed stand next to a glass half full of scotch.

Officer Archuleta said they weren't sure if they were looking at a robbery or a suicide or some combination of both. It seemed to be a very bizarre case. Signe explained the Chloe Patterson murder case to the officer including the possible role of Dirk Patterson in the crime. Signe also explained that Svelty had told her she was afraid of Dirk, and that he had a large life insurance policy on her. Officer Archuleta said that Mr. Patterson had been nothing but polite and helpful. Signe asked the officer if she and one of her CSI's could come right down and go through the crime scene with him and one of his CSIs. Jack loaded the Crown Vic and put Valerie's crime scene gear in the trunk. They headed for Albuquerque's north valley.

Officer Archuleta met them at the house and helped them through the yellow tape. Signe started in the bathroom where pill bottles were everywhere. Bottles of tranquilizers, anti depressants, sleeping pills and diet pills were scattered across the travertine floor. Every prescription was for Svelty. Next to the bed was a large brown empty plastic bottle that was labeled 'Seconal' and a tumbler half full of liquor. Officer Archuleta said their lab found only prints from Svelty on the bottle and tumbler.

In the den, books and files were scattered across the floor several inches deep. The safe stood open and empty. Jack, Valerie and Signe all sat on the Turkish rugs and started going through the material file by file and paper by paper. After three hours Officer Archuleta excused himself. He was replaced by an APD officer on the next shift. They found information about the purchase of Hercules. They found expense vouchers for Anthony Squitero, but nothing incriminating. Finally in the last stack Signe found two slender files with an upside down capital 'F' in the corner that matched the symbol from the raid on Squitero's office. There was nothing out of the ordinary in either one. Signe took them both.

It was 6:30 p.m. and they were tired. Jack, Valerie and Signe loaded their gear into the Crown Vic and headed home. Signe did not know how to put this crime together or how to fit it into Chloe's murder but she did have some evidence to work on.

Svelty was still in a coma and on a respirator when Signe called the St. Joseph's ICU the next morning. When she spoke with the doctor he said that she had taken much larger than lethal dose of secobarbital or Seconal. Her blood pressure was labile and kidney and liver function had deteriorated some. She had vomited after she became unconscious and some of the vomit had gone into her lungs creating aspiration pneumonia. He thought her chance for survival was less than 50%. The treatment for now was supportive care and antibiotics for her pneumonia; application of hemodialysis might play a necessary role at some point in the future. Her young age was in her favor and, hopefully, if the doctors could prevent a catastrophe for the next four to five days she might wake up and then recover fully.

Signe read about the Seconal. It was a potent sleeping tablet but was also used recreationally to produce intoxication like alcohol. After an overdose death was usually caused by shock or cardiopulmonary arrest.

It was definitely an old fashioned drug popular for suicide in the 50's and 60's. Signe read that Marilyn Monroe, Jean Seberg, Judy Garland and Jimi Hendrix had all died of barbiturate overdoses. Whether Svelty had swallowed the pills voluntarily or with someone pointing a gun at her, and threatening her was, so far, unknown.

CHAPTER 38

Signe set to work with Valerie, the CSI, on the evidence they had collected last night at the Patterson home. They made a list of all of Mr. Squitero's expenses paid by Dirk according to date and amount. They totaled $179,000. They swabbed the safe and found traces of cocaine and evidence of printers ink suggesting cash had been kept in the safe. Chemical tests for gunshot residue suggested that bullets and most likely one or more guns were kept in the safe. The two slender files with the upside down capitol 'F' in the corner were baffling to both Valerie and Signe. Valerie had tried heating the similar files taken from Tony's office. No secret writing appeared. Exposure to several other chemical 'developer' also revealed no secret messages. Valerie exposed the papers to ultraviolet and infrared light with no effect. She finally sent an inquiry to the National Crime Data Base about methods of secret writing. Signe felt frustrated again, and realized that if Svelty died another important witness and source of information would be lost.

The next morning Signe and Vincent headed off to Cochiti Pueblo for the annual piñon dance. The notices said the dancing would start at 1 p.m. and Vincent knew that it should last for several hours.

"Are we going to this Indian dance for fun, or as part of your endless need to work?" Vincent teased.

"Both." Signe said airily.

When they pulled up in Vincent's pickup the large dirt lot was already full of dirty, beat up trucks and cars. The central plaza of the pueblo was crowded with Indians and a few Anglos. Obviously, Indians from other pueblos up and down the Rio Grande were attending and probably also some Hopis and Navajos. The sides of the plaza were surrounded by weathered one and two story brown adobe houses. A kiva was located in the center of the plaza.

Log ladders went up the sides of the houses and some people were already sitting on the roofs. Blankets were spread along the two shaded sides of the plaza and Indian women were selling jewelry, blankets and pots.

The jewelry was unlike that displayed by Wanda in the Taos plaza. The pieces of turquoise were large and sky blue colored or blue green with twisted veins of brown or gold through them. The stones were surrounded by heavy hand wrought ropes and leaves in delicately designed silver. Signe glanced at the rugs and the jewelry but focused on the pottery. She had no pots from Cochiti. She knew this pueblo was the home of Helen Cordero, a kindly and innovative potter who had died in 1994. Helen was only an average potter even into her 40's when she suddenly began to make clay figures, a huge innovation at the time. The figures evolved into a fat seated Indian woman with tiny figures of children in her lap, up and down her arms, on her shoulders on her knees, and even on her feet. This was the beginning of the famous ceramic 'storyteller'. Most were now in museums or private collections and much too expensive for Signe to buy. Signe wished she had had a chance to meet Helen.

One other potter was even more famous than Helen, Signe knew. It was Maria Martinez of San Ildefonso, a nearby pueblo. With her husband she had created the strikingly modern looking black wear. It was based on 2,000 year old potsherds found by the Smithsonian. Maria already made the thinnest, most beautiful polychrome pots in the village. It took her a decade of experimentation, with her husband's help, to make the beautiful black wear. It was rich and lustrous and very smooth. Signe had seen one of Maria's pots in a museum.

Signe studied the modern Cochiti pots. There were traditional polychromes and interesting animal shapes. She always thought of Axel when she shopped for a pot. It was something they had done together many times before. She saw pots in the shape of owls with round feet and curving wings, raccoons with big black eyes and even fat little quails. She began bargaining on a small polychrome pot, orange on the inside with a simple black and white geometric design on the outside. The asking price was $400; she offered $100. It was nearly 2 p.m. and the first older men with their large cottonwood drums were just arriving. Indian time Vincent thought to himself. The seller said $325; Signe offered $150. Just then a distinguished elderly gentleman approached Signe. "I am Mateo Romero, detective," The Indian said. "Did you wish to speak with me?"

"Yes. I am Detective Sorensen and this is Private Jaramillo of the New Mexico State Police," Signe replied. "180 dollars, that's my last offer. Signe shouted over her shoulder as she walked away. Then turning to Mr. Romero, she said, "Is there somewhere we can talk in private, sir?"

"Please. My house is just off the plaza." Mateo Romero said. "Follow me."

Mr. Romero threaded through the hawkers and observers gathered on the plaza and walked down a narrow lane to his house. The old wooden door was a painted a worn turquoise blue. He led the way through a cluttered sitting room and through a low door way. It was dark in the house and Signe had trouble making out objects. The second room came into focus slowly. Brown, gray, and yellow powders sat in odd shaped jars along a shelf. Herbs were hanging upside down in bunches tied with twine from the vigas. Old leather bound books lay about in odd stacks. Mateo Romero cleared papers from the seats of two chairs for Signe and Vincent. After they were comfortably seated, Mr. Romero spoke, as a means of introduction, about his life in the pueblo as a governor and a medicine man.

"One of Chloe's girlfriends gave us your name, Mr. Romero as a possible acquaintance of hers," Signe began.

"She was much more than an acquaintance," Mateo began. "I had a son Juan who had a drug problem. He met Chloe in a rehab program, and when I visited him on family day we spent time together having picnics and taking walks. Chloe's family didn't visit her in rehab. After several visits Juan, Chloe and I got to be friends. When the kids got out of rehab, they continued to meet for lunch or a movie in Santa Fe. Both started using drugs again, and Chloe went back into rehab but Juan didn't. He was under a lot of pressure from me, his family and the people of the pueblo to quit. He took a bus to Los Angeles and was found there dead, in an alley, from an overdose of 'ecstasy'. Chloe came to his funeral and then disappeared. I didn't think I would ever see her again."

"Did Chloe every mention anyone she was afraid of?" Signe asked.

"No, she didn't. And then about six months after the funeral she came here for a visit," Mateo continued. "She sat in this very room. She was high on drugs, dirty, and her clothes were soiled and torn. She said she had no where else to go. Her parents refused to help her, and all her close friends were users, so she thought of me. My wife and I took her in and nursed her for two weeks. When she was better she said she wanted to learn the Cochiti way of the spirit. She said that she and Juan had had long talks about the Indian path, and she felt it might help her stay off of drugs even though it failed Juan. She started coming every week and I taught her the Cochiti way. She was smart and learned quickly and she always seemed drug free during her visits. About two months ago she reached the end of her training with me. I told her she needed to meditate in a sweat lodge, and that in our pueblo that usually was only done with braves. Even though I supported this purification, I said, I would have to ask the elders of the tribe for permission."

"I've never heard of women even being allowed to be in the vicinity during a sweat lodge meditation," Vincent said.

"We are an advanced pueblo and two other women have been initiated in this way," Mateo said. "But the elders were badly split, initially. Not only was this a woman but she was non-Indian. We had several long meetings in the kiva about Chloe. Finally they assented, I believe, because they knew I had lost my only son to drugs and she was an addict trying to seek a higher way. I took her into the hills by *Kasha Katuwe* where our tribal sweat lodge is located and we built a fire. When the lodge was hot she stripped and went inside. I noticed a tattoo in the fold of her leg. She said it was the Japanese symbol for 'serenity'. I hold her that magic might interfere with 'the way'. She said she would have it removed, but she was murdered before she could do that. She stayed in the sweat lodge for five hours meditating. She came out about every hour dripping with sweat and I lashed her back with willow switches. It was dusk when she finished. She looked very tired but peaceful. I wrapped her in a blanket and drove her to the house. My wife bathed her and fed her broth before putting her to bed. She slept for sixteen hours."

"Thank you for telling us that story Mr. Romero," Signe said. "It always puzzled me that I hadn't met anyone who was close to Signe and now I find that you were. She seemed like such a lost soul. I hope to come back soon and talk some more with you about Chloe."

"You and Vincent are always welcome here, Detective," Mateo said as he walked them to the front door. As they walked toward the plaza Signe and Vincent heard the rhythmic beat of the drums before they saw the dancers. The men and women were colorfully adorned with feathers, colored yarn, animal skins and horns. Their movements were animated and yet at the same time stately. Signe and Vincent stood to one side holding hands and watching the ceremony. At a break in the dancing Signe wandered over to the potter's blanket, and found that she had successfully purchased a Cochiti pot.

CHAPTER 39

Signe got up early the next morning and drove to Albuquerque. She wanted to assess for herself how Svelty was doing. She parked behind St. Joseph's Hospital, one of the taller buildings in midtown, and rode up to the eighth floor. Svelty was in the twelve bed ICU which at that morning hour was a beehive of activity. Nurses, lab techs, x-ray techs and respiratory therapists were scurrying around the unit. A couple of late rounding doctors were in the unit but most had already left for their offices. Svelty was in cubicle #5 an alcove with partial walls on each side. She looked horrible. A large tube came out of her mouth and was taped securely to her swollen face. A smaller tube came out of her nose. IVs ran into both arms with little machines on poles to control their flow.

Signe found the machinery sterile, complex and foreign. She overcame her dread and walked up to the bedside, and took Svelty's swollen hand. An oxygen monitor glowed red on her index finger. Signe held the outside of Svelty's hand gently and spoke her name in a loud voice. She had to speak up because every little life saving machine in the room had its own voice and there was a constant cacophony of beeps, squeaks, and chirps with the loud steady whoosh of air from the respirator in the background. The detective noted no movement from the patient. She gripped her hand more firmly, and spoke in a louder voice but to no avail. Somewhat resignedly she pulled up a chair and just sat quietly by the bedside for a few minutes. Try as she might she was unable to see any voluntary motion from Mrs. Patterson. While sitting there she did notice a series of small round bruises on both side of Svelty's neck. She suspected photos were forbidden without written permission. She took her Nikon out and snapped some pictures when the nurses were distracted.

She had spoken with Dr. Mark Josephson, a pulmonologist, who was Svelty's attending doctor. He had offered to meet with her. She took the elevator down and walked across the driveway to the medical office building adjacent to the hospital. He interrupted his office to speak with her. He was a badly dressed young man who needed a haircut. When he turned around she noticed that his shirt tail hung out of his rumpled brown corduroys.

He was not encouraging about Svelty's prognosis. She had not awakened from the coma. Her liver was functioning better but her kidneys were worse. Worst of all the aspiration had now turned into ARDS, a major killer of patients in her condition. Dr. Josephson explained that ARDS or adult respiratory distress syndrome occurred in unresponsive patients with pulmonary insults, such as pneumonia. Surfactant, the liquid interface in the lungs between air and tissue disappeared. Oxygen could not get into the blood stream despite setting the respirator for large, fast, high pressure breaths. Settings were nearly maximal for Svelty already, and if there was no improvement she would succumb to a low oxygen state called hypoxia.

Signe didn't know enough about medicine to ask an intelligent question about Svelty's state, so she asked about the bruises on Mrs. Patterson's neck. Dr. Josephson confessed that he had not noticed them. Signe thanked him for his kindness in talking with her and left. Signe had a quick pleasant lunch with Bernadette at the Artichoke Café nearby, with hand holding and two tender kisses. Then Signe drove back to Santa Fe.

When Signe got back to the station house Valerie brought some sketches to her desk. Mr. Stephen Samuels had come in that morning and Valerie had worked with him on the computer sketch artist selecting eyebrows and noses. They were looking for the face that Mr. Samuels saw in stall #17 the afternoon of the murder. Valerie showed Signe three different printouts. All were heavy set males with dark brows and some facial hair. Signe thought it could be Anthony Squitero or Dirk Patterson, but not Johnny Armijo or Richard Lederback. However, it could also be someone else that she didn't even know about. Signe thanked Valerie for her efforts.

Signe wanted to keep the pressure on her suspects so she and Jack drove over to 'Tony the Squids' office. Tony was in the back room working on his electronic gear.

"Yo, detective, did ya bring my files back?" Anthony yelled over his shoulder at her as he put down a soldering gun.

"I'm afraid I didn't, Mr. Squitero. The department isn't quite finished with them. There are some important leads in that material that we need to follow up on," Signe said trying to suppress the amusement in her voice.

"Have you found Wanda yet?" She continued now that she had Anthony mentally on the run.

"I was with that woman for years and I thought I knew her." Anthony said. "I knew her friends, her aliases, her family, her hiding places, and I thought I would find her in a couple of days in New Jersey. That broad is puzzlin' me."

"Let's see, Tony, you've been investigating this crime now for over five weeks. I thought you would have it all solved by now, and hand the perpetrator to me on a silver plate."

"Ya know, detective I followed a lot of leads that went no where. I think the guy who did it is a pro," Tony continued.

"Do you have anything for me?" Signe said as she headed for the door.

"No, I don't detective," Tony concluded without trying to conceal the amusement in his voice.

Signe spent a quiet evening at home cooking Danish chicken soup with tiny meatballs in it, and writing Axel a long letter. She called the ICU and the nurse confirmed that Svelty's condition was the same.

In the morning Signe got to the Police station early. She had a meeting with Dirk Patterson and wanted to review her files before they started. She had to admit that he intimidated her. She hoped to put a little pressure back on him by having the meeting in Santa Fe. Mr. Patterson wanted to put pressure on Signe so he rented a conference room at the Eldorado, another downtown hotel, for the meeting. Signe took Jack to the get-together mostly for moral support. When they walked down the carpeted hallway and turned into the Onate conference room; Dirk was already there with another well-fed man in an even more expensive looking suit and wide suspenders. Introductions were made. The resplendent man was Mr. Patterson's attorney Ruben Pelicanto. So I've been 'one upped' again Signe thought.

"I hope Detective Sorensen you have called us here to reveal who murdered my daughter," Dirk began in a loud, aggressive voice.

"I'm sorry to say, sir, that the murder remains unsolved." Signe replied.

"Surely, you have someone in custody or at least a person of interest detective," Mr. Pelicanto chimed in.

"Your client, sir, and his employee, Anthony Squitero are both persons of interest," Signe said. "Your client had a hate filled relationship with his daughter and a $2,000,000 motive. Your client may also be involved in the near fatal overdose his wife recently suffered." Mr. Pelicanto rose and motioned for Mr. Patterson to rise also.

"We're done here," Mr. Pelicanto yelled, spraying spit on Signe. "My client came to this meeting in good faith, to learn more about the tragic death of his beloved daughter, not to be insulted by a small town detective with bad English."

"Tell your mouthpiece to sit down, Dirk!" Signe yelled back in anger. "I have something to tell him about Chloe which I won't reveal unless the insults stop. Everything that I have said at this meeting is true and you know it, Mr. Patterson."

"Okay, okay," Dirk sputtered and at the same time pulled Mr. Pelicanto down.

"Do you know Mateo Romero, the medicine man at Cochiti Pueblo?" Signe asked.

"Never heard of him," Dirk replied.

"Did you know Juan Romero, his son?" Signe continued.

"No," Dirk answered clearly getting exasperated again. "What is the purpose of these questions, Detective?"

"Chloe was heavily involved with the medicine man, and asked him to teach her the Indian way to help her overcome her drug addiction," Signe began. "She was receiving extended weekly instructions in the secret ways of Cochiti Pueblo, ways usually only revealed to young Indian males. She underwent a purification ceremony in a sweat lodge just before her death. I'm afraid she may have stirred up deep resentments in some of the elders of tribe, and they may have lashed out to protect their secrets." Mr. Patterson sat in stunned silence.

"I want you, Sir, to rack your brain for any hints you have about this or the names of any persons who might know about it," Signe said forcefully, as she stood and motioned Jack out of the conference room.

As they walked down the hall, Jack said, "That went well," in a sarcastic tone.

"Actually, Jack, that's the best I've every done with Mr. Patterson," Signe replied. "He is so aggressively contentious and easy to dislike. He bested me twice before, and I think this scuffle was a draw."

Jack wheeled the Crown Vic up to the front door of the station and Signe slid her long legs on to the ground and marched through the front doors. She called the ICU at St. Joseph's and spoke with Svelty's nurse. Svelty wasn't any better. In fact her lungs and kidneys were a little worse. Mr. Patterson had been in with his wife's living will and asked about turning off the machines. The nurse heard Dr. Josephson say it was too soon. He thought her chance of recovery was 20-30% now, but that they needed to wait a couple of more days before making that decision.

CHAPTER 40

Sven Torvaldson took Signe to dinner that evening. He always brought her a single rose. She remembered the day she had flirted with him in front of the other detectives. She had been caught necking with Bernadette the night before, and wanted everyone to known that she wasn't gay, even if she wasn't sure herself. Sven had never forgotten her long slender legs or her soulful and attentive gazes. He took her to the severely modern Santacafe with its excellent food, obsequious service and high prices. He held her hand through dinner with occasional squeezes for emphasis.

They talked over the Patterson case in great detail. Signe gave him a follow up on her meeting with Dirk and Anthony. She told him in a sad voice about Svelty and her slim chance for survival. Sven reported that his company had paid Mr. Patterson $2,000,000 in cash. They had run out of excuses not to honor the policy. Sven also reported that Wanda had decamped from New Hampshire and then his tails had lost her. They lingered over coffee and Crème Brulee that they shared off of one spoon. Sven had mentioned during dinner that he had another appointment in Santa Fe in the a.m; so he would be staying in town. He invited Signe to his hotel for a night cap, and not being tired, she accepted.

She'd been on enough of these late evening escapades in Denmark so that she insisted on driving. She met him at the bar of the Eldorado Hotel for a drink. It was modern Indian in décor and opened onto a large unadorned lobby. It was not *hyggelig* in Danish or cozy in English. Sven ordered a bottle of champagne and suggested they go up to his suite on the sixth floor. The rooms were very masculine with orange, red and brown tones in the Indian décor. A small balcony with a ramada on top looked out on the lights of Santa Fe. Signe and Sven kissed each other and caressed each others arms shoulder and backs. Sven slipped Signe effortlessly out of her dress and slip. They snuggled on a large sofa kissing more deeply and fondling each other. Signe played with his wavy blond hair and hairless but muscular Scandinavian chest. He felt very familiar to her. She removed the rest of his clothing with gentle kisses, licks and tugs.

Sven excused himself to get a condom from the bathroom. While he was gone Signe stretched her nakedness on the sofa enjoying the warmth of human contact, the tingling in her loins and the feeling of gradually getting very wet. Then she had a thought of recent lovers—Vincent, Bernadette and especially Juan. Suddenly she realized that she wasn't ready for what was about to happen. She grabbed her dress and pulled it on while stepping into her shoes. When Sven came out of the bathroom with a very nice erection he was surprised and disappointed to see Signe with her dress on.

"I'm just not ready, Sven. You were perfect. Give me some time." Signe sputtered as she walked quickly to the door. He was too surprised to say anything. She put some more clothing on in the elevator. When she hit the lobby she flipped a twenty dollar bill at the sleepy bellman.

"My car please," She shouted imperiously over her shoulder as she strode toward the front door. She knew she had made the right decision but she still felt alone.

The next morning at the station, Signe got a surprise call from Hector Fortuna. He reported that Hercules was doing well in Argentina and that they had bred him to four of their finest mares. He said that Juan Vivendi had visited for a weekend and reported that the authorities would not prosecute the Fortuna's for currency fraud. He called to thank Signe for her visit and because he had an idea for her. He had been thinking about her predicament. Jose reported after she left Argentina, that a policeman came into the stall just before he put on the helmet with the blinders and earflaps. He wasn't sure he could recognize a picture of the officer but he had the best memory of the three brothers. He remembered his last name began with a capital 'G' little 'a' and next a little 't' or an 'l'. Signe said she would mail pictures to Hector but she was already pretty sure she knew who it was. She thanked him for his hospitality even though she had already rewarded him with a leisurely naked walk down the long hallway in his house.

Signe called Vincent first to ask some more questions about Sergeant Raymond Gallegos his superior officer and cousin.

"We grew up together, so sure we were close," Vincent said. "He was older. We got into the usual trouble as teens. We vandalized some cars, did some underage drinking and sporadic shoplifting. My dad was a violently abusive drunk so I spent a lot of time at Raymond's house often staying for weeks at a time. Raymond was four years older and eventually he and another cousin got caught stealing a car. Ray was still a minor and he got sent to the State School at Springer for a year. When he came back we weren't as close. He seemed kind of wary and distant. He finished high school and then went right to the State Police academy."

"Did he get in anymore trouble with the law?" Signe asked.

"Not that I know of," Vincent replied. "He was always complaining about the low pay, particularly, when the victims of the crimes he was working were rich like Chloe Patterson."

"Did he ever take kickbacks or bribes while he was on the force?" Signe asked.

"Honestly, Signe, not that I ever saw or even heard about," Vincent replied. Signe told Vincent about Hector Fortuna's call and what Jose had seen.

"If he was there before I found the body, Signe, he never let on to me then or since," Vincent replied.

Signe decided she had to put heavy pressure on Raymond Gallegos if she was to get the truth. It seemed he had lied to her on four separate occasions, if she was counting correctly. Signe asked Chief Detective Hartford to call the Sergeant in for a conference. She didn't say anything further to Vincent for fear he might tip Raymond off, if only by accident.

Signe grabbed a quick lunch with Jefferson at The Shed. They both spoke poetic words about the lovely blue corn red enchiladas. Signe got back to the office thirty minutes before the meeting with the Sergeant and put in a quick call to St. Joseph's. Signe's favorite nurse was working, and she said that Svelty stabilized over night and as the day wore on had gotten a little better! Dr. Josephson decided to do hemodialysis to remove the waste products her kidneys weren't excreting yet. They still had a long way to go but she was even starting to make random movements.

The meeting with Sergeant Raymond Gallegos began promptly at 1:30. Chief Hartford weighed in first.

"Sergeant. We have a reliable witness that will place you in stall #17 at the State Fair before the murder on October 3rd," the chief began sternly. Signe recollected that the witness was one continent away and that the witness had not seen pictures of the sergeant just yet, but it was a strong start.

"Despite multiple meetings with Detective Sorensen during which you were helpful in other ways you failed to mention this fact," the chief continued sternly.

"I'm sorry, sir," Sergeant Gallegos began. "But I felt that at anytime this case would be turned over to the State Police since we have always had jurisdiction at the fair and I could correct the oversight. When that didn't happen it became too late to fix without it looking like I was complicit."

"You have every opportunity to tell me about this Raymond, and you know it," Signe added.

"I hope by making a clean breast of it you will be lenient, chief," Raymond said contritely.

"Tell me the whole story, now, Sergeant Gallegos!" Chief Hartford said in a voice too loud for the room they were in.

"I was assigned to the north side of Santa Fe on October the 3rd, which includes the fair, as you know. It was about an hour before I had to go on duty. Vincent had told me that there was a horse in Stall #17 that was worth hundreds of thousands of dollars and I wanted to see it for myself. I wandered in from the sunlight into the anteroom of the stall and introduced myself. A man was over in the corner. He seemed distracted but said I should just go over to the fence by the other side of the stall. He told me not to reach into the pen or make any noise because the horse was 'spooky'. I took a look and left. As my eyes adjusted I realized there were two men in the anteroom. One had his back to me. I felt like I was interrupting. Just as I stepped out into the sunlight I saw a piece of neatly folded white paper on the ground. Without even thinking I stuffed it in my pocket of my uniform. That's everything that happened chief."

"When did you look at what was written on that paper?" Chief Hartford asked.

"I live alone and do my own laundry about every three weeks. I checked the pockets then and found the paper," Sergeant Gallegos replied. "It was a series of numbers. I didn't think much of it. I thought perhaps it was a judge's shorthand for the contests he officiated or a tally of horse races from the fair track."

"Where is the paper?" The chief asked impatiently.

"Here," Raymond Gallegos said sheepishly as he took the paper out of his pocket. Signe took the paper in a gloved hand in case there were any fingerprints which seemed very unlikely at this point.

"Thank you, officer. I will speak with your superiors and they will be in touch with you," Chief Hartford said curtly and rose, indicating that Signe should do the same. The sergeant walked out of the conference room head down.

PART 5

CHAPTER 41

Signe got up very early the next morning for the drive to Albuquerque. She was anxious to see Svelty. How many trips had she made to Albuquerque in the last three months? She found she had lost count. Of course, she hoped to get some information about her case but she suspected she would get nothing from a woman who had been so desperately ill. More than anything she wanted Svelty to see a familiar face amongst all the tubes and machines of the ICU. She had a strong feeling that Dirk wasn't visiting much.

When she entered Svelty's cubicle, Dr. Mark Josephson was examining Svelty's heart and lungs with his stethoscope. He listened carefully for several minutes, and then casually draped the stethoscope around his neck. He turned away from the bed and was surprised to see Signe standing by the door.

"Good morning, Detective Sorensen," he said in a deep cheery voice. "Our patient is much better. I am very surprised and relieved. I didn't think this was possible two days ago. As I told you I think her young age of thirty-three and lack of a smoking history must have really helped. Medicine is so much art and so little science. The ARDS, I'm sorry to be talking jargon, the lung condition, has almost completely resolved and now her kidneys are working. The x rays of her lungs taken two days ago and compared to this morning are like night and day. What brings you by?"

"I heard how much she had improved, Dr. Josephson, and I thought she might want to see a recognizable face." Signe replied. She moved to the bedside and took Svelty's left hand and looked into her eyes. Svelty didn't squeeze Signe's hand but her eyes turned in the detective's direction. Signe thought that was a good sign.

"Will she recover fully, doctor?" Signe asked.

"I certainly hope so, Ms. Sorensen." Dr. Josephson said, motioning her away from the bedside. Then in a low voice he added, "Some unforeseen complication could cause a set back or still take her life. Art not science, detective. I'd best finish my rounds."

"Thank you, Dr. Josephson. You've been more than kind." Signe said, as she turned back toward the immobilized patient. She pulled a chair to the bedside and sat quietly amidst the beeping of the heart monitor and the sighing sound of the respirator; holding Svelty's hand firmly for ten or twelve minutes.

On the boring drive back to Santa Fe, Signe got a call on her cell phone. "Yo, detective this is the Indian squaw from Taos callin'." The voice said.

"Hello, Wanda, or is this Rosie or Sandra?" Signe remarked sarcastically. "I thought I had lost you for good. Where are you?"

"Can't say, girlfriend, and I don't want this call traced, so it'll be short. I'm in the land of enchantment, though. I'll be in your office at nine tomorrow." Wanda replied and then the line went dead. Good, Signe thought the two *hetaerae* are suddenly back in play.

Signe stopped on the plaza at a rolling white stand for a quick chorizo burrito and lemonade. She knew it wasn't safe to eat food from such a place, but she needed something hot and fast, Vincent came to mind, as she bit off the warm folded end of the flour tortilla and the hot red chile and the sausage bits spilled into her mouth.

She drove quickly to the station and sat down at her desk. This was her 'new' desk now piled high with reports, brown manila folders, photos and yellow legal pads. Not one square inch of the desk top was visible. She looked hopefully over to the other side of the room at her 'old' desk. The piles weren't quite as high. She transferred several stacks of paper from "new' to 'old' and then sat down at her newly created work area. She pulled out the numbers that she had gotten from Sergeant Gallegos. 363351-1052418 was written in pencil on a folded piece of old worn paper. She wondered if this was the same number that Johnny Armijo had died trying to give her.

After fifteen minutes of searching through piles of folders on both desks, she could not find Johnnie's folder. She felt her anger and frustration rising. She wanted to scream and throw things. Maybe this was PMS, she thought, but no, it was just her sloppy filing habits biting her sharply on the ass. She sat down with a cup of coffee and within minutes, as the caffeine traveled from stomach to brain, she felt soothed and sharpened. What a wonderful drug! She was an addict. She knew it and she liked it. After her caffeine hit she resumed her search. There it was, plain as day, on the bottom of a pile in a corner of the 'old' desk. She pulled the number out from among the loose disorganized papers. It was 8142501-153336. She recognized it instantly as the same number, reversed, with one pair transposed. I wonder, she thought is this just dyslexia? Were either Dirk or Johnny left handed? Or had Johnny's drug addled brain simply transposed two numbers?

At least two players in this murder thought the number was important and she wanted to let her OCD trait loose on this number. First though, she gave Valerie, the lab tech, a copy of the number to puzzle over.

Signe left the station and found a heavy wet snow falling in Santa Fe. It was cold and windy. She drove to the Coyote Café and sat in her favorite corner by the fireplace. While sipping a Kahlua and cream she played with the numbers. The seven digit string could be a phone number. If that was so the telephone number couldn't start with a one—there were no letters with it on the keypad. How about starting at the other end? Then the exchange would be 814. This wasn't a Santa Fe or Albuquerque exchange. She could puzzle this out some more, but why make it hard? She had a cell phone on her hip. She dialed the number adding the New Mexico area code-505. On the third ring a woman answered. It was a pet store in Alamogordo. Signe asked a few pointed questions mixed in with some questions about a fictitious cockatiel, and decided this was a dead end. So the seven digit string probably wasn't a phone number and it still left the six digits that followed or preceded unexplained.

Sometimes her best ideas came when she unfocused her mind and let it just wander. After drifting for twenty minutes nothing seemed any clearer. She would check the local banks for safe deposit boxes and accounts. She scooped up her papers and slid home on Santa Fe's snowy streets.

The next morning Wanda arrived forty minutes late. Signe was beginning to think she wouldn't show. Then Wanda popped into the station house in fur lined boots and a parka with an outrageously tight purple sweater on. She plopped into a chair snapping her gum.

"Good morning, detective," Wanda chirped. "The roads were hell. I'm living in the boonies, and I don't think they have a snowplow in the state."

"That's okay, Wanda. I'm glad you're safe. Where are you staying?" Signe asked.

"Just between you and me, Detective, I rented a place in Algodones. It's in the middle of nowhere," Wanda replied. "Tell me how I can help."

"I want you to get together with Anthony and wear a wire," Signe said. "Then see if you can get him to talk."

"I'll try anything you want, detective." Wanda began. "But if Anthony doesn't tell me to go to hell, he'll have me naked in two minutes. I can't really have a mike taped between my tits."

"Any chance he'll let you leave anything on? We have some pretty small transmitters now." Signe inquired.

"Not a chance, Signe. Can I call you that, detective?" Wanda queried.

"Sure," Signe replied.

"No way! He doesn't even let me keep anything on when I'm on the rag. It's a mess." Wanda replied disgustedly. "Can you hide it in my hair?"

"Perhaps we could build it into a barrette," Signe relied. "Don't you still wear a firearm on your ankle?"

"Yeah. But I usually take it off in bed." Wanda said. "I can't move very quickly with it on."

"Let me think about this problem, Wanda." Signe said. "Have you heard anything else, since you got back, which might help us solve Chloe's murder?"

"Sorry Signe, I'm really out of the loop," Wanda said. "But I'll bet Tony will be happy to see me. I think I can get him to open up in more ways than one."

Signe thought Wanda looked scruffy. She had a shapeless skirt and rundown heels on.

"Here's some money, Wanda, you must be about out," Signe said. "There's a Victoria's Secret at the mall where you can buy some lingerie. Come back after lunch and we'll wire you up."

Signe popped into Chief Hartford's office to give him an update. She told him about the resurrection of both Svelty and Wanda.

"I've got to admire your persistence, detective," the chief said. "This is one convoluted and complicated murder. You've hung in real good on this case. You know Chief Nielsen in Copenhagen thinks the world of you. He told me you are clever, innovative and resourceful. He also said that you had great legs. But he didn't mention this determination that I've seen. You're a damn good detective."

"Thanks chief," Signe said. "I value your opinion. I need to go and figure out where to put a wire on Wanda so I can hear what her partner is saying when she's in the buff. Excuse me."

On the way to the lab she made a mental note to visit with Dr. Goldiamond about her two resurrected *hetaerae*. Valerie had been working with her collection of mikes and transmitters for the last hour since Signe called for help.

"The new microphones won't be an issue," Valerie began. "I have some that are high quality and are no bigger than a lady bug. The transmitters are a lot bigger. The smallest is about the size of a butter scotch candy but the battery only lasts for 35 minutes. I can stretch the components out so it's more the shape of a piece of licorice and about an inch and a half long. I don't think the barrette ideas will work—too heavy especially if the client is rolling around. How about a choker or a waist ornament?"

"Can you really do that, Valerie?" Signe asked.

"I never have, but yes," Valerie answered with an 'anything for you' voice.

Just then Wanda walked it carrying four large pink sacks with V S printed on the sides. Signe explained what they were thinking.

"I need to measure you so I can figure out where to hide the transmitter. Please take off some of your clothing," Valerie said.

Wanda set her sacks from her shopping spree on the floor and slipped nonchalantly out of all her clothing leaving them in a pile on the floor in the middle of the lab. Well she's not very modest, Signe thought. Valerie and Signe noticed that she had a great body despite her short stature. Her waist was small measuring only nineteen inches and could easily accommodate a jeweled hip hugger but, Signe thought, a heavy weight on top of her might interfere with the reception of sound from the mike. Above her unbelievably large breasts, which Valerie managed to brush several times, Wanda's neck measured twelve and a half inches. A choker would work even though it might get some low hum from proximity to Wanda's larynx. Valerie told her to come back in an hour. Signe wandered over to Dr. Vivian Goldiamond's office.

CHAPTER 42

Dr. Goldiamond's office was like an oasis in the department. She had serious looking books on her shelves, drapes over the windows and small figures of men and women, alone and together scattered about. She often burned scented candles. Signe entered after knocking and sat down on a small dark blue loveseat.

"I'd like to bring you up to date on the two *hetaerae* that I spoke with you about," Signe began. "And get some more ideas about how to use them to advance the investigation of Chloe Patterson's murder."

"I'd like to help you Signe," Dr. Goldiamond said sliding forward. She was wearing a stylish black suit. As she leaned forward she showed some décolletage and the top of a real silk stocking came into view. Rather than ignoring the flirtatious signs as she did regularly with Valerie, Signe decided to confront the issue head on.

"Are you gay Dr. Goldiamond and are you coming on to me?" Signe asked without trying to be confrontational.

"Wow. Let me answer the second question first, Signe," Dr. Goldiamond began. "Yes I am coming on to you. I am very attracted to you, and Art Johnson told me you were gay before he was killed. The answer to the first question is that I'm married and enjoy sex with men but also with women. So I guess you would say I'm bisexual. Could we discuss a possible relationship in a different venue sometime?"

"No, I don't think so," Signe replied quickly. "I'm heterosexual and Art simply caught me experimenting one night. Besides I really need your help with these two women."

Vivian was taken aback. Signe had given her a very straight, in both senses of the word, and quick answer. But, of course, Vivian was a professional and she wanted to help Signe with her two fascinating women

"Okay, my mistake. Tell me about them," Vivian replied.

"Wanda, you'll recall, is the young brunette from Newark," Signe began. "She lived with the mob guy-Anthony." I got permission to talk to her parents and her sister. The father was a longshoreman, hard drinker, physically abusive to everyone in the family. He didn't have much to say. The mother said Wanda was a good kid who suddenly got 'wild' when she was twelve. She started drinking, using drugs and running with older boys. The sister says both girls were sexually abused by the mother's brother from about age eight in Wanda's case. Wanda ran away from home when she was fourteen."

"I remember you telling me about her," Dr. Goldiamond said. "You have more information now but it's consistent with what we talked about with some added fillips. She grew up powerless, physically abused, sexually abused and without a strong nurturing relative. Her sister was too young to support her. The only real attention she got was the wrong kind. She grew into a rescuer, often of the wrong type of person, because that's what was modeled for her. I'll bet that Mr. Squitero, the guy she's with physically resembles the uncle that abused her."

"But she's trying to break away from him," Signe broke in.

"That may well be, but it is going to be very difficult because of her dependent personality," Vivian continued. "She sees Anthony, and most of the world, for that matter, as black or white as I already told you. So he is either very, very good when he nurtures her or buys her gifts or very, very bad when he hits her. She sees you the same way. Right now you are 'good' but that could change in the blink of an eye. You need to go out of your way to support her as you try to get her to help you. Borderline personalities don't usually have close friends. You may be her only girlfriend. I think you can handle her but don't ever forget how quickly she can flip."

"Wanda does have friend in New Jersey, Michelle" Signe offered.

"But is she really close with her or is she just someone she uses in an emergency?" Dr. Goldiamond queried.

"I suspect she's an acquaintance. It's not easy for me to be phony with people but the advantage I have with Wanda is that I genuinely like her," Signe replied. "She's a fighter and I respect that."

"Before we go on to the second, what do you call them? *Hetaerae*? Tell me how you are doing, detective." Dr. Goldiamond said. Signe thought for a moment not sure where to start.

"I'm doing well. I have a young boyfriend who's attentive and affectionate." Signe began. "I'm teaching him what I want. He wishes to get serious but

I don't. I still miss my son Axel terribly and daily. I don't have any close girlfriends. Does that make me a borderline personality?"

"No," Dr. Goldiamond replied. "Aside from your fear of commitment you are pretty normal."

"I eat well, sleep well, and insist on being satisfied sexually, which by the way is getting better and easier, and occasionally I drink too much." Signe replied in the terse complete way that Vivian loved. "Now, how about my other courtesan?"

"You mean the upscale one that you find so similar to Wanda? What was her name?" Vivian asked.

"Svelty," Signe replied.

"Where did she ever get that name?" Dr. Goldiamond asked.

"Katherine was her given name, but her mom says they called her Svelty in training as a stewardess because she was always so beautiful and smooth even when descending those ridiculous rubber slides they have for escaping airliners." Signe replied. "We just about lost her to a secobarbital overdose that was either self inflicted or forced on her. I don't know which yet. She is still very ill, but we should be able to talk soon. I talked with her mother about Katherine's past. She had a perfectly boring and normal upbringing in rural Oklahoma except for the two years between ages seven and nine. Suddenly she began bed wetting and she started several fires. One fire burned down the family garage with a car in it. Except that she did torture two family cats. Her parents had high hopes for her and were devastated when she married Dirk Patterson. They saw him as an old, ill mannered, schemer.

"I said before that I think Svelty is the one to worry about," Dr. Goldiamond began. "That triad of pyromania, animal cruelty and bedwetting is very predictive. Later we see deceitfulness, consistent irresponsibility, disregard for others and irritability. It's true most of these traits relate to the marginal behavior of her husband, but she has known about and participated in that for years. She just turns a blind eye to all the suffering he causes and goes on shopping sprees in New York. I think she is a sociopath, which is a rare diagnosis in a woman. She has no empathy for other people. You need to be very careful around her. She could be dangerous."

"Thanks, Vivian," Signe said as she looked down at the notes she had scribbled in Danish.

Signe was tired of thinking and dreaming about this case. She put in perfunctory call to Sven Torvaldson just to bring him up to date. Then she called Vincent to see if they could spend the evening together. She suggested a snowy drive up to Chimayo for a dinner of the hottest Mexican food she had ever eaten. Chimayo is a small village on the high road to Taos. A twisty road cuts to the east from the main road and winds through little villages on the shoulder of the Sangre de Cristo Mountains on its way to Taos. It is one of the most picturesque drives in the west. Chimayo is nestled in the hills at the beginning of the drive. The restaurant is called Rancho de Chimayo and is an old adobe pitch roofed building set among large oak trees. It claims to have been run by the Jaramillo family for eleven generations. Vincent, a distant relative, feels that claim is embellished. Signe knows they have the best green chile enchiladas she has ever had. However, they are so hot that it takes her an hour to eat them. She has the waiter bring half of the entrée, and asks him to return with the other half in thirty minutes so the food stays warm.

Vincent and Signe started with margaritas in the bar with freshly toasted chips and bowls of thick homemade salsa. Vincent talked about a major robbery of a savings and loan that he's working on. Signe brought him up to date on the murder case; she describes in detail the recent events that relate to Svelty and her overdose. Just as they are going into the dining room, Signe mentioned the puzzling numbers she had gotten from Vincent's uncle. She pulled a copy of both versions out of her pocket and shows them to Vincent.

"I can't make anything out of the number you got from Johnny, *querida*," Vincent said. "But the one you got from Uncle Raymond makes me curious. I just spent the last two days in courses on tracking and orienteering. We talked a lot about GPS, you know, global positioning systems, and those numbers look like the longitude and latitude numerals they kept showing us for New Mexico. You know longitude is the distance from the equator and latitude is the angular distance from the prime meridian."

"Vincent, that's not what I learned in school." Signe began again thinking that schools in Denmark were more rigorous than those in the US. "Longitude is the angular distance from Greenwich and latitude from the equator."

"Okay, wise ass," Vincent retorted. "But if you add north and west to Uncle Raymond's numbers you have the approximate coordinates of Santa Fe. Maybe it's just a little north and east of the city."

"You have beautiful brown eyes, and you are also a genius!" Signe replied as she kissed him on the mouth. She called for the check even though they weren't half through eating and bolted for the exit.

"Where are we going?" Vincent called from behind her as she darted out the door.

"Back to headquarters so you and I can look up these coordinates," Signe replied over her shoulder. Vincent wasn't quite sure if he had ruined their evening together or if she had.

CHAPTER 43

The station house was quiet when Signe and Vincent got back to Santa Fe at 9:45 P.M. Signe woke up the computer with the broken key and Googled a map site for GPS coordinates. When she entered 36°33'51" north and 105°24'18" west the Pecos Wilderness came into view. As she enlarged down from the satellite picture, Beattie's Cabin appeared at those coordinates in the north central part of the wilderness. Signe looked at Vincent who was still miffed about his interrupted dinner.

"It's a remote hiker's cabin named after an early hermit," Vincent said.

"What does this rustic cabin in the middle of a wilderness area have to do with Chloe's murder?" Signe asked.

"I don't know, Signe. I haven't been there in years," Vincent said. "It's a very old log cabin with a small horse corral that's often used by backpackers for shelter. There is a beautiful mountain lake right next to it. It's deep in the wilderness on the north side, probably closest to the village of Truchas or Peñasco."

"Can you take me there?" Signe asked without hesitation.

"I don't think you know what you are asking, Signe," Vincent said in a weary voice. "You don't have wilderness areas in Denmark. The Pecos is over 200,000 acres of rugged mountains, forests and lakes with no roads and no motorized vehicles allowed." Vincent flashed back for a minute to his ATV adventure with the piñatas at the state fair. "Plus the Pecos is at high elevation in northern New Mexico and it is winter. It would be very possible in late spring, say, around May 20th."

"Can you take me there?" Signe said, again, in that maddening, demanding tone that Vincent had heard before.

"I suppose so," Vincent relented. "It will take two horses and a mule, tents, sleeping bags, food and lots of permits."

Something about this sounded familiar to Signe after her adventures with Juan in Argentina.

"I can't wait until spring, Vincent." Signe said. "I could take Jack but his shoulder isn't fully recovered. I don't think he could saddle a horse or lift packs, and I can never remember which strap to hook to what. Can we go this weekend?"

"The answer is yes, *querida*," Vincent said resignedly. He was already making lists of supplies and the permits he would need in his head. He drove Signe to her apartment. She invited him in, kissed him deeply, and caressed his tight ass. They made love hurriedly. Signe was tense and she thought the sex might relax her so that sleep would come easier. She was exactly right.

The next morning she told Chief Hartford about her discovery and her plan. By this time Gerald knew her too well to try and discourage her. He wished her luck.

Vincent spent the day securing two stout horses and a mule. He filled the back of his pick up with supplies and borrowed a horse trailer from a friend. Signe told Vincent that Mr. Torvaldson would pay for the expedition. However, she wasn't as confident of his support since she had come on to Sven, and left him naked and aroused when she fled from the Eldorado Hotel at the last minute.

Before heading into the Pecos Wilderness, Signe drove to Albuquerque to check on Svelty. When she first got to St. Joseph's ICU she found Svelty's cubicle empty. Signe's heart sank for a minute. She was afraid that some unexpected complication had taken her witness. However, Signe found her favorite nurse who told her that Svelty was extubated, and so much better that they transferred her to the fifth floor. Signe found Svelty in her new room, very pale and drowsy looking, but sitting up in bed. There was remarkably little equipment around her, just one IV.

"Mrs. Patterson, I'm Detective Signe Sorensen of the Santa Fe Police. Do you remember me?" Signe asked in a rather loud, slow voice.

Svelty seemed to be trying to focus on her guest but her eyes wandered some and she didn't speak. "You have had a terrible illness brought on by an overdose of pills. Do you remember any of that, ma'am?" Signe thought that Svelty was going to speak but she didn't. "I had a very nice visit with your mother and dad. I look forward to seeing them again," the detective said as she rose and left the room. Discouraged, Signe walked down the hall and at the nurse's station was surprised to see Dr. Josephson.

"Good morning doctor. I just visited Katherine Patterson." Signe said.

"Yes. She is remarkably better and will be able to go to a rehab hospital soon." Dr. Josephson said cheerily. "She's way ahead of schedule on her recovery."

"She doesn't seem to be able to speak, doctor," Signe said in a disappointed voice.

"I wouldn't be too worried about that at this point, detective," Dr. Josephson said in a kind voice. "She is still foggy from the barbiturate and the hypoxia; I'm sorry, low oxygen, from her lung problem. Her metabolism, that is her body chemistry, is just getting back to normal and that also can affect cerebral function. Moreover she had a tube down through her vocal chords for nine days which will impair her ability to speak. In addition, she is socially isolated—no one is visiting her, except you."

"Will she recover her mental capacity and be able to converse?" Signe asked now in a worried tone.

"I'm very confident she will recover fully, although she will have some amnesia for her hospital stay. Be patient detective. I would give her another week or two," Dr. Josephson said. "Say, could I buy you lunch?"

"Sure," Signe said surprising herself. Dr. Josephson took her to The Quarters on Yale for what, he thought, were the best ribs in the southwest. They had a companionable meal without innuendo or flirting. Signe felt so relaxed that she got the delicious tangy claret colored barbecue sauce all over her face and blouse. She felt completely relaxed and a little bit sleepy on the drive back to Santa Fe.

When she returned to her desk she had a message from Christopher Malloy of the *New Mexican* Santa Fe's local newspaper. She had received two other phone messages from a reporter that she had simply crumpled up and tossed in the wastebasket. Signe felt she had to return his call. Signe Sorensen did an inventory of her soul frequently and when she did so she found only three areas of prejudice. Each seemed well founded in her experience. She hated criminals especially ones that hurt, raped or murdered others. She liked their lawyers even less because they made money helping the undeserving. Also, unlike criminals, lawyers typically came from the middle and upper class not from the dirt poor, child abusing, and poorly educated underclass. In other words, lawyers had a choice about how they spent their lives, and many criminals didn't. A lawyer could have actually chosen to do something helpful with his or her life.

She saved her deepest prejudice and derision for newspaper reporters. She found them intellectually deficient, expedient, flashy and never held to account for what they wrote. When Mr. Malloy sat down next to her desk Signe was already seething.

"I'm here Detective Sorensen about the death of Chloe Patterson which occurred over seven weeks ago." Mr. Malloy began. "Her father tells me she was a healthy young woman and that her tragic death still has not been explained by you. I plan on running a front page story on this tragedy."

"I'm afraid, Sir, I can't tell you anymore about this on going investigation," Signe began. "Your approach, frankly, sounds like a threat, Mr. Malloy. I don't wish to compromise any of my witnesses or leads unless you have something to offer me, right now."

"I don't have anything to offer you. You're the detective," Mr. Malloy spit at Signe. "Yet, you aren't successfully at solving crimes, and your department is inept. I've read about your exploits in the Copenhagen papers. Three high profile unsolved murders in two years. You let the trail go cold and now there is little hope of ever catching those Danish miscreants. The Santa Fe Police file yearly reports with the state which I have access to. Only 74% of murders in the county have been solved in the past five years. Here is a possible headline—'Nineteen Murderers Still on the Streets of Santa Fe Today.' I could make this into a ten part series and get nominated for a Pulitzer Prize. I will smear you all over the front of my paper in hopes of apprehending this young woman's killer."

"Get out of my office you disrespectful, foul mouthed, loser," Signe shouted as she pushed a pile of folders in his direction. Christopher Malloy dodged the falling folders and sauntered out of the station house. Signe followed behind the reporter just wanting some fresh air. However, as she walked by the lab Valerie called to her.

"I got the first transmissions from Wanda's choker just now," She began. "Reception is only fair, but I can tweak that."

"What did 'Tony the Squid' say?" Signe asked as her anger started to abate.

"There was a long 'I missed you', 'can you forgive me?' preamble. I'll spare you that drivel," Valerie began. "Then she asked some questions about a kidnapping in New Jersey I think. He was pretty forthcoming. Then there was another long section of cooing. Wanda talked about her fears of getting hurt by someone here in New Mexico and brought up Chloe's death. Anthony told her not to worry and then changed the subject."

"It's a start," Signe replied. "Have her in and give her some praise while you are improving the equipment. By the way, good work Valerie." Signe fled to the coziness of the Coyote Café.

CHAPTER 44

Vincent spent all day Thursday collecting and packing gear. The trail from Santa Barbara Campground to Beattie's cabin was twenty-two miles long and uphill. Vincent figured, the trip should be one day in and one day out with two strong horses and a pack animal. So to provide a safety margin, he packed enough food and fodder for four days. Each horse would carry a rider and eighty pounds of supplies. The mule would carry 210 pounds of supplies. Permits from the Department of the Interior for the trip required long forms but were quickly granted.

Signe and Vincent left Santa Fe Friday morning at 8:30 after a large breakfast. The horse trailer was actually large enough to hold four animals. It was long and heavy and slowed Vincent's pick up. The high road to Taos that led to their starting point was narrow and curvy which also slowed their progress. They drove through a series of small villages—Nambe, Las Trampas, Truchas and Peñasco. Each village was a scattering of old adobe buildings centered around a small but well kept church, which acted like the hub of the wheel. Traffic through each village wasn't heavy but was slowed by farmers, often with their families, driving in and out of town usually in 20 or 30 year old Ford pick up trucks. The trucks were dented and the hoods and fender had lost most of their paint to the sun or frequent polishing. At Las Trampas they got behind a small truck pulling a homemade trailer with 'in tow' spelled out in black electrical tape across the tailgate. The old truck could barely go up hill. Signe could feel Vincent's impatience rising. After that truck turned off, Vincent quickly caught up to a large black road resurfacing vehicle. It had two dishes stuck on the top and large black rhomboids angling toward the rear, with pipes and gauges everywhere. Vincent thought it resembled the starship in *Star Wars*. It was only going nine miles per hour.

Finally, Vincent turned south along a twisty dirt road out of Peñasco to the Santa Barbara Campground wilderness trail head. Once at the campground, it took Vincent an hour to saddle and load the horses and mule with Signe's help. Finally, they climbed into the saddle with relief and headed south along the trail. However, it was nearly 1 p.m. The trail was initially wide and, at first, rose gradually through a grove of cottonwood trees, bare of all their leaves. The snow was only nine inches deep. However, the sky was filled with dark gray low hanging clouds. Soon it began to snow hard with large soft flakes falling everywhere.

As the trail rose even further a small icy stream appeared on the right side of the trail. In spots where it wasn't frozen over it gurgled pleasantly. As the horses moved upward the snow got heavier and deeper. The 13,000 foot tall Truchas Peaks on their right hand side showed gray rock on the bottom but the peaks were lost in the heavy clouds. Occasionally the horses slipped on the ice underneath the snow. Signe and Vincent were both heavily dressed in down jackets with hoods and heavy insulated gloves, but they weren't moving, just sitting in their saddles adjusting to the shifting gait of the horses, so they both got cold. The horses moved heavily uphill and snorted huge clouds of steam. After going only five to six miles the sky began to darken and the snow fall got even heavier.

Looking at the ominous clouds in front of them, Vincent suggested turning back and trying again in a few days. However, Signe had studied reports about moisture in the Pecos Wilderness. She pointed out that, if this was an average year, in only two weeks the northern part of the wilderness would have six and a half feet of snow pack, and would only be accessible by snow shoes for the next six months. She felt this was their only real chance to get the evidence.

Over the next several miles the trail traveled along a ridge where the snow was blown away and they made more rapid progress. By six p.m. it was totally dark. Vincent and Signe both used headlamps to spy out the trail ahead, but the going was slow. Huge snow covered limbs stretched across the trail above them looking like grasping beasts in the harsh artificial light from their headlamps. Finally at 11 p.m. when both were tired, wet, and very cold the lake and then the cabin came into view. Vincent unsaddled the animals quickly while Signe built a large fire. Both crawled into their sleeping bags by the fireplace and once they were warm went to sleep quickly without eating.

The next day broke grey and the snow was still falling hard. Vincent stirred the embers of the fire and added wood. Both were ravenously hungry and as soon as the fire burned down Signe began cooking. She fixed large pancakes with warm maple syrup and slices of ham. Vincent came in from tending the horses and the mule and wolfed his food down. With his mouth full of pancake Vincent reported that two feet of snow had fallen during the night and that, with the snow still falling, they wouldn't be going anywhere soon.

After washing the dishes Signe put on sterile gloves and began searching the cabin. Old supplies, bedding and some clothing were stacked on shelves and in cupboards. She went through every item carefully and methodically. Nothing struck her as being important or useful in her investigation. To be safe, she had Vincent sort through the same old and worn materials. He came to the same conclusion.

After lunch Signe found a tattered pack of playing cards. Dozens of games of fish, war and gin rummy followed. When they got bored of cards, Vincent threw several logs on the fire and Signe piled their sleeping bags near the flames. They fondled each other and then made love more leisurely than they had in weeks. After three orgasms Signe decided Vincent had proven to be an excellent pupil. Finally, Vincent was sitting cross legged in front of the flames with Signe facing him with his erection deep inside of her. As he started to move faster and deeper he took her left arm in his right hand and put her arm behind her back. Suddenly as his breathing quickened he pulled her arm upward and she felt a sharp pain in her triceps. He had never hurt her during sex or any other time. She reacted with surprise and pain bringing her right elbow into his face as she fell back off of him.

"What happened? I was sooo close." Vincent panted.

"You hurt me. My arm doesn't bend like that." Signe replied still annoyed.

"Can we try again? It really felt good." Vincent replied.

"No thanks, Vincent," Signe huffed as she stood and pulled on her long underwear. Signe got all of her clothing on and went for a walk around the lake on her snowshoes. They spent the rest of the evening lost in thought and not speaking to each other.

By the next morning another foot of snow had fallen but the storm was over and the sky was now blue, cold and clear. Vincent felt the two of them could walk out on their snow shoes, but he worried that the snow would now be up to the horses' chests preventing them from leaving the wilderness. He walked all three animals around the lake and found that they could still navigate, particularly if he alternated the lead between the three animals. The lead animal broke a path through the snow but tired quickly. He planned to take the stock halfway down the trail one day carrying some feed, then he would head back to the cabin and they would all walk out bareback the next day. In the meantime Signe and Vincent redoubled their efforts to find the clue. Just before Vincent was ready to head out, he discovered a small package wrapped in plastic on the lake side of the porch. Inside was a large goblet like those used for margaritas with lipstick on the edge. It was wrapped in a small woman's black cashmere sweater. Signe was delighted. She wrapped the goblet carefully in a blanket and placed it gingerly in her backpack.

Vincent left with the three animals each carrying only one day's food and led them half way down the trail. The animals seemed tired but in good condition; the trail was down hill. He placed hay and oats within reach of each animal after clearing a spot in the snow around each animal. He tied them there securely and then walked back up on his snowshoes. His only worry was coyotes but he felt the deep snow would limit their mobility even more than the horses. The next morning before first light Signe and Vincent started snowshoeing down. They reached the stock at noon. Vincent feed them the last of the forage and then all five, two humans, two horses and one mule walked out with no supplies. They reached Vincent's truck at 6 p.m. The slow dark ride home took two more hours and then Vincent dropped Signe at her apartment. She was cold, sore and tired and upset that Vincent had hurt her. She hoped it had really been an accident like he said when he apologized. She took a long hot bath and fell into bed.

CHAPTER 45

The next morning, on rifling through her accumulated mail for a letter from Axel, Signe came across her face on the front page of the Sunday *New Mexican*. The title was 'Murderers on the Streets of Santa Fe'. In a four page article Malloy had done every sleazy thing that he said he would. The first page had a picture of Signe and Chloe's heads side by side facing each other. First, Malloy told about the murder victims whose cases were unsolved in the county. He had quotes from orphaned daughters and depressed, nonfunctioning widows. The article went on to the failings of the Santa Fe Police in solving local murders. The next section went, into agonizing detail, about Signe's unsolved cases in Copenhagen. All in all it was a sensational pile of muckraking without any attempt at balance. Signe threw the paper down in disgust and for the first time thought seriously about fleeing back to Denmark.

While ruminating about how she would torture and murder Christopher Malloy, Signe was startled by a call on her cell phone. It was Dr. Mark Josephson and she suspected it would be bad news.

"Good morning, Signe," He said cheerily and she was relieved. "Thanks for letting me take you to a 'dive' for lunch. Can we do that again?"

"I can't tell you how much I enjoyed the time," Signe said in a sleepy husky voice. "Of course we can do it again. How's Svelty?"

"Oh. She's the reason I called." Dr. Josephson began. "She woke up yesterday and she's totally clear even though her voice is still just a whisper. She should go the rehab hospital in two or three days. The reason I called is that I think now is the time to ask her some questions about what happened. Sometimes mental state deteriorates again with barbiturate overdoses. Some of the large quantity of drug is stored in the bodies' fat and can come back in to the blood stream unexpectedly with recurrent coma or mental confusion. I don't want you to miss this lucid interval."

"I'll get around and come right down," Signe replied. "Thanks for the info." As she punched the 'end' button on her phone, she jumped out of bed and headed for the shower. She was on the road in twenty minutes. When she got to the fifth floor and slipped into Svelty's room she noticed that the patient was sitting up in bed, alert and wide awake. Signe pulled a chair to the side of the bed and scooted the chair up toward Svelty's head.

"Good morning, Mrs. Patterson, I'm Detective Sorensen," Signe began speaking slowly and loud. "I'm investigating your daughter Chloe's death."

"I know who you are detective," Svelty replied promptly in a coarse whisper. "Thank you for coming to see me in the hospital"

"I've been visiting you for the past three weeks. You were critically ill," Signe began. "I'm so glad you are better."

"I'm sorry, but I can't remember anything during that period," Svelty said. "It's all a blank. They say I took a bunch of pills. I can't remember that, but it doesn't sound like me. I've been upset about Chloe's death and Dirk's erratic behavior but I wasn't depressed. I've never attempted suicide."

"I'm wondering if someone forced you to take those tablets, Svelty," Signe replied. "Don't worry about it. Maybe your memory will return with time. Right now you should just focus on getting better."

"I feel stronger and more alert every day," Svelty said.

"I got to talk with your parents when you were in the coma, Svelty," Signe said. "They seem so supportive and kind."

"They have been great and when I'm better I will probably go to Oklahoma to recover," Svelty said.

"I'm going to go now and let you rest," Signe said. "Here's my cell number. If you remember anything, call me."

Signe went across the driveway to Dr. Josephson's office. They had a cup of coffee together and talked. Mark thought there was a good chance that Svelty's memory would improve with time. They had their usual pleasant conversation and just enjoyed each others company.

Signe drove over to the Office of the Medical Examiner and picked Dr. Gilchrist for an early lunch. They went to their favorite, The Artichoke Café, for cold asparagus with hollandaise sauce and seared tuna. They held hands and agreed to spend an evening together soon. Signe felt upbeat and positive on her drive back north.

On the way back to Santa Fe Signe called a group of people on her cell phone. She checked in with Jefferson Barclay who hadn't heard anything new about the murder. She asked Vincent to check up on Irma Perez's pregnancy. She also called Chief Hartford to let him know about the trip to the Pecos and Svelty's condition since she hadn't been in to the station house since the weekend. The chief wanted to know all about the Pecos Wilderness trip so Signe played it up a little bit. She told him all about the snow storm and getting trapped at the cabin with Vincent. She told him about their difficulties on the trail due to the snow and the wind. Finally, she told him about the goblet that she found. He seemed pleased.

When she got back to the station house she checked into the lab. Valerie had been working on the goblet all day. The goblet was wrapped in an expensive cashmere sweater that was not worn or dirty. It contained no stains or chemicals. However, the inside of the goblet had traces of chloroform in it. After forty-five minutes of searching Valerie found one blond hair on the inside of the sweater. She would check the DNA against a known sample from Chloe's body.

She checked the goblet under visible light and found lipstick on the rim. She saw some greasy areas on the goblet that might be fingerprints, however, they were faint. She applied a powder but the prints were too faint to yield a complete print. She tried a modified and filtered xenon light source to improve resolution and felt that she had eight good finger prints and one smeared print. However the resolution was still not good enough to match to the prints in the National Criminal Data Bank and other collections of finger prints. She would do the DNA analysis that afternoon and take the goblet to Albuquerque in the morning. The FBI there had a new argon ion laser that was supposed to be fifty to seventy times more sensitive for analyzing weak or old finger prints.

After rewrapping the goblet, Valerie sat Signe down with a bunch of transmissions from Wanda's wire. Aside from frequent episodes of intercourse, Signe decided they really did miss each other, there were several substantial transmissions. Both talked about a kidnapping back in New Jersey. Signe decided she would have that info transcribed and sent to the FBI in New Jersey. Both Anthony and Wanda talked about their tailing efforts in Santa Fe. They verbally agreed on who they would continue to tail and monitor with bugs. Of course, Signe was high on the list. Both the BMW and the Crown Vic were slated for transmitters the next day. Little came up about the murder until the end of one long recording.

"I think the police will try to pin this murder on me," Anthony blurted out.

"I know you are too smart to let that happen, Tony," Wanda began. "Look at what you got away with in New Jersey. Besides I thought you told me that you had an airtight alibi for that afternoon."

"I did, but now my cover guy is starting to seem a little shaky and undependable," Tony said.

"Tell me you didn't kill that poor girl, Tony," Wanda said in a pleading voice.

"You know me better than that," Tony said emphatically. "But I do work for Mr. Patterson and you do know how much financial and other troubles he's gotten into. We've talked about it, baby. It's my job the help him with everything, legal and illegal, you know that."

"I don't like the sound of that, Tony," Wanda replied. "Do you want me to fix dinner?"

"Ya, I'll be home around seven thirty." Anthony replied.

Signe decided to call Wanda in and see if she could get her to push Anthony Squitero harder. Wanda's remark about dinner broke a valuable line of questioning about Anthony and Dirk and what Anthony would and would not do.

Signe called Vincent to chat and also to find out about Irma. Vincent reported that the young woman had gotten large very quickly and there was the possibility of twins. Irma had had an ultrasound last week and it was only one large fetus. Vincent volunteered that perhaps the reason she looked so alarmingly large was because she was only four feet ten inches tall. Otherwise mother and baby seemed to be doing well. Irma wasn't married but she had been seen repeatedly with a young man at school and he had come over to the Perez house. Signe wondered if she should try to give the young man some money to marry Irma. However, again she couldn't think of a way to do it without getting dragged in in the end. Perhaps she ought to have feelings about her potential grand child, but she searched her soul and found none.

CHAPTER 46

She arranged to have dinner that night with Sven Torvaldson. He was balking at paying for the Pecos trip and she felt badly about the way she had treated him. She suggested an early dinner and a movie to keep it light. They met at the Palace. Sven brought the traditional single rose. Signe thought that was a good omen. After the traditional pleasantries Signe plunged in.

"I want to apologize again for the way I ended our last meeting at the Eldorado Hotel," Signe began. "I find you very attractive, and I enjoy being with you. I acted on my true feelings all of that that evening. However, then I got anxious and uncertain. It might have been easier to just go ahead that night and sort it out later, or never see you again. But you have been a good friend and support and if nothing else I was being honest."

"Thanks for bringing it up, Signe," Sven answered. "Despite your assurances that evening I was afraid I had made a misstep or read the signals wrong. You are a friend and I want to have a deeper association with you on your terms. However, as you saw that night, I find you very sexy and want a physical relationship with you. In point of fact, I still think about you every day and often replay that evening together."

"Ever since we first met Sven there has been one question bouncing constantly off the walls of my brain," Signe said urgently. "Are you married?"

"Sort of," He replied evasively. "Well, yes. I have a wife and a daughter. We have been together for six years but the last two or three have been bad. No affection, lots of arguing and almost daily fights. We've been to counseling but it hasn't helped. I've asked for a separation but Jessica is worried about the effect on our daughter. We haven't had sex in years."

"Thanks for your honesty," Signe replied earnestly. "Maybe, we should just be friends until you get this sorted out?"

"I'd like that," Sven replied. "Shall we go to that movie?"

Signe had suggested dinner and a movie when she had called Sven earlier that day. They walked down the street to an old nearby theatre and saw *Unfaithful* with Diane Lane and Richard Gere which was set in a dark Greenwich loft filled with old books. Signe wasn't sure she'd made a good cinematic pick as the adulterous tryst between Diane and her young French lover got more graphic and urgent. At one point he slid his long slender fingers under the band of Diane Lane's white suburban panties. However, Sven kept his arm discreetly on her shoulder throughout the show. They kissed once when they got back to her car. The kiss was a little long for friends but Signe enjoyed it and didn't end it first. She was still tingling from watching the young actor's erotic touches in the movie.

Valerie called Signe from Albuquerque the next morning.

"You are not going to believe what I have found!" Valerie shouted excitedly into the phone. "You will have to take me to lunch!"

"Okay, okay, what?" Signe replied.

"First, I did the DNA analysis on the hair from the sweater late last night and it's a match with the victim." Valerie said. "I used the cool argon laser the FBI has to lift images of the prints from the Goblet. It's awesome. The laser enhanced the ridges so they were as clear as a freshly painted center line on a blacktopped road."

"And?" Signe said impatiently.

"There are five fingerprints on the goblet from Anthony Squitero's right hand and four other finger prints on the goblet. One is badly smeared, however the other three are from Chloe Patterson's right hand!" Valerie screamed into the phone.

"Get back here right away, Valerie," Signe said. "You have the murder weapon. Protect it."

Signe burst into Chief Hartford's without coffee and after a cursory knock. She told Gerald Hartford what she had just heard about the goblet. They decided together to bring Anthony Squitero in for questioning before they called the district attorney.

First, Signe had to catch up on her partner. While she was buried in snow in the Pecos, Jack had been working an armed robbery at a local saving and loan. The lone robber had only partially covered his face so there were lots of pictures and crime stoppers led them to the robber's trailer in La Cienega. Jack was ready to throw himself back into the Patterson murder.

Signe and Jack took the Crown Vic to Anthony's office and escorted him to the station house without hand cuffing him. Jack put him in an interrogation room and read him his rights. Signe put the chief and one other detective behind the large one-way mirror before she went into the room.

"We have brought you in today, Mr. Squitero, to question you about the murder of Chloe Patterson," Signe began. "We have new evidence that links you to the crime. Tell me what you know about her death."

"I have been checkin' on this case since it happened, as you know detective," Anthony began. "I think it is complicated and not the work of one person."

"What was your role in it?" Signe enquired.

"I am innocent," Anthony replied without hesitation. "May I go now?"

"No," Signe replied. "I feel I have enough to hold you. Lock him up Jack. You may have your one call."

Jack decided to handcuff Mr. Squitero before taking him to booking.

"God damn it, detective I'm innocent!" 'Tony the Squid' yelled over his shoulder as he was propelled down the hallway toward the holding cells. "You've got the wrong man!"

An hour later Anthony Squitero was out on bail and his arraignment was scheduled. Christopher Malloy from the *New Mexican* called ten minutes later. He had heard that they had arrested a suspect.

"I see that I finally got you guys working on the Patterson case, detective," Chris began insolently. "What can you tell me about the person you have arrested? I'll put the story on the front page."

"No comment," Signe said with delight as she slammed the phone down. Three other detectives and several uniformed officers congratulated Signe on the arrest. Signe went to her 'new' desk and organized all the folders there that related to the Patterson. As she was walking out of the station house she got a call on her cell phone.

"Hello detective. This is Svelty Patterson calling," Svelty began in a hoarse voice. "My memory has come back and I need to talk with you as soon as possible about what happened to me."

"I want to hear what you have to say in person," Signe replied. "May I come and visit you in the morning?"

"That would be fine," Svelty replied. "I'm still at the rehab hospital getting my strength back. Do you need directions?"

"Yes, just give me the number on your bedside phone and I'll get them from the staff." Signe said. "I'll see you in the morning."

Signe got up early and drove to Albuquerque once again. As a precaution she put in a call to the Albuquerque Police and contacted Lisa Gonzalez. Lisa was a detective second grade that Signe had worked with on a case right after her arrival in Santa Fe. Signe asked Detective Gonzales to accompany her to the rehab hospital to hear what Svelty had to say. Signe picked Lisa up at headquarters and after a swing through Starbucks, she drove to the Rehabilitation Hospital of New Mexico located on the south side of town. Svelty was sitting up in her room in a dressing gown with her makeup on.

"You look so much better, Mrs. Patterson, than when I last visited," Signe began.

"Thank you, Signe," Svelty replied.

"I'd like you to meet Detective Lisa Gonzalez from the APD," Signe said. "She might be able to help us."

"I hope so," Svelty replied. "The reason I called you is that I've had a sudden return of memory. I can't remember anything during the two weeks I was in the hospital but I do recall the events that led up to my almost dying in the hospital. Dirk and I had had a terrible fight. He had received $2,000,000 from the insurance policy on my step daughter's life. He hid the money and I suspected he was using it for barely legal ventures. I confronted him and he became furious. He hit me and then dragged me into the den by my hair. He got his gun out of the safe and threatened to shot me. I backed down because he was in a black rage. He asked for a few minutes to cool down. When he came back he seemed calm. He had two scotches in his hands. He offered me one and apologized which he had never done before. I was still anxious and afraid and I drank the scotch rather quickly. That's the last thing I remember."

"So you think that the potentially fatal dose of barbiturates was in the drink, Mrs. Patterson?" Signe asked.

"Yes," Svelty said with conviction.

"And you believe that Mr. Patterson tried to murder you?" Signe asked.

"Yes, for the insurance money," Svelty replied.

"If I take you down to the station house, now, will you sign a statement to that effect, ma'am?" Detective Gonzalez asked.

Svelty nodded her head vigorously up and down. Her damaged vocal chords had given out. It was the most talking she had done since the overdose. Once Mrs. Patterson was dressed the two detectives took her to headquarters. Signe left Svelty with Lisa and drove back to Santa Fe. On the way she called Dr. Josephson and Bernadette just to chat.

Driving along the massive west face of the Sandia Mountains she found their dark peaks less foreboding than usual. She reflected on the change in fortune she had experienced in the last 10 days. Suddenly, after weeks of frustration, her murder case had cracked wide open. A suspect was charged with the crime. Anthony and Dirk, the two men she had suspected from the beginning, were both charged with crimes. No wonder the Sandia Mountains looked friendlier.

CHAPTER 47

When she got back to Santa Fe, Signe told her partner, Jack, about Svelty's revelation. Then she brewed a fresh pot of extra strong coffee and took two cups into Chief Hartford's office. He wanted to hear all about the meeting with Svelty. Signe told him how much she had improved since their last visit and how physically she was back to her gorgeous 'trophy wife' self. She said that Dr. Josephson had predicted that Mrs. Patterson might recover more of her memory as time went on. Signe was surprised that the fog had lifted so completely but Dr. Josephson said, on the phone, that it often happened just that way.

"Do you believe her, Signe?" The Chief asked.

"Oh, yes. I think she's telling the truth," Signe replied. "Her story really fits. Dirk Patterson was probably involved in Chloe's murder and he got what he wanted out of that—$2,000,000. But the insurance man, Mr. Torvaldson says that he is still in bad financial straits. Remember he had another policy on Svelty that was only voided by suicide if it occurred in the first year after the policy was issued. He needed the cash. Svelty was also furious at Dirk about Honey, the stripper from The Wild Pony, that Dirk gave a job at his firm."

"I have a major problem with Mr. Patterson forcing Svelty to take those pills, Signe," Chief Hartford replied.

"What is it?" Signe retorted.

"Didn't you tell me that Dirk called 911?" Chief Hartford said.

"Yes," Signe said.

"Why would he do that before she was dead?" The chief responded.

"For two reasons," Signe responded. "First he had run out of an alibi. His gun club meeting, where dozens of people would see him, was over and he only needed twenty-five minutes to get home. I drove it. Secondly, I think he made a mistake. When he got to the house Svelty was probably pulse less and barely breathing. He expected her to be dead by the time the EMTs arrived, so he called. In reading about Marilyn Monroe and all the other secobarbitral suicides, an unusual contradictory effect has been found. One to two hours after ingestion of a lethal dose the victim wakes for an interval before slipping back into a coma followed by death. Have you every noticed that if you drink too much you fall right to sleep only to wake completely for an hour or so at 4 a.m.? I think Svelty was bouncing back up, and the EMTs caught her on the upswing."

"That's a very clever explanation, Signe," Chief Hartford said. "But, I'm not sure a jury would buy it."

"At least I convinced you, Chief," Signe replied.

The next day, Anthony Squitero was indicted on first degree murder charges in the death of Chloe Angela Patterson. Mr. Ruben Pelicanto, who was also retained by Mr. Patterson, entered a plea of not guilty for the defense. Stung by recent negative publicity in the *New Mexican* about their inability to solve murders, the police pushed hard on their friends in the judiciary for a speedy trial. Mr. Squitero, confident of his innocence also wanted a speedy trial so he could get on with his life. Judge Manny Ramirez was selected for the case. Both sides were pleased. He was new to the circuit court but thought to be fair and bright. The murder case was assigned, to a recently vacated block on Judge Ramirez' docket. Jury selection went quickly. Signe wondered to herself what a jury of peers in northern New Mexico would look like for an overweight Italian man from New Jersey with mob connections.

The state's side of the case, as presented by the District Attorney, was compelling. What was known about the who's and where's of the case were laid out by the DA in the first two days of the trial. Large poster boards summarized all the known facts. Detective Sorensen was the first witness called. After being sworn in she testified about finding the body. Signe had reviewed her notes from that day the night before and told about what she had seen and heard that day. She emphasized how sad it had been to come across such a young victim, until the defense objected.

Mr. Pelicanto's cross examination had been intense.

"You failed to mention a large hoof print on the victim's chest, Detective," he said. "In striving to give us a complete picture how could you over look this?"

"It was later determined that no damage had been done by an equine," Signe said. "I'm striving to give you a full picture, not bury the jury in irrelevant detail."

"Just give us the facts, Detective!" Pelicanto shouted. "And let us decide what's important or not."

"Yes sir," Signe replied. Well, there goes my credibility. Signe thought to herself.

"Was the body moved after the victim's death?" Mr. Pelicanto asked.

"I believe it was," Signe said. "Sergeant Gallegos of the New Mexico State Police may have moved it inadvertently."

"Do you know that for a fact, Detective?" Mr. Pelicanto asked.

"No I don't. I didn't discuss it with him." Signe said.

"Do you know who committed this murder, Detective Sorensen?" Mr. Pelicanto asked.

"No I do not, sir," Signe answered.

"Have you considered any other suspects for this murder besides Mr. Squitero?" Pelicanto asked. "And is it possible that someone else committed this crime?"

"Yes and yes." Signe answered.

"It seems to me that you have conducted a very incomplete investigation and now you are blaming this murder on my client because you are feeling pressure from the press," Mr. Pelicanto said rapidly.

"I object," the District Attorney said.

"Sustained," Judge Ramirez replied.

"We are all here today because of a goblet," Mr. Pelicanto began. "This goblet was found beside a snowy cabin deep in a wilderness area and purports to have finger prints from my client on it. This evidence was found by Detective Signe Sorensen. I will later demonstrate that this goblet is a fake, a plant, a hoax and tells us nothing about who committed this murder. Please tell us the preposterous story of how you found this evidence, detective."

"While I was investigating another crime involving a relative of the victim a number turned up," Signe began. "This number turned out to be coordinates from a global positioning system which pointed us to the evidence. After struggling for over a day through heavy snow we got to the cabin and Officer Jaramillo found the goblet. Analysis by the FBI lab showed finger prints on the goblet."

"Who put the goblet in this implausible place and why, detective?" Mr. Pelicanto asked his voice dripping with sarcasm.

"I do not know, sir. Perhaps it was hidden in an out of the way, but safe place, by an as yet unidentified accomplice. If that person was charged with the crime the goblet would exoneration him," Signe replied in measured tones.

"No further questions," Mr. Pelicanto said.

Sergeant Raymond Gallegos was next.

"How long have you been on the force, Sergeant?" Mr. Pelicanto began.

"Fourteen years," Raymond replied.

"When did you learn proper crime scene management?"

"At the academy, sir."

"You don't seem to have learned it very well, Sergeant," Pelicanto shot back. "How many crime scenes have you completely disrupted, as you did this one?"

"Objection," the DA said.

"Overruled," said Judge Ramirez. "Answer the question."

"Perhaps two or three because it was necessary to extract a victim that was still alive," Gallegos answered.

"So you admit to moving the corpse, and disturbing evidence in this case," Pelicanto retorted.

"Yes," Sergeant Gallegos mumbled sheepishly.

"In summary, because of you, we don't really know what happened in stall 17 that afternoon and anything further said about this case is pure conjecture. You have violated the most fundamental rules of crime scene management. After watching CSI on television, a ten year old child would have done a better job than you did on that October afternoon," Mr. Pelicanto concluded.

Stephen Samuels, CPA, was called next and answered questions about what he had seen that afternoon. His description of a heavy set swarthy man arguing with Chloe just before her murder bolstered the DA's case. After his testimony court was adjourned for the day. Despite attacking two witnesses Signe didn't feel that Mr. Pelicanto had scored many points. Even though the crime scene had been disrupted a body was still found there. The key piece of evidence in this case—the goblet was derided by Mr. Pelicanto. However, its smooth hard surface carried strong evidence of a link between the victim, the murderer and a poisonous substance. It had not been broken, figuratively, into shards by the defense. Signe reported the proceedings to Jack and the chief and then called to check on her *hetaerae*.

Svelty was back at home and getting stronger every day. Dirk was out on bail but Lisa Gonzalez had helped Svelty get a restraining order. It seemed that Dirk was staying at Honey's place. Wanda had been in court all day playing the part of Anthony's devoted and distraught companion. She was wearing a black sweater two sizes too small that focused attention on her gigantic boobs. She felt safe in Algodones with Anthony locked up, and would return the choker with the transmitter in it the next day.

CHAPTER 48

The next morning dawned cold and clear. A dusting of recent snow remained on the streets of Santa Fe. The upper half of the Sangre de Cristo Mountains was blanketed in several feet of glaringly white snow. This was Signe's first winter in New Mexico. She had never seen anything so evocatively stark. She seemed compelled to look to the east again and again. In her country when it snowed the heavy concentration of people and vehicles turned flurries instantly to a brown gruel. She was also very grateful that she wasn't still at Beattie's cabin in the depths of the wilderness. She imagined that the snow was now up to the tops of the windows and doors of that rustic log cabin. She wanted to put on her heavy clothing and walk the hills to the north and east of town. Instead she put on a black suit and raced over icy streets to the courthouse.

Vincent Jaramillo was the next witness called and sworn. He really should have been called first because he was the first one in the stall, Signe thought. Signe suspected Mr. Pelicanto changed the order to revisit the series of embarrassing questions that he fielded yesterday about the disruption of the crime scene.

"What were your first thoughts when you saw the victim, Officer Jaramillo?" Mr. Pelicanto began.

"I was anxious, Sir," Vincent began. "The victim looked small, young and very dead to me, even though it was my first murder."

"How long have you been on the force?"

"I started active duty on April 1st of 2002, sir."

"So, you would describe yourself as very inexperienced for such a complicated case?"

"Yes, sir."

"In other words you had no business being there. You were over your head. You were out of your depth," Pelicanto retorted.

"Objection, calls for speculation," The DA said.

"Overruled, goes to competence," Judge Ramirez said. "You may answer."

"I am inexperienced," Vincent began. "But I didn't disturb the body or violate protocol in any way, Sir."

"You were in over your head, as I said," Mr. Pelicanto. "The whole Santa Fe Police Department and the New Mexico State Police were in over their heads here. It resulted in multiple gaffes, missteps, and lost opportunities which I will enumerate. The final result was to accuse an innocent man of this heinous crime!" Mr. Ruben Pelicanto shouted as he looked toward the jury.

Signe knew Vincent well enough to know he was blushing under his even brown skin. She could see perspiration on his upper lip as he stepped down from the imposing elevated dark oak witness stand.

The next witness called was a total bolt from the blue for Signe. Tommy Rice walked up to the witness box in an ill fitting suit. Signe had only seen him in an orange suit at the jail. He looked better despite his fallen nose and nearly dissolved teeth from the chronic use of crystal meth. After he was sworn in the DA began questioning him. He went through Tommy's drug history in detail so that it couldn't be used to impugn him later.

"Tell us about your relationship with the victim, Mr. Rice," the DA began.

"I was her drug dealer," Tommy began. "I sold her marijuana, cocaine and crank. She had been a customer of mine for years, but she had only recently started buying crystal meth."

"You had seen her a few days before her death, is that right?" The DA asked.

"Yes."

"How did you find her?"

"She was usually smiley and flirty. This time she seemed real shifty and suspicious. She said she felt like a man was following her, and she was afraid."

Tommy had been called to shed light on Chloe's state of mind prior to her murder. It could have been done better by Chloe's fancy dancer boyfriend Johnny Armijo if he had only been alive, Signe thought to herself.

"Did she talk about going to the authorities?" The DA asked.

"No. She was too much of an edge player to do that and she didn't even know what the man looked like. She was looking forward to being out of Albuquerque at the State Fair for a few days." Tommy replied.

"It is well known that crystal meth makes its users paranoid, Mr. Rice," Mr. Pelicanto began. "You said that you sold this drug to her. Her mental state was affected by it. I have nothing further."

Judge Ramirez ordered a lunch break. Signe and Vincent sought some comfort in the fiery hot, red enchiladas at The Shed. Both agreed that the DA was doing a good job of tightening the noose on 'Tony the Squid'.

The afternoon in court was given over to expert witnesses on both sides. The DA's expert on fingerprints talked about the ion laser technique for reliably enhancing prints and the uniqueness of a person's prints. He emphasized the near infallibility for identification if prints from three or more fingers are recovered.

Mr. Pelicanto's expert from the prestigious Johns Hopkins University told about the fact that many people, we now know, have the same finger prints and reviewed all the problems with laser detection. Signe found both experts more boring than Dr. Larry Abramowitz. However, after three hours of droning on she decided they had argued to a draw, and the goblet remained intact in all its fragile, shiny hardness. At the end of this dueling expert diatribe Judge Ramirez dismissed court for the afternoon. Mr. Anthony Squitero would take the stand in his own defense the next morning and Signe was sure there would be no empty seats in the courtroom.

After he was sworn in at 10 a.m. the next morning, Anthony Squitero was questioned by the DA.

"Sir, you told Chief Hartford that you arrived in New Mexico on or about October 8th to investigate the murder," The DA began. "When in fact, you came to Santa Fe in early September. Why did you feel it necessary to lie about this?"

"It really wasn't a lie so much as my not wanting to tip my hand until I knew the players better," Anthony replied. "I would have corrected this as soon as I got a chance."

"You stated you were in the employ of the victim's father, Dirk Patterson," The DA queried. "Is that correct?"

"Yes, I was hired to look into his daughter's tragic death."

"Did he pay you to put bugs on Chief Hartford and Detective Sorensen's cars?"

"No, that was my idea."

"Did he pay you to hire Richard Lederback, an attempted assassin?"

"I don't know a person by that name, Sir."

"Mr. Lederback attempted to kill Detective Sorensen in a car wreck, shot and killed Officer Art Johnson, and then wounded patrolman Jack Gallegos.

Does that bring back any memories of him? I believe all of those crimes were committed at your instigation, Sir."

"That is a fucking lie."

"Watch your mouth on the stand Mr. Squitero," Judge Ramirez boomed. "Or I will find you in contempt of court."

"When did you first meet Dirk Patterson, Sir?" The DA asked.

"I did investigative work for him on a freelance basis starting around three years ago," Mr. Squitero replied. "He often needed help with accident cases he was working on, and we got to be friends. I was spending two to three months a year in New Mexico until this fall when I relocated here permanently."

"How much of that relocation was prompted by difficulties with the authorities in New Jersey over their high profile kidnapping cases?" The DA asked.

"Objection!" Mr. Pelicanto shouted as he jumped up.

"I'll allow it," Judge Ramirez said. "Goes to intention."

"I was never charged in any of those kidnappings and disappearances," Mr. Squitero replied.

"You carried out extensive investigations into Ms. Patterson's murder," The DA responded. "You carried out numerous bugs of phones, placed transmitters on police vehicles, and tailed official vehicles. All of these are felonies for which you may be prosecuted in the future. After all this effort what exactly did you find out about the person that committed this murder?"

"I think that they were brainy, well heeled, and covered their tracks well. I didn't even get close."

"Or was that because you actually committed the crime and were only pretending to look for the culprits?" The DA said.

"I swear to you and everyone in this room—I didn't kill this beautiful young lady," Tony said vehemently.

"How do you explain the goblet?"

"I'm been set up!" 'Tony the Squid' shouted. "I've never seen that goblet. I have done some illegal things in the past. When I came out here I turned over a new leaf. I have violated no laws since coming to this state."

Mr. Pelicanto spent fifteen minutes highlighting good things that Mr. Squitero did in his life, including working for the Bonaventure Orphan's Fund back in Newark. Sven had previously told Signe that this was a Mafia front organization for laundering mob money. Then Mr. Pelicanto focused on Tony's alibi.

"Where were you Mr. Squitero, on the afternoon of the murder?" Ruben Pelicanto began.

"I wasn't even in Santa Fe. I was in Albuquerque at an off track betting parlor." Tony began. "I spent the afternoon picking losers at Hialeah and Santa Ana. I lost about $700 on a series of ten or eleven races over four hours."

"Can anyone vouch for your presence there?"

"Yes. I was with my friend, Mr. Michelangelo Bachechi the whole time."

"Is he here today?"

"No. Unfortunately, he got tangled with the law back in New Jersey and couldn't be here. But I have letter from him supporting what I said."

"Are there receipts or other documents from the OTB showing that you were there?"

"Unfortunately, no. I bet with cash and the establishment was operating without a license and has since closed."

"I would like to enter this letter as evidence judge," Mr. Pelicanto said.

During closing statements, he DA summed up the motive and opportunity the defendant had for committing the crime. He made light of an alibi letter from a previously convicted felony. He reviewed the evidence and finally held the goblet up gently thrusting it toward the jury in the dim courtroom as he asked for a conviction. Mr. Pelicanto spoke the concluding words of the trial, using his years of courtroom experience in New York to speak eloquently about this case. He started by admitting the problems with Mr. Squitero's defense—a history of illegal activity, a weak alibi, and a potential motive. However, he concluded by claiming vehemently that the state had not proved its case beyond a reasonable shadow of a doubt.

"If a speck of doubt remains, and it does, about my client's guilt then, ladies and gentlemen of the jury, you are obligated to acquit him!" Mr. Pelicanto concluded with his arms spread in supplication and his upper body thrust into the jury box.

Judge Ramirez instructed the jury and sent them of to deliberation. Signe and Vincent shuffled slowly out of the crowded courtroom as shafts of winter sun from two high windows flooded across the polished dark wood tables where the attorneys had so recently debated.

CHAPTER 49

The next day while a heavy snow fell in Santa Fe from low soft grey clouds, the jury deliberated. Signe heard that the jurors asked for the goblet to be brought to them and that they also wanted a transcript of her testimony to be delivered to the jury room. Her imagination went wild, something it almost never did. She imagined an acquittal even though, to her, the evidence seemed overwhelming. She remembered how much she hated the operating principle in this large, very tolerant country-'beyond a reasonable shadow of a doubt'. In Europe a perpetrator such Anthony Squitero, known to his friends as 'Tony the Squid' would already be serving a long sentence. After the acquittal she imagined a juror talking to the press about her dubious and flawed testimony. Christopher Malloy would concoct another muckraking story for the *New Mexican* and entitle it, "Incompetent Detective Frees another Murderer".

Just as an even worse scenario was building in her brain, Signe heard a murmur go across the detective's bullpen. The jury was in. Signe and Jack slid across slippery snow packed streets to the old courthouse and Signe jumped out at the front door. Signe was walking through the thirteen foot tall oak door in the back of the courtroom as she heard Judge Ramirez say,

"Members of the jury, have you reached a verdict?"

"We have your honor," The jury foreman said. "We find the defendant Anthony Squitero guilty of murder in the first degree."

The gallery erupted in mixed gasps and cheers that filled the chamber the judge banged his gavel ineffectually.

Signe burst out of the courtroom with a horde of people. Christopher Malloy faced the crowd on the courthouse steps with a pencil poised over his notebook. He nodded in Signe's direction and smiled as if he wanted a word. She gave him a look of pure unadulterated hate and hurried on by brushing his shoulder in the jostling crowd. Signe was simultaneously elated and let down. After all those months of work when at times no one, not even Detective Hartford, believed in her she felt vindicated. The other side of the coin was the realization that she had had devoted every waking hour to working on or thinking about this case. What would she do now? She was a veteran and she had been here before and of course she would move on to a new case. It would preoccupy her and give her a new excuse to continue to avoid her demons and refuse to move ahead with her life. She had always done that. There was time to worry about that tomorrow. Right now she needed some oblivion. She invited Vincent to the Coyote Café for drinks and then to the Pink Abode for chicken Marengo. She doubted that Napoleon Bonaparte felt any more triumphant after his victory in Italy than she did that night. She took Vincent to his apartment and pleased him sexually in every way she could think of, but she didn't spend the night. At one point just before he came, for the third time, he held her left wrist too tight hurting her again if only for a few seconds.

Signe needed to get out of Santa Fe for a few days. In the past she would have gone with Axel, but of course, he was no longer at her beck and call. Vincent gave her things that she needed, but now he had hurt her twice. He was always probing her for commitment which caused her to push him away. She cast her mind about for someone to accompany her on a trip to the healing wilderness of New Mexico and she saw the wrinkled brown face of an older man.

She called Mateo Romero and he said agreed take a road trip with her. His only condition was that they head to the south where it was warmer. She packed her camping gear and then went to Albertson's early the next morning for food and supplies. She picked Mateo up at his home in Cochiti Pueblo and they headed south on I-25. They started to drive prior to picking a destination. They talked about Carlsbad Caverns, the ghost town of Mogollon and the Gila Wilderness. After driving nearly two hours they passed through the small dusty town of Socorro still without a destination. The geographical center of New Mexico, the fifth largest state is Gran Quivira a Tompiro Indian ruin that began in 600 AD and flourished from 1000 to 1600 AD. Several hundred Indians lived there in multistory dwellings with several kivas for religious and clan ceremonies. The modern day town of Socorro is only fifty miles to the south and west.

Major roads sprout off the freeway below Socorro so Signe and Mateo stopped beneath a large leafless cottonwood for some herbal tea made by the medicine man. They spread Signe's worn and soiled map of the state on the picnic table and contemplated their destination. Bosque Del Apache was nearby and flight of snow geese and sandhill cranes would be arriving daily, as winter progressed but there was little hiking. Elephant Butte Reservoir was not far to the south but without a boat it was hard to navigate. Mateo moved his index finger down to an irregular area to the south and east outlined in purple—White Sands National Monument. He thought this the perfect place to be alone with the New Mexico earth and sky. After gathering their things, Signe drove there following Mateo's directions.

The monument was largely deserted and they easily escaped a few recreational vehicles from North Dakota and Montana. As a Native American, Mateo Romero was allowed unrestricted access to the back country. He and Signe camped in a primitive campground with no other occupants. Each morning the sun rose over the Sacramento Mountains and warmed their tents. They hiked each day over the crystalline white dunes of calcium carbonate. A rare yucca or Jimson managed to survive in the white, nutrient poor chemicals, but otherwise rank on rank of undulating white dunes stretched away into the distance mostly vegetation free. The shadowed back sides of the dunes were a surprising royal blue color Signe noted.

As they walked Mateo talked about the Indian ways and how the Cochitis fit into the universe. She imagined that Chloe had heard much of this from the medicine man. Signe felt her mind relaxing even as the muscles of her legs got sore from all the hiking. At night Mateo was allowed to have a fire and he laid it carefully before sunset. When the sun sank behind the San Andres Mountains at this time of year it colored the dunes a bright orange and then a soft pink color. At night the heavens were lit with stars as thick as she had seen in another hemisphere, on the pampas in Argentina. After five days in the austere white dunes Signe felt like her old self. She drove home reluctantly and she stopped at every possible point of interest along the way to postpone her arrival. When she dropped Mateo Romero off at the pueblo he gave her a slender turquoise necklace as a remembrance.

Signe found it jarring to enter her old life the next morning. Papers relating to the Squitero conviction littered her 'new' desk and a large stack of messages sat on one the corner. Many of the messages were congratulations from co workers and friends over the conviction. There was a long effusive and flowery message from Jefferson Barclay which Signe read twice. Both of the *hetaerae* had called and there was even a note from Chief Nielsen in Copenhagen.

Signe called Svelty first. She was getting stronger daily. Her memories of the assault that led to her taking the pills were even stronger. Every night she had vivid nightmares about that evening. She awoke panting and sweating and going back to sleep was difficult. She was seeing a therapist twice each week. She was sure her anxiety level would skyrocket if Dirk came back into the picture but so far he was observing the restraining order. Dirk stopped by once a week to get things from the house. She easily arranged to be gone at those times.

Signe called Wanda next and Anthony's young accomplice jabbered excitedly on the phone. Signe thought perhaps she hadn't talked to anyone in a few days. She invited her to lunch at the Ore House. She knew Wanda didn't like Mexican food. Signe reflected on the way detectives got intimately involved in suspects and witnesses lives while the investigation went forward, only to drift apart quickly after the case was solved. Signe kept tabs in the Danish newspapers on the soprano who lived with Herr Müller, the German banker. Ironically, since the publicity about the crime Inge Johannsen's career had soared. She had signed a contract with Duetsche Grammophon perhaps the most prestigious classical label recoding in the world. She now was mentioned with Renee Fleming and Cecelia Bartoli in the ranks of worldwide soprano superstars.

Wanda was late to her lunch date and seemed anxious and distracted.

"I haven't been sleeping since Anthony's verdict," She said. "I'm afraid they will give him the death penalty. I love him! He's been better to me than any other man in my whole life. Hell, he's been better than any other *person* to me."

"Please don't forget the times he abused you, Wanda," Signe pleaded. "Also, he happens to be a convicted premeditated murderer, and the person that he killed in cold blood was a lot like you. I'm sorry, Wanda but you are talking crazy. What about your boyfriend from The Compound, Roger?"

"Roger is very sweet and always nice and supportive," Wanda began. "But he is soo boring. There isn't any edge to him. I need the excitement and the unpredictability! Without it I feel like I'm dying, Detective."

Signe didn't say anything further, but then she recalled Dr. Vivian Goldiamond's words about Wanda's borderline personality. Signe recollected the doctor's warning that Wanda could flip at any time.

CHAPTER 50

In two days time both Wanda and Signe would be back at the courthouse for the sentencing of Mr. Anthony Squitero. Signe knew that New Mexico was one of the few blue, that is, democratic states in the west. It was surrounded by a tidal wave of, red, republican states that voted for George W. Bush in 2000 and supported the death penalty. In a sea of red the nearest support for New Mexico was Iowa far to the east and California far to the west. Signe felt the chance of 'Tony the Squid' getting the death penalty, despite his life of misdeeds and the heinous crime he had committed, was very small.

That night Signe went to supper with Jefferson, Jack, Dr. Goldiamond, Dr. Abramowitz, Dr. Bernadette Gilchrist and Sven at the Pink Adobe. It was a celebration of the conviction organized by Signe. She wanted to thank all of them for their help bringing this very frustrating case to a conclusion. She ordered a special menu of Caesar salads made table side, artichokes and chateau briand. They all started off with cocktails and lots of cabernet sauvignon was served during dinner. By dessert everyone was happy and loud and glad to be celebrating. Signe sent everyone home in a taxi, kicked off her shoes and wandered into the kitchen with a large fresh glass of wine to talk with Dmitri, the chef. Signe hadn't felt so relaxed in a long time. She got some cooking tips before stumbling into a taxi for home.

Signe worked on cleaning up both of her desks the next day. She started with the new desk first putting all the material about the Patterson case in boxes. After she did that the desk was nearly clean. She was so pleased that she started on her old desk. Things didn't go as well there. Some of the material was from Chloe's murder but much of the clutter was from unrelated cases. As she pulled one brown folder out the contents spilled to the floor. It held the clues she had found in the stall on the very first day after the murder. First she picked up a piece of red paper which she later identified as part of the Fortuna's plane ticket from Argentina. Next she picked up a piece of milky plastic that she had identified as part of a syringe. She had put a piece of note paper in the folder that described a thumping noise. Several witnesses later identified it as the sound of the trailer hitch coming on done when Hercules was being taken away. Finally there was a slender cable tie that she remembered finding but never fully explaining. Had it been used to restrain the victim or to hold the syringe and vials of medicine or poison together? She wasn't sure but it didn't seem to matter anymore. The crime had been solved. She put the cable tie back in the folder and placed the folder in a storage box.

The next morning Wanda came by early and they both went to the sentencing. Judge Ramirez spoke about the crime and the findings of the jury and then turned to the punishment phase.

"Please stand Mr. Squitero," the bailiff said.

"Mr. Anthony Squitero the law allows me some latitude in sentencing you for the crime of first degree, or pre meditated murder," Judge Ramirez began. "I may sentence you to 30 years in jail, to life in prison or to death. First, though, is there anything you wish to say?"

"Yes your honor. I am innocent of this crime," Anthony began. "I did not kill this young woman and I ask for your mercy."

"I hereby sentence you, Anthony Squitero, to life in prison without the possibility of parole for the murder of Chloe Angela Patterson."

Wanda gripped Signe's arm with both of her hands and leaned against the detectives shoulder with relief. Wanda pushed her way quickly to the wooden rail that separated the spectators from the lawyer's tables. She leaned over the railing and hugged and kissed Tony while his hands were being cuffed behind his back. As they walked from the courtroom Signe had to support Wanda who seemed truly strickened. Wanda had just escaped from the grasp of a murderer who had used and abused her and yet she could only see this as a huge loss. Signe took Wanda back to the station and sat with her until she was calm.

Signe took two large cups of coffee into the chief's office. She told Chief Hartford about the sentencing and about Wanda's emotional response. They went back over the case to look for loose ends. They both felt that Richard Lederback, who was now dead, had been responsible for Signe's accident, Patrolman Art Johnson's murder and the ambush that wounded Jack at the Otowi Bridge. The horse had been legitimately sold to the Fortuna brothers for a large sum of money. Juan Vivendi had written Signe that he wouldn't go after the brothers about currency fraud. He would hold that charge as a bargaining chip if there was future trouble at the Terra Grande Ranch. At one point, Wanda would have implicated 'Tony the Squid' in money laundering since she was the mule who carried the money from the sale of the horse to the Barbados. However, Mr. Squitero was already sentenced to life in prison.

What about the shootout at The Wild Pony? Witnesses had all described two men and perhaps a getaway driver. More importantly, Dr. Bernadette Gilchrist had found bullets from two 9mm guns either at the scene. One of the shooters may have been Richard Lederback. Who was the other man? Perhaps Anthony or even Dirk with his new found love of guns. In any case, the murder was outside their jurisdiction and Chief Hartford doubted the Albuquerque Police would spend a lot of resources solving the crime. The victim was a drug addicted gambler and Albuquerque had a murder rate last year that was higher than New York Cities'.

Should Wanda be charged? She had admitted to tailing the police and putting transmitters on official vehicles. These were minor felonies and without Anthony's financial and emotional support seemed unlikely to continue. Neither Signe nor the chief seemed inclined to go after Ms. De Berneres. Perhaps, if left alone, she would find something constructive to do with her life. Signe thought she was smart and resourceful.

Chief Hartford reported that Sergeant Raymond Gallegos of the New Mexico State Police had gone before a review board. He had been found guilty of disturbing a murder scene, withholding evidence, and lying about both. He had been demoted from Sergeant and was on probation for one year. Gerald Hartford was surprised that he hadn't been thrown off the force.

Svelty would soon testify if Dirk were tried. Chief Hartford wasn't sure she was telling the truth. Perhaps, she was just trying to get out of a bad spot. He said that clearly she didn't trust Dirk, and was afraid of what he had become. Signe tended to believe Svelty mostly because she had been through a devastating coma and a prolonged recuperation. In any case, Signe would be attending Dirk's trial and have a chance to observe her more closely. Chief Hartford also admitted he had been wrong about Signe's trip to Argentina. He had thought it would be a wild goose chase and it had yielded valuable clues. Still reviewing the past three months Chief Hartford continued to wonder out loud if they were all wrong and that Svelty Patterson was really a cold blooded psychopathic killer. Maybe she had murdered Chloe, Art Johnson, and Johnny Armijo and had tried to kill Signe in the car wreck. Signe was so shocked at this revelation that her mouth dropped open.

PART 6

CHAPTER 51

Signe had trouble wrapping her mind around the idea of Svelty Patterson as an emotionless psychopathic killer. Despite her line of work she still saw people as basically good. However, in her fourteen years as a police officer and a detective she had seen her share of depravity. There was real cruelty and pain toward victims and often within families. She remembered one fifteen year old Danish boy who hadn't received a motorbike, a gift that he had his heart set on. He stabbed his mother, father, and two beautiful young sisters to death in a society where hand guns were hard to come by. When Signe helped take the young man in he had shown no sadness or remorse over his horrendous crime. So she decided she would have to give herself a chance to process the chief's intuition about Svelty. Keeping in mind that Dr. Vivian Goldiamond also felt that Svelty was possibly dangerous and unpredictable. Signe would watch Mrs. Svelty Patterson closely over the next few days.

Dirk Patterson's trial began in Albuquerque the next day. Signe was assigned to the trial by Chief Hartford. They both hoped she might uncover accomplices involved in Chloe Patterson's murder. Rather than drive back and forth, Signe decided to stay in the Duke City for a few days. Driving the dark stretch of I-25 where her accident occurred still made her anxious.

The District Court was held on the fifth floor of a twenty story building on the north side of Albuquerque's downtown. Signe thought the city center of Albuquerque had a confusing mix of two story and twenty story buildings with no coordination of style, size, or orientation. Looking at it, even from a distance always jarred her eyes. She thought it resembled a jagged, irregular, untended forest. It was America's 'every man for himself' and 'to hell with the neighbors' gone wild. In Copenhagen the city planners made the builders construct uniform buildings with a common architectural style all six stories tall. With her European sensibilities she found such a downtown warm and inviting instead of jarringly angular and disarrayed.

Signe took a seat in the back of the gallery before the trial began. She looked around and didn't recognize anyone. Dirk Patterson was charged with the attempted murder of his wife, Svelty Patterson. Svelty's attorney, Robert Van Meritt, was a young Albuquerque district attorney. Signe had heard that he was good and that like most Albuquerque barristers, disliked Dirk for his intrusive advertising and sleazy ambulance chasing.

Mr. Van Meritt presented the case against Dirk Patterson simply and clearly. The state contended that Mr. Patterson had attempted to murder his wife for $2,000,000 in insurance money of which he was the sole beneficiary. He tricked his wife into taking a barbiturate overdose. The amount he gave her in a glass of scotch was twice the lethal dose for a person of her size. Then when she was almost dead he called 911. When the EMTs arrived he was sure that she would be dead, and they would be unable to save her.

Mr. Van Meritt called Svelty to the witness stand. As she walked toward the front of the courtroom, Signe noticed her expensive coordinated outfit and perfect make up. She was beautiful and Signe knew she was very vain about her appearance. Detective Sorensen suspected she would do almost anything to preserve her showy and expensive life style.

Once she was sworn in, Mr. Van Meritt started with questions about the day of the alleged crime.

"Mrs. Patterson, please tell us, in your own words, what happened on the evening of your overdose," He began.

"We had a fight," Svelty began. "We had been fighting almost everyday since our daughter Chloe died, but this one was worse. Dirk was having terrible financial difficulties. He has mortgaged everything we owned. He had forty credit cards and he was still sinking. He got so angry that he pushed me and hit me repeatedly. One of his PIs taught him how to do that without leaving any marks."

Svelty began to cry and Mr. Van Meritt offered his handkerchief. Once she stopped crying, Svelty continued, "Then suddenly his mood switched. He seemed to take pity on me. He sat me down and was very comforting and soothing. He listened patiently as I shared my concerns. After a while, he went in the other room and came back with a glass of scotch for each of us. I was very upset and drank it quickly."

"What happened next?" Mr. Van Meritt asked.

"I began to feel dizzy almost immediately," Signe said. "I got nauseous and then my legs got numb. Dirk helped me lie down. Then he brought me an Alka-Seltzer. Within a couple of minutes I felt even worse. I couldn't move my arms or legs or even talk."

"What happened next?"

"I passed out."

"What is the next thing you remember?"

"I woke up in the hospital. People told me it was three weeks later."

"Have you ever considered or attempted suicide?"

"No. I mean sure I get depressed sometimes and I have always had trouble sleeping, but I've never even thought of suicide. I think it's a sin."

"Your witness," Mr. Van Meritt said.

Mr. Pelicanto, both Anthony and Dirk's lawyer, got to his feet.

"Mrs. Patterson, the police report says that there were twenty seven bottles of prescription medicine in your bathroom," He began. "They included oxycodone, Valium, Xanax, secobarbital and a variety of other what I would call 'psych meds' from several different doctors. If you we such a stable upbeat person why did you need such things? And so many of them?"

"I didn't say I never had problems," Svelty retorted. "I have had anxiety and panic attacks for years. Living with my husband is very stressful, and according to my years of therapy I have unresolved issues from my childhood. I'm very high strung."

"Do you remember an episode in Oklahoma where you were rushed to the hospital and had your stomach pumped?"

"Yes. I was fifteen and I took nine aspirin tablets. They didn't even keep me overnight."

"Were you trying to commit suicide?"

"In a way, yes. I had been dumped by my boyfriend before the prom. Do you remember being a teenager? I didn't think I would ever recover from it. But I never did anything like that again."

"Are you saying that the recent death of your only step-daughter, your violently dysfunctional marriage, and your impoverished financial condition haven't sent you into a depression?"

"You are an ass, Mr. Pelicanto and you have always been one," Svelty replied in an acid tone. "Of course I am affected by the tragedy in my life."

"You didn't answer the question, Mrs. Patterson."

"I was profoundly saddened by those heartbreaking events. I cried myself to sleep on many nights, but I didn't attempt to take my own life."

"No further questions, your honor," Mr. Pelicanto concluded.

Signe had watched Svelty closely and thought that she had done well. She saw no sign of psychopathology or mental illness. The judge called for a recess.

After lunch Dirk Patterson, esquire was called to the stand. Signe thought he looked puffy and slightly disheveled. He appeared very unlike the brash, rude, arrogant man she had met the night of Chloe's murder. The district attorney questioned Dirk about his background, his law practice, financial problems and marital difficulties. The DA went into great detail. The courtroom was hot. Signe had already sat through one long trial and she was tired of sitting. She had picked her line of work because she got to move around and be involved in several things at once. Despite her intelligence she had deliberately avoided more academic pursuits because she didn't like inactivity. She may have elected not to go to the university simply because sitting in class made her bottom hurt. During the testimony her mind wandered, she drifted off and was jolted back awake as her head came up with a violent jerk.

By the end of the questioning Signe decided that Dirk came off as a sleazy opportunist but also as a person with no criminal or violent behavior in his past. Signe didn't feel the DA was doing a good job of pinning the crime on the defendant.

Mr. Pelicanto's cross brought up every even marginally good deed done by Dirk and the list wasn't long. He stated repeatedly that Mr. Patterson had made the emergency call that saved his wife's life. Signe walked outside for a cup of coffee, and when she got back the judge was adjourning court for the day. Signe decided that they had battled to a draw. It was a case of 'he said, she said'. The next day experts for both sides would testify.

Mr. Pelicanto's expert spoke about the popularity and reliability of barbiturates for a successful suicide. His research focused on basically stable people who had reverses in their lives and drank to relieve the pain. He argued that once the alcohol lowered their inhibitions, they took medicines they often didn't understand well dying shortly thereafter. In his opinion it was almost an inadvertent death. He was convinced that this is what he thought happened to Mrs. Patterson.

The DA's expert was Dr. Bernadette Gilchrist, MD, FACFP and medical director of the Office of the Medical Investigator. She agreed with the previous expert's description of the frequency and method of death with barbiturates. However, she focused on the excitement phase of the overdose before the plunge into coma and death.

"Dr. Gilchrist, please tell us about your investigations into 'self-killing' or suicide," the DA said.

"I have published four papers on the pathologist's perspective toward suicide," Bernadette began. "Two focused on drug overdoses which are more common in young females."

"What is important about the way secobarbital behaves in the body in understanding this case, Doctor?"

"After the initial ingestion the person falls into a profoundly deep sleep. Then there is an excitement phase, at a variable time, where the victim is fully awake and actually hyper vigilant. This is followed by a prompt spiral into coma and death."

"Would our victim have experienced this excitement phase?"

"Almost certainly."

"How does what you have described fit into our crime?"

"It is my contention from reviewing the record that Mrs. Patterson was deeply comatose and seemed near death when her husband called the emergency network. He gave her no CPR. I believe he was confident she would be dead by the time help arrived. Instead Mrs. Patterson went into the excitement phase, a phase which her husband had no way of knowing about, and she was physiologically intact enough, if only briefly, to be saved."

Signe found Bernadette's proposal about what happened that night believable. After Dr. Gilchrist left the stand, both lawyers summarized their cases with compelling examples and passionate pleas. As the judge instructed the jury, Signe thought that the case against Dirk probably hadn't been proven. After all, the case rested on Svelty's admittedly unbelievable testimony. Signe felt the jury deliberation would be short so she decided to stay in Albuquerque one more night. Signe had a pleasant dinner with Bernadette and headed back to the hotel early.

When she got to her room she was suddenly wide awake. She hadn't brought a book. She called Vincent and told him every detail of the trial so far. Then she lamented that they hadn't seen each other in over a week and that she was horny. Vincent suggested phone sex. That's something I've never tried Signe thought as a slipped out of her clothes and jumped in bed with the phone. Vincent set the scene at the Kokopelli Bed and Breakfast where they had spent their first night together, and Signe's active imagination did the rest. She felt sleepy and pleasantly satisfied when they finished.

CHAPTER 52

Early the next morning, after starting some coffee in the room, Signe grabbed the *Albuquerque Journal* by reaching her arm far out into the hallway while pressing her nakedness against the inside of the door. The front page had a large black block headline, "Killer Flees Prison". The byline was Santa Fe, New Mexico. Signe threw her robe on grabbed a cup of coffee and sat down to read. The article told of a daring raid last evening that freed convicted murderer Anthony Squitero. Details were still sketchy, but some type of light aircraft had swooped in the exercise yard of the New Mexico State Penitentiary and air lifted the criminal over the prison walls. The prisoner was still at large.

Signe threw the paper down and called the police station in Santa Fe. Luckily Jack was there.

"Is Anthony still in the wind?" Signe asked.

"Yes, Signe. Law enforcement is in an uproar up here," Jack began. "We spent the night running roadblocks for the State Police. All leave and vacation days have been cancelled until further notice."

"How did he get out?"

"The State Police and prison officials are still investigating, of course, but it seems like a well thought out escape. It happened about 5:30 p.m. yesterday afternoon just as the sun was setting. The prisoners from cell block C were exercising in the central yard. You've seen the yard. It's a large space, perhaps half an acre, surrounded by the cell blocks which are three stories high on all sides. About forty prisoners got in a fight in the northwest corner of the yard. They were punching, yelling and throwing pieces of weight lifting equipment at each other. While the guards were distracted, an ultralight aircraft came in low over the west wall. The noise from the ruckus was so loud that no one seems to have heard the sound of its small engine. It landed

240

near the southeast corner where Squitero was hiding under a camouflaged tarp. He climbed aboard and the craft went over the wall to the southeast. The guard in the south tower saw the ultralight lift off and fired two rounds from his rifle, but he was too far away. he reported that the aircraft was staying low and going fast by then. He didn't think he hit them."

"Who was behind this?"

"No one knows. The guard said the pilot was a small person about one third the size of the prisoner. Something about the pilot made the guard think it might be a young female. However, the authorities think that he is mistaken."

So Wanda De Berneres sprang her loser lover from the State Pen and disappeared into the New Mexico night Signe thought.

"Thanks, Jack. I'll be back later today."

"I wouldn't come in if I were you, Signe," Jack replied. "You'll just get put on one of those tedious road blocks or sent to comb the hills south of town."

Signe decided immediately that Jack was correct. Let's see if I can help from Albuquerque she thought, heading to the business center of the hotel as she flashed her badge. In minutes she had three phones and a computer. First she pulled up a map of the area around the penitentiary. She suspected the felons would head to the south. It was the quickest way of getting away from population centers. The previous day's paper said that sunset was at 6:02 p.m. So she thought an inexperienced pilot like Wanda could fly for about 75 more minutes before the daylight would have completely failed her. A quick call to the Santa Fe airport located her pilot friend who that had advised her about aircraft when Hercules disappeared. He reported that most ultra light aircraft went 65 to 80 miles per hour. Signe printed out a map of northern New Mexico and drew a circle 90 miles from the penitentiary on the south side of Santa Fe. If she were Wanda she would avoid Albuquerque directly to the southeast—too many aircraft, military installations and people. There was little to the west except the small town of Grants. Also if she flew that direction she would have to fly over the San Mateo Mountains in the fading light. If she were Wanda she would fly down little used state route NM-14 over Cerrillos, Madrid and Golden for lights to guide her to I-40 and then fly east staying a couple of miles north or south of the interstate to avoid detection. The steady ribbon of lights from the traffic would have provided an infallible guide for the pilot. Just as it got really dark Wanda and Anthony would have arrived at Santa Rosa, NM with its unmanned airstrip. Signe called the State Police. Just her luck, Private Raymond Gallegos was patrolling near there as the search for the fugitives widened. She sent him racing to the airport with sirens blaring and lights flashing. He found an ultralight up against an old hanger under a camouflage patterned tarp. Signe suspected that she had found the escape vehicle and she asked Raymond not to touch it.

The airport had no permanent employees and no control tower. Signe asked Officer Gallegos to talk to the people that lived in nearby houses particularly at the west end of the runway. The prevailing wind in New Mexico was from the west and a pilot would use that to his advantage in getting airborne. Raymond radioed back in twenty minutes. Two people that lived just off the east end of the runway heard a multi-engine plane take off at 8 p.m. the night before. Signe put in an emergency call to the FAA. So far she had been able to think like Wanda and track her moves. Now she realized that no one knew what she had uncovered so far. She put in a call to Chief Gerald Hartford. After explaining what she had found, he said he would pass the information on to the chief of the State Police.

"Please get up to Santa Fe as quickly as you can, Signe," Chief Hartford said. "If you are going to solve this case all by your self you could at least do it from our jurisdiction."

"Yes, sir," Signe replied with pride in her voice.

Signe exploded out of the business center of the hotel yelling 'thank you's' over her shoulder, dragging her suitcase stuffed with tangled clothes and started driving north. On the way she called the FAA back. As she suspected there was no flight plan filed for a Santa Rosa departure the night before. She was again reminded of the transporting of Hercules from New Mexico. Had Wanda planned and coordinated that departure? Signe realized that she had never asked her that question. Why leave the ultralight where it could be found? Perhaps it was a way of thumbing her nose at the authorities. Wanda probably planned on it not being found for a few weeks at such a remote location. Then it would remind the police of her cleverness in escaping with 'Tony the Squid'.

Signe concluded that most likely Wanda didn't want to land at the next airport, one that came equipped with prying eyes while she had an ultra light in the cargo bay. Signe thought the best solution would have been to push the incriminating ultra light out of the aircraft over west Texas or wherever they headed. But when she called her airplane advisor, he reminded her that opening the cargo door while flying would dangerously destabilized the craft. Everyone in the country knew about the daring escape. The story had been featured on CNN with a picture of the penitentiary and an ultra light aircraft. The last report Signe saw showed Suzanne Malveaux, for CNN, standing next to the penitentiary wall with microphone and camera in the bitter winter morning cold. Clearly, Signe thought, Wanda's decision to abandon the ultra light had been a wise one.

When Signe got to the station house everything was in an uproar. She could only image what the State Police headquarters, across town looked like. The road blocks had been closed and the search parties were just coming in cold and tired from the hills south of the penitentiary. All available patrolmen and detectives were working on the fugitive's next move from the Santa Rosa Airport. Roadblocks were now set on I-40 as it reached toward Amarillo to the east. Signe thought that a waste of time. Three officers were working on all morning flights that were leaving the country for any foreign destination. This involved checking the passenger lists for 1100 flights.

The television was on in the detective's bull pen and the Chief of the New Mexico State Police was being interviewed. He took credit for having discovered that the fugitives had gone from the prison by ultra light aircraft to Santa Rosa. He had a crude map that showed the possible path of the escaped murderer and his accomplice. It was exactly the route that she had originally proposed Signe thought. They showed a prison photo of Anthony Squitero and listed Wanda De Berneres as his presumed companion and mastermind of the audacious prison break. The chief said both were presumed to be armed and dangerous. A $50,000 reward was offered for information that led to their apprehension. Authorities in 159 local and 87 international airports were on the lookout for the two fugitives.

Signe felt that Wanda had the jump on everyone. She thought that Anthony and Wanda had probably left on an early morning flight overseas with plans to travel to two or three other countries over the next few days as the heat diminished. She checked the passenger manifests herself using Wanda's name and the alias she knew—Rosie Bachechi and Sandra Vitari. She drew a blank. However, she knew enough from her search of Anthony's office that he had the sophisticated computer equipment and state of the art copying machines to make passports and other travel documents. She suspected that Wanda knew how to make a fake passport that would pass for authentic.

Signe worked late into the evening with the other officers but nothing seemed to indicate where her *hetaera* had gone next. Wanda knew that Signe had heard about her Barbados trip when she was the carrying the cash to an offshore bank. Signe had also easily found Wanda when she tried to disappear in New Hampshire by The Old Man of the Mountain. Wanda might also have seen CNN already. If she had, she would know that it was Signe that tracked her so quickly to Santa Rosa. Wanda probably expected it would take the police at least two weeks to find her aircraft in Santa Rosa and by then the trail would be very cold. Based on her knowledge of Wanda, Signe expected them to fly to somewhere like Russia with falsified passports, then Cuba, then maybe Guatemala to hide in the hills. On the other hand, it was conceivable that Wanda would do something completely unexpected.

The possibilities were endless Signe Thought. Perhaps Wanda would fly to New Orleans and take a freighter to Suriname. Or she might fly to Miami and take a yacht to Venezuela. After all, that was a country without an extradition treaty with the US. Signe knew she needed to find the final destination of the plane that took off from Santa Rosa. She contacted the border patrol. They had recently installed a series of blimps with down looking radar across the New Mexico/Mexico border. She hoped that they kept records of planes flying out of the country even though they were really looking for low flying planes loaded with cocaine and marijuana coming into the country.

Signe also contacted the FAA. Their Albuquerque Center controlled flights of aircraft over 18,000 feet in altitude for a five state area. She hoped they kept records on lower flying craft. While Signe worked to get 'Tony the Squid' behind bars again, a part of Detective Sorensen wanted Wanda to get away with her bold and daring jail break.

CHAPTER 53

Detective Lisa Gonzalez called Signe the next morning with the outcome of Dirk Patterson's trial. The jury had deliberated for two days. They had that twelve copies of Dr. Gilchrist's testimony brought to the jury room for review. In the end, they reported to the judge that they were hopelessly deadlocked. Asked if further deliberation would result in a verdict, the foreman said that the answer was 'no'. The judge declared a mistrial and Dirk was a free man. That sent a shudder down Signe's spine. Inside information, Detective Gonzalez reported showed the final vote for conviction was ten to two. Two older white males held out for acquittal and wouldn't budge. So far, Signe had seen no evidence of the craziness that Dr. Goldiamond said might lurk in Svelty. However, Signe wondered if this very public trial was Svelty's way of guaranteeing that Dirk would never lay one of his sleazy fingers on her. Even more, Mrs. Patterson had assured that Dirk would not be tempted by the huge insurance policy on her life.

Signe was sure that every meeting and hospital visit that she had had with Svelty was reported to Dirk by his private detectives. He was a vengeful and unscrupulous man who might try to seek revenge on her, Signe thought. Signe felt her best defense was to get damaging evidence on Dirk before he came after her. She turned to Sven Torvaldson. She knew he had done extensive research on Dirk's background, which they had discussed together. She called him.

"How are you, Sven?" Signe asked.

"I'd be better if I were having dinner with you tonight," Sven.

"Done. But I need you to work on something for me, today," she replied.

"Okay."

"Dirk Patterson was the most successful ambulance-chasing lawyer in the state and probably the richest lawyer in Albuquerque when suddenly, for no apparent reason, his empire collapsed. It's as if a monster wave comes ashore on a beach and a multistory, turreted sand castle, which had been there for years, instantly becomes a flat featureless piece of beach. What was that event and when did it occur?"

"I can help with that. The company stopped working on Dirk after we paid him the settlement, but there are two bright investigators in the home office who already have a lot of material on him. Perhaps the dinner should be tomorrow night to give me some time, Signe."

"Thanks. I'll meet you at The Palace at 8 p.m.," Signe concluded.

Signe called the Border Patrol back. They were instructed to note low level flights out of the country as a matter of record but they reported no unregistered flights from the New Mexico sector into Mexico on the night Anthony escaped. So, Signe thought, the pair didn't flee south of the border. They might have holed up for a few days somewhere but surely Wanda would realize that by then the search for the two of them would be even more intense.

Next Signe called the Albuquerque Center. An air traffic controller trainee had spent the last two days reviewing tapes from the night in question. He had found an unidentified aircraft that was picked up on radar just east of Santa Rosa at 8:07 p.m. that flew at 9,000 feet in an east south easterly direction. Signe's mind jumped to Atlanta or Miami as possible destinations. Houston or New Orleans seemed less likely targets because they were smaller airports with fewer overseas flights. Signe was surprised to learn that the student controller had taken the initiative to contact the next center east and that the unidentified plane had headed for Miami. Atlanta would most likely have meant a flight to Europe. Miami made South or Central America a more likely destination. Signe called Chief Hartford and told him what she had found.

The day after the prison escape there were several flights to Caracas and Maracaibo from Miami. American Airlines, Aeropostal and Lacsa accounted for most of the flights. Signe decided that Wanda would avoid an American carrier. There was an 8:20 a.m. flight on Lacsa, the airline of Costa Rica, which departed Miami for Caracas that immediately caught Signe's eye. After getting permission, she called the chief of the New Mexico State Police and told him about her hunch. He asked her to follow-up. She contacted the Dade County police and requested they set up interviews with the Lacsa check-in personnel, flight attendants and customs officers for Flight 716 to Caracas.

Signe and Valerie spent the next day examining the ultra light found in Santa Rosa. The State Police had relinquished it to their more modern lab for investigation. It was brand new, and was out of fuel just as Signe had suspected. It was actually a kite plane. The cockpit was painted a bright yellow and white. The bottom looked like a baby carriage with three wheels for landing and two small seats. The engine was behind. A large pole stuck up from the "baby carriage" with wires that went to two large cloth wings. Signe thought the whole thing looked preposterous and unwieldy but Valerie said that with little training and no license they flew well in light air.

The two women spent hours going over the craft. They searched for fibers, hair, residue of any kind and fingerprints. The night of the escape the temperature in Santa Fe dropped to 20 degrees Fahrenheit, Signe was sure that Wanda and Anthony wore gloves but a print found anywhere on the craft could prove to be invaluable. Valerie finally found one middle finger print on a strut and Signe found a sticker under the seat for Canyon Runners an aero trekking club in Animas, New Mexico. Animas is a rural village in the extreme southern part of the state near Arizona and Mexico. Signe faxed a picture of Wanda to them. Yes, they confirmed that she was a student there and had been a quick study at flying. They knew her as Rosie Bachechi. Valerie quickly matched the print she had found to the middle finger of Anthony Squitero's left hand.

Signe was early for her dinner with Sven Torvaldson. She was enjoying a martini when he sauntered in with one yellow rose in his hand. After some small talk he launched into what his investigators had found. The date that Dirk's sandcastle collapsed was March 14, 2002. Sven's investigators detected a reduction in Dirk's income starting in 1999 that accelerating over the next three years. Everyone in Albuquerque knew he had very high fixed costs. They could simply look up and see his huge face on numerous bill boards. He had dozens of employees, an elegant office and huge advertising expenses. By 2002 he was still handling lots of accident cases but none of the multi-victim horrendous crashes that had filled his coffers in the 1990s like a rain barrel during a deluge.

Dirk had skated on the edge of the law with many of his clients but in 2002 it appeared he had decided to cross to the other side. Somehow Dirk's people had found out that the Albuquerque Bus Company was self insured for accidents up to $10,000,000. Yet over the past five years pay outs for accidents had been abnormally low and only amounting to about $450,000 each year. Dirk set about trying to tap this large tank of money.

After weeks of searching, Dirk's investigators had found Sharon Thompson. She was a cash strapped single mother of three who was a student at the University of New Mexico. Better yet she had been in a wheelchair since age 12 due to an inherited bone disease. Dirk planned to involve her in a fake bus accident, simulate her death and relocate Sharon and her three small children. In return he would pay her $10,000 dollars a month for 10 years and immediately pay off her $28,000 dollars in high interest loans and credit card debt.

Dirk's accident reconstruction expert found a sidewalk ramp where Sharon could roll in front of a very slow moving bus. He built a special wheelchair out of stainless steel rods rather than tubes with a concealed six point safety harness. The wheelchair weighed 215 pounds but only had to roll a few feet downhill as part of this charade. The accident expert arranged for a pair of EMTs to arrive at the scene right after the accident and remove the victim, now covered in blood along with the fake wheelchair.

A day for the accident was set. At the last minute Sharon got cold feet. Two other days were scheduled at times when the correct number of witnesses was likely to be at the intersection. Sharon cancelled both at the last minute. She told Dirk's expert that she was afraid she might actually die during the accident. She insisted on talking to the person in charge of the scheme. Sharon wanted assurances that if she were to die her children would be provided for.

Dirk reluctantly met Sharon at his office one evening and using his most supportive lawyer tone gave her every verbal guarantee that he could dredge up. He explained the danger to both of them if anything about the whole caper was written down. She wheeled out of the office seemingly reassured. However she missed the 'accident' that was scheduled for the next day. Two days later she came to the office alone and demanded to speak to Mr. Patterson. She told him that she had been wearing a wire during their meeting and that she wanted $30,000 dollars a month in cash for her silence. If he was late with one payment she would go to the authorities with the tape and have him disbarred. Perhaps, for the first time in his life, Dirk Patterson was completely surprised. He reluctantly agreed.

In all of the investigations of the bus company, armored wheelchairs and accident scenarios Dirk's people had not investigated Sharon Thompson thoroughly. For one thing she was a pre-law student at the University. She had also sued a professor, a fast food chain and a department store. She had won three times citing sexual harassment once and violations of the Americans with Disabilities Act twice. Sven thought, when Sharon turned on him, it really took the wind out of Dirk's sails and the firm went into a steep downward spiral.

"That's an amazing story," Signe said. "And you managed to come up with that in two days."

"We had some parts of it from our previous investigation," Sven said proudly. "Also everyone that works for Dirk will talk for a price. Dirk had a falling out with a crime scene investigator and Dirk threw him out of the office without his last paycheck. He was very willingly to talk to us in detail about his former employer. Dirk Patterson has lots of enemies."

Signe and Sven had worked their way through a several course meal while Sven told his story. They each had lobster bisque, a Caesar salad and a Porterhouse steak. They went to the bar for a nightcap and then he walked Signe to her car. They had a lingering goodnight kiss, but after all that she had heard, Signe's mind was elsewhere.

CHAPTER 54

Signe told Chief Gerald Hartford about Dirk's nefarious plot to scam the bus company and how it had run amuck. The chief could only shake his head in disbelief. He also agreed with Signe that this tale suggested Dirks high level of desperation. Dirk was angry, feeling hounded and without his main henchman and sidekick 'Tony the Squid'. Both Signe and Chief Hartford agreed, he was even more dangerous now. Chief Hartford said he was taking his wife to Florida for ten days and outlined the things he wanted Signe to work on while he was away. This was done a little tongue in cheek because Gerald knew that Signe would head off in her own independent direction as soon as he was out the door.

Signe and Jack loaded the evidence collected from the ultra light used in the escape into the Crown Vic. They planned to drive it to the laboratory at State Police Headquarters so they could share their findings. They were talking about basketball as they usually did. The University of New Mexico's season was just starting and they both had high hopes for a successful year. Traffic was light and Jack slowed to a stop at a red light by the old drive in theatre on Cerrillos Road. Just as the light was turning green a bullet tore through the right rear window of the Ford lodging behind Signe's seat. Granules of glass splattered across the back seat as the bullet tore into the inside of the door.

"Here we go again Jack," Signe shouted.

They both ducked to the right and spilled out of the passenger's door clutching Kevlar vests, binoculars, and the .223 sniper rifle. Jack checked every morning to make sure their emergency equipment was in easy reach in the back seat. Since the last attack they decided they needed to stay together in emergencies for better communication, and not be separated by the twenty-two foot length of their steel cruiser. Jack's shoulder was completely healed from the last attack, but Signe wondered how he would hold up psychologically. She thought the busier she kept him the better.

"Once you have your vest on, scan those old buildings by the drive-in," Signe shouted. "Here are the binoculars. I'll crawl back in and alert dispatch."

"This is a busy area, Signe," Jack yelled back. "There could be innocent people in any of those old houses even though they look deserted."

He seems to be handling this well, Signe thought to herself. She crawled back out the driver's door and laid half beside and half on Jack so she could peer around the front tire. Everything was quiet to the east. Traffic whizzed by behind them oblivious to what was going on on the shoulder of the road. Jack and Signe had seen and heard nothing since the first shot. A gentle breeze rustled the Russian olive trees that grew in poor untended ground around the drive-in. Plastic bags and pieces of waste paper blew lazily by the unkempt structures near the old theater. Each little movement drew their eyes but there was no sign of the shooter or his weapon. Three squad cars arrived simultaneously. Even though it had only been ten minutes Signe was impatient. Without waiting, she spread the officers out in a long irregular line and started across the field. She invented a reason for Jack to stay with the Crown Vic. She liked working with him and didn't want him incapacitated by this event which began to seem to her less a real attempt on their lives than a warning. Who is doing this and what is this criminal trying to tell me Signe wondered?

The six officers found no one. Eventually a shell casing was found on a scaffold behind the dilapidated old aluminum drive-in movie screen. Jack and Signe went ahead and delivered their evidence to the State Police and then returned to headquarters to start filling out the piles of paperwork generated by such an incident. Both had the obligatory psychology evaluation sessions with Dr. Goldiamond and then went back to work. Signe left as soon as she could and retreated to her corner at the Coyote Café. It was a cold winter's day. The place was empty. She curled up by the fireplace with a Kahlua and cream to think. The shot looked more and more like a warning to her. The car was stopped. She would have been clearly visible in the front seat. The officers measured the distance to the movie screen and it was only 120 yards. It would have been an easy shot even for an amateur with a high powered rifle and a good scope.

Signe started through her list of players first. Richard Lederback was dead. Wanda De Berneres and Anthony Squitero had successfully escaped the country, were probably in Caracas, and would gain nothing by coming back to Santa Fe. That left Svelty and Dirk. Signe had been warned about Svelty but she couldn't picture the trophy wife climbing up on a dilapidated drive-in movie and shooting from ambush. That left Dirk Patterson, Esquire, a member of the Albuquerque Shootist's Club as the prime suspect. However, what was his motive? The disappearance of Hercules turned out to be a sale even if he handled in a furtive manner. Anthony had been convicted of Chloe's murder. Dirk had been acquitted for the attempted murder of Svelty in a case that Signe still thought might have been a clever diversion by Svelty to bring Dirk to the attention of the authorities after she failed in her attempt to kill herself.

As she inched closer to the fireplace, Signe wondered why Dirk would take a shot at her. He was in the clear for now, at least criminally. His major problem was financial destitution, and that showed no signs of getting better. There must be someone or something out there that was beyond Dirk Patterson's control that was sucking him back into the maelstrom. Who was it? What was it? It had to be something that happened in Santa Fe or he wouldn't be trying to scare off a Santa Fe Police detective.

As the fire warmed her, Signe began to daydream. She got lost in a revelry of having sex with Juan, from Argentina, and then looking over her shoulder to see Dirk approaching. Both Signe and Juan nonchalantly picked up their pistols turned their heads and shot the lawyer repeatedly causing him to sprawl on his back, dead behind them, as they continued their dalliance. Signe's cell phone rang, dissolving her daydream. It was Detective Lisa Gonzalez of the Albuquerque PD.

"I am investigating the accidental death of a Sharon Thompson, Signe," Detective Gonzalez began. "She was in her thirties and a prelaw student at UNM. She'd been in a wheelchair since she was a teen. Sharon rolled off an icy curb by the University into the path of an oncoming bus this afternoon and she and her wheelchair were crushed beneath it. It wasn't a pretty sight. Our computer said she was a person of interest for an investigation you were conducting."

"I never met her detective, but I'm sorry to hear about it," Signe replied. "I believe she was involved in a scam with Dirk Patterson to fake an accident for insurance money. She turned it into a blackmail scheme. You should probably investigate her death as a murder. I may even know how to tip you off as to what happened."

"That would be great. I was just making a courtesy call," Lisa replied.

"They constructed a special armored wheelchair for the accident so the chances of Sharon getting seriously injured by the bus would be less. Have your lab people look at the chair. If it weighed over two hundred pounds and was made out of solid stainless steel rather than hollow tubes it was the insurance scam. If she was in a regular thirty some pound wheelchair it was murder."

"Thanks for the tip, Signe," Detective Gonzalez replied. "I'll call back when I know more."

This was more evidence that Dirk Patterson had suddenly become active again. Signe needed to know what was driving him to this frenzy of activity. Normally, a large cup of coffee in her hand, she would have discussed the situation with Chief Hartford. However, he was in Florida. In his absence she realized how much she used him as a sounding board for her ideas. Instead she spent the evening with Vincent. Things were good between them again. She explained the Dirk dilemma to him in detail but he couldn't come up with any cogent ideas about the sudden commotion. He did ask her to drop the case for her own safety.

"You have been assaulted with murderous intent four times, since this case began, Signe" Vincent correctly stated. "You were in one car 'accident' and three attempted shootings. That's not even counting the shootout at The Wild Pony that I was involved in. So far you haven't even been wounded. You've been extraordinarily lucky and you should quit while you're ahead. Besides, I love you and I don't want anything to happen to you."

"That's touching, Vincent," Signe began. "But I guess I don't look at it that way. I suppose I just sweep all that stuff under the carpet. Sometimes I don't feel that anyone really needs me. Look how well Axel has done with his dad and you, like most law enforcement people, are very independent. I promise I will reconsider the whole unsatisfying investigation from the beginning. Thank you, darling."

After Vincent left, Signe called Axel. It was early morning in Denmark—eight hours later. Axel was getting ready to go to apprentice school. He liked the wood working more and more and his skills were improving rapidly. He was operating the bigger power tools like the planer himself now. He had met a girl from Odense named Birgit and they were seeing each other two or three nights a week. His Dad had counseled him to go slow but he really liked spending time with her. He found her funny and pretty. Signe also threw in her two cents worth about taking his time since he was only seventeen, though she worried that her advice fell on deaf ears. In any case she loved hearing his voice. She even felt a twinge of homesickness for the very first time in months.

CHAPTER 55

As he came back into play Signe needed more intelligence on Dirk Patterson. The next morning she called Sven Torvaldson and asked for tight surveillance on the flamboyant barrister. Sven knew that if Signe could charge him with a crime and get him convicted that his company might get at least some of their money back. He said that he would be happy to help. Then Signe called Detective Lisa Gonzalez of the Albuquerque Police Department to get an update on Sharon Thompson's unfortunate death.

"Thanks for the great tip, on Miss Thompson, Signe," Lisa Gonzalez began. "She was in a standard Invacare wheelchair when she was crushed. They weigh 31 pounds new. I saw what was left of it. It was folded up like a pretzel. It was only five inches tall when placed on a flat surface. It didn't even resemble a wheelchair."

"I think you have a murder on your hands, detective," Signe replied.

"Unfortunately we didn't process the crime scene as a possible murder. I thought it was just a tragic accident caused by a slippery curb until I talked with you. We lost a lot of potential evidence."

"But you have the advantage of knowing who the perpetrator is, Lisa."

"Speaking of that, can you guess who filed a wrongful death suit against the city for $10,000,000 yesterday? It was filed on behalf of Sharon Thompson's three underage children."

"So you say Dirk Patterson has already raised his slimy head? Someone helped him commit this crime. You just need to find out who it was."

"I'm on it detective. I'll keep you posted."

Signe was afraid that Dirk was about to get away with another crime and have an even bigger pay day. By her calculation he had already received almost $500,000 by selling Hercules and $2,000,000 from the insurance policy on Chloe. Now he stood a chance at getting $5,000,000 or more from

Sharon's death. Signe was sure he would cheat the three children out of as much of the settlement as he could.

Frustrated, Signe put in a call to the Miami-Dade Police about Wanda and Dirk. Their detectives had shown pictures of the two escapees to dozens of airport personnel. The desk clerk for Lacsa remembered them. They had looked haggard and were arguing loudly as they checked in for flight 716 to Caracas, Venezuela. A check of the log showed they sat in seats 2A and 2B. Just like Wanda to sit in first class, Signe thought. She had panache. Signe called Sven back asking him to have some private investigators scour Caracas for the pair.

"I'd start with five star hotels and residences knowing those two," Signe told Sven.

Signe thought it less and less likely that Anthony Squitero had actually killed Chloe Patterson but she wanted to make contact with him so she could learn what had really happened. Even if he didn't administer the fatal dose of chloroform she suspected that he was involved in the crime. She couldn't believe that she was still at the vortex of this murder investigation after thirteen and a half weeks of toil, travel, expense and danger.

Jefferson Barclay had called and wanted to take Signe out of town for dinner and a surprise. Signe decided such a break might be perfect. She quickly called him back and accepted. Jefferson said he would pick her up at six that evening. He wanted her to wear a dress but bring some heavy outdoor clothing. He wouldn't tell her anything more and wouldn't give any hints.

Jefferson picked Signe up at her apartment in his SUV. She wore her favorite sapphire blue dress and he wore a smartly tailored pinstriped suit. He headed north out of town and Signe suspected Tesuque or Pojoaque was their destination. Los Alamos was that direction also but there was not one restaurant there that Jefferson would grace with his big toe let alone eat a full meal there. Jefferson sped past the turnoffs for all the places Signe guessed and then headed north through Espanola. Signe gave up trying to puzzle out their destination and relaxed into the pleasant conversation.

After an hour and twenty minute drive, Jefferson pulled the vehicle into the snow packed parking lot of Lambert's in Taos. Signe had heard it was famous for its modern American cuisine. Jefferson sent people there all the time from La Fonda and they raved about it. Signe had pumpkin soup, fiddlehead fern salad and pork tenderloin. She found each dish to exceptionally tasty and visually appealing. Jefferson Barclay chuckled telling Signe that she sounded like an advertisement in *Gourmet* magazine.

After dinner they sat beside the big stone fireplace and had coffee and warm cognac. When she was totally relaxed Jefferson brought in Signe's winter clothes and ordered her to change. When she came out she was dressed in a parka and mittens and he escorted her to the front door.

A sleigh drawn by two white horses was waiting. They sat in the back under blankets and a bear skin rug. The coachmen headed off to the east on back roads toward the mountains. It was very cold, crisp and clear. There was no moon, but thousands of stars lit the sky and the white driven snow had a bluish color. The only sounds were the clop of hooves, the runners cutting the snow and the gentle ringing of the bells on the horse's harnesses. Jefferson babbled on about his current boyfriend and then turned to Signe.

"Are you still seeing that young man from the State Police?" He said.

"Yes. Why?" Signe asked.

"I never thought you'd last this long," Jefferson replied. "I'm just surprised."

"That is not the real answer, Jefferson," Signe said. "I know you too well. Come on."

"Well, when he was in high school, he used to spend time with some of the older queens in Santa Fe," he began. "He did it for cash. I doubt it meant anything. He was cute and poor. I'm sure he needed the money."

"You mean to tell me that my Vincent, Vincent Jaramillo spent time having sex with aging homosexuals?" Signe asked with a concerned voice. "And he wasn't just experimenting?"

"I know he did it for three or four years. It's unusual for a young stud to do it for that long unless he gets something out of it, if you know what I mean."

"I have never sensed any of that in him when we are together. He seems very masculine and completely heterosexual. I'm shocked Jefferson."

"He probably had a conversion, Signe. I've seen it, but only rarely."

"In all the times we've been together I only had a problem once when he was close to an orgasm. He twisted my arm really hard and I sensed it was helping him get off."

"Signe, I have to tell you something I wasn't planning on sharing. Toward the end of this period Vincent got involved with a pair of homosexuals named Steve and Dan. They were into masochism and took turns hurting each other for their partner's pleasure. The rumor was, and it was only a rumor, that Vincent got mixed up with that sick pair. He would inflict the pain with whips, tight ropes and nipple clamps to heighten their sexual pleasure. This went on until Steve got hurt so badly, by Vincent that he had to go to the hospital. The story was covered up in straight society as Steve was on the city council at the time. However, the story spread like wild fire through the gay community."

"What a violent and perverted saga. It makes me feel anxious and a little bit physically ill. Could we just not talk for a while?" Signe said snuggling up against Jefferson's padded shoulder.

"Of course, my dear," Jefferson replied. "I'm sorry. The rumor may not even be true. Shall I check it out further?"

"No, Jefferson," Signe said. "I appreciate your being so forthcoming. I will take care of it."

Signe put Vincent out of her mind and they both enjoyed the rest of the sleigh ride. Signe pretended she was the Julie Christie character, Tonya, in the movie *Doctor Zhivago* and that she was gliding over the Russian steppes. It fit with the cold, dark, stillness of a northern New Mexico night. They slid over the deserted country roads behind the tireless horses for another hour before returning to Lambert's. They talked pleasantly of other things on the drive back to Santa Fe. Jefferson dropped Signe off at her apartment. Cold and tired she fell sleep quickly.

Vincent had told Signe that Irma Perez was planning to marry the young man she had met at school. Signe thought that the ceremony would be soon, as Irma's pregnancy was advancing. The brides true condition would be revealed by the thickness of her waist as her father Manuel Perez escorted her down the aisle. Signe checked the papers and found that the wedding would be Wednesday in the chapel of St. Francis Cathedral rather than in Irma's neighborhood church. Signe decided to go.

The cathedral itself seats 1200 people but there is room for only one hundred worshippers in the chapel. A modern building constructed on the south side of the cathedral, the chapel is decorated simply except for a large crucifix over the altar. Signe arrived at the last possible minute and sat in the far right rear pew. She enjoyed the rich organ music that filled the chapel. Despite her white dress and many layers of lace Signe thought the bride looked very pregnant. Signe was surprised at the length of the Catholic service and the amount of kneeling involved. She meant to slip out just before the end of the service but missed her cue. As she turned to exit, one of Irma's older sisters recognized her and glared. Signe smiled back as blandly as possible and hurried out into the weak winter sun.

Vincent was away on an assignment for the State Police. As soon as he got back into town, she set up a meeting at the Coyote Café. She wasn't taking any chances. She knew she needed to confront him, and she wanted a public place so they wouldn't be alone and so that she could escape easily if it became necessary. At four in the afternoon the restaurant was deserted. They sat in a corner and ordered drinks.

"I was in Taos while you were gone, Vincent," Signe began. "And I heard some disturbing things about your past."

"I already told you I was wild, darling," Vincent replied somewhat defensively.

"It wasn't about shoplifting or even stealing cars," Signe replied. "It was about bizarre sexual behavior and it made me feel frightened. You need to tell me about the sexual things that you did before we met."

"I'm not sure I know what you are talking about," Vincent said looking earnest. "But I will tell you everything. You are important to me and I love you."

"It had to do with sex that you had with other men, Vincent," Signe replied abruptly.

"That was a long time ago. I'm sorry you heard about it and that it hurt you. When I was fifteen my parents were poor and a friend told me I could make easy money kissing and hugging certain men. I didn't believe him but I tried it even though I didn't like it. He turned out to be right. I could spent two or three hours with a man and make $100. I was only fifteen and I had to work three long days in the stables or the fields to make that kind of money. I did it on and off for about three years but by the end I just hated it. The money just wasn't worth it. So I stopped. I've never been with a man since. We've been together for three months and you know what I'm like, darling. If I were gay or bisexual you would sense it."

"I believe you, Vincent," Signe replied softly. "But what I heard was very upsetting. Did you ever injury any of those men?"

"There were two men toward the end that used me," Vincent began. "There names were Steve and Dan or Don. They were masochists. I learned the word later. They had to have pain to get off. I spent time with them. They paid very well. Usually they would have me tie one up and then I would use a whip on one or both of them. Once when I was with them Don hurt Steve with a pronged trident that he swung against his flank. There was a lot of blood. Steve passed out. When he recovered consciousness Don blamed the accident on me. I was young. There wasn't much I could do. I never saw either of them again. I swear."

"Thanks for being so open about it, Vincent," Signe said. "That must be hard for you. I appreciate your honesty."

She leaned over and kissed him. It hadn't been as much of a confrontation as Signe had feared. Vincent seemed honest, open and contrite. They spent the evening together and Signe felt closer and more committed to Vincent than she ever had before.

CHAPTER 56

Detective Lisa Gonzalez called early the next morning to talk with Signe. The Albuquerque Police had gotten one of Dirk's disgruntled employees to testify that Dirk had helped plan the contrived accident involving Sharon Thompson. The district attorney planned to charge Dirk Patterson with murder in the death of the young wheelchair bound mother of three. Lisa was sure it would be front page news the next day in *The Albuquerque Journal.*

"I just wanted to thank you for the tip," Lisa said. "We couldn't have done it without you, Signe."

"I love to see the bad guys go down, Lisa," Signe replied. "Thanks for following up. I'll be down for the trial."

After she finished talking to Detective Gonzalez Signe checked with Sven to see if Wanda De Berneres and Anthony Squitero had been found. Sven had just gotten a call from one of his Venezuelan stringers. Apparently, Wanda and Tony were living at Tamanaco Intercontinental, an upscale golfing community on the outskirts of Caracas. They seemed relaxed, affectionate and tan according to the report. There was no way to bring them back to the states as Venezuela had no extradition law with the US. Out of other ideas, Signe asked Sven's investigators to dream up a way to put pressure on the two.

Ironically, the very next day Signe got an e-mail routed through Egypt and Russia from the pair of fugitives. Anthony stated that while he had done a lot of illegal dirty work for Dirk Patterson, he hadn't killed his daughter. Since he was safely hidden now and would never come back to the United States he said that he had no reason to lie anymore. He thought that Dirk had hired someone local, in Santa Fe, to commit the murder. He had seen Chloe the afternoon of her death, however, he was simply there to make sure that the transfer of Hercules went as planned. They had had a loud disagreement because Chloe wanted him to give her money. He said they often argued when she was on drugs. He said she looked very strung-out that day. He also said that the goblet presented at the trial was a totally bogus piece of evidence perhaps fabricated by the real killer. Even allowing for the fact that he was a prodigious liar, the things that 'Tony the Squid' said made some sense to Signe.

Four days later Signe found herself in a district court room in Albuquerque for Dirk's trial. The DA, stung by Dirk's previous mistrial wanted swift justice. Opening arguments by both sides took up most of the first morning. The prosecutor revealed that a man in Dirk's employ, Bob Huffman, would detail the insurance scam planned by Patterson and also tell how Sharon Thompson blackmailed him. Ruben Pelicanto was back to defend Dirk, and he explained that the prosecutions case was a house of cards. The afternoon docket was a series of background and character witnesses which Signe decided to skip. She had lunch with Dr. Mark Josephson and went to Old Town in search of Indian pots. Then she drove back to her own apartment in Santa Fe. Since their heart to heart talk, Signe had been letting Vincent stay the night and she was enjoying their new closeness.

The next day Bob Huffman testified about planning the fake lawsuit against the bus company. He had detailed notes, with diagrams, about building a special wheelchair, timing the accident so there would be witnesses and an analysis of several sites where the accident could be staged. Mr. Huffman had taken the files when Dirk Patterson fired him abruptly over a disagreement about a motorcycle accident scene reconstruction Huffman had conducted. He explained that Sharon wore a hidden recording device to a meeting with Dirk. Bob Huffman said that the scam was put on hold because Sharon was blackmailing Dirk over what she had recorded. Signe found him an accurate, credible witness with lots of documentation. Signe thought that Mr. Pelicanto's cross examination didn't shake the witness's testimony or cast real doubt on any part of what he said about the planning of the scam and Sharon Thompson's efforts to blackmail Dirk Patterson. Several other corroborating witnesses from the Patterson law firm were called to give testimony in the afternoon. Signe drove back to Santa Fe after a long day of sitting, confident that this time Dirk would be punished.

Signe was enjoying an early dinner with Vincent at The Pink Adobe. She had eaten her salad and was waiting for the Chicken Marengo that she almost always ordered when she got a call, on her cell, from Detective Lisa Gonzalez.

"Dirk Patterson is not going to get convicted on this murder charge," Lisa began.

"I hate it when guilty bastards get off Lisa," Signe replied. "What happened?"

"He was murdered. I just got the call. You know him and his wife so well. I want you to help me work the crime scene."

"I'll be right there. Where is the body?"

"He was found in his old house on north Rio Grande Boulevard."

"I'll be there in fifty minutes."

Signe jumped up from their table and hurriedly explained to Vincent what had happened.

"I'll tell you all about it tomorrow, darling," Signe said over her shoulder as she rushed out of the restaurant. The drive to Albuquerque went quickly. On the way she wondered if she had overlooked something. Was there some clue to this unanticipated event that she had missed? When she arrived three Albuquerque Police cars were still on the scene. Technicians were collecting evidence and taking photographs. Detective Gonzalez took Signe into the library where the victim's body was located.

"This is how we found him," Lisa said gesturing toward the body.

Dirk Patterson, obviously dead, was bound hand and foot in a large leather chair with wooden arms. There was blood in a three foot circle around him. He had been shot several times—both knees, one shoulder, abdomen and perhaps finally in the center of the forehead. He was wearing underwear and there looked to be some knife wounds also. Signe could also see dark ligature marks around his throat and wrists. The murderer had methodically tortured the victim and then killed him. Signe thought immediately of the warnings she had received from Chief Hartford and from Dr. Vivian Goldiamond about Svelty Patterson. Could that petite woman have physically done all this Signe wondered?

The victim's mouth was stuffed with cloth that was taped in place perhaps to muffle his screams. A piece of the victim's own expensive stationary was held to his chest with a slender knife whose bloody handle protruded from between his ribs. A message in block letters was written on the stationery in thick dark red blood—'FOR C'.

"How long has he been dead?" Signe asked Lisa as she fought down a feeling of dizziness and nausea turning deliberately away from the body.

"Liver temperature suggests twelve to sixteen hours but I'm afraid he was tortured for many hours or days before that," Lisa said in a soft voice. "This is the most vicious and psychologically perverted killing I've ever seen in this violent little city."

"I hope there are lots of clues here that will lead you to the killer," Signe replied. "However, this looks so methodical that I suspect you have one intelligent perpetrator that covered his or her tracks well."

"Do you really think a woman could have done this, Signe?" I mean physically and psychologically?" Detective Gonzalez asked.

"Yes, I do. If I were going to commit the crime I would lure the person here under false pretenses," Signe began. "You know either sex or money. Give him both. Then slip him a sedative or inject him with something fast acting. Given his size I'd try to paralyze him right in that chair. Failing that, I would move him using ropes, ramps of plywood and a small wheelchair. Once I had him bound in that big chair I could proceed to slowly torture and kill him even if I only weighed a hundred pounds."

"The way your mind works, is scary sometimes Signe." Lisa Gonzalez replied.

"Are you saying that you think I would make a good criminal?" Signe replied.

"Just a diabolically crafty one, that I would not like to try and catch," Lisa replied. "Is that shot to the forehead what killed him?"

"You mean the COD or cause of death?" Signe replied.

"Yes."

"Do you see how much blood is on the floor?" Signe replied. "I think he exsanguinated and the gun shot was just insurance."

Detective Gonzalez sent two of her officers to check for suspicious items in the alley of the Patterson house and around the neighborhood. They found a variety of junk and amongst them were some old rope and a dilapidated old wheel chair. Lisa asked the officers to check for blood on the items but Signe felt they were more likely to find DNA that belonged to Dirk and Svelty or some unknown perpetrator on the rope or wheelchair.

"What about the macabre note on his chest, Signe?" Lisa asked.

"I see it as a clear reference to his murdered daughter, Lisa," Signe answered. "You may not know her name was Chloe. A man was already convicted of her murder. However, I had already begun to think that he didn't do it. I'm struck by the premeditation of this crime. Whoever killed Dirk didn't do it as an act of passion. It was a cold, calculated torture and murder carried out by a psychopath. It gives me a chill to even think about it. If you ever get close to this suspect, promise me you will call for back up before trying to apprehend this person."

"Of course," Lisa Gonzalez replied. "After all, you've been right about everything, Signe."

It was late and Signe still wasn't comfortable driving that stretch of I-25 after dark but she headed home. It was a cold January night and an atypical wind blew from the east steady and hard down off of the Sandia

Mountains. The more she thought about it the more Signe felt that Svelty had committed this heinous crime and that she had ignored the warning of two smart people—Chief Hartford and Dr. Goldiamond about her *hetaera*. Of course, she had never been concerned about protecting Dirk. She had hated him from the moment she first met him. Had her prejudices cost the life of a disreputable lawyer who was none the less still a human being? She was afraid they had. She was sure she wouldn't sleep well. She called Vincent on her cell and invited him over to her apartment for the night so that she wouldn't be alone.

CHAPTER 57

The next morning, Vincent suggested a night at their old haunt the Kokopelli Bed and Breakfast in Pojoaque to celebrate their new closeness. Unlike the first time, he would make all the arrangements. He said he would even get two bottles of the Malbec wine from Argentina that she liked so much. Signe remembered that the Fortuna brothers had taught her about that wine when she visited them on the Pampas. She eagerly agreed to Vincent's proposal.

Vincent arrived at her up at her apartment the next evening. He said his truck was in the shop and asked if they could drive Signe's BMW. She tossed him the keys. She followed him out to the vehicle carrying her small backpack.

"Can we have dinner at El Nido?" Signe asked. "For old times sake?"

"I thought of that but I want you all to myself," Vincent replied. "So I got a cold supper that we can share in the room. There is smoked salmon, vichyssoise and cold curried chicken salad. I brought some champagne to go with the Malbec."

"How delightful," Signe said as Vincent gunned the BMW up the and out of Santa Fe. "Before we get there I want to tell you some new things about the Patterson case. Then, I hope, we can have a relaxing evening and night free from work."

"Okay," Vincent replied in a disappointed voice.

"I got another e-mail from Wanda and Anthony and despite his conviction, I don't think he killed Chloe," Signe began. "They are sure that Dirk ordered the killing of his own daughter for the insurance money, and said that he didn't use Anthony as the contract killer. Dirk and Anthony were too closely linked. They believe that Dirk Patterson hired someone local to commit the crime. Since Wanda and Anthony Squitero worked as moles and investigators for him for so long they both can burrow into his financial records and they've already started on it. Talk about identity theft. They have all his personal information, account numbers and PIN numbers. They think they've found an account at the Bank of Santa Fe that was used to pay the killer. They should have the account number tomorrow and I can get the name on it from a vice president I know there. I hope to pick up a suspect or even make an arrest tomorrow."

"I still wish you'd drop this case, Signe," Vincent said. "It has dominated your life for the past four months, and it impacts our relationship in a very negative way."

"I feel like I'm very close, honey" Signe replied. "You of all people have some idea of how much physical and emotional energy I've put into this murder."

"You've been consumed by it. And that's not a compliment."

"I even had a dream about Chloe last night. I had forgotten how beautiful she was. She floated in on a cloud. She was dressed in a long white gown. Her blond hair was curled and piled elegantly on her head. I knew it was a dream because a soft gold light shown out around her eyes. She came very close to me and said, 'Catch him. Give me peace.' Then she floated away. I awoke shivering with cold. Do you remember the shivers I got when I first started working this case, Vincent?"

"Of course."

"I need to solve this case and put it behind me. Then I want to take you, my love, on a trip to Denmark."

"No more work talk, then?" Vincent asked in an imploring tone.

"No more, my dear," Signe said softly.

Vincent was driving onto the crunchy gravel parking lot of the Kokopelli Bed and Breakfast.

"Will you check us in, dear?" Vincent asked. "I want to unload the food before it gets warm."

"Sure," Signe replied. "But how do you know which bungalow we're in?"

"I asked for number five," Vincent replied. "The one we had last time. I said you wanted it left unlocked."

"I'll be right there," Signe shouted over her shoulder as she strode toward the office. With each step across the wide grey gravel parking lot her work shoes made a loud crunching sound, which was almost too loud. Something about the sound gave her a vaguely uneasy feeling. She signed the guest register and picked up the key before heading back to bungalow number five. She was feeling happier than she had since Anthony's conviction.

When she arrived Vincent had the food attractively laid out on the table in front of the antique sofa. The days were short and it was already nearly dark outside. He had lit four tall white candles which were placed symmetrically around the food. When she entered he popped the cork on a bottle of smooth, fruity Roderer champagne. Signe silently patted herself on the back for teaching her young lover so much about food and wine in the last four months. She took the flute that he had poured and took a long sip and then kissed him tenderly. She sat on the edge of the sofa and took the plate that he handed her with a portion of smoked salmon on it. They finished the champagne quickly.

Vincent served the vichyssoise and opened the first bottle of Malbec at the same time. He handed her a large wine goblet with an ample amount of the rich dark red wine in it. She swirled the glass and stuck her small Danish nose into the orifice of the glass to appreciate its bouquet. Then she took a large swallow of the wine. She took two bites of the delicious cold potato soup and suddenly felt lightheaded. The room spun and she felt overwhelmingly tired. She could barely sit up. She excused herself and walked haltingly into the bedroom and flopped down on the bed on her back without even pulling the covers back. She must have lost consciousness.

Sometime later she half awoke, in the dim light of the bedroom, to find Vincent kneeling over her legs with surgical gloves on. He had a cable tie in his mouth and in this right hand he held Signe's .38 caliber pistol which she had placed on the lamp stand by the front door. She thought she must be dreaming but as he grasped both of her hands and bound her wrists tightly with the cable tie she realized she wasn't. She had been given a sedative but Vincent must have under dosed her. She was just barely awake. Once her hands were bound, he stood over her and placed the muzzle of her gun in her mouth.

"You wouldn't stop!" he yelled. "Even after I framed Tony, you wouldn't stop! If you opened that account tomorrow, you are going to find that only Dirk Patterson and I had access to the $250,000 in it. I killed Chloe Patterson. She was a worthless drug-addicted loser. Her life was meaningless! I'm not sorry I did it, but I am sorry I have to kill you. You are beautiful, smart and resourceful but you didn't know when to stop."

The cold muzzle of the gun touched the back of her throat and stimulated her nervous system. She kicked upward using every ounce of strength that she had left in her right leg as her left leg pressed into the bed for support. Her sharp shin bone caught Vincent's soft gelatinous testicles and compressed them violently against his pubic bone. He winced in pain. Then cried out and rolled back toward the right side of the bed. He had not taken the time to disarm Signe. With her hands bound together she reached down to the .32 caliber pistol on her ankle. She drew it swiftly and despite blurred vision fired quickly. Her drugged brain told her she would only get one shot off. The slug caught Vincent in the right shoulder pushing his whole body back, but he recovered quickly. He lowered her pistol toward her mouth again. With her last bit of consciousness Signe fired again catching Vincent in the center of his chest. He gave a surprised look and fell backwards.

The dose of sedative welled up again in Signe's brain and she was unconscious again for the next four hours. Sometime during the middle of the night she awoke slowly, with a vicious pounding headache. In addition to the headache, as she became gradually became more aware, she discovered her aching and swollen hands were bound with a cable tie. She sat up with difficulty because of her tethered hands. She noticed blood on the foot of the bed and quickly checked herself for wounds. She found none. As she swung her legs to the floor she saw Vincent's crumpled body lying on the polished hardwood floor. His eyes were wide open. He was dead. He had surgical gloves on and her .38 caliber Smith & Wesson lay near his right hand. Signe staggered into the sitting room on numb clumsy legs and slumped down on the antique sofa. She picked up the receiver of the phone with her bound hands and squeezed it between her right ear and right shoulder. She dialed 911.

"This is Detective Signe Sorensen of the Santa Fe Police and I would like to report a fatal shooting at the Kokopelli Bed and Breakfast on County Road 29 in Pojoaque," Signe said in a wavering voice. "There are no other injuries."

Signe tried clumsily to cut the cable tie binding her wrists with a dinner knife. She soon discovered the knife was too dull and she couldn't bring pressure against the plastic with her fingers bound together in such a fashion. Finally, she lay back on the sofa with her bound hands resting by her right shoulder and waited. Her head throbbed less when she was still. She heard the faint sound of sirens in the distance first and she found the rise and fall of the wailing as it got louder and louder very reassuring. Jack was in the first squad car that arrived shortly after 5 a.m. He took out a knife to cut the cable tie but Signe motioned him away.

"Thank you, Jack," Signe began in a tearful voice. "But we need pictures before these *knep* painful things are removed. Also there is DNA evidence on them."

"I'm so glad you're okay, Signe," Jack said with relief in his voice. "The call I got was pretty scary."

While they were talking Chief Gerald Hartford burst into the bungalow looking tan from his recent trip to Florida.

"Thank God, you are okay, Signe," the Chief began. "Let's get that cable tie off your wrists."

"We can't Chief until she's photographed," Jack piped up.

Valerie came through the door as if on cue. She was already gloved. In her right hand she carried her Nikon and in her left hand a large black case of crime scene material. She photographed Signe's hands and then cut the cable tie and placed it in an evidence bag. The pain in Signe's wrists and hands got better quickly with improved blood flow. Valerie sprayed Signe's hands for gunshot residue. Both of her hands turned a dark blue which the crime scene technician photographed. Signe was taken into the large black and white tiled bathroom. Valerie and another female officer helped her out of her clothing and bagged and labeled each item. They helped her into a hot shower. She stood for several minutes allowing the hot water to pulsate against her head, neck and upper back. Then she washed herself vigorously everywhere with mounds of soap and bubbles. Valerie, thoughtfully, had brought a pair of surgical scrubs for Signe to slip on. When she came out of the bathroom she noticed that, mercifully, Vincent's body was gone. Two officers were gathering evidence in the bedroom.

Jack and Chief Hartford stood in the sitting room. An officer had just reported that Vincent's Ford pickup had been found concealed behind some brush a quarter mile down the road. The chief offered Signe an ambulance which she declined. She had hated the cold emptiness of St. Vincent's Hospital when she had gone there after her car wreck.

"Would you just drive me home in my own car, Jack?" Signe implored.

"You've got it, partner," Jack responded promptly.

He was as anxious as she was to escape the scene of the shooting.

"I don't want to see you for at least two days," Chief Hartford said as Jack placed his jacket around Signe's shoulders and guided her toward the door.

CHAPTER 58

Epilogue

When she got to her apartment Signe had a headache and still felt drugged although the effects were wearing off. She decided to sleep for a while and asked Jack to stay around until she woke up.

"For the very first time in my life, Jack, I'm afraid to be all alone," Signe lamented.

"I'll just curl up on the sofa, Signe," Jack began. "I can stay as long as you want."

"Thanks, Jack," Signe replied as she stumbled into her bedroom.

She slept fitfully for four hours. He sleep was disrupted by bad dreams and chills. When she awoke Jack made her some coffee and fixed some eggs. Signe ate greedily.

"Vincent had me take my car to the B and B so that my death would look like a suicide," Signe began. "And he made some excuse so I went to the office alone to register. That way the manager wouldn't even know he was on the premises. Just before he tried to shoot me he said his name was on the account in Santa Fe that Dirk set up for his perpetrator. Vincent killed Chloe and I was just about to uncover it. I want to search his apartment Jack."

"That can wait until tomorrow, Signe," Jack replied. "You'll be thinking more clearly."

"Okay. But I want to meet you and Valerie tomorrow morning at Vincent's apartment at eight. Here's the address," Signe said scribbling the number and street name on a scrap of paper.

"Deal."

Signe spent the rest of the afternoon and evening studying her collection of Indian pots and consulting books about what she wanted to purchase next. Before bed she had a long phone conversation with Axel. She went to bed early and slept surprisingly well. Jack picked Signe up the next morning and drove her to Vincent's apartment.

"Do you remember how impressed I was with the information and communication between the criminals?" Signe said. "I even suspected that Chief Hartford was the leak at one point. *I* was the leak, Jack. I told Vincent everything immediately and he just had to contact the other perpetrators."

Valerie was already gloved and waiting. Signe had spent several nights in the apartment and knew the layout. Nothing suspicious turned up as they rummaged through cupboards and drawers. Jack wondered aloud whether Vincent had a secret lair somewhere. They tapped the walls and measured the rooms looking for areas that didn't fit the dimensions correctly. They found nothing. Then Signe remembered that once Vincent had mentioned a storage shed.

They found the aluminum shed double locked in the back yard. Inside was a treasure trove of criminal tools and evidence. Large satchels of burglary tools were against one wall. Hand guns and rifles, many with telescopes on them, were displayed on another wall most had their registration numbers filed off. Stacks of dusty gay men's magazines and magazines glorifying sadism and masochism sat in the corners. They gave Signe a creepy feeling after all the times she had slept with Vincent. She would have felt better if she had found just one *Playboy,* but she didn't.

"I think Vincent fabricated that goblet, Valerie," Signe said. "You know, the one we used to convict 'Tony the Squid' with the fingerprints on it. Vincent probably carried it into the Pecos Wilderness himself in the saddle bag of his horse and then pretended to find it when I didn't look in the right place."

"He was crafty, Signe," Valerie replied. "I let him in the lab, in violation of the rules, all the time and never suspected a thing."

Valerie was taking pictures of the items when she found a small medical bag under a bundle of cable ties. She opened it and passed it to Signe.

"Weren't some strange chemicals found in the vic's body at autopsy?" Valerie asked.

"Yes. Including one we never explained," Signe replied.

Signe opened the kit and found a gold stud, a surgical tenaculum for holding tissue and two small dark bottles. She opened the first bottle. It smelled like chloroform. She opened the second one and it had musty ammonia-like smell that she recognized but couldn't place at first. Then it came to her. It smelled like the hydrazine that Dr. Abramowitz had given her when she visited Los Alamos. Signe sank to the dirty floor holding the small kit as she realized that this was what Vincent had used to murder Chloe.

"Now I know how Vincent murdered Chloe," Signe said to no one in particular. "He sedated her with the chloroform and then, when she was unconscious, grasped Chloe's tongue with the tenaculum. He made a small hole in the center of her tongue and inserted the stud that we found on her body. Bernadette and I thought the tongue stud was an old adornment like her tattoo. Then he poured the hydrazine around the stud. The potent poison entered the fresh hole in her tongue. It went immediately into her blood stream because of the rich supply of blood to her tongue. Poor Chloe. Vincent must have gotten the rocket fuel in his high school science class and kept it all these years after hearing what a deadly poison hydrazine was."

While Valerie and Jack collected the rest of the evidence, Signe's mind wandered. Vincent had put on such a façade of perfection, she thought, while underneath he was so perverse. Signe knew she would spend months replaying every conversation she had ever had with Vincent looking for clues she had missed.

Two nights later Jack and Chief Hartford hosted a celebratory dinner for Signe. Signe invited Jefferson Barclay, Mateo Romero, Sven Torvaldson, and Lisa Gonzalez to attend. She secretly hoped that Wanda De Berneres and Svelty Patterson were hiding nearby. Christopher Malloy had written a factually accurate article that morning in the *New Mexican* about Signe's brush with death. At the end of the meal Signe announced the formation of the Chloe Angela Patterson Foundation to aid in the prevention of drug addiction in local teenagers. She would use the blood money that Vincent received for killing Chloe and a large donation from Johnny Armijo's parents to start programs in the schools in the Aqua Fria neighborhood of Santa Fe. The foundation headquarters would be located in Anthony Squitero's old offices since the lease had been prepaid for a year. At the end of the dinner Signe Sorensen hugged each of her friend's goodnight. She knew she would sleep well that night for the first time since Chloe's death in early October.

ACKNOWLEDGMENTS

I am deeply indebted to Blythe Hoekenga for her constant encouragement and suggestions. Thanks to Britta Hoekenga and Bob Sanchez my sharp-eyed editors who have even sharper teeth. Thanks to Brandt Hoekenga for his effortless and catchy cover. June Shaffer and Marilyn Muehsam deserve thanks for helping with my egregious punctuation. Thanks to Marty Enright for showing me the little known natural delights of New Mexico. Thanks to Pat Conway and Dorothy Webb for their many helpful suggestions, and kind support. I've been inspired by the work of Antonya Nelson and Mari Ulmer. Thanks to Hilary Hoekenga for being my favorite gadfly. Finally, thanks to my wife Dona for tolerating the many new characters, such as Signe Sorensen, that now inhabit our lives.

LaVergne, TN USA
21 March 2010
176620LV00002B/12/A